THE FOUND OBJECT SOCIETY

"*The Found Object Society* is a sly, subversive exploration of our obsession with death. The intriguing concept of Maryk's speculative suspense debut is as utterly unique as her audacious protagonist. A profound yet pacey ride you won't soon forget!"

—K. T. Nguyen, Agatha Award–winning author of *You Know What You Did*

"From the moment I heard the premise of *The Found Object Society,* I wanted to read this book, and it did not disappoint. The addictive pull to the Found Object Society that drives the main characters to the brink of self-destruction is palpable, but as delightfully surreal as the concept is, the questions Michelle Maryk explores about grief and regret are grounded and so human. A truly original book that focuses not on the *why* of death but on why we can't look away."

—Jennifer Fawcett, author of *Beneath the Stairs*

"A roller-coaster speculative novel that keeps you guessing, Michelle Maryk's sharply crafted debut, *The Found Object Society*, kept me intrigued until the final page turn. Evocative, unafraid of big questions, and entertaining as heck, Maryk shines brightly with this novel."

—Alex Segura, bestselling and award-winning author of *Secret Identity* and *Alter Ego*

"*The Found Object Society* is a master class in speculative suspense—an intricately woven story that will stay with you for a long time."

—Sarah Lawton, author of *All the Little Things* and *A Drowning Tide*

"A sexy, speculative thriller! In her imaginative debut novel, Maryk has invented an elite secret society that allows her to explore the universal desire for love, purpose, and meaning in the shadow of mortality—our own and that of those we love most. A moving rumination on the power of regret, and the promise of second chances, as well as the surprising ways both can rewrite our fate."

—Sarah Tomlinson, author of *The Last Days of the Midnight Ramblers*

"*The Found Object Society* is a mind-wreck in the very best way. Wholly original and intoxicatingly hypnotic, Maryk's debut will sweep you into a lush and dangerous world where nothing is as it seems. Prepare to be spellbound."

—Kathleen Barber, author of *Truth Be Told*

"*The Midnight Library* meets death tourism in Michelle Maryk's dark and spellbinding debut. A secret society offers its wealthy members a one-of-a-kind experience: a glimpse into someone else's final moments. Like the society's voyeuristic patrons, I found myself completely riveted, unable to look away. *The Found Object Society* is a wild ride."

—Allison Buccola, author of *The Ascent*

PRAISE FOR *THE FOUND OBJECT SOCIETY*

"Michelle Maryk's debut novel begins with a stunner of a premise when Greta Davenport is offered the chance to experience death without dying. *The Found Object Society* is a compelling story as much as it is an exploration of regret, mortality, and the flawed nature of the human heart. A stunning debut novel."

—Danielle Girard, *USA Today* bestselling author of *Pinky Swear*

"Michelle Maryk demonstrates her versatility and virtuosity in this genre-blending book that defies categorization. Razor-sharp observations, mordant humor, and a surprising plot make this one of the most daring and original books I've ever read. If you love secret societies and are convinced the death drive powers us all, you'll be obsessed with *The Found Object Society*, a rare book that combines wisdom and spine-tingling chills."

—Ashley Winstead, *USA Today* bestselling author of *Midnight Is the Darkest Hour*

"Like classic *Tales from the Crypt* with a dash of *The Substance*, Michelle Maryk's genre-bending and original debut takes you on a ride through the darkest depths of voyeurism with a new take on addiction. *The Found Object Society* will have readers wondering what price they'd be willing to pay for the ultimate trip."

—Vera Kurian, Edgar Award nominee for *Never Saw Me Coming*

"*The Found Object Society* hits the target as both an engrossing speculative tale where a select few can experience the death of another human being and a profound study of trauma and loss. It made me think hard about the extent people will go to escape emotional pain and the irresistible urge to change the dynamics of our own humanity. Inventive and wholly original, fans of Matt Haig will devour."

—Wendy Walker, bestselling author of *All Is Not Forgotten*

"*The Found Object Society* is a speculative novel for our new world, one in which we are so spoiled by the access we're granted with technology, we've become bored with reality. A deft satire of the ultra-wealthy and an irreverent love letter to New York City, Maryk shows us that in a world of billionaires taking thrill rides to space, the final frontier, truly, is our own mortality. But how closely can we brush with death before it consumes us entirely? Don't be fooled by the novel's dark humor or addictive pace—underneath there beats a warm, grief-stricken heart."

—Melissa Larsen, *USA Today* bestselling author of *The Lost House*

"*The Starless Sea* meets *The Lost Apothecary* in Michelle Maryk's nuanced and ambitious debut. *The Found Object Society* is a richly drawn story of loss, grief, and humanity's obsession with death, told through the eyes of a plucky protagonist I won't soon forget."

—Tessa Wegert, author of *Death in the Family*

"Rendered in a whirl of rich imagery and lush prose, and featuring an utterly captivating narrative voice, *The Found Object Society* is a triumph of a novel. This speculative marvel deftly explores questions of mortality, regret, and desire while doubling as a sly interrogation of wealth and privilege. Michelle Maryk is an author to watch."

—Greg Wands, internationally bestselling coauthor of *Trust Issues*

"In *The Found Object Society*, Michelle Maryk brilliantly executes an intriguing premise: What if you could experience someone else's death without dying? For Greta, the story's memorable protagonist, the answer is both thrilling and profound. Utterly enthralling, deftly plotted, and wholly original, *The Found Object Society* has all the makings of a major breakout book. I loved it."

—Laura McHugh, award-winning author of
What's Done in Darkness

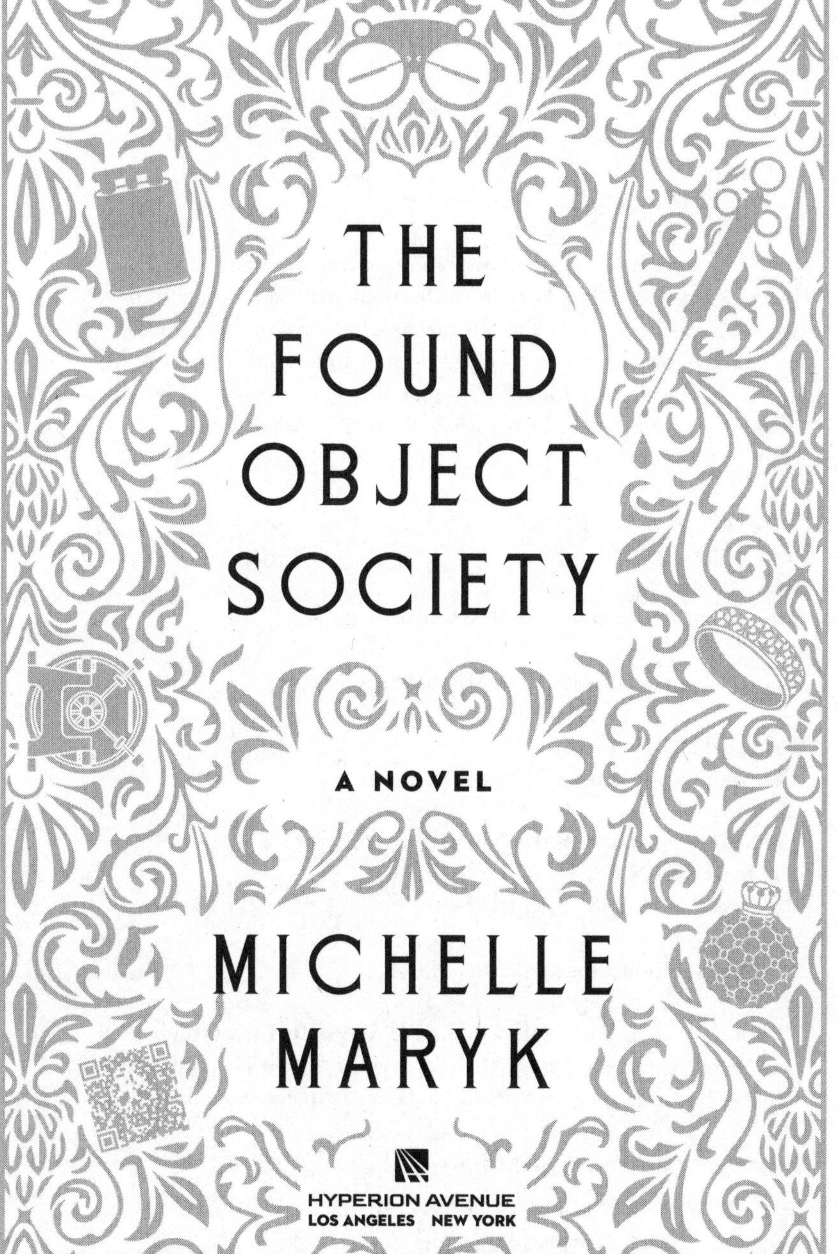

THE FOUND OBJECT SOCIETY

A NOVEL

MICHELLE MARYK

HYPERION AVENUE
LOS ANGELES NEW YORK

For information address Hyperion Avenue, 7 Hudson Square, New York, NY, 10013.

First Edition, February 2026
10 9 8 7 6 5 4 3
FAC-004510-26159
Printed in the United States of America

This book is set in Hoefler Text, United Sans, Mystery Show JNL

Designed by Amy C. King
Illustrations by Spencer Fuller and © Shutterstock

Library of Congress Control Number: 2025945035
Hardcover ISBN 978-1-368-11474-5
Paperback ISBN 978-1-368-11475-2

Reinforced binding for hardcover edition

The authorized representative in the EU for product safety and compliance is Disney Trading B.V., Asterweg 15S, 1031 HL, Amsterdam, The Netherlands, email: DCP.DL-EU.bookscontact@disney.com

www.HyperionAvenueBooks.com

Logo Applies to Text Stock Only

For Tom. *Everything right time.*

When we concentrate on a material object, whatever its situation, the very act of attention may lead to our involuntarily sinking into the history of that object.

—VLADIMIR NABOKOV, *Transparent Things*

PART ONE

Blank Card
6 × 6 inches
Origin: Unknown

CHAPTER ONE

This version of Greta Davenport doesn't care that she's about to drive drunk.

She doesn't care that she's made a scene at the annual Ellery goddamned Heyward Mansion fundraiser gala for local wildlife preservation—the one that *she* helped organize. Doesn't care that the board, rods up their asses, took her aside and said that, in their opinion, *it would be best if she left the premises. All things considered.*

What's happened here tonight is their fault, not hers. *Jerks.* If the board hadn't insisted the gala fall on this very date—despite Greta's best efforts—things would be different. But no, her dread of this night has become a self-fulfilling prophecy. The interminable toasts. The smug, self-absorbed, and self-congratulatory speeches. The grinning-until-her-jaw-hurt small talk with socialite idiots like herself. Greta's biggest lapse in judgment (until this moment) was thinking she could put on a brave face and drink her way off the precipice from which she now so publicly dangles.

All things considered.

Please. That's the part that pissed her off. Of course, they all think it has to do with her ex-boyfriend Ryan showing up with his new *girlfriend.* Gal pal? Arm candy? Whatever. Did Greta happen to flip a tray full of champagne flutes in their general direction? Sure she did. That was cathartic. Therapeutic, even. But Greta couldn't give two fucks about Ryan (after all, *she* dumped *him*). He was as disposable as all the others.

What the board and the pompous attendees don't know—and she'd never give them the satisfaction of telling them—is that today happens to fall on the twentieth anniversary of the darkest day in her seemingly privileged life. How fun. Yippee. So that's why Greta has decided to drink up, get rowdy, and create an overall cringeworthy situation that will most certainly end up in some gossip column in the local white-as-white-can-be monthly magazine: *Goings-On About Town* or *Town Talk* or *Societal Fucking Sycophants*. And that's where things stand.

She grabs the keys from the cute parking valet, who, other than suggesting he call her a cab while he scrolls idly through his phone, looks through her—*through* Greta Davenport! No checking her out. No admiring her fine-tuned shoulders, her regal clavicle. No following the round of her sculpted ass. This sexy valet has aged out this former showstopper who could bring a room to its knees simply by entering it. To him, she's some broad approaching middle age who's too sloshed to drive.

Goddammit.

Greta doesn't feel old. In fact, she still *feels* like her teenage self—the one whose parents were still alive. When she looks in the mirror, however, her reflection begs to differ. To someone like this twentysomething parking valet who could stay up all night fucking and then want another go when the sun comes up, her thirty-seven years seem ancient.

She gets into her vintage burgundy 1968 Mercedes SL convertible and slams the door. Unfortunately, she's slammed it onto the long silk shoulder sash of her strapless jumpsuit and now she's like a dog tied to a fence. Greta doesn't want to pull an Isadora Duncan—the dancer famously strangled to death in

1927 with her own scarf while driving along the windy roads of Nice, France. Gertrude Stein said of her death (as only Gertrude could), "Affectations can be dangerous."

As she reopens the door to set herself free, she notes the small crowd of bemused partygoers who have drifted out to watch the grand finale of *The Greta Davenport Flameout Show*. If any of them take out their cell phones to film this, Greta is prepared to run them over. She puts the car in gear and speeds around the fountain of the mansion's circular driveway, making a beeline for the gate and then the darkened rural roads of Litchfield County, Connecticut.

Now, after midnight, the winding country road is even darker than usual under the moonless sky. It's been a while since Greta's driven this drunk. Last time she was this bad was way back in college. Greta's always taken a certain amount of pride in being a *good* drunk driver. Still, some fresh air couldn't hurt, so she rolls the windows down, swerving over the center line and back again in the process. No matter how many times (and there have been many) Greta has tested the boundaries of her own mortality, she's always come out ahead. It's a fact that's haunted her since she lost her parents in a car crash twenty years ago tonight. By all accounts, the accident should've taken her life, too. It's what she deserved. But it didn't. Greta's blamed herself for their deaths, swallowing down that guilt with booze, drugs, and men ever since. If she hadn't lied, they would never have gotten into the car that night. If they hadn't gotten into the car, they wouldn't have crashed. Wouldn't have been lost.

Lost is a weird word to describe the dead. Like her parents had wandered off at the county fair and she'd reunite with them eventually at the Lost Parents booth. She'd scold them for not holding her hand like she'd told them to do, and then they'd walk off and get a corn dog. But saying they're *lost* is easier. When you're lost, there's always the chance you could be found.

Greta tests her Teflon mortality as she takes the curves too fast. A Gatsbyesque mansion and its quarter-mile-long driveway hulks on the right side of the road. One lone window is illuminated, thirty or so more dormant.

The Mercedes fishtails for a moment as she takes her eyes off the road. Anyone else would proceed with caution—not Greta. To her the rush is addictive, dancing on the edge, testing the limits of life itself. *Poor, poor, rich me*, she thinks. Has she always been this much of a douche?

Gnarled trees, thrown into sudden relief by her headlights, flash past like tentacled giants. A yellow sign indicates a sharp bend approaching. Greta slows only slightly. An immortal needn't worry too much about their speed, after all.

The headlights catch the reflection of something in the road ahead. A pair of tightly spaced black eyes look back at Greta. A possum freezes its glacial lumbering as it crosses the roadway. Greta may be immortal, but the possum isn't, and she's just come from a fundraiser to preserve local wildlife, so she'll be goddamned if she's going to run over one of His creatures. She slams the brakes. The Mercedes's tires lock. Greta overcompensates with the steering wheel as the convertible lurches right, then left, before going into a sideways skid, sailing toward two budding maple trees.

Her careening is endless. The brakes have slowed not only the car, but have handcuffed the passage of time. The cold, early-spring air combs through her hair like sticky fingers. Greta no longer feels that she's the driver; instead, she's a passenger draped across the minuscule back seat, unable to control the vehicle. An observer. A child.

Is this it, then? Is this how it ends? Greta joining the ranks of the *lost* along with her parents. Smashed up and broken into bits against a tree in her 1968 Mercedes. *At least it will be instant*, Greta thinks; airbags weren't mandatory in 1968, and the seat belts are as useful as those in a plummeting 747.

The surrounding mansions are too far away to hear a crash or the scream—the one that she's emitting right at this moment—so there's no one to find her until they drive past and see the grisly aftermath. Maybe her ex or another partygoer will discover the wreckage. They'll pull over to call 9-1-1—if they can get service—embarrassed by the predicament that dead Greta Davenport has put them in: her bloody, boozy mess. The hassle of speaking with the police and recounting Greta's behavior at the party. Lying and saying they didn't know she was drunk. Or better yet, placing the blame firmly on the young valet who should've known better than to give the keys to someone so inebriated.

Greta's immortal, though, remember? At least she's thought so in the twenty years since the accident. So, instead of wrapping her beautiful Mercedes around a tree, she does a one-eighty, slides between both maples, and comes to a stop.

The beams of the headlights now shine back the way she came. Greta is still alive (and, apparently, screaming). She closes her mouth and runs her hands across her face and torso. Her neck and shoulders burn from whiplash, but there's no sign of trauma, not the physical kind at least. Near silence surrounds her. Off in the distance she hears frogs in a marsh, their spring awakening underway. The car's engine idles. Her breathing is heavy. In the road, the possum is either *really* dead or just, well, playing possum.

"Fuck!" Greta calls out to the night.

She rests her arms on the steering wheel and shifts the car into neutral. The motor is left running, the lights on. Her neck jolts as she opens the door to step out. Her heels sink and crunch into gravel as she walks the perimeter of the car to check for damage. Noting none—and what a fucking miracle that is, in and of itself—Greta, still panting, makes her way toward the possum in the road. The adrenaline courses through her body, giving her a buzz that borders on the erotic.

"Hey, buddy, you okay?" she says, and pauses as if the possum may respond.

The animal is frozen in a cartoonish rictus, mouth partially open, revealing rows of pointy teeth. She inches closer, her silk heels dragging and clacking against the asphalt. As much as her neck hurts, it's only now that she realizes the ache of her feet, her toes crammed and funneled into the torturous culs-de-sac of her Manolo Blahniks. She stops short of the possum and leans over it, one hand bracing her neck.

"Hey, are you dead?"

Greta should clear it out of the roadway, but she's not about to nudge the thing with eight-hundred-dollar heels. There's nothing worse than roadkill: an innocent animal plowed down because of humanity's stupid inventions. Smashed, mangled, then flattened repeatedly until it resembles a bloody doormat instead of a raccoon, or fox, or groundhog, or whatever lovely pure thing it once was (maybe not in the case of the possum, but still). It felt as disrespectful as turducken. A chicken stuffed into a duck shoved up the butt of a turkey, and then roasted and eaten. Really? There should be a universal karmic payback coming over that travesty alone.

The possum's legs twitch back to life and it rights itself. Greta and the creature size each other up. The possum gives her a half-hearted hiss and waddles off the road, into the black of the meadow and out of the view of the headlamps.

"Thanks for trying to get me killed. It didn't work," she says, waving goodbye. "It never does."

She walks back to her idling Mercedes and leans against the driver's-side door. The headlights illuminate the path of her slide, and the skid marks form a near perfect arrow that points back to her and the mammoth trees she so narrowly averted. Weird. She's pretty sure she's sober now. The near-crash has baby-shaken the drunk right out of her. Easing back into the car, she takes off her shoes and tosses them onto the back seat. She rests her pulsing left foot on the clutch and slides her right onto the gas. Barefoot, like when she was a teenager driving back from the beach in her VW bug, sandy toes and horsefly-bitten ankles at one with the rubber.

Not a single car has driven by since her skid. It could have been hours, but it was probably only minutes.

Like it never happened.

CHAPTER TWO

Greta drives the next five miles of roadway with remarkable caution and deliberation. Yes, she feels sober, the torrential downpour of fear chemicals washing the booze out of her like a deluge through a gutter, but she's not going to get into another near-death situation, neither for herself nor an animal (or human, for that matter). Not tonight.

She may feel less drunk, but any Breathalyzer would say otherwise. She bribed her way out of a DUI once with a deft combo of money and eyelash batting. The whole thing made even Greta feel like she needed a *Silkwood* shower, so she'd rather not repeat it. And frankly after the way the valet *didn't* check her out tonight, she's not so sure that tack would be effective anymore. Fucking depressing.

Greta pulls into her driveway and cuts the engine. She heaves her stiff self out of the Mercedes and cranes over the back seat to grab her torture shoes and purse. The pebbles of the driveway are cool and smooth under her feet. Forsythia bushes and rows of fragrant hyacinths line the path up to the front door of the stone Davenport millhouse. The house she inherited at seventeen and renovated to look as little as possible as the same one she grew up in after the age of ten. Ryan moved in for a short while—what a raging mistake that was—but it was otherwise hers, and hers alone, these past twenty years.

She taps the entry code on the front door keypad and lets herself in, then deactivates the alarm. Ryan always creamed over electronic gadgets, especially when buying them with Greta's not-so-hard-earned money. Though an IT guy by trade, he's not the bloated, Rush T-shirt–wearing kind that rarely ventures outdoors, but the effortlessly good-looking, back-slapping, Ivy League bro kind. Tech gadgets are his life. Talking about them and to them. Telling them what to do, what he wants to listen to, which lights to turn off and on, how warm or cold it should be in the house, and on, and on. Ryan thought that being the boss of his gadgets could also translate to his treatment of Greta—but she's no gadget.

Once he was gone, one of the first things she did was deactivate as many of the gadgets as possible. The keypad lock and the alarm are all that remains. The rest were tossed into the garbage, lithium batteries and all—so much for living "green."

Flipping the light switch on the old-fashioned way—with her fingers—is another newfound pleasure. She tosses her shoes on the tile and her purse on the vestibule table. She unzips the side of her jumpsuit and leaves it in a pile on the floor. Her neck is too stiff from her almost-crash to bend over and hang it. Besides, who cares? She's about to walk into the kitchen when she hears the metallic *clink* of the mail slot in the front door.

A six-by-six bright white square made from heavy cardstock drifts from the slot like a feather and lands at her feet. Gingerly, Greta picks it up by the edges, like maybe she doesn't want to get fingerprints on it, or maybe it's been laced with anthrax. Both sides are blank. She rushes back to the door and flings it open.

"Who the fuck's out there?" she yells.

Still and quiet greet her. She listens for the telltale crunch of the stones on the path and driveway or rustling in the forsythia—there's nothing. She flips the switch to the floodlights over the driveway hoping to catch someone in the act, but still, no one. No sound of a broken twig or the hoot of an owl to startle her before she's able to breathe that faux sigh of horror movie relief. Nada.

The spring night air gives her gooseflesh. She's standing on the front landing in her sexy thong and strapless bra—a sight that no one else will be enjoying tonight. She goes back in and closes the door, shuts off the outdoor lights. To be safe, she throws the dead bolt and sets the alarm for Home.

She has a thought and takes her cell phone from her purse. She types in a text.

Very funny, asshole. Not letting you in.

She hits Send.

The little dots roll back and forth. Her ex, Ryan, is typing. Thinking.

What are you talking about, Crazy?

He was never the best liar, but it's hard to tell from a six-word text.

She types again.

I think you know.

She's trying to call his bluff, catch him in a lie. In truth, it doesn't make sense that Ryan slid the card through the slot. He would've had to dash out of the gala and follow her along the road. He'd have seen her near miss with the tree as she tried to avoid the possum. Plus, Greta hadn't noticed any headlights other than her own.

Rolling dots. Rolling dots.

(Pinwheels-for-eyes emoji.)

He's telling her she's drunk. More pulsing dots.

(Martini glass emoji.)

More stupid dots. He's on a roll.

(Champagne glasses emoji. Showerhead emoji. Crooked head laughing tears emoji.)

Ha-ha, very funny. Even in emoji-speak Greta can feel Ryan's permanent smirk. Greta's turn.

(Middle-finger emoji x3), Dick. (Eggplant emoji.)

Message delivered. Message read. Rolling dots. Then nothing.

If it wasn't Ryan, who was it?

Maybe it got stuck in the mail slot and only fell out when she opened and shut the door. That's the most likely explanation. Even then, who sends a blank card? And what the hell is it?

She holds the card up to the table lamp in the entryway and turns it over in the dim light. There's no writing, no images. Blank. There's *something* to it, though. It's not just a six-by-six white card. The surface is pearlescent, reflective—maybe there's a subtle pattern. In the low light, it's hard to see. She's tipping from the outer edge of drunk into hangover-land. It's too late for parlor tricks.

Card in hand, she zombie-walks into the kitchen. She fills a coffee mug with ice water from the fridge and gulps it down. Fills it again. She leaves the card on the island and turns off any remaining house lights. At the foot of the stairs, something stops her. She looks back toward the kitchen.

In the inky black, the white square glows in the dark, like a tiny window carved into the marble surface, lit from within.

Upstairs, Greta takes a Tylenol PM for her neck pain. She lies naked and spread-eagle on the California king-size mattress. Now that she has the bed all to herself, she likes to occupy as much real estate as possible. It's her nightly *fuck you* to Ryan. She flicks the switch of her bedside lamp. If Greta thought she was sober after her game of chicken with the possum, she was dead wrong. The room begins a slow rotation that turns into an outright spin. She shuts her eyes tight, trying to slow her descent.

Her sleep is fitful. Dreams filled with scattered images of yellow road lines hurtling past, silhouettes of bare trees, tentacled branches extending toward her. All the while, a white card gyrates like spin art in front of her, just out of reach.

CHAPTER THREE

It's shortly after nine a.m. when Greta finally stirs. Her whole body feels like she's been whacked with a pillowcase full of oranges.

She usually tries to work out first thing in the sunny home gym she'd had built on the first floor. Just another idle rich lady, hell-bent on sculpting her body into perfection, no matter her age. Or maybe it's *despite* her age? It's what's expected. You certainly can't wear a strapless jumpsuit to a gala with flabby arms or a wide, flat ass. This morning her regimen ain't happening, though.

Pasty-mouthed and head weighted down like wet oatmeal, she reaches for her water glass. Empty. She stumbles to the bathroom, her lips and tongue dry as dust. Some fluids remain in her body, though, since she's having a pee that may never end. The mirror is not her friend. Her auburn hair looks like she got stuck inside a wind tunnel; makeup from the night before is smeared, her lash extensions clumped together. Today is not one of those days she sees her seventeen-year-old self looking back at her. What she sees is an aging woman who can ill afford to get drunk and sleep with her makeup on like she's in college.

"You look like holy fucking hell, Greta," she says to her reflection.

After an aggressive face washing and brushing of teeth, she pops a few ibuprofen, ties the belt on her robe, and heads downstairs. She goes into the kitchen to make a coffee with the built-in Keurig that came with the wildly expensive fridge that Ryan insisted they—meaning Greta—buy. (Okay, so Greta didn't get rid of *all* of Ryan's gadgets, even though she's more of a pour-over or French press gal herself.)

She's almost forgotten about the spooky white card that appeared through the mail slot last night. Yet there it sits, eye-balling her. She leans against the cool stone of the kitchen island to take a closer look, but the nag of a headache behind her eyes stops her.

"Coffee," she says to the universe, hoping that one will magically appear in front of her. She places a mug under the Keurig spout, pops in the strongest espresso pod she can find, and taps the button to brew.

The ingenious little contraption emits a high-pitched whine and then, little else. She tries it again. The Keurig lets out a final death rattle before the *clonk* of some bit of machinery crashes its way down the inside of the fridge door. She opens it, trying to find the part, but it's stuck in the interior bowels of the door, rattling around like a tubercular cough.

Obviously, this is Ryan's fault. The fancier the parts, widgets, and doodads there are to a thing, the higher the likelihood of it breaking. She's out of regular coffee grounds, so the press is out of the question.

"Just kill me already," she says, and opens her Uber Eats app.

A mere three minutes later, there's a tap at the door.

Could the delivery have come that fast?

Greta shuffles to the entryway and opens the door. She catches the delivery driver's profile as her dilapidated compact sputters down the driveway. There's something familiar about her. On the ground by her feet sits the Samuel's Coffee Shop delivery bag.

Thank God.

Greta plunks back down at the kitchen island. She brushes the blank white card aside and reaches into the bag from Samuel's. The cup scorches her fingertips and she lets out a yelp. Cursing under her breath, she pops the lid off to cool it down.

The design of the foamed milk is extraordinary. Tendrils of foam, expertly manipulated into bare branches of a massive tree that overlap one another until they appear almost three-dimensional. They remind Greta of her reckless drive home last night, the ghostly trees embracing the edge of the road, the lifesaving space between them, allowing scant inches for Greta to slide through unscathed. The foam twists into a tremendous trunk down the center and splays into an elaborate root system. One root forms a large arrow that points directly at Greta. It's unnerving.

The white card pokes out from under the Samuel's bag. Greta slides it out and takes a cautious swig of her latte. The shimmery square is hypnotic. She raises it level with her eyes and squints at it skeptically.

"What are you? *Why* are you?"

There's no response, but she confirms that it is, in fact, still a six-by-six white card—no change from last night's drunk goggles. She picks it up, and there's a noticeable heft to it. She flips it over. Other than an opalescent sheen, there's not much to see.

Her cell phone vibrates, distracting her.

At some point, Greta will have to face the music from her melodramatic outburst at last night's affair. She cringes as she plays back her performance. Has her life become such a dull blade that she must resort to soap-opera diva antics?

Greta has always craved *more* but been at a loss—or simply too lazy—to seek it out. So instead of *more* taking the form of picking up the pieces of her orphaned life with a worthwhile career or doing anything to benefit humankind as a whole, she's done what most other privileged white girls do: attend private school, go to an Ivy League college as a legacy admission, date a good-looking series of bros, sit on the board of a couple of philanthropic organizations, and throw a drunken hissy fit in a crowded black-tie affair.

To the uninformed eye, last night's outburst looks like jealousy.

In a way, it's boredom, and boredom is the easier pill to swallow. But when she scrapes away the grief of losing her parents as a teen (*lost, lost, lost*), that's where the truth lies. Beneath the surface of Greta's clichéd life, there's a yearning for a darkness and danger she can't define. The need to test boundaries, even those of mortality (especially mortality), and get lost herself.

The caffeine clears Greta's mind and a deep valley replaces the haze. Her sternum caves, making it hard to breathe. At thirty-seven, she's more restless than ever. Unmoored. With each passing year, the cement she slogs through gets heavier, grabbing hold and anchoring her to the ground. Pointless. She slows her breathing and focuses on what's left of the milk design on her coffee. The beautiful tree is mangled, now resembling a drowning Medusa head. Only the arrow remains intact, still pointing at her.

Greta grabs her phone and unlocks it with her hungover face. An impossible number of texts and emails greet her, but she's not ready to tackle them. Instead, she opens her camera roll and swipes through the photographic timeline of the previous night. The throngs of elegantly dressed fundraiser attendees. Greta striking her signature pose, the perfected slight smirk of her profile, her body angled favorably toward the camera, one foot crossing the other, standing next to the event co-chairs—the ones who hours later suggested that *it would be best if she left the premises. All things considered.* Behind them, gown- and tux-wearing attendees blur past. As she scrolls, she sees herself grow progressively drunker. Her finger stills when she reaches a selfie with her best friend, Lisbeth Carr. Her eyes are slightly glazed, but that's not what's caught her attention. It's the woman behind them—she's sure she's never met her before, but there's something unsettlingly familiar about her profile.

Greta deletes the photo with an exaggerated tap and inadvertently activates the camera. The screen lands on the white square that's sat patiently on the marble countertop through Greta's existential crisis. She's about to turn the camera off when four yellow corners appear around a Bitly link.

The camera has locked onto a QR code.

"What the fuck?" Greta says.

Well, this isn't boring. Greta leans back in the barstool and contemplates her next move. Her heart beats fast, the cement around her feet loosening.

There's no doubt what she's seeing: Hidden in the pearly white of the card that materialized through her mail slot late last night is a QR code, just begging for Greta to click the link.

Think this through, Greta. She hops down from the barstool and paces as her mind grapples with an explanation.

This could go a few ways. The most banal would be that this is merely a cheesy marketing flyer for a spa. Another could be a too-cute-by-half invitation to a party. But what if it's something more sinister, or intending to damage Greta in some way? What if one of Greta's porn-worthy trysts was caught on camera and the blackmail bill has come due?

Or . . . ?

It's an understatement to say that Ryan is a tech-savvy guy. Maybe he's playing a nasty trick on her? Not a little *ha-ha* trick, but something bad, something that could, what? Corrupt all her files? Access her accounts? Fuck her over in a way that she can't even imagine and will never recover from?

The spa possibility is the most appealing and also the most *bland*, the most *banal*. What she *should* do is throw the damned card away and forget about it. Greta isn't going to do that, though. Of course she isn't. She wants excitement and here it is, at least the possibility of it.

She brings the card and her phone to her cavernous living room and sits on the couch, placing them both on her lap. The stone chimney shoots through the center of the room like it's erupted from the Earth's crust.

Maybe she needs glasses, but, honest to God, she can't see the QR code with her own eyes. It's there, though, it must be. Unlocking the phone, she activates the camera, and once again, holds it over the card.

Nothing happens.

"No, no! It has to be here."

She moves the phone across the card. Still, nothing appears.

"Duh, there are two sides, idiot," she mutters, flipping the card over and readjusting the camera. "Come on, you bastard, you know you want to."

Sure enough, the telltale yellow corners and link materialize. Greta holds her breath and taps it with a shaking finger.

"Here goes nothing. Or everything."

For an eternal moment, the screen goes black—like *the phone has died* black. Then it bursts with blinding white light. By reflex, Greta pulls it away from her face. The light pulses like a resting heartbeat.

"Holy shit, what is that?"

As though it heard her, a soothing, female AI voice coos, "Hello, Greta."

Greta laughs. A nervous kind of a laugh. Keeping the phone at arm's length, she stares at the throb of bright light.

The voice repeats, "Hello, Greta."

Okay, she'll play.

"Uh, hi? Who is this? What is this?" Greta says.

"Put the phone closer to your face, if you would."

That seems like a bad idea. Greta fumbles to find the words. "Um, I don't understand. Why?"

Was she having an actual conversation with an AI voice on her phone?

"Don't worry, Greta Davenport. I want to show you what we have to offer."

We? *You mean there's a* we*?*

Tossing away common sense and all she's learned about cybercrimes, identity theft, and whatever other dark matter exists out there in the ether, Greta pulls the phone closer to her face. Not *bland*, right?

"Thank you, Greta. One moment, please."

The white pulsing light collapses in on itself and the screen explodes with image after image of . . . *things*. Objects. One after another. Old things, new things, mundane and indescribable things of all shapes and sizes, man-made and natural. They're all flashing by so quickly it's hard to focus on any one object. It's like the torture sequence in *A Clockwork Orange* but with photos of ordinary objects instead of violence and warfare. Behind the images, the sound of a human heartbeat grows louder and louder, crescendoing until it turns into a dull tone. The images stop. A single line appears and moves across the blackened screen.

It's a heart rate monitor, and it's flatlined.

The line dissolves and forms the words:

Welcome to the Found Object Society, Greta

CHAPTER FOUR

Greta receives instructions and an address in Manhattan. Tomorrow at two p.m. she's scheduled for a preliminary interview to determine if she's a suitable candidate. There's no explanation of what the Found Object Society is, what it does, or who does it.

All the voice says is "Come see for yourself, Greta. We can change your life," followed by "Do not speak of this to anyone, please. This is important."

After Greta disconnects their link, she's about to google the Found Object Society when panic sets in.

Has she completely lost her mind? She opened a link that was so suspicious it'd never make it past her email spam filter. She allowed it to scan her face. It used a kind of facial recognition ID to confirm it was her. It knew her voice. Greta had what was an almost normal, albeit brief, chat with an AI. In all likelihood, her bank accounts (of which there are many, some even Swiss and Caribbean, and all very robust) are being drained at this very moment. Passports and identity cards are being created in some obscure Baltic nation, all bearing Greta's likeness. Her voice is being manipulated and saved so that it can be looped, spliced, and used to do God only knows what.

"I'm a fucking idiot."

Greta opens her laptop and starts frantically logging into all her accounts—credit cards, checking, savings, mutual funds.

All of them. One after another, she sees that there's no suspicious activity. Zero. Status quo. She checks her social media accounts and other than some very unflattering photos and comments from last night's train wreck at the gala, there's no sign of anyone trying to steal her identity.

Greta jumps when her phone rings. It's Lis.

"Hey, Lis," Greta answers.

"Where the hell have you been? I've been texting you since you ran out of the party. That wasn't pretty."

Greta puts Lisbeth on speakerphone and rubs her face in her hands.

"I know, I know. I lost my shit. What can I tell you?" Greta says.

"Why didn't you at least text me back? I know what that was all about last night, even if no one else does."

It's true. Lis knows Greta down to the molecule. She's the only one who does.

"I couldn't deal. I'm sorry. And I got this . . . this . . ." Greta lifts the white card and reexamines it.

"Yes? You got what? What did you get?" Lisbeth says.

Do not speak of this to anyone, please. This is important.

"Nothing. I got too drunk, that's all. I should've made an excuse not to go in the first place. Since I'm one of the gala chairs, I couldn't. Then Ryan was there looking so goddamned smug, I just, you know."

"Oh, I know. Everyone knows. Honestly, G, it wasn't your best tantrum. It was kind of lame. I've seen you do much better."

Lisbeth laughs that laugh of hers. The one she uses whenever Greta's done something publicly regrettable or embarrassing. Lisbeth has been privy to all of Greta's shenanigans, her private suffering. They met as roommates freshman year in college, the

September after the accident, and have been like sisters ever since. Lisbeth is Greta's anchor.

"Yeah, yeah. I mean, we're closer to forty than we are to thirty, and what's changed?"

"Are you going to get all midlife-crisis-y on me now?" Lisbeth says.

Greta's dying to tell Lisbeth about the invitation. What if she got one, too? Maybe they could go together? Instead, she obeys the AI. "You're right, maybe that's all it is."

"Take a trip or something. It's not like you have a real job. A few weeks off to Italy or Croatia again would do you good. I can probably meet you somewhere if you want."

Italy or Croatia—*again*. Boring. Greta remains silent, staring at the card.

"Hello? You there?"

Greta lifts the white card by two corners with her index fingers, shifting it back and forth. The sun bounces off its pearlescent surface. Maybe Greta can dance around the subject, fish, without telling Lisbeth about it outright. "You get any interesting invitations or, I don't know, cards lately?"

"We get zillions of invites a month. Why? Is there some awesome party you aren't telling me about that I wasn't invited to?"

"No, no. Just wondering. Listen, I've gotta go. I have a doctor's appointment in the city tomorrow, so I'm crashing at my SoHo place tonight."

"Everything okay?"

"It's just a checkup, no big deal."

"As long as you're sure," Lisbeth says. "Keep me posted, okay?"

"I will." Greta runs her fingers across the surface of the card. "Thanks for the call, Lis. I appreciate it."

"Always. Bye, G."

"Bye."

It's true. A trip isn't a bad idea, in fact. Only the one Greta's planning to take isn't to Italy or Croatia; it's to the Found Object Society.

Greta bought the loft on Greene Street right out of college with money from her trust. The trust that she was supposed to get access to when she became more of an adult. Instead, she got *all* of it at seventeen, when her parents died.

By the time she closed on the loft, she was twenty-one. It's hers and hers alone. Her parents have never been in it. They've never sat on the couch working on the *New York Times* crossword together, her mother with the uncanny ability to see the words appear so clearly before her in the little white boxes that she'd brazenly fill them out with pen. Her parents have never leaned on the railing of the balcony, arms loosely around each other, sipping coffee as the traffic blinked and blared below. Her mother has never left her trademark scent of Coco Chanel there, the one she left on everything she touched. For days after they'd died, even their cat, Murphy Brown, had that warm amber smell on her head—Greta's mother would often kiss the flat space between the cat's ears as she slept on their bed. Murphy Brown is long gone now, too. The relief, the sanctuary of the loft on Greene Street, is that it holds no echoes of her parents. Any memories, any traces, are all her own.

Greta tried to do the same with the Connecticut house. She peeled away the layers of life her parents had left behind, planed down the living flesh of them and the identifying features of their existence, until all that remained was clean white bone. If she couldn't see them, smell them, taste them, then they'd never existed. And if they didn't exist, then the memories were all that remained, and those she could tame with alcohol, with drugs, with the incessant noise and clatter of high society, faux friends, and parties. The anonymous bones of her parents turning to dust and blowing away.

Greta had told the contractors in Connecticut to take down the walls in the living room and leave only the enormous chimney. She'd hired movers to box up her parents' books, trinkets, and art pieces that they'd collected over a lifetime of travels around the world, and then asked the estate planner to do whatever she wanted to with them—sell them, donate them, Greta didn't care, she just wanted them gone. She'd wanted to see only bone.

When Greta bought the place on Greene, most other college grads were scraping by with their first jobs, cramming four roommates into spaces meant for two. Greta's loft was the kind of New York City apartment you see in movies where the main character is supposed to be broke yet still lives in a sixteen-hundred-square-foot palace a couple of blocks from Balthazar.

Yeah, right.

Greta's been googling all evening trying to find something, *anything*, about this so-called Found Object Society. Other than *found object* being a literal translation of the French term *objet trouvé*, there's zilch. Objet trouvé refers mostly to an art movement where *found* or discarded objects are turned into "art" by an artist.

So, what is this *society*, then? She's tried every combination possible in her search: She's written it out in French, La Société des Objets Trouvés; in English; a combination of both; even abbreviated it to FOS—fructooligosaccharides came up (whatever those are).

There's no online record of something called the Found Object Society.

Pouring herself another glass of wine, she fishes out the last of her Szechuan cold sesame noodles with her enameled chopsticks. Tomorrow at two o'clock she's going to the address in Tribeca to find out, though. Will she get kidnapped? Chopped into bits? That's not the kind of life change she's looking for. She's come this far, though, and her curiosity is beyond piqued. Any hesitation is momentary. She wanted to shake up her dull life and this'll *shook* it good.

In less than twenty-four hours, she's going to go through with it.

CHAPTER FIVE

Greta's been pacing in front of the nondescript building on Duane Street for the past fifteen minutes. This morning had been an agony of checking the time, fussing around the apartment, cleaning (which she loathes), and endless primping and outfit changes. In the end, she went with a pair of rough-hemmed jeans, vanilla suede sneakers, a T-shirt, and a stupidly expensive Etro trench coat.

Despite her efforts to kill time, she still showed up outside the building at 1:40 p.m. It's now 1:55 p.m. and she has five minutes to go before she's due inside. She leans on a parking meter. Though the last thing she needs is more pep, she sips her latte—with disappointingly unadorned foam—from Hungry Ghost. Her stomach squirms with a blend of predawn Christmas-morning excitement and dread.

She focuses her thoughts on the building.

It's one of those cast-iron, sturdy builds from the early twentieth century that Tribeca and SoHo are known for. Bluish gray, with enormous arched windows. Most of these stalwart beauties have been converted into primo condos for people like Greta. Some house the occasional artist holdout who started renting the space in the 1970s—paying a pittance in rent at the time because *who the hell wants to live in Tribeca?* Little by little, the expanding world of the wealthy encroached on their sanctuary, the place where they could roller-skate down the hall, stretch canvases the size of a Westfalia bus, and host parties that lasted for days. Now those folks are old and the last ones standing. Maybe they'll stay until they take their last breath, or they'll cave and accept the outrageous sum of money that a guy like Ryan might offer them, then scurry off to find the last of their species in Woodstock or Saugerties.

Greta checks the time on her phone. It's 1:58. Close enough. The front door is locked and there's no doorman, only a coded entry box. She types in the number for the suite on the third floor and taps the bell icon. On the keypad is a domed camera. A blue light comes on and Greta leans in.

"Hi, my name's Greta Da—"

Before she can finish, the door clicks. No buzz, just a click. She gives it a tug and walks across the unremarkable vestibule to the elevator, which slides open before she can push the Up button. Inside, the elevator is an empty metal box—no buttons, not even an intercom or a glass panel that shows the last time the elevator had a safety inspection. *Great.*

"Now what?"

The door closes. The Christmas-morning anticipation that Greta felt is replaced by that deepwater dread. The elevator ascends to what she believes will be the third floor. But who knows?

The doors open and Greta is met by a dark hallway. She steps out. A line of bluish motion-activated lights dots the ceiling and come on, one by one. Greta is again reminded of the arrow etched out of the foamed milk from yesterday's latte as the line of lights guides her, like a runway. They point her to a large metal door—the only door—at the end of the hall.

If Greta's going to change her mind and back out, now's the time to do it. There's no fire exit or stairwell (code violation, anyone?) for a quick escape. She could turn around, go back into the elevator, and hope it'll take her down and out. Back to the land of *bland*. She's come this far already, though. If she turns back now, she'll always be left wondering, *What if?* There'll be no one to blame for her rich-orphan-girl ennui but herself.

"Let's go, Greta. You can do this," she mutters.

The door at the end cracks open. The room that lurks behind it must be a bright one. A shaft of white etches an elongated triangle onto the linoleum floor. Greta picks up the pace. She places her hands on the cool metal and pushes it all the way open. Engulfed by light, she has to shield her eyes to see. She steps in and closes the door behind her.

Greta allows her eyes to adjust.

She's in what she figured would be a reception area of a posh doctor's office or a spa—instead, it's empty. Everything is white—the floors, the walls. There are no visible light fixtures, as if the room luminesces without the help of electricity. There's no desk. No artwork. No pamphlets or posters declaring *Welcome to the Found Object Society*. The metal door she entered through is missing. Gone. Greta runs her hands along the wall and eventually finds its nearly invisible, four-sided seam. There's no doorknob. It feels like an alien-abduction holding cell.

"Jesus Christ, what is this place?"

"Welcome, Greta." The familiar AI voice startles her. Where's it coming from? She quickly whips her head toward the ceiling, looking for an intercom speaker. "Please take a seat, and we'll be with you shortly."

What seat?

She noticed no furniture when she walked in, so where's she supposed to sit?

Greta turns. Behind her, a vintage-looking leather chair has materialized (which is impossible, of course). How did she miss it? She walks over, touches it to make sure it's real, and sits down. The leather is buttery and well-worn. Next to the chair is a narrow side table, its diameter only wide enough to hold a candlestick-type telephone from the early 1900s. The kind where you pick up the receiver from its hook and lean in to speak into the mouthpiece.

The ring of the telephone makes Greta nearly jump out of her skin. Goose bumps cover her arms, run up the back of her neck. It's just a telephone ringing, for crying out loud. Man, she's on edge.

Taking a breath, she announces to the empty room, "Uh, I guess I'll get that?"

She's never answered this kind of phone before. Greta lifts the earpiece off the cradle and picks up the sticklike base.

"Hello?"

Static chatters in her ear, like whoever's on the other end is far away, or, she thinks, from another era long past.

"Would you please place your mobile telephone into the table drawer?" the voice says.

The voice is steady, serious, almost monotone. It's a woman's voice, but not the AI one.

"What? My cell?" Greta cradles her phone in her hands, like the precious infant it's become. "I don't really . . . Do I have to?" Greta says.

Distant crackling. "Yes. Please place your cellular telephone into the drawer in the table. Electronic devices are not permitted in the interview room."

Interview room? Maybe cell phones interfere with the machinery or something. Though what the hell kind of machinery would they even need? This is just a screening for some society or club, right? Greta's anxiety factor ratchets up to seven. *This was a bad idea.*

"Sorry, there's no drawer, and I don't understand why—" The narrowest of drawers slides open of its own accord. A drawer that wasn't there a moment ago.

"Do you see it, Greta?"

"Uh, yeah, I see it, but—"

"Don't worry, you'll get your phone back when you leave. Please place it inside."

Greta complies. It's not like her to be so . . . obedient.

The sober voice says, "Thank you. Please enjoy the candy that we've left for you."

Looking down, Greta sees a candy wrapped in waxed paper resting next to her phone in the drawer she'd sworn had been empty when it first opened. Her stomach drops. A memory shoots up from a great depth, and she gasps for air. The recollection is one she hasn't thought of in years. Decades?

The candy looks like the saltwater taffy she had as a child with her parents on the Mystic boardwalk. She picks it up, smells it. *Blackberry*. Her favorite flavor. The one they'd always buy her. Greta unwraps it. It's even the same color. She rolls it across her finger pads before raising it to eye level, examining it as though she'd be able to spot traces of a drug if it were present. She can't.

"In for a penny . . ." Greta says, and puts it in her mouth. The taste is at once sour and sweet. It *is* the candy from Mystic. *Exactly.*

Greta's feet in flip-flops, squishing into the wooden boardwalk, the *scree* of seagulls lunging for bits of greasy funnel cake on the sand below, the *dunk-dunk* of sailboats bobbing, tied to the dock. The flavor washes over her tongue. Envelops her. Sends her through time.

And now I'm probably going to trip balls because it's made of LSD.

Mouth full, she says into the phone, "How did you know?"

The woman on the line is no longer there. The only sound is a distant static beaming in from what feels like another century.

CHAPTER SIX

"Welcome, Greta. Thank you for responding to our invitation."

A Black woman, impeccably dressed in a beige pantsuit and a lab coat, appears and gestures for Greta to follow her. Where did she come from? As was the case with the chair and the table with the old-timey phone on it, Greta hadn't noticed the doorway this scientist or doctor (or actor?) came out of. Not until now, when she holds it open for her and they enter what looks like a treatment room at a swanky spa.

Greta's still chewing on the luscious candy.

"Was that you on the phone out there? This taffy, it's amazing. How could you—"

"Please get comfortable and we'll have a chat," the woman says, almost mechanically. She holds a computer tablet and gestures toward the center of the room.

There's only one place for Greta to *get comfortable* in this stark and windowless space: An inviting white leather Le Corbusier chaise longue beckons her. The last remnants of tangy blackberry dance across her taste buds as she reclines onto the mid-century lounger. The curves follow her spine and cup under her knees. A cylindrical cushion cradles her neck.

Greta's starting to think there really was something in that taffy. She's floaty, calm. The sounds of the Mystic Seaport boardwalk close around her.

The woman taps and swipes on her tablet before presenting it to Greta.

"If you could sign this waiver, please," she says.

Greta's signed plenty of waivers in her time—before spa laser treatments, dental X-rays, entering a construction site. Any time anyone is worried about getting their ass sued for any reason whatsoever: *waiver.* Greta's not going to let it kill her boardwalk buzz. All that fine print strikes her as banal, beneath the expectations that have been set for her so far. Screw it, though. Greta has the lawyers and financial muscle to buy her way out of their legal gobbledygook.

She scrawls an illegible signature at the bottom without so much as a glance at the language and hands it back to the woman.

"Thank you." The woman tucks the tablet under her arm. "The Found Object Society is an elite and special club—*very* special. Before we continue, I must emphasize the importance of secrecy."

"So far, I don't know anything at all, so keeping it a secret isn't going to be that hard," Greta jokes. Her attempt at levity falls like a deadweight. The woman's expression remains flat, neutral.

Greta adds, "In fact, I don't even know your name?"

"Please call me Eileen."

"Okay, Eileen. I have some questions—a lot of them. First, what is the Found Object Society? Why did you pick me? *How* did you pick me? Was it some Instagram thing or that aging app that me and every other doomscrolling idiot did and then it turns out it's some kind of Russian spyware or something? Not that you're Russian. And who delivered that invite the other night? And that *taffy*?"

"Everyone always has questions."

Greta waits for Eileen to continue, to fill in some blanks. She doesn't. The end of her nonresponse hangs in the air, limp. Eileen simply looks at Greta and smiles. Even her grin comes off as robotic—albeit a very lovely robot, but still. *Robot*.

If she's being honest, Greta's so far unimpressed with this person the Found Object Society has chosen to be the introductory face of their organization. She'd been expecting more. Eileen comes off as more of a pencil pusher than a showy salesperson. Maybe someone called in sick?

Greta idly wonders if any of her friends or acquaintances have come to this place. Has anyone she knows sat in this very chair and looked into Eileen's deep brown (if not bored) eyes, questioning what it is they're doing here and why? Maybe this is like *Eyes Wide Shut* and it will turn out to be some masked, anonymous sex society. Greta's feeling so chill from the taffy, she kind of doesn't care.

Sitting on a white stool, Eileen rolls closer to Greta and places a hand on top of hers. It's an awkward gesture. This must be the *make human contact* part of the training manual. Skin on skin. Look the client in the eye. Woman to woman.

"The Found Object Society offers members an experience beyond imagination. It's for people like you, Greta, where life as you know it simply isn't enough. Our members can afford almost anything, yet life disappoints. Numbs. You're never as alive as you hope to be, as you *need* to be." Eileen squeezes Greta's hand. "When you were driving two nights ago, driving under the influence, speeding along the darkened roadway—"

Greta sits up, interrupting. "I can explain that. I realize it was reckless, and I almost plowed into a tree and killed a possum—" Greta pauses. "Wait, how do you even know that?

I was alone. Did you guys plant a camera on me or something? That's not okay—"

Eileen pats Greta's forearm. "Lean back. It *is* okay, Greta. There was no camera. We're not the police, and you aren't being recorded. You are safe. Tell me, as you were driving, what did you feel? Be honest now."

Greta's head is spinning. This is a crazy dream. Doorways and furniture, *an invitation*, all appearing out of thin air. A woman who she's only just met knowing that she was driving drunk two nights ago. What is this? Entrapment? Blackmail?

"Think about it, Greta."

The candy has dissolved, yet the taste lingers on Greta's tongue. Salt air. Hand in hand with her parents. The *scree* of gulls.

Greta thinks about it. She does. What *was* the feeling she had while driving like a drunken bat out of hell? Taking each curve in the road faster than the one previous. Testing the limits not only of the car but of her own innate survival instinct. How far was she willing to take it? She'd come close to the edge before, yet never that close. Is it that she wants to be *lost* like her parents?

Deserves to be?

If Greta hadn't lied that night twenty years ago, hadn't gotten into a vicious argument with her mom over something not worth remembering and then stormed out into her friend Bridget's waiting car, if she hadn't told her parents (yelled at them, really) that she was sleeping at Bridget's place (and Bridget hadn't told her parents she was staying at Greta's), they'd never have driven out in the middle of the night in search of her.

They'd be alive if it hadn't been for Greta. Their lying, scheming, always-angry-for-no-good-reason teenage daughter, Greta.

Phone calls had triangulated from house to house, and Greta's parents caught them in their lie. They extracted Greta from a house party amid a game of strip quarters. Drunk, naked except for a thong, and humiliated in front of her so-called friends. Her mom dressed her before pouring a seventeen-year-old Greta into the back seat, where she promptly passed out.

After that, Greta has no memory of what happened. Of what caused the accident, of why her mother, the driver, swerved suddenly, losing control of the car and crashing into a maple. It wasn't cold or icy, there were no apparent mechanical issues, no sign of speeding. The police could find no evidence of what made the car lose control, and her parents weren't around to tell her. The *why* of the accident has always remained a mystery.

Greta's limp, alcohol-drenched muscles were what saved her from the crash, her parents dying on impact. Greta came to in a shower of glass like sleet, blood warm as summer rain. She woke in the middle of a nightmare, screaming for the eternity it took for the police and ambulance to arrive. But it was too late, all was lost.

They were lost.

Two nights ago, the possum cut her rush short. Unlike her parents, she managed to elude death, by skidding between the trees instead of into them. The surge, the unspoken wish for self-harm, was like autoerotic asphyxiation, where climaxing—having the orgasm of your fucking life—was heightened because you almost died in the process. La petite mort. The little death.

"Immortal," Greta blurts out. "That night, I felt immortal. Like I was testing the boundaries of life and instead of crashing, I was fine. I teetered on the edge and caught my balance. It was . . . it was exhilarating, yet somehow disappointing."

Greta has told this stranger something she's never dared utter aloud to anyone, not even Lisbeth, not even to herself.

Eileen types something into her tablet.

"Very honest. Good. When you're lucky enough to be able to afford everything in life, what is there left to explore other than the great unknown of death? What could be more exciting than straddling the canyon between living and dying?"

"I don't really want to die, if that's what you're saying." *That's not entirely true, is it though?*

"Of course not, Greta. I said *straddling* the canyon, not plunging into it." Eileen winks, like she's just learned how to and is trying it out for the first time. "What if I told you we could offer you the *experience* of death without actually dying?"

Greta shakes her head in disbelief.

"In certain circumstances, the energy released at the moment of a person's traumatic death can be transferred to whatever that person was touching. By you simply holding that object, Greta, we enable you to live the moment their life was extinguished, and then bungee-cord back out, if you will."

Experience death by holding an object? That can't be.

"I guess I'd have to say: *You're crazy*."

"I assure you, we are not crazy." Eileen smiles that weird smile again. She's leaning in hard, closing her scripted sales pitch, trying to make Greta feel at ease so she can seal the deal, meet her quota. "It's an experience that will change your life. We *guarantee* it. If you're looking for more, Greta, then the Found Object Society is the *most*."

CHAPTER SEVEN

Eileen leans in beside Greta and fiddles with something beneath the chaise. Greta's so relaxed she doesn't budge and lets Eileen get on with whatever the hell it is she's doing. It's not like Greta to be this trusting, this *sedate*. She can't move. Doesn't want to. Eileen's cheek is close and Greta marvels at her near-poreless skin. She'd thought Eileen was in her forties or fifties. Now she's not so sure.

Eileen unfolds an armrest of a sort from behind the chaise. It extends out at the level of Greta's shoulder. It's like nothing she's ever seen. A human arm–size trough (if that's the word?) filled with quicksilver. That's it. It's a liquid metal mold for Greta to place her arm into. Um, no thank you. Quivering, expectant, the shape hints at the round of a bicep, the point of an elbow, a narrowing channel for a wrist, and finally extends into a hand with five slots for fingers. The thing is alive. Humming.

"There *was* acid in that taffy, wasn't there?" Greta says, again trying for a joke. But this isn't funny. It's terrifying, yet Greta's mesmerized.

"You're being humorous, Greta," Eileen says.

"Kinda? But seriously, what is that? It looks like that Han Solo carbonite cast crossed with that bad guy from *Terminator 2*," Greta says, pulling her arm tight to her chest, reluctant to come into contact with whatever that stuff is. *No fucking way*.

"I'm not sure what you're referring to—however, I can assure you this is safe."

Who doesn't know who Han Solo is? The *T2* movie, maybe . . .

Eileen continues, "The Obitus Mold measures your body's reaction to specific imagery. This way we can see how pliable your mind is to what you'll be experiencing at the Found Object Society."

Obitus Mold?

"Can't you just use some good old-fashioned electrodes or a heart rate monitor?"

"No, Greta. Our technology is well beyond any of that." Eileen coaxes Greta's right arm away from her chest. "Please relax. You'll be fine. Most people find this very pleasant."

"What if I'm not *most people*?" Greta says, acquiescing to Eileen's touch.

Eileen holds Greta's forearm above the Obitus Mold like an offering. The liquid metal reacts to the proximity of Greta's skin. It ripples and lifts upward as though gravity has reversed direction. The substance seems almost sentient. Snaking through the air, it stops short of Greta's flesh. Eileen lowers Greta's arm until she's in contact with the otherworldly substance. The liquid swoops around her forearm in an abrupt embrace.

Greta gasps, though not from pain. It's cold *and* it's warm. Unearthly. Soothing and disconcerting. It's everything all at once. She looks down as the mercurial mass rushes over her skin like the rapids of a river around a rock. Even if it were possible for Greta to pull her arm out, she's not sure she'd want to.

The room goes black. Eileen is gone.

Greta's body and mind are a sieve—words, faces, landscapes sift through her. She's no longer a single entity, but thousands of pulsing pieces flowing together, bouncing off one another, emitting heat, light, sound. Each one a tantalizing tongue flicking across her body. Teasing. No single delicious image lingers long enough for her to hold on to it, no matter how badly she wants to—needs to. It's the place of half sleep, where part of the mind is connected to the outside world while the other half luxuriates in decadent, near-pornographic images that are so of the moment that surely there could be no way of forgetting them—yet if awakened before dropping down into a complete dream state, they disappear, and upon fully waking there's nothing left but a notion, an echo. A longing for the thing that had been so clear and now is gone. The vision that had been so present only moments before simply evaporates.

How long Greta remains in this state, she can't be sure. The black recedes as the room's illumination rises like the sun, the lights of an airplane cabin easing on as dawn breaks on the other side of the Atlantic. The Obitus Mold is gone and both her hands lie slack in her lap. She examines her arm for traces of the molten metal. Blue fluorescence dances across the skin of her forearm—the Obitus Mold's lingering lover's kiss like a breeze across a sand dune.

The lights are fully up and Greta tries to remember, to catch the pieces of what was surely a kind of dream. She closes her eyes tight, grasping at the images, like trying to hold on to water. What had she seen? Felt? The experience falls through her fingers. What were the sensations? Each becomes a slippery notion, a fading impression, taunting inklings. There was comfort at times, bits of terror, snippets of languages that weren't her own, yet she understood them nonetheless. That she remembers. What words? She tries to extract the memory. She can't.

Gone.

There's nothing left except the longing to live it again. The *need.* The high of something so foreign from any experience she's ever had. More. Greta wants more. It wasn't like being drunk, or on molly or ketamine. This went deep, nesting in her soul and leaving her hungry. Starving. Even though this was no more than a test of some kind, and not the real Found Object Society experience—if today is even *close* to that—Greta's all in. What was the joke about trying a drug for the first time?

The first taste is free.

That's it. This one is free, but she's willing to pay anything—*anything*—for the next one.

Eileen is by her side, materializing from nowhere, like everything else: the card through the mail slot, the QR code, the chair and the old-timey phone. The taffy.

"How are you feeling, Greta?" she says.

"Like I've been teased to the point of no return." Greta watches the blue electrical storm recede from her arm, retreat into her fingernail beds. "And this wasn't the actual Found Object Society experience, right?"

"That's right. This was a test for us to see how you'll react. How open your mind is to things that defy explanation," Eileen says.

"You're telling me the Found Object experience is even *more* intense than this?"

"There's no comparison. You'll see for yourself on your first visit to the Found Object Society. That is, if you're approved to become a member."

Eileen helps Greta up from the chaise.

If? What the fuck? "What do you mean, *if*? Sign me up."

"In due time, Greta. You'll find your phone in the elevator," Eileen says, like that's a perfectly logical thing. "We'll be in touch."

"Wait, *be in touch*? Hang on. I passed the test, right?" Greta's feeling twitchy, unaccustomed to the possibility of being denied anything.

"Don't worry. You did fine. We'll contact you when it's time," Eileen says.

Greta turns to go to the door she entered from. It's not there.

"The exit is here," Eileen says, pointing to a different and very obvious doorway that Greta's positive wasn't there before.

The fog lifts from Greta's mind. She stops at the threshold of the door and turns back to Eileen. "The taffy. How did you know about the taffy? It's the same one I had as a kid. Not similar, it's the *same*. Even that blackberry flavor. How is that possible?" Greta says.

"You may ask yourself how any of this is possible, Greta. Yet here we are," Eileen says, as the door closes between them.

CHAPTER EIGHT

Greta's in the hallway again, standing outside the elevator door. It slides open, and she steps in.

As Eileen promised, her cell phone is inside. It leans against the rear wall like it's been hanging out behind the school gym having a smoke, waiting for her return. Greta picks it up, activating the home screen.

2:08 p.m.

That can't be right. She walked into the office at two p.m. She had to have been there for at least an hour. Thirty minutes, *minimum*. The elevator deposits her back into the nondescript vestibule and, dazed, she walks out onto Duane Street. She looks back up at the building and counts to the third floor. Is that where she's been for the past . . . *eight minutes*?

A FedEx truck is pulled up in front of a fire hydrant, music blaring. Greta can hear the delivery person in the back of the truck, banging around. The woman bounds out of the back door like a linebacker, balancing several boxes.

"Excuse me," Greta says. The FedEx lady keeps walking. "Excuse me? FedEx person?"

That gets her attention. She turns to face Greta, boxes swaying in her arms. "What?"

"Sorry. What time is it?" Greta says.

"You kidding me?" the FedEx lady says, indicating the boxes. She glances down at her Apple Watch. "Two ten."

"It's two ten? You're *sure*?" Greta says.

The FedEx lady huffs and keeps walking down the block.

It was true, then. All that had just transpired: the old-fashioned phone call, the Mystic boardwalk taffy, Eileen, the Terminator-liquid-metal-arm-wrap Obitus Mold, and the subsequent salacious-dream-slash-acid-trip had been compressed into eight minutes. Eight fucking minutes.

"Impossible," Greta says out loud.

You may ask yourself how any of this is possible, Greta. Yet here we are.

This is all too strange, too crazy. There has to be a logical explanation for it, but Greta's having a hard time figuring out what that could be. She ambles up West Broadway, shoppers weaving in and out of the tony boutiques, café dwellers with blankets on their laps, huddled under heat lamps with their tiny dogs, sipping Aperol spritzes and Negronis, forcing spring out of hiding.

Ever since that card came through the mail slot . . .

Since the appearance of the card two days ago, the focus of her life has shifted and landed squarely on the Found Object Society. Was it real? Have these people—people like Eileen—really figured out a way to tap into the energy (or whatever the hell it is) a person gives off as they're dying? *Our technology is well beyond any of that.* Our? And if there is a palpable energy, how does it transfer, like Eileen said, into an object—the last one they touched before their death?

Greta's never been into paranormal or supernatural stuff, especially since her parents died. If they are hovering around somewhere, Greta doesn't want to know about it. The finality of death being the end, and nothing more, holds appeal—at least as it applies to her parents. She can't bear the thought of them observing her stumble through her embarrassing life without them. Lisbeth Carr had been the only person who cared enough to keep her anchored, from floating away. Lis understood the broken shards of Greta's heart. Most other people thought of Greta Davenport as the rich party girl who would buy your drinks or dinner if you hung around long enough on a Friday night.

No, if Greta's parents have been silent observers of her life for the past twenty years, it'd be unbearable. The idea of it is nauseating. That's nonsense, of course it is. And maybe the Found Object Society is nonsense, too. Maybe it's a brilliant ruse to get rich people like Greta to pony up for a supposed *experience of a lifetime*. Like all those billionaires lining up to fly into space in that turd Jeff Bezos's Blue Origin, or the other turd Elon Musk's SpaceX rocket. The Found Object Society is no more than a genius sleight of hand, a series of Hollywood special effects, a lab-engineered drug that taps into the pliability of people's minds. Greta's been handpicked based on her social media interactions and bank accounts. Period. There's a clever bunch of Gen-Z researchers, holed up in their bedrooms, wearing pj's, gathering data, and creating lists of suckers like Greta.

If that's true, and if her little interview today is any indication, they've done a great fucking job. Because they've got her, hook, line, and sinker.

CHAPTER NINE

Greta can't sleep.

Her neck is still stiff, and it's what-the-fuck o'clock. There's a couple arguing down on the sidewalk below her on Greene Street and she's watching them from her balcony. They're both gesticulating like drunken marionettes. Every so often, one will lean on a lamppost or the brick wall. It's hard to hear what they're saying ten floors up, but it isn't pretty. This probably isn't the way they'd planned for their night to end. Or maybe it's their thing: argue, have makeup sex, argue again. All the corners humans paint themselves into. The comforting loops and repetitions of life, even when they're as ugly as a public altercation on a sidewalk (or a good old-fashioned champagne bath at a gala). Change is the real enemy, not the cheating boyfriend nor the soul-crushing job. The fear of breaking the pattern, trying something new, even if it holds the promise of something better.

She's in her robe, feet bare, wearing a path into the floor as she paces back and forth between the loft's living room and the balcony while she replays her experience in the office (or was it a lab, or a stage set?) of the Found Object Society. That broke the pattern, no doubt about it. It'd been out of this world, anything but *bland*. She pushes aside the doubts and second-guessing that it's an elaborate hoax, a party drug, and instead she focuses on what it felt like.

Greta's taking a shot in the dark, trying to make sense of what seems like a sci-fi movie. The Obitus Mold sensed when her skin was near. Maybe it was heat sensitive. The silvery liquid approached her like a cautious dog before it enveloped her arm with its metallic pudding. It was an entity in and of itself. A presence that read her thoughts and showed her things that went by so fast, she can't remember more than slashes, lurching emotions, and the need to feel it again. When she'd first clicked the link on the QR code, there'd been a montage of objects that were hard to make out but must've registered somewhere within her brain's hippocampus.

And the taffy. Had the candy been the delivery system for whatever this drug is they've cooked up? The taste transported Greta back to that long-forgotten memory of walking the Mystic boardwalk with her parents. The same way smell can return you to a different place and time—one whiff of apple pie, or the smell of warm summer rain, and *poof*, you're there again with those same people, in that same place, maybe even decades past. It's time travel. Your own personal time machine thanks to your olfactory system.

The human mind's a hell of a thing. Greta isn't wide awake because she's trying to find the wizard behind the curtain. No, she's awake because she needs to get to Oz. The officious Eileen had showed her the tantalizing path and now she wants to walk it the whole way, to live someone else's death, to plunge to the bottom of that canyon before snapping back up again.

We'll be in touch.

Isn't that what people say when they mean they most definitely will *not* be in touch? She couldn't have failed the test—could she? Eileen said she'd done *fine*. Greta has to keep her shit together and be patient. Will it be a day? A week? Months?

If she has to wait that long, she'll go bonkers. Will they call her, or deliver another card through the mail slot?

An idea stops her interminable pacing in its tracks: What if Greta installs a security camera outside the house? Then she could catch them in the act. Greta had been hasty in her slaughter of almost all things tech and Ryan-related. Now she regrets throwing the surveillance system out. No matter, she'll buy a simple one she can hook up herself.

She's about to leave the balcony to place an order on Amazon when she gets the distinct feeling that she's being watched. Greta turns to face the apartment window across from hers. In the dark of the balcony, two people stand side by side, silent, watching. They're two-dimensional black silhouettes, like cutouts. One figure has an arm draped across the shoulder of the other. Like her father would do with her mother. The simple gesture that meant, to a young Greta, everything was right in the world. Greta's breath catches in her throat, skin flaring with goose bumps. A light comes on in the apartment across, illuminating the balcony. Not people, after all, but two potted shrubs.

Greta's mind is playing tricks.

How many days has it been since the gala? Three? Maybe it's three. No, maybe two. Or three. Greta is losing track of time. It's become elastic.

Greta's back home in Connecticut. After what she thought she saw on the balcony across the street, she was unable to sleep. There'd been no point in trying. So instead, she made her way home from the Greene Street loft before the sun had even come up. *By train.*

That fact alone demonstrates the level of her restlessness, desperation. There are few versions of Greta Davenport that would deign to take public transportation, and in the wee hours last night, she was one of the few, the unproud. True, she could've called Carl, her longtime driver who takes her back and forth between the city and Litchfield County. Calling him at that hour would've been a bridge too far, even for Greta. Not when he's fast asleep at home with his wife and kids in whatever weird-ass, hive-inducing neighborhood he lives in, in Queens. A borough she's never so much as set foot in unless she was at LaGuardia Airport—which, until its eight-billion-dollar renovation, had been the suckiest of all the New York City airports. The near-empty train ride from Grand Central had been a blur, and same with the Uber ride home from the station.

Greta can't shake how real those figures on the balcony had felt. Chalk it up to lack of sleep and the rush and comedown after her visit with Eileen—her *eight-minute* visit—and that could explain what she thought she saw. The hallucination of her parents across the way makes sense. Anytime death becomes a topic of conversation, it gets Greta thinking of her parents. The Found Object Society is all about the dead and the experience of dying. That's its raison d'être. So, it's only natural that Greta's mind would go that way, right?

She's wearing the same clothes she wore to her meeting with Eileen. Greta hadn't bothered changing when she left a few hours ago. That's not like her. She's getting ripe, but slowing down enough to strip and shower doesn't appeal. A dangerous energy is crackling off her as she wanders the vast house she grew up in.

She comes to a stop by the living room window. The sun rises behind the fields and woods of the property. Low light filters through a fog that hangs above the pond behind the house. Rays of sunlight slice through it, breaking it apart. A pair of mated swans paddle through the miasma. Greta half expects her parents to emerge from the mist as well, followed by Murphy Brown the cat, and a parade of other lost souls. *Lost.*

"Keep it together, Greta," she says.

She slides herself down the wall and sits on the floor, checking her phone for any word from the Found Object Society. Crickets.

It's barely after six in the morning, way before business hours. Then again, the original invitation came after midnight. There's no way of knowing what to expect, or when. Greta needs to do more than live in limbo until she hears from them. *Them?* Or is it a one-woman operation? Eileen and an AI voice. *Our technology*, that's what Eileen had said, so it has to be more than just her. Especially for an organization as elaborate as this one appears to be. Eileen never asked for Greta's cell number or email address. They seem to already know everything about her, so they'll find her when they're good and ready. To be safe, Greta switches her phone off vibrate and turns the volume up as high as it can go. God forbid she misses them when the time comes.

From her vantage point, seated on the wide-plank floors, the open expanse of the living and dining area looks even bigger, hollow. Greta feels like a child, sitting in the wide emptiness that she's created. The guts of the house were scooped out in the remodel. The comforting nooks and walled-in spaces sloughed away. The baubles, the albums, the *stuff*—all the things that had defined the house of her parents, the house where they had existed together—were erased. Gone. Little else remains, save for the soaring stone chimney.

Most days it's a relief, but here at daybreak, after an interview that has altered the course of her life in a way she has yet to define, she struggles to breathe. Ghosts surround her, filling the void, stealing her air.

CHAPTER TEN

What are you up to? Want to come over?

Greta sends Lis a text. She can't be alone today, not like this. It'll be good to see Lisbeth, talk to her. Lis can drop that anchor for Greta, the one she needs whenever she floats off. And, man, is she adrift.

Greta's going to tell Lis about the Found Object Society. At least that's what she's decided at this moment. She may chicken out. The AI's instructions were clear: *Do not speak of this to anyone, please. This is important.* Greta's afraid if she doesn't tell Lis, she's going to lose her shit waiting. Lis is the keeper of Greta's darkest secrets, her fears. So telling her is almost like talking to herself. If Lis keeps quiet about it, they'll never know.

Lis's response is swift. She'll be over soon. Greta looks like crap. She has to tidy herself up before Lis gets here or there'll be hell to pay. Hot water pounds Greta's neck and shoulders. The much-needed shower kneads away the achy stiffness from her near-crash the other night.

More humanized, she gets dressed. Her jeans hang looser than usual, her eye sockets deep and sunken, cheekbones jutting out, trying to escape through her skin. How does she look this withered after only a couple of days? It's like the morning after she tried molly for the first time. Little sea monkeys of methylenedioxymethamphetamine swam in her spinal fluid, gnawed away at her vertebrae. She had looked and felt like death.

It was worth it, though, for the high. That delicious buoyancy, the absence of sorrow and regret, was worth every moment of the comedown.

It's what kept her coming back to molly, time and again. *Will it be the same, the thing that keeps her coming back to the Found Object Society?* she thinks.

"Well, don't you look like a smack addict," Lis declares, when Greta opens the door. "What the fuck, G?"

"Great to see you, too," Greta says.

Lisbeth strides in like she lives there, and in a way, she does. She's been coming over to the Davenport house since that first Thanksgiving of their freshman year at college. Lis drove Greta home for the break, and when she realized she would be alone—not even an aunt or uncle or cousins to be thankful for—she dragged her to her parents' place.

Greta had been orphaned the year before and had little family to speak of—none who cared, at least. Then again, Greta hadn't been the ideal niece or granddaughter. She was a spoiled, cavalier rich kid and couldn't be bothered with relatives. Her father's sister, Aunt Tilly, had been designated as her guardian for the short period before she turned eighteen. Once Greta officially became an adult, they'd had a big falling-out, and Aunt Tilly's obligation was over. Tilly took her chunk of the inheritance and signed the rest away to Greta without a thought for how that might affect a grieving teenager. So Greta and Murphy Brown were left to fend for themselves in the big stone house. A girl, her parents' cat, and piles of inheritance money.

Lis heads into the kitchen to make herself a coffee. She takes out her favorite dumb mug, the one that reads *Someone's got a case of the Mondays!* in red letters across it. Greta braces herself as she watches her prop it under the spigot of the built-in Keurig and pop in a pod.

"It's broken," Greta warns.

Lis collapses against the refrigerator door and moans, "Ryan and his goddamned gadgets."

"My sentiments exactly."

Lis roots around in the cabinets, leaving all the doors open in the process, as she is wont to do. Greta follows behind her, closing each one, like they're an old married couple.

"There's, like, no coffee here at all," she says.

"I know. I need to go shopping."

"You suck."

Greta nods. She does, in fact, suck.

Lis throws some Earl Grey tea bags onto the counter and takes out another mug for Greta. She fills the kettle with water and plunks it down on the stovetop.

"I hate tea," Lis reminds her.

Greta shrugs. "I forgot about the broken Keurig. Sorry."

"There's nothing to eat either," Lis says.

"Yeah." Greta makes a half-assed attempt to look through the refrigerator. She knows there's not much in it.

"Peachy," Lis says.

She shoves Greta to the side and reopens cabinets, taking out anything resembling food and dumping it on the kitchen island. Stale stoned-wheat crackers, jam, peanut butter. In the fridge she finds a stick of chorizo, adding it to the mound.

Lis gets out two plates and cutlery and makes something out of nothing. Cracker halves with dollops of peanut butter and jam, slices of chorizo. Their pas de deux continues as Greta closes what Lis has opened.

They both sit on stools at the kitchen island, picnic rations before them. Lis gives Greta a long, hard look.

"Okay, seriously, what's going on with you? Ever since the gala, you've been in a weird place," Lis says. "It can't be about Ryan. Wait, you went to the doctor yesterday. Is something wrong?"

Greta had invited her over so she could tell her about the Found Object Society. Now she's finding it hard to muster up the courage. She should just show her.

"Of course it's not about Ryan." The invitation from the Found Object Society beckons, tucked in her back pocket. "And there was no doctor's appointment." Greta pulls the card out, holding it up for inspection. "It's this."

"A white card? What am I looking at here?"

Greta lays the card flat on the island and pushes it toward Lisbeth. "You have your phone?"

"There's a dumb question. Why?"

"Turn on your camera and hold it over the card."

Lis takes her phone from her bag, unlocks it, and activates the camera. Greta's heart is thumping so loud she's sure Lis can hear it. This is probably a mistake, but she has to tell someone.

The kettle whistles, and they both jump at the sound. Lis gets up and pours the water over the tea bags.

"Let me make the lousy tea first, okay? Then I'll play your little game."

Lis sips from her novelty mug and pans the phone camera above the card. Nothing happens.

"What am I doing here, Greta? What am I looking at?"

"You're doing it wrong. Stop moving it around so much—hover."

"Take it easy. I think I know how to use my phone."

Greta gets up and stands behind Lis, looking over her shoulder. She reaches around her and flips the card. Her hands shake.

"This side. Try this side," Greta says.

"Okay, okay. Calm down. You're looming. You're weirding me out a bit."

Lis makes a show of holding the camera over the card. She moves from one quadrant to the other. Each time she moves and holds the camera, she looks back at Greta, shrugging—nothing is happening.

"I don't understand what I'm doing with this card, or what you think I should be seeing. Give me a clue?"

"Let me look at it." Greta grabs the card back and walks to the far end of the island to retrieve her phone. She unlocks it with Face ID and holds it over the white square. Instead of the usual QR code, an image pops up, followed by a message that makes her stomach drop. *How on earth . . . ?*

Greta's ears ring and the room goes white. She tosses the phone down like it's burned her.

Lis jumps up. "Jesus Christ. What happened? What is it?"

Greta takes the card and tosses it into the garbage bin under the sink.

Lis walks over and grabs Greta by the shoulders. "You're white as a sheet, G. What's going on here? I'm your best friend. Tell me." She focuses on Greta's eyes, but Greta won't look at her. "Are you on something? Is that it?"

She kind of is. Greta's coming unhinged. Lis's camera didn't lock onto anything when she looked at it, though Greta's did, and there's a message. Loud and clear.

On Greta's phone is an image of Lis holding the *Someone's got a case of the Mondays!* mug, taken what must only be moments ago. Beneath the photo are seven words:

We told you not to tell anyone.

For the next hour, Greta backpedals. She makes excuses for her erratic behavior: Her lack of sleep (which isn't a lie). Even her drunken near-crash the night of the gala. Anything. *Anything* to steer Lis away from a truth about the Found Object Society that's starting to crystallize in Greta's mind: Somehow, the operators of the society are watching her movements, are *documenting* missteps with photographic evidence. If that's true, where are the cameras? How are they here?

Lis reluctantly buys what Greta is selling. There've been enough times in their relationship when Greta's gone off the deep end and Lis has pulled her back to safety. Greta hopes Lis thinks it's one of those times and nothing more.

To be safe, Greta takes Lis's mug before she's finished and puts it in the dishwasher.

"You don't want this anymore, do you? You hate tea, like you said."

"Whatever. It's cold anyway," Lis says.

What sort of game are they playing here? With a lurch, Greta imagines every ounce of Lis's vivacity extinguished with a mere flip of the switch and forever trapped in that stupid mug. She gets Lis to touch as many other non–novelty mug objects as possible before she leaves. It's manic. Photographs that she's seen a million times before, the Manolo Blahniks she wore the other night, a houseplant in a long line of murdered houseplants.

"Jesus, if I didn't know any better, I'd think you were trying to get my fingerprints all over everything so you can frame me."

Greta's laugh is stilted.

Lis continues, "Oh, wait. That's *good*. Who're you gonna kill?

Is it Ryan? Please tell me it's Ryan. I won't take the fall, though. I'll tell the police that the murderer is Ms. Greta Davenport, with a dead houseplant in the study."

"Don't tempt me, Lis. Sorry about today. I just need sleep. Okay? I'll make it up to you, promise."

Greta pushes her toward the door.

Lis steps out onto the pea gravel walkway. "You're trying to get rid of me. I get it. Please take care of yourself. Go grocery shopping. Eat the food you buy. Sleep. Don't drive drunk. Blah, blah, blah." Lis makes an abrupt turn back to Greta and hugs her, whispering in her ear, "You're up to something. I know how you operate. But I'll let it go for now. I love you. I'm not going anywhere, okay? You need me? I'm here."

"I know that. I do," Greta says. "Text when you get home, okay?"

"Sure, *Mom*, will do."

Lis gets into her green Porsche 911 and drives off.

The familiar sound of tires crunching on the driveway brings Greta back to her childhood. To when she'd wait in bed for her parents to come home from a party, unable to sleep until she heard the refrain of treaded tires rolling across gravel. It wasn't until then—until she knew her mother and father were safe and home—that she'd allow herself to drift into slumber.

As Lis turns out of the driveway and onto the road, Greta's head swims with panic. Is her best friend safe? Did she endanger her life? It's nuts. Greta has to get some sleep, get her shit together, and think about what she's gotten herself into. This is turning into a *Twilight Zone* episode. But it's real. Greta's nearly 100 percent sure that it is. If not? Then she's well and truly broken with reality.

Eileen told Greta that the energy released at the time of a traumatic death could transfer into the last object a person had touched—like, say, a novelty mug? There's no denying the intent of the Found Object Society's message: *Tell anyone about us, and there will be consequences*.

CHAPTER ELEVEN

With Lis gone, Greta retrieves the card from the kitchen garbage. The tea bag has stained it like a Rorschach test. Greta tries to wipe it—it's too late.

"Shit," she says, wondering if it'll still work.

Work? How this two-dimensional card functions at all is a complete mystery. Somehow, it knew that Greta was trying to get Lis to look at it, that she wanted to tell her all about this crazy, not-of-this-world experience she's having. Not only did it know, but it could see—the card could *see*, dammit—the mug that Lis was holding, and it threatened her best friend with imminent death. Is there a microscopic camera woven into the fibers of the paper? How stupid is that? How outright bananas?

What if Greta had disregarded the warning? Would a wooden beam have fallen from the ceiling and clocked Lis in the head? Would she have been electrocuted by a faulty outlet near the sink when she was washing out the mug? That Greta is entertaining the idea that a *piece of paper* has sway over life and death is absurd.

It's bullshit.

Greta wants out, to go back to her boring, predictably louche life. She picks up the card and tears it in half.

Greta's functioning on no sleep, no real food. She's dehydrated, and now she's ripped in half what she believed to be the portal to an experience unlike any other. She wants to cry, but she doubts there's enough fluid in her to squeeze out any tears.

Her phone chirps. It's Lis.

Home. Thanks for "coffee" (rolling eyes emoji) Talk tomorrow?

She's home safe.

(Thumbs-up emoji)

There's a clunk at the front door. Greta starts at the sound, knocking over a barstool in the process. She bounds over toward the noise like Pavlov's dog. Deflated, she realizes it's not another invitation, but the night-vision trail camera she ordered from Amazon Prime. She watches the UPS truck cruise out of the driveway and back onto the road.

She opens the box in the kitchen, ignoring the tea-stained remains of the card. The directions to install the camera are convoluted and stilted, riddled with excessive capitalization and superfluous exclamation points. Still, the camera proves easy enough to set up, and she connects it to her phone via the app. Now, where to put it?

The point of the exercise is to film someone as they deliver another card—Greta's convinced there will be one—through the mail slot. She can't imagine the Found Object Society calling or texting instead. When Eileen said *We'll be in touch*, Greta should've asked more questions. *We'll be in touch.* Vague, vague, vague.

She straps the camera to a dogwood tree that faces the entryway and front door. It's not exactly *hidden*, but the placement is right. Greta sets it to detect motion and shoot video for up to thirty seconds. That should be enough time to catch someone in the act.

The picture quality is impressive as she activates the app. Greta can see herself standing there and looking at her phone in the live playback. She waves at the trail camera. She's watching herself waving while she watches herself on the phone. *Bizarre.* Walking in and out of frame, she makes sure the camera view is wide enough to get someone approaching from several angles. There's a slight delay between when Greta moves and when it's reflected in the live video on her phone—like near past tense.

Greta walks out of the camera's line of vision and past the forsythias that stand guard around the front door. She looks back down at the screen.

The on-camera Greta is still anchored in the same spot, unmoving, like a sentry. How can the delay be that long? There must be a glitch. On-camera Greta stands there, looking directly at the trail camera lens. She hasn't moved, but the image isn't frozen. Real Greta can see on-camera Greta blink. Breathe. Doppelgänger Greta is gaunt to the point of transparency. Real Greta looks over to where the on-camera Greta appears to be standing. There's no one there. She looks down at her phone in time to see the other Greta mouthing something—several words. Then she pauses, and then seems to say them again, like her needle is stuck. She's emphatic, but there's no sound. Doppelgänger Greta repeats the words—whatever they are—again and again.

Then she's gone.

CHAPTER TWELVE

Greta's on the couch in the living room, hiding under a blanket. Body shaking, she can't stop thinking about the version of herself she saw on the app. The horrifying impossibility of it. On-camera Greta was wearing the same clothes that the real Greta was wearing earlier, but they hung loose, like she still had to grow into them—or like she'd shrunk.

There was a frailty about that version. A body bending, ready to break. Was she old or young? How the fuck was she there at all? There should've been sound, but there wasn't. Greta hadn't been recording, so she can't watch it again to read camera-twin Greta's lips. The more she replays it in her mind, the more the memory smears and the more her grip on sanity loosens. The words had come out of her mouth rapid-fire, as if they were being directed at the real Greta. Imploring her to listen.

Again, she closes her eyes and tries to picture it, to picture this crazy, impossible thing, that there was another version of herself looking back at her, speaking, trying to tell her something. Greta's world over the past several days has been a series of impossible things. Difficult-to-explain events. An hour compressed into eight minutes. Greta's never been one to believe in ghosts or UFOs, yet here she is embracing the possibility of the impossible.

If she can figure out what the other Greta was saying, maybe it'll make sense of the rest of this. Her own mouth, a version of it, at least, had been forming words. Not screaming or yelling, simply repeating a series of words over and over again—that's what it looked like, anyway. A song? A poem? A call to action?

Exhaustion overwhelms Greta. At least she's on the couch, near the front door, so she can hear the metallic *clank* of the mail slot. This puzzle won't get solved tonight, not right now. She reaches out from under her blanket tent and opens the bottle of Tylenol PM she's left on the floor. Greta has to shut off her brain, to push herself down into the deep end of sleep. . . .

Seventeen-year-old Greta's topless, wearing only a thong that she secretly purchased. Her mom would not approve of a thong. Her mom would not approve of her lying and saying she was staying at Bridget Bower's house when they were really going to a party at Todd Daehler's, his parents away in Palm Beach. Her mom never approves of anything Greta does. Fuck her mom.

Greta's drunk, way drunk, a quarter between her thumb and index finger. She bounces it on the tabletop and it lands with a splash in a cup of beer. Everyone cheers. Todd Daehler leans in and kisses her neck again. He smells sour, skin hot. Under the table, his hand fights against the current of Greta's clenched thighs, trying to work its way upstream, prying apart the channel between her legs, meeting with resistance. Heat radiates from her center. She considers loosening her grip.

The group of seven other drunken teens, all seated in a circle and in varying states of undress, yell and chug in response to Greta's bull's-eye with the quarter. Some remove a piece of clothing. A clove cigarette smolders on a plate. The teenagers' voices echo through the adult-free house. Another braless girl across from Greta holds an arm across her nipples. Two lacrosse boys on either side of her stare. One puts a hand on the girl's forearm to move it away and she shrugs it off.

A beam of light cuts across the room and a lacrosse boy looks away from the braless girl.

"Hey, whose car is that? Isn't everyone here?" he slurs.

Their reactions are unified, but slow. They jump up from the table, revealing exposed body parts. Pert breasts in motion, a hard-on in tighty-whities, six-pack abs on a boy that doesn't have to try. Greta's the last to stand, and when she does, the booze rushes through her bloodstream and whacks into her brain like a two-by-four. Her clothes are behind her and commingled with pants and socks that belong to someone else. She reaches for them as the other bodies scatter, grabbing for theirs.

When a boy calls out *Holy Shit, it's Greta's parents!* seventeen-year-old Greta freezes where she stands. She's topless and wearing her illicit thong. She can't move and her parents have found her. Deer in the headlights.

A sound wakes Greta from her Tylenol PM–induced slumber on the couch. Fog grips her thoughts. The cloying stink of clove. The smell of hormone-jacked skin. Cheap beer like shag carpet across her tongue. The headlights of her parents' car.

She emerges from under the blanket. Eyes open, she takes in her surroundings. The colossus chimney shoots through the center of the living room, no walls or shelves flanking it on either side. She's in the present. Greta rolls onto her back. Her neck catches. The whiplash from her near-crash reintroduces itself.

The ceiling is unchanged from when she grew up. If she'd woken and looked up instead of out, she might have thought she'd gone back in time. The same series of spidery cracks stretch from the top of the window frame and spread toward the center of the room. A family tree of fractures that's never extended any farther.

Wait, a sound woke her up.

She sits bolt upright, disregarding the pain. Her mind clears. A noise had pulled her to consciousness. What was it?

The metallic clank *of the mail slot.*

She frees herself from the tangle of blankets. Sweatpants twisted, socks hanging off, Greta makes her way to the front door. Cautiously, she leans against the doorjamb that leads to the entryway. Her breathing is rapid and shallow.

It's another card. The square has landed in the same spot as the other one. Though the size is the same, the color is different. This one is black.

CHAPTER THIRTEEN

The card is black as a death notice. Sooty, dark, a starless sky.

Lis got home safe. She'd texted and said as much. Greta isn't sure what to do first: Check the card for a message, or check the trail camera footage? Either way, she needs her phone and scrambles back to the couch, where she fell asleep with it next to her. Frenzied, she tears off the blanket and digs between the cushions. She yanks them off the couch and finds her phone resting in the hammock of cloth that stretches across the sofa's frame.

Holding the phone to her face to unlock it, she walks back to the entryway. Greta's moving too fast. It doesn't recognize her. The screen asks for the passcode instead. She's walking and typing at the same time. Greta types in the eight-digit code and the dots shudder in discontent. She tries again, tapping imprecisely. Same result. Third time's the charm? Again, the disgruntled shimmy from the screen.

"Fuck!"

Greta takes a deep breath, forcing herself to slow down. She's got three more attempts before the phone locks her out. Her fingers tremble. Tapping with caution, she hits each of the eight digits of her passcode.

Finally.

Now, which to do first? Check the card for a QR code. Shoveling the black square off the floor, she swats aside house keys and lipsticks from the entry table and lays it on the flat surface. Like the first one, this card has no discernible markings, all black with a diamond dusting of luminescence. Camera on, she hovers it above the square, waiting for the telltale nibble of a QR code. It locks on right away, displaying four yellow brackets, one at each corner, the link at the bottom.

Greta's been dizzy with need ever since she tore the other card in half. It'd been the equivalent of flushing a stash of perfectly good coke down the toilet when the cops busted the door down. Here it is again, though. The fix. The promise of something even greater than her experience in the chaise in Tribeca with Eileen—the stoic and well-coiffed pusher.

Link activated, Greta's screen explodes in a supernova of light hurtling through space. The animation is brilliant, taking her on a ride through a twisting flume of stars, then depositing the viewer inside a core of white. It holds for a few seconds, bright, throbbing. It gives Greta a chance to catch her breath.

The familiar, soothing AI voice returns. "Congratulations, Greta. We would like to invite you to become a member of the Found Object Society."

Greta shrieks with delight, overjoyed by the acceptance into a society that not only has upended her life and made her feel like a junkie, but has even threatened to hurt her best friend should Greta speak of it. She's come undone. No doubt about it.

"Hi? Yes! I accept. Of course!" Greta sounds like an overeager schoolgirl getting asked to the prom.

The light pulses again. Is it thinking? "Thank you, Greta."

The screen bursts with a flurry of numbers and symbols, thousands of them running vertically, a waterfall of numerical gibberish.

"In a few moments, you will receive an encrypted link to make a payment for your membership."

Payment. Duh, of course there's a fee. Whatever it is, she'll pay it.

"To secure your place, we will expect a payment of five hundred thousand dollars by the end of the business day."

Holy. Shit.

Five hundred thousand dollars. Still, a fraction of the cost for a ride on one of the douchebag billionaire's space buses. Her wealth adviser won't like it. Screw her. It's not like Greta has children to send to college (or to pass a trust fund to). If Greta dies, Lis gets everything. Until then, it's her money.

It's before sunrise and Greta is awake. Is it Wednesday morning? Just four days since the gala, four unbelievable days since this madness started. Out in the predawn dark, a mockingbird is the only sound. Songbirds shouldn't sing in the dark, yet that's what a lovelorn mockingbird does.

Phone in hand, Greta walks through the gaping cavity of the downstairs level to her desk. She opens her laptop and logs on to one of her bank accounts to prepare to transfer funds.

Transferring five hundred thousand dollars to an account belonging to a company—a *society*—that, as far as the world wide web is concerned, doesn't exist. It's reckless. But Greta figures if they were out to get her money, they could've cleared her accounts a few days ago, after she'd scanned that first QR code.

The shower of numbers slows to a trickle and, as promised, a link appears with bank information. If Greta was a detective, or half as tech savvy as Ryan, maybe she could trace the IBAN number to see where the money's landing. The Found Object Society surely has triple-scrubbed, five-times-removed accounts scattered throughout Switzerland and the West Indies. If the CIA breaks down her door in a few hours, well, then she'll know she's fallen for some secret weapon–funding scheme for Putin or North Korea. She takes a breath, then approves the wire.

Transfer complete.

Five hundred thousand dollars travels through the ether, soon to land in a bank tucked into an Alpine mountainside or a palm tree–laced beach. Now she just has to wait for confirmation the funds were received.

. . . Then what? Greta supposes she'll get her appointment for the real deal. The actual Found Object Society experience that's gnawed away at her for the past almost seventy-two hours, since she read that first card.

All she has to do is wait.

The trail camera footage. Greta forgot about it with the excitement of the official acceptance into the Found Object Society.

Remembering to disarm the alarm, she opens the front door and walks in her socked feet onto the dew-covered pea gravel. The moisture seeps through, chilling her. She opens the security cam app and waits an eternity as it loads. Both trail camera and Bluetooth source need at least twelve feet between them to connect, so she walks out farther. The first hints of sunrise etch around the trees and forsythia bushes. The mockingbird's lonely refrain continues, his efforts unrewarded.

"Better luck tomorrow, bird," Greta says.

Trail cam and phone linked, Greta scrolls to the video library. There are seven videos of half a minute each, ranging in time from 10:13 p.m. to only twenty-nine minutes ago at 4:47 a.m. That's the one. It has to be. The hairs on the back of her neck stand on end.

She scans the murky grounds and gets the sense she's not alone. Since she received the first card, there's been a shift in the atmosphere in and around her house. It crackles with a new and unnerving energy. The air is haunted, inhabited by the invisible past.

Greta downloads the videos and goes back inside. Locking the door behind her, she resets the alarm to Home. Her stomach growls. When's the last time she had a proper meal?

Videos first, and then she'll think about breakfast. Greta nestles herself into the sofa cushions that she's tossed on the floor. If she was a kid, she'd build herself a pillow fort, hiding from the monsters she imagines patrol the grounds outside. Instead, she's wedged into a failed Tetris of pillows and hoping to find something very real, very human, in a thirty-second clip of video from 4:47 a.m.

She scans the first videos from earlier in the night. Night-vision imagery further amplifies the ghostly vibe. A colorless kingdom of darkness, the world inverted. The carpet of pea gravel glows white and part of the rear of her Mercedes is visible in the background, along with the first few letters of its Connecticut license plate: *JRZ*.

The first two videos show an errant branch falling from a tree. The third startles her. A raccoon's eyes glow as it walks straight toward the lens and galumphs out of view. A world of nocturnal activities Greta doesn't know about. Next, a doe and then her fawn nibbling tender shoots. The sixth clip is a cat that reminds her of Murphy Brown, mouse in mouth, tail hanging down.

Tongue stony dry, Greta hits Play on the seventh video, the one she hopes will reveal whoever delivered the latest card from the Found Object Society. She taps up the volume. A high-pitched screech makes Greta cover her ears. There's a glitch as the screen flashes with electric-blue static before returning to the regular empty frame. No sign of a person walking into view or out. Someone (or some*thing*) must've activated the camera, though. The frame is off, different than it was a moment ago. Greta can't put her finger on why. She follows the glowing ash of the pea gravel until it leads to the back of her car. Nothing unusual. The video ends.

Unease crawls across Greta's skin as a thought emerges. She replays the video. The screech, the momentary angry azure static. Once again, her eyes follow the path of the gravel up to her car. Ears ringing, she hits Pause. In the frame is the rear of a car, same as before, but the first three letters of the Connecticut license plate now read *T3R*.

The first three letters from the plate of her parents' car. The one they died in twenty years ago.

Greta lies down on the cool tiles of her bathroom. She's been dry heaving. Greta's empty inside. Her throat burns from the stomach acid and tears stream down her cheeks, not only from the physical exertion, but from what she saw—what she thinks she saw—on the seventh video. Like so many other things over the past few days, it couldn't be real. There's no way that her parents' car from twenty years ago could appear in a video from a trail camera from this morning. No fucking way.

She had run out to the driveway to check, but it was her Mercedes, no other tire tracks or signs of a car that was totaled long ago. Then, when Greta rewatched it, the mirage was gone. Except for the sound and the blue static that followed, it was her car in the video again, not her parents'. For the camera to activate, there had to have been a motion trigger; whatever it was, it hadn't been visible to the naked eye. Did the tech geniuses at the Found Object Society see the trail cam and use a kind of focused electromagnetic field device to disrupt it? That was a thing, wasn't it? Very *Bourne Identity*.

This has gotten out of hand. Greta needs to take control of her mind and body and get back on track. She drags herself to the kitchen and guzzles down most of a bottle of Sanpellegrino. The die's been cast. The absurd sum of money paid. She's going to go through with this. It's a society, right? So that means there are other members, not only Greta, she reasons to herself. Maybe there's even a lounge where they can all gab about their deaths after the fact. They can commiserate and laugh about how they received their first invitation, about meeting officious Eileen and putting their arm into the Obitus Mold.

This is good. Smart. This is a healthier way of thinking. The Found Object Society isn't a club of one. There are people like her out there—somewhere. Greta's got to go with the flow, accept that this is no more than a five-hundred-thousand-dollar joyride for the rich.

Embrace it. This is going to be the adventure of a lifetime. A goddamned, morbid, crazy motherfucker of an adventure.

PART TWO

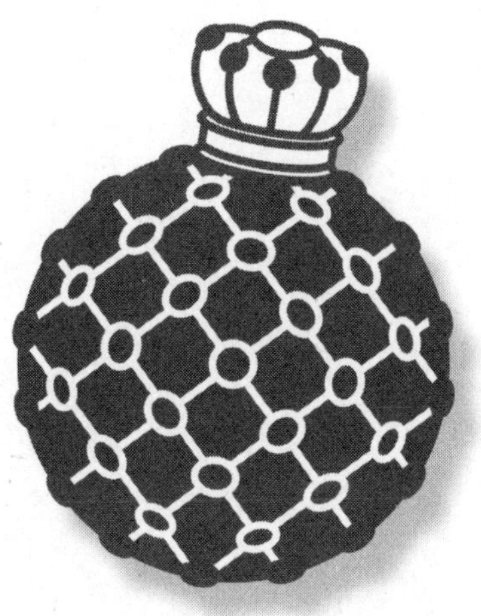

Found Object #1
Origin: Western Europe, France,
19th Century

CHAPTER FOURTEEN

South Street Seaport. One of the oldest neighborhoods of New York City.

Its cobblestone streets and brick-faced low-rises burrow in the crook of an elbow, right below the Brooklyn Bridge. The area's fortunes have fluctuated: As far back as the seventeenth century, it served as a port for the Dutch West India Company, the air thick and toxic with smoke from burning drifts of oyster shells; in the 1800s it was a thriving commercial hub of docking schooners, the city's unfortunate children swimming in its greasy waters; and the rise of the Fulton Fish Market, the most important wholesale fish market in the United States, inked the reek of fish guts into the landscape, where it held court for 183 years, survived four major fires, and was controlled by Mafia families for much of the twentieth century, before packing up and moving to Hunts Point in the Bronx in 2005. Like so much of the city, wealth and the need for square footage squeezed it out.

It seems only appropriate to Greta that the Found Object Society be located here, hidden in a subterranean basement of an imposing Georgian brick town house, surrounded by the ghosts and stories of a part of the city centuries old. If she could block out the jags of skyscrapers that surround it, the elevated FDR Drive, and all the noise of the twenty-first century—the pounding techno from an open-air café on Fulton Street, the clash of car horns at ten o'clock at night—she could picture

273 Water Street as it had been when it was built, horses clopping past on cobbles, whale-oil lamps illuminating the windows.

In the thirty-six hours before her driver, Carl, drove her down to the city, Greta had googled the shit out of the address. Of course she had. The history of Manhattan's third-oldest building at 273 Water Street—also known as the Captain Joseph Rose House and the Rat Pit (among others)—is so Dickensian, it verges on the absurd. The East River used to run right behind it when Captain Joseph Rose built it in 1773, before they brought in the landfill. He even had a dock in the backyard, where there are now tony restaurants. Then, in the nineteenth century, it was a cobbler shop, an apothecary, a boardinghouse. It was in 1863 that the place descended into the hell that bordered the notorious Five Points section of Manhattan. A skeezebag named Christopher "Kit Burns" Keyburn—who later disappeared without a trace—turned the basement into the Sportsmen's Hall, where lowlifes bet on how quickly a dog could kill one hundred wharf rats thrown into the ring. (Under twelve minutes was the record.) Greta hopes they've tidied the place up since. If traumatic death can transmit energy to an object, as the society says it can, imagine what it could do to a place. Crack open the earth beneath it like a ship's bilge and allow the past to seep in, taking hold for an eternity? And now, in the shiny twenty-first century, 273 Water Street is (what else?) home to four luxury condominiums—oh, and a society that dabbles in death.

After the sum of five hundred thousand dollars had landed in its secret account, the Found Object Society had sent Greta another message later that same morning. It gave her the address on Water Street in the South Street Seaport, Thursday's date, and a time. Nothing more.

So, for the past day and a half, Greta has tried to embrace this as an adventure, as opposed to the mind-fuck it feels like. Since her discovery of the QR code in that first invitation, her life has undergone a seismic shift. She's seen and felt things that can't be possible, and that have picked at the twenty-year-old scab of the death of her parents. She's forgotten to eat and drink, gone without sleep, and she's lied to her best friend. Was what she was experiencing outlandish? Scary? Yes and yes. Hasn't she also been craving something to bend the norm of her life? Yes, again.

Instead of fighting it, questioning her sanity, today Greta's decided to go with it.

Like the time Greta tripped on mushrooms in college and it went badly. *Very* badly. That is, until a senior named Wade—a guy she'd always dismissed as a hacky sack–playing granola head—coaxed her out of hiding and became her guide. He led Greta on a tour of Georges Seurat's *Un dimanche après-midi à l'île de la Grande Jatte*. The poster of the picnic scene along the Seine hung on a wall.

"Can you hear it?" he'd asked.

Greta stared and listened. At first, she couldn't hear anything, but then . . .

It was the monkey she heard first. A capuchin only an aristocrat like the woman holding the leash could afford. The sound began as a distant murmur, a kind of *eh-eh-eh* until it erupted into a full screech of a primate. Greta laughed and turned to Wade.

"The monkey!" she'd said.

Wade nodded in agreement. "The monkey."

Wade had showed her how to give in to what she saw that night. To not fight it. Had it been real? In her mind, it had been. And that's what Greta has decided to do with the Found Object Society: Submit. Allow it to wash over her. She will not be afraid. She will take the ride all the way to its final destination.

Greta watches as a shambling man, too well-dressed to be homeless, shuffles past and sits down beneath the scaffolding of a construction site for a future glass tower. His eyes are sunken, face waxy. No one is immune to addiction.

Nourished, hydrated, and ready for the ride, Greta leans her face in front of the blue domed camera outside the anonymous, subterranean door at 273 Water Street, six steps down from street level and invisible to the casual pedestrian strolling past. The windows of the house itself are dark. None of the four owners of their luxury apartments above the Rat Pit are home. Are the rich occupants aware of the secret society that conducts its business below them? The narrowest of alleys is carved on either side of the Georgian beauty. The discreet bronze plaque affirms it to be the Captain Joseph Rose House (ca. 1773), the oldest building in the Seaport Historic District.

Click.

Like the office on Duane Street, the dome recognizes Greta's face and unlocks the door. Her heart's racing. Most of the day, she's managed to remain calm, but it's finally happening. This place has infested her thoughts for the past several days. And now she's going in.

Other than a naked blue light bulb, the vestibule (if that's what you can call it) is black. The walls, the floor. It looks like the backstage at an off-off-Broadway theater, where the only people that can find their way around are the unpaid actors and stoned stagehands. Adjusting to the low light, Greta rests her palms on both sides of the wall. The space is a scant four feet wide.

She moves away from the entrance and walks toward another door twelve feet ahead of her. It's no regular door, though. Focusing her eyes, she looks at what seems to be a massive bank vault, far wider than the corridor itself. That can't be, can it? It must be a trick of the light.

The entrance is a Goliath of rectangular metal, its borders etched with one layer of delicate filigree, followed by another perimeter of songbirds, leafy vines grasped in their beaks, linking them to one another. Bolted across the right side is a tremendous hinge mechanism shaped like the letter *T*. Hardware the size of fists attaches it to the door itself, a round crossbar cutting across it horizontally. Above the crossbar is a gleaming handle a foot in length, buffed smooth from oil-slicked hands opening and closing it over years of use.

Placing her hand on the handle, she mutters, "Wish me luck."

The handle glows at her touch. Smelted metal, but it doesn't burn.

"Stand back, Greta," a disembodied AI voice instructs.

Greta obeys, and there's a great shifting of gears and cogs as the vault mechanism unlocks. When it cracks open, the air gasps with the sudden change in atmosphere.

"Holy. Shit."

Greta looks back toward where she had come from. She's alone. There's no one else to bear witness to this technological wonder. Part antiquated apparatus, part Richard Dreyfuss walking into an alien spaceship holding hands with childlike aliens.

Instead of a hairless, giant-eyed extraterrestrial greeting her, she's met by an absolute house of a man decked out in late-nineteenth-century formal wear (at least, that's what it looks like to Greta). His suit jacket is made from the deepest of crimson silk, paisley dancing in gold and evergreen in the background.

A smoking jacket? Maybe a dinner jacket, since there are long tails in the back, secured by one button in the front. Under that, a vest of pale silver, cut wide and low, which barely restrains his very twenty-first-century pecs. The pants are of the same cloth as the jacket, but charcoal gray and shimmering like a panther. His shirt is plain white and immaculate, an ascot matching the color of his pants pinned to his collar with a square-cut emerald.

The man's neck erupts from the collar. If it weren't for his costume, he'd look like any given bouncer at a strip club. Face flat, punched in—like Daniel Craig—and even more beautiful for it. Greta's taken aback.

"Jesus. No one said there was a dress code." She looks down at her appallingly casual modern-day attire: expensive jeans, designer sneakers, a white T-shirt, and a black leather jacket. Society giving fewer fucks with each passing year until we'll all be walking around in pajamas and Uggs.

"No worries, love. No dress code at the Found Object Society."

Of course he has a cockney accent. Why wouldn't he? Now Greta finds him that much more attractive. Put the same man in a shitty, collared polo shirt, khakis, and white sneakers, tell him never to speak, and she wouldn't even look at him twice. What a world.

The vault sucks closed behind her and emits a light gasp that makes Greta think of sex. This hyperbolic Daniel Craig has got her horny.

Greta tears her eyes away from the man and tries to make sense of her surroundings.

This must be the waiting room. The opulence is over the top. Walls covered in ornate, patterned wallpaper depicting hallucinogenic-worthy scenes: peacocks and tropical flowers, their pistils dripping with apricot-colored pollen; monkeys with tails curled around branches clutching at fruit—*monkeys again.* Images of horse-drawn chariots; every type of couple combo in the throes of passion; the chiseled face of a man who must be Tupac Shakur; banquet tables overflowing with rotting food; a cliff on Mount Everest dotted with dead bodies; Apollo 1—three figures writhing as fire swirls around them in the capsule.

No one pattern repeats, which is a daunting task on walls this large. The scenes depict an indecipherable story; there's no real narrative beyond excess passion and tragedy. A gorgeous vomit of sex and death. A patchwork history of everything. The effect is the opposite of the intent of hospital decor. Instead of soothing an anxious patient, this wallpaper agitates, titillates.

The furniture is an amalgam of eras with the focus being pre-twentieth century: scalloped wood and velvet-upholstered chaise longues in burgundy and pine green, rugs in animal stripes covering hardwood floors of exotic tigerwood, asymmetrical chairs and lampshades of deep pink silk. Part bordello, part opium den, all ne plus ultra, yet exactly how a place called the Found Object Society should be.

Everything from the bouncer to the decor to the heavy smell of jasmine is meant to arouse, incite, entice. Neurons and synapses fire in overdrive. If Greta's experience ended right here, at the society's entrance, it could be enough.

An old-fashioned phone rings and the cockney bouncer starts at the sound, his response reflexive. It's a candlestick phone, like the one on Duane Street. He lifts the phone—dwarfed in his meaty hands—off the table. The earpiece looks like a thimble next to his face.

"Yes, miss?" he answers, then listens for a moment. "Of course. I won't." He drops his head like he's being scolded. "Not again. I understand—"

He stops midsentence and turns his back to Greta. The behemoth of his torso acts as a sound barrier. Though the words are muffled, his conversation with *Miss* no longer sounds like English.

Greta scans the room and takes the chance to touch the wallpaper. She runs her hands across it. It's more than images printed on paper. The depictions are embossed, like welts, and soft as flower petals. Tactile, begging to be touched, stroked, inhaled. *Erotic*.

Hand on the wallpaper, she continues to look around, make sense of this surreal environment. A bronze-framed list of rules for the Found Object Society's members hangs on the front wall. Greta reads them while the bouncer remains on the phone.

Rules of the Found Object Society:

1. *Interfering or tampering with the vessel of your voyage is strictly prohibited. You are a passenger ONLY. This rule will be enforced to its full extent.*
2. *Absolutely no photography or cellular or recording devices of any kind are permitted. Cell phones must be handed over and secured before entry.*
3. *Posting on social media or discussing the Found Object Society with anyone who is not an employee or fellow member is strictly forbidden.*
4. *Members must wait a minimum of seventy-two hours between voyages.*
5. *Do not loiter in the waiting area.*
6. *A member who appears to be intoxicated, high, or otherwise impaired with any controlled substance will be asked to leave.*
7. *No refunds will be given for any reason.*

Vessel? Voyage? Passenger? Rules that will be *enforced?* Greta's never been good at rules.

"Greta Davenport," the bouncer says.

He's standing behind her, his body emitting heat like a furnace. She turns around, embarrassed at being caught in what feels like a private act of stroking the wallpaper.

"Yes? Sorry, I shouldn't be touching things," she says.

He looks bemused and shakes his head. "Don't be silly. Touching the wallpaper is fine." His face shifts back to serious bouncer face. "Just nothing else beyond this room."

"Oh, um, roger that," she says. *Roger that?* Big Daniel Craig has her tongue-tied, talking like an idiot. Ha, *Big Daniel Craig.*

"Your phone, if you please, Miss Davenport." His hand extends toward her, a shovel in the air.

Right, rule number two.

"Sure, of course." She takes the iPhone out of her purse and pauses, rethinking giving up her umbilical lifeline.

He waves his fingers at her. "Miss?"

Greta relents and places it in his palm. Part of her thinks he may crush it into dust in front of her.

"Much obliged," he says. He goes back to the area by the phone and spins a combination lock that's camouflaged within the wallpaper.

He opens the safe and places her phone inside. Greta cranes her neck to see how many other phones are in there, how many other patrons there may be in the Found Object Society tonight. It's hard to see, and he closes the safe quickly, giving the numbers a spin. The safe disappears into the debauchery of the wallpaper.

"Miranda will be out in a moment to take you back for your voyage."

"Voyage. I see that on the sign with the rules. What does that mean? And what's with these rules and the enforcement stuff?" Greta says.

He scratches his cheek with a liverwurst-size index finger. His eyes dart over to a curtained section of the wall. "Yes, Miss Davenport, that's what we call it. A *voyage*. And, uh, as for the enforcement"—the drapes part and Big Daniel Craig shifts his body to attention, changing his tone—"that's for Miranda to tell you about, miss, not the likes of me."

A woman Greta assumes is Miranda emerges through the oxblood-colored velvet. A jaw-dropping Oaxacan goddess birthed in front of her—the diametric opposite of the bureaucratic and lackluster Eileen.

"At long last, Greta Davenport. I'm Miranda. And yes," she says, giving the bouncer a steely look, "please direct any questions you may have to me." She holds out her hand.

Greta is so flummoxed by this gorgeous creature standing before her that she's tempted to genuflect and kiss her hand instead of shaking it. Reaching for Miranda's hand, Greta is painfully aware of how unmanicured and rough her nails are. Miranda's fingers are elegant, delicate as bird bones. Each digit is adorned with a ring, each one more eye-catching than the one before it; bands of gold and platinum, dolloped with gemstones.

The one on her thumb freezes Greta. It's an elaborate tree, a network of branches woven from gold, a multitude of emeralds for leaves, a snarl of roots that extend past her knuckle, the thickest root in the center, made of saffron-colored topaz and forming an arrow that points toward her wrist.

It's the same design as the foamed milk of her latte.

Greta keeps her grasp and looks up at Miranda's face. Could she be the delivery driver? The profiles are alike, but the similarities end there. Greta's mind is trying to make connections where none exist.

"That's quite a ring." Greta taps the pad of her thumb on top of the bejeweled tree.

"Thank you." Miranda extracts her hand and smiles.

Greta's surprised that Miranda's voice is unaccented. She had assumed the *Miss* whom Big Daniel Craig was speaking to on the phone in what sounded like a foreign language had been Miranda. Her mistake. Miranda's dressed to the nines in voluminous layers of blood-orange silk, crinoline, and muslin that wrap around what must be a spectacular body. There's a bustle in the back and either she's naturally wasp-waisted or she's wearing a corset (an actual freaking corset). Like a sugar cone, it pushes her Goldilocks "just right" bosom up and over the fabric. A long gold chain hangs down between her breasts, the pendant disappearing among the cloth and soft flesh. Even standing still, her clothing rustles and murmurs. A breeze in the forest.

"Have we met before?" Greta says.

Evading the question, Miranda says, "I'm sure you're eager to begin, Greta." She parts the velvet curtain from where she emerged. "Shall we?"

"Enjoy your death, Miss Davenport," Big Daniel Craig says with a smile, and waves.

Greta notices a blue light come on by the vault entrance. Another society member arriving.

Greta follows Miranda through the blood-colored velvet, the cloth caressing Greta, depositing its intoxicating scent of jasmine onto her clothing and hair. The room she enters is massive. The proportions are off down here—way off.

How can this be a basement below the Captain Joseph Rose House? The vastness of the Found Object Society's guts is overwhelming. Someone built this place, planned it, rendered drawings, had an architect. Who, though? Captain Joseph Rose himself? Or maybe Christopher "Kit Burns" Keyburn, the sicko? That's a bad thought. A very bad one. A labor of this magnitude couldn't have been done in secret. Several subway lines slice across lower Manhattan, tunneling like moles, yet there are no vibrations, no noise to indicate the cacophonous, modern world outside or below.

With the lullaby of her shifting dress and bustle, Miranda leads Greta into a cavernous chamber she calls the Collection Room. They walk down a narrow corridor along the wall. To their left are rows upon rows of shelves that extend so far that Greta can't see their end point. They're not metal shelves like you'd see in the tombs of microfiche and files at a library. They're wooden, like apothecary ones, consisting of hundreds—thousands?—of cubbyholes of varying dimensions, shrouded in darkness. Though they are in silhouette, Greta can see that each cube holds a single object, each one a different size and shape. A *found* object. The illumination is as dim as a museum protecting priceless works of art from incandescent light. Miranda walks backward, facing Greta, and speaks as a docent would, explaining the particulars of the wing they're in.

"As I mentioned, this is the Collection Room. The heart and soul of the Found Object Society. Within these shelves and display cases are the objects that you will choose from for your voyage."

"Big Daniel Craig said—" Greta blushes at uttering her nickname for the bouncer out loud. Miranda smiles and Greta continues. "Sorry, I read your rules sign and the *gentleman* up front said you called this experience a voyage. Why is that?"

"It's the best name for what it is. It's a journey you'll be on soon. You are a passenger along for the ride—nothing more."

"Is that what rule number one's about? *No interfering or tampering with your vessel*, or whatever?" Greta says.

"Correct. The person whose death you will experience is your vessel. You'd never interfere with the work of a plane captain or a train conductor, would you?" Miranda says.

Greta shakes her head.

"No, of course you wouldn't. You allow your vessel to take you to your destination—to their own death. Shall I continue?"

Greta nods. Miranda's answers and speech sound rehearsed. But it's silly to think that Greta is so special, that she's the only member. Miranda must give this spiel a lot. After all, hasn't Greta hoped to find other members of the Found Object Society to confab with?

"As I was saying, Ms. Davenport, this is where all the found objects are stored. They are cataloged by regions and time period."

"Like a wine store," Greta says.

"Exactly right, like a wine store," Miranda says, as though she's heard the comparison a million times before and grows less impressed with each repetition.

She leads Greta to the aisle in front of them and waves her hand along its side. Sensing the motion, a pin light from above focuses on a placard that only now becomes visible. Written in fine calligraphy are the words *Western Europe, 1750–1850*.

Miranda walks Greta over to the next aisle and waves again, illuminating another card. "And here you see *Asia, 1611 to 1700*."

"Interesting," Greta says. Yeah, *interesting*. Everything inside Greta is shrieking with excitement, wonderment, and the best she can come up with is *interesting*?

Miranda roots around in the deep pockets of her skirt and petticoats and pulls out a tablet much like the one Eileen had on Duane Street. This is all so steampunk.

"I see you signed the waiver already. Good," she says.

Greta signed it, sure. Did she read it? Not so much.

Miranda continues to swipe and then taps seven different locations on the screen, as though she's ticking boxes. Miranda swipes and then places her finger in the center of the screen for a couple seconds before releasing.

A gentle bell rings once, and a minuscule spotlight above them points into one of the aisles of cubbies. Another bell rings and points to a different aisle and shelf. It continues until a bell has sounded seven times and there are an equal number of spotlights cutting through the dark. Some crisscross one another. Each one points to a specific cubby in an aisle. The lights pierce the dark like bullet holes through a black curtain. Black has substance here.

"Voilà!" Miranda beams. When smiling, she's more beautiful than any human has the right to be. "Based on the data we gathered from your Obitus Mold, Greta, any of these seven objects will provide you with a most satisfying voyage."

Death, Greta thinks. What Miranda really means to say is a *most satisfying death*.

CHAPTER FIFTEEN

This is no quaint museum, and Miranda's no docent.

The Found Object Society is a club dedicated to members whose lives have become so dulled by wealth and excess that only experiencing another human's death—and surviving it—will sate them.

This is so fucked up.

It's too late to change her mind and demand a refund (not that they'd give her one). Truth be told, Greta doesn't want one. Will acknowledging the depravity of what she's about to do suffice? It's not like *she's* going to kill anyone. They're already dead. All Greta's going to do is live their death through that person's eyes. They're gone and Greta can't change that. Miranda says she's only allowed to be an observer on her *voyage* inside her *vessel*, not alter any outcome. Greta still has so many questions, but she's hell-bent on going with it. Like tripping to the Seurat.

"How much time do I have to make my selection?" Greta asks.

"As much as you need. Your first voyage is your most important. It will set the tone for the rest."

The rest. The first taste with Eileen was free, but *the rest*? Those will cost you five hundred thousand dollars.

Greta catches Miranda checking the time as she pulls a fobbed pocket watch on a chain from between her breasts (maybe Greta doesn't quite have *all the time she needs* after all). She drops it back in like a coin in a fountain. What else does she keep in her multitudinous skirts?

"Miranda, how many, um, *voyages* can I take in one night?"

"Ah, that's rule number four. One. Tonight you have your first, then you must wait at least three days, seventy-two hours, until the next one. We've discovered it can be *risky* for your psyche to have too many too close together. The mind needs time to recover."

"Makes sense," Greta says. Does it? Make sense? Does any of this?

She leans in to read the label attached to the outside of the cubby in front of her. *WEGer17C-41511*. Inside is a five-sided wooden spinning top, with basic drawings of farm animals on all sides. A child's toy.

"Is this a toy? And what do these letters and numbers mean on the label?" Greta says.

Miranda rustles over to Greta. "Yes, it is a young child's toy." She points to the label. "These are our abbreviations. *WEGer* stands for *W*estern *E*urope, *Ger*many. *Seventeen C* is the seventeenth century. The five digits are its catalog number in our library."

Greta is stunned. "Wait. You mean there are over forty-one thousand objects in the collection?"

"Many more than that, yes."

It's ghoulish being surrounded by tens of thousands of objects touched by people at the moment they died. The Found Object Society is a vast catacomb, the dead stacked one on top of another for what seems like miles.

Greta looks at the toy again as a sickening thought occurs. "Does this mean a child was the last one to touch this before they died? That my voyage would be experiencing the death of a little kid?"

"No, Greta. All the objects in *this* area, and handpicked for you, were last touched by people above the age of sixteen. Specialty voyages—like voyages of children, for instance—are kept in separate areas and for a very *specific* type of clientele. Those cost more." Miranda's expression shifts. "Are you interested?"

Is Miranda trying to upsell her? You'd have to be a pretty sick individual if you want to feel a child die, if you're willing to pay extra for that privilege. Greta shudders to think of what the other *specialty* voyages might be. Death by execution, perhaps?

Greta's heart rate quickens: *Death by car crash?* She pushes the thought back.

"No, no. Absolutely not. I'm just curious. What sicko wants that?"

"Don't be too hasty to judge. You never know what a member's intentions are. What they may have suffered to bring them here."

So, is that a requirement of membership, in addition to truckloads of money? Suffering? Grief? Greta has that in spades. If that's why she was targeted for membership, it gives her no peace. She continues to explore the seven objects chosen for her based on the information the Obitus Mold gathered.

"What if the death I get is a dud? You know, some happy old man who lived to ninety-three and died in his sleep?" What a question. Here Greta is, concerned that living through the death of another person may be too boring for her. Is she that much less demented than the client who wants to experience a child dying?

"A scientific impossibility, Greta. The energy required to have a death transfer to an object comes from trauma, stress—never peace or tranquility. We don't understand why, but that's how it works." She smiles. It's unnerving. "Plus, you are not only experiencing the death itself, but the crucial period that leads up to their demise. Our voyages are always dramatic, entertaining. You won't be disappointed. I can guarantee you that."

"Of course, thanks," Greta says. She feels dirty, like she's been caught enjoying hardcore porn or a snuff film (and in a way, she has).

She goes from lit cubbyhole to cubbyhole: a broken, ivory-handled hairbrush; a greasy Rubik's Cube; a brass pestle. In the background, Greta hears the occasional clang of pipes, followed by a *whoosh-whoosh* sound. Heating pipes?

Greta walks deeper into the aisle of nineteenth-century Western Europe. The pinpoint of light shines into a small cubby, four rows up from the floor. Looking back down the aisle, she notices Miranda has disappeared from view. Greta gets on her toes to take a closer look. The card reads, *WEFr19C-12716:* Western Europe, France, nineteenth century, item 12716.

It's an ornate bottle. A handblown glass ball encased in an elaborate cross-hatching of woven gold thread and mesh. In the center of each golden *X* rests a pearl-size piece of turquoise. What appears to be the cap of the bottle is shaped like a five-sided crown of gold, also studded with turquoise, with a deep-red stone on top in its center. This enchanting three-inch-tall object draws Greta in—like *it* has chosen *her*, and not the other way around. She reaches to touch it. Before she can, the blackness surrounding the bottle stirs, restless, and extends a fraction toward Greta, as though the very presence of her skin has awakened it. She backs away.

"Oh, that's a juicy one."

Greta jumps at Miranda's voice and the black void retreats back into the hole. She's imagining things. Miranda's appeared from nowhere to Greta's right. The nearest entrance to the aisle is way down to Greta's left. So how did Miranda come up on her right?

"Is this the object you've selected?"

"I think *it* chose me."

"That's often the case. You'll have an excellent first voyage with this one—*very* melodramatic. You won't be disappointed."

What a thing to say about someone's death. Miranda extracts a wooden box from her downspout of skirts.

"I'd hate to see what the inside of your purse looks like," Greta says. She's nervous, twitchy, making a crap joke that falls flat.

Miranda opens the box lined with the same material as the Obitus Mold. There's a depression in its center, in the same shape as the object Greta has chosen for her first voyage. That can't be a coincidence. Miranda pulls a pair of golden forceps from her skirts as well and grips the turquoise-studded bottle by its neck, placing it into the box. She lays it down and light hits the bottle, revealing an amber liquid inside. Miranda closes the box.

"Let's take you to your cabin, Greta," she says. "It's time to set sail."

Miranda and Greta enter another hallway, a capillary off the aorta of the Found Object Society. To the right, ten wooden doors with brass fixtures and rounded windows line the narrow corridor. The glass windows are opaque. The feel is that of a ship, cabin doors one after the other. Above each is a set of three colored lights: green, blue, and red.

The green bulb is illuminated above the door they're standing in front of. The blue and red lights are off. Greta peers down the hall and notices that three of the doors have their blue lights on.

"What do the different light bulbs mean?" Greta asks in a whisper.

"Green means that a cabin is available for a member. Blue indicates a guest is on their voyage," Miranda says.

Three other members of the Found Object Society are here—right now. What are they like? Will she meet them? Does she know any of them already?

"How about the red one?" Greta doesn't like that Miranda hasn't mentioned the red one.

"Let's go into your cabin, shall we?"

Greta's expecting Miranda to wave her hand in front of the cabin and for the door to magically open. Instead, she grips the heavy brass handle with her bird hands and pulls. Like the vault entrance to the Found Object Society, this door comes ajar with a sigh of air. This one is more sleepy than aroused.

Greta and Miranda step into the cabin and the door sucks shut behind them.

What the hell does the red light mean?

CHAPTER SIXTEEN

The interior of the cabin is snug. A womb of plush navy velvet. There's room for Miranda and Greta, a carved, wooden-framed chaise (the kind you'd see in an old-fashioned psychiatrist's office), a small bar-type cart, and little else. The cushion of the chaise is inviting, curved to fit the human body. On the wall above it is an illuminated porthole, the shape of a round-edged rectangle. If this were a cruise ship, Greta would expect to look out at the ocean. Here, there's no sea view, only an emerald-green glow, nothing else visible beyond it.

"Have a seat, Greta," Miranda says.

Greta hangs her jacket on a hook on the wall and then sits on the edge of the chaise, her butt sinking into the sumptuous cushioning. Her breathing quickens and her heart beats high in her throat. She thinks of the wallpaper, Miranda's ring, the illuminated cubbyholes. Everything about the Found Object Society vibrates with life and excites—even the shadows. What's she about to get herself into?

Miranda wheels the cart alongside her. It's covered in a tasseled swath of cloth. She sits next to Greta. The folds of her voluminous skirts rest against Greta's thigh and her fragrance cloaks them. The moment is intimate, the heat of their bodies twining in the air.

Uncovering the cart, Miranda reveals a porcelain saucer with a piece of the same wax-wrapped taffy from the office in

Tribeca. The one that tasted like Greta's childhood. She offers the candy to Greta.

"This will help relax you and prepare you for what's to come," Miranda says.

"How is this happening? How are you doing what you do here?" Greta says.

Miranda winks.

Greta takes the taffy, unwraps it, and places the lavender-colored chew in her mouth. Blackberry rushes across her taste buds. The smells and sounds of the boardwalk in Mystic return with a gentle ferocity. Before Tribeca, Greta had all but forgotten this memory. It makes her feel safe, loved, hand in hand with her parents, hot sugary funnel cake wafting around them, seagulls cawing, carnival barkers calling out a winner, blackberry spilling across her tongue like a tipped can of paint.

Greta's lying down now, Miranda by her side, watching her.

"You asked about the red light, Greta."

Greta's head is heavy and, with effort, she nods in agreement. "Yes."

"The three lights outside the door signal the status of the room to those of us who work here. Red indicates . . . a problem. That, for one reason or another, the client requires assistance or has strayed from the rules we've set forth. It's very rare and shouldn't be of any concern to you as long as you follow the rules."

Greta's brain and mouth are slow to respond. The taffy continues to melt on her tongue. "Right. The rules." There was so much to absorb when Greta walked into the waiting room. Had she paid enough attention to the rules? She thinks she had: No phones, no social media, no interfering with your *vessel*. You're an observer only.

"You'll be fine, Greta. You were meant to be here."

Was I? Greta thinks, her mind floating away.

Miranda reaches underneath the chaise and Greta hears a *click*. An armrest extends from below Greta's right shoulder. It's the Obitus Mold again, but this time, the metal appears solid.

"Is that the same one from the other day?" Greta says.

Miranda nods. "Indeed it is. Can you place your arm in the Obitus Mold for me?"

Greta does and her arm nestles into the folds made to fit her anatomy. The metal feels like sun-warmed clay. Reacting to Greta's skin, it tightens its grip. The mold is snug and comforting. Greta's hand rests palm up.

"How are you feeling? Are you ready to begin?"

Greta should be panicking. She's about to undergo something that can't be possible. That must be a trick. A remarkable experiment in the power of suggestion, replete with splashy special effects of living wallpaper and dark spaces, mysterious players and locations, and stellar production and costume design. An immersive encounter made possible with the introduction of a candy-like drug that opens the mind. That makes you believe. That, and five hundred thousand dollars.

What does she have to lose, really? The answer is, *not much*.

What has Greta done in the twenty years since her parents' deaths? Since the accident that took them to wherever it is they went: The vacuum of space? Pure dark? The reliving of life's sweetest moments, strolling hand in hand on a boardwalk? She's skated recklessly through the years. Tested boundaries that only someone as rich as she can afford to test and still come out on the other side of it unscathed. Skittered along the surface of her existence and bathed in the shallow end of societal excess. If this all goes wrong tonight, if she never comes back, what is there for her to lose? Who'd care?

And what if it's real? Her insides tremble with the possibility. If the Found Object Society is what it says it is, and not some parlor trick, then tonight will be more speed, more death-defying bends in the roadway than she could ever inflict upon herself. It'll be the ultimate drug, and there'll be no looking back.

Greta takes a deep breath in. She's okay with that, she is.

"Yes, Miranda, I'm ready."

Miranda opens the wooden box and reveals the bejeweled golden bottle that promises to take Greta on a *juicy* first voyage. She notes that Miranda's put on latex gloves, a stark contrast to her Victorian costume.

"Relax your hand for me, please."

Miranda rests the bottle in Greta's palm, the nubbins of the turquoise beading pushing into her skin. The cross-hatching of gold thread is like a raspy cat tongue on her flesh.

Miranda's taken out an antique-looking hypodermic needle, more like a telescope-size thing, with three metal circles on top—one central ring to depress the syringe and two anchored on each side. The liquid inside is silvery and opaque, like mercury.

"Please make a loose fist around the object." Miranda quickly wipes an alcohol-soaked cotton ball across Greta's forearm and then holds up the hypodermic contraption. "This looks scary, but it's a very fine needle. You'll barely feel a thing. This will take you where you need to go. It's the steering wheel for your vessel."

More nautical metaphors. The Found Object Society is a mash-up of eras and themes, mixed metaphors aplenty.

"Why do I feel like you're about to put me out of my misery?" Greta says, only half joking.

Miranda's right. Greta can't feel the needle going in.

"Because in a way, I am," she says. "Bon voyage, Greta."

CHAPTER SEVENTEEN

It didn't work.

The lights are off in her cabin and Greta is lying there in the dark. Five hundred fucking thousand dollars and nothing happened.

"This is bullshit," Greta says. The words are in her mind, not coming out of her mouth.

She tries to sit up. She can't. Her head knocks up against something. It's pitch-black and she can't make out any details of her surroundings. What did she bump into? The ceiling is high in the cabin, so it can't be that. She tries to move her hands, but they're pinned to her sides. Blinking hard, she refocuses her eyes. There's only black. The darkness is complete. Her breath, hot and rapid, blows back at her from whatever lies above. Wiggling her feet and fingers, Greta realizes it's not only above her, but all around. She's in an enclosure. Entombed.

A coffin?

"Miranda? Hello?" Why isn't her mouth moving to speak, yet she can hear the words?

Something's gone wrong. Greta's trapped. Is this what Miranda meant by the red light? It's too soon, isn't it? Her voyage hasn't even started yet, and she seems stuck in between. Is the red light on now and Miranda and Big Daniel Craig will come and help her?

Greta can't see her own hand in front of her face. For fuck's sake, she can't even *move* her hand. This must be what claustrophobia feels like. She's vacuum-sealed. Greta tests the side of whatever she's in with her fingertips. The material isn't solid; it has give to it, elasticity. Greta senses that whatever she's in, it's starting to move.

Her enclosure tips forward, angling her downward, feetfirst. There's a muscularity to her encapsulation. It's contracting, pushing her out and down.

Jesus Christ. Jesus fucking Christ. No, no. Hello? I want out! Words in her head, not leaving her mouth.

Greta's body accelerates downward. She's in a flexing chute. As her body follows its twists and turns, Greta's taken by the silence. How can she be moving this fast without at least the sound of air rushing past her?

Jettisoned from the confines of the tube, Greta floats in darkness. A portion of her, at least. Disembodied, it's her mind that's adrift. Her alarm subsides. She bobs for a moment as an unseen force takes hold and pulls her toward two round windows in the distance. Closer and closer they come, the light pouring through them, blinding after so much black.

Greta's seen enough sci-fi movies to know that it feels like she's docking onto something. Some*one*. Pulling up to the windows, she locks in place. There's movement in front of her. Bodies in motion.

These aren't windows, she realizes. They're eyes.

CHAPTER EIGHTEEN

Sixteen-year-old Zephyrine stands transfixed outside the ajar door to her master's bedroom, disgusted at the sight.

In the four months since she and her brother, Gilbert, arrived at Château de Barbitière, Zephyrine has witnessed many times the comings and goings of the man and woman who perform in private for the master (even in the middle of the night). Master Auguste is seated, fully clothed, in a chair of gold velvet, his considerable midsection hanging off to either side. Next to him, a small table with a vial of clear liquid. In his swollen hand, he dabs a peach-colored silk handkerchief with the frolic-inducing ether and brings it to his bulbous nose, inhaling deeply. His eyes are glassy and rheumy. The master half watches the couple in their languid sex act on his bed, giggling as he sings a children's song:

Il était une dame Tartine
Dans un beau palais de beurre frais
La muraille était de praline,
Le parquet était de croquets,
La chambre à coucher
De crème de lait,
Le lit de biscuits,
Les rideaux d'anis.

Zephyrine knows the song well. It's a happy one about a palace made of fresh butter, walls of praline, floors of croquette, a bed made of biscuits. On his tongue, it's poison. Her mother used to sing it to her to induce dreams of delicious things when her own stomach had been empty, sating her to sleep. Why should he sing such a song in the midst of such wantonness? Zephyrine can't say.

How she'd love to kill him, so she and the mistress Claudette could be alone together. Zephyrine can't afford the luxury of such thoughts. It is insanity to even consider it. Love can make you do and think insane things. And what if she followed through with this bloodthirsty fantasy of hers? She would all but guarantee an end to her own life and ensure her ten-year-old brother's place in the purgatory of the master's sordid château.

Tonight, before the dinner party, she will tell her beloved mistress how she feels about her, and Mistress Claudette will reciprocate. Zephyrine is certain of it. Her wish to do away with the mistress's husband is something she should keep to herself, for now.

Wouldn't it be wonderful, though? Then they could be together and free from his perversions, even if their love must be kept a secret. Has Mistress Claudette had the same thoughts of killing her beast of a husband? A wretched man, gluttonous in all his appetites, an addict. Unlike their—Zephyrine and Gilbert's—parents, he deserves to die.

Sometimes she thinks they would have been better off fending for themselves in Belleville, but that's foolhardy. She and her brother are well fed, have a roof over their heads, and small change in their pockets. They are alive and more fortunate than most.

And Zephyrine loves Mistress Claudette, and she loves her back. She knows she does.

Château de Barbitière was to be Zephyrine and Gilbert's salvation from a bleak future on the streets of Paris. With both of their parents dead from consumption, the family doctor had taken pity on the siblings. He told them that the mistress Claudette was in search of a new lady's maid—someone young and beautiful who would represent her well. Zephyrine fit the bill. It should have given Zephyrine pause, the way the slack-jawed doctor had held her wrists and looked her body up and down, turning her around, evaluating her like a colt in a stable. He had even checked her teeth, his breath soaked in tobacco and sardines, thick digits exploring her gums, his skin a bitter sting on her tongue.

What other choice had there been? Their parents had been ill and unable to work for weeks. Their meager savings had dwindled, and Zephyrine and Gilbert would have joined the ranks of the destitute in a matter of days after they had passed. They would have had to leave their village of Belleville for the downtrodden alleys of the city and the Quais de la Seine, with only one way to keep them alive until her brother could fend for himself—by using the body that she had come to realize held value while she was still young and healthy.

With her beauty, Zephyrine could easily be mistaken as having been born into the aristocracy. She'd grown into her long limbs and transformed from awkward girl to enchanting woman. Her appearance was her dowry—not jewelry, nor money, but her physical self. In life, her dear parents had worked hard to keep the family afloat. In death, everything but Zephyrine's beauty went along with them into their common graves, tossed like refuse amongst the near 30 percent of the population of Paris who had succumbed to the ghastly disease.

Four months ago, the doctor packed the brother and sister into a carriage and took them on the two-hour journey to Château de Barbitière. Neither had ever been in a horse-drawn carriage like that one. *A Citadine carriage*, he called it. It was majestic, shiny and black, with red-bordered windows on the doors, two magnificent white horses in front, the coachman looming above them, whip in hand, his cape hanging heavy as crows' wings. Gilbert moved from side to side within the coach, peering through the windows, watching as Belleville and the smog of Paris disappeared into the distance.

When they approached the château, Zephyrine couldn't believe her eyes. They entered a long drive, a citadel of plane trees lining the path on either side. At the end, the Château de Barbitière revealed itself to them. A monolith of limestone and windows, elaborate capillaries of gardens stretching in all directions, a path connecting with a pond in the distance, the sun reflecting off it like bits of broken glass.

Gilbert had fallen asleep, the adventure getting the best of him.

"Wake up, child!" the doctor barked.

Brother and sister descended from the carriage and were welcomed by an army of staff. They then were separated and handed off to servants whose task it was to get them acclimated to their new home. Her brother was taken by the stable master and shown where the horses were kept and where he'd sleep.

An elegant woman with a ramrod-straight spine took Zephyrine by the arm and introduced herself. "I am Sylvie, the head of the household. Come with me, young lady. We must make you presentable for the mistress."

She brought Zephyrine upstairs to what would be her sleeping quarters. The room was small yet comfortable. The ceilings low, the bare minimum height, as though it was all that could be spared for the help. The tiny window looked out to the pond with its bridge in the distance.

"Does the pond belong to the château?" Zephyrine asked.

"It does," Sylvie said. She opened a hand-painted wardrobe and shuffled through a line of dresses. She held one made of navy silk in front of Zephyrine. "This one will suit you fine."

"Whose clothes are they?" Zephyrine asked.

"Yours now."

"Whose were they before?"

Sylvie hesitated before answering the question. "The mistress's lady's maid before you. Enough questions. Let's draw you a bath."

Where had this other girl gone? Why had Zephyrine replaced her?

Zephyrine had never undressed in front of a stranger before. Sylvie seemed unfazed. Zephyrine tried to cover herself with her hands.

"We're both women here. No need to be shy. Step into the tub."

Zephyrine did as she was told and lowered herself into the velvety warmth of the bath. Sylvie placed drops of lavender oil into the soapy water and swirled it with her hands, brushing against Zephyrine's thigh. She knelt beside the tub and tucked Zephyrine's hair behind her ear.

"I can see why the doctor chose you for the mistress. You're a lovely girl," she said through gritted teeth.

The way Sylvie looked at her—like the doctor had—made her uneasy.

"Thank you, madame," she said.

Sylvie took hold of her ankle.

"You may call me Sylvie when we are alone. You are the lady's maid to the mistress. An important job. Do as you are told, and you will do well."

She released her grip and dried her hand on a towel.

Before walking out, she said, "Finish your bath and I'll lay your clothes out for you. Please come downstairs as soon as you're dressed. Then, lucky you, you'll meet the mistress Claudette."

CHAPTER NINETEEN

Zephyrine descended the staircase that first day, clean and smelling of lavender, the dress of the previous lady's maid rustling with her every step. She was afraid but full of hope that she and her brother would make proud the memory of their parents. Zephyrine, a lady's maid to a mistress of high society. Gilbert, working with the animals that he had always admired. Her parents' deaths would not be the end of them as her mother had feared as she took her final breaths, her father having died only the month before.

"What will become of you when I'm gone?" she'd asked, the words rattling from her lungs.

At her mother's deathbed, the terror of an unknown future had eclipsed Zephyrine's sorrow. Yet, there she was, walking down a staircase, smelling of flowers. It was the day she met Mistress Claudette for the first time. The woman she would come to love.

The mistress sat in an extravagant room cluttered with varieties of furniture to drape a weary body across—sofas, wood-carved chairs with elaborate armrests—and cushions abounded, even on the floor in front of the fireplace, which roared like a dragon's mouth.

The rich lived in garish color and comfort while the unfortunates, like Zephyrine's family, existed in shades of gray. Mistress Claudette sat on a strawberry-colored chaise, either side of her body propped with green silk pillows. She held a crystal glass in one hand, barely larger than a thimble, inside it a rosy elixir. Her golden dress spilled across the cushions, her narrow torso sprouting from the waves of cloth. She faced the fire, her near-black hair in a luscious mound atop her head, tendrils dropping around the nape of her long neck.

Without turning to look at Zephyrine, she spoke. "Please come sit across from me, Zephyrine."

This meant sitting in the chair directly in front of the fire. Zephyrine was already warm from the heavy layers of clothing she was unaccustomed to wearing. Still, she obeyed and gave a slight bow before she sat.

Then she saw the face of her soon-to-be beloved for the first time.

"Mistress," she said.

Fantasies of murder continue to infiltrate Zephyrine's thoughts as she stands. The naked couple collapse from their animalistic effort onto the bedsheets as the master's eyes roll back, still singing the child's song.

The staff pretends not to notice the comings and goings of the master's bedroom. Though she's never stated as much, the mistress must loathe her husband. How couldn't she? Zephyrine has come to know the mistress better than anyone. Their secret moments together are proof enough to Zephyrine that the mistress has fallen for her, too.

Was it any wonder that the lady's maid who had come before Zephyrine was gone? Surely, she too could no longer withstand the profligacy that existed under this roof thanks to the master's immoral inclinations. Zephyrine is stronger than her predecessor. She will fight because she has something to fight for: her brother, and the woman she loves. The woman she craves. The one who makes her explode with color.

That first day, her back to the fire, sweat roped down Zephyrine's spine. The mistress turned her gaze to her for the first time. Her skin was translucent, with a cherry stain across her high cheekbones; her upper lip was more prominent than the lower, a bewitching scar, round like a pea, giving her a permanent pout. Her dark gray eyes, edging on black, made Zephyrine's stomach flutter.

Zephyrine was only sixteen, and though she'd never so much as kissed a boy, she knew it wasn't a boy she was after. She'd never entertained other possibilities for love, but seeing Mistress Claudette for the first time that afternoon was a revelation.

"Aren't you even more lovely than the doctor promised?" the mistress said.

A flush spread across Zephyrine's neck and chest. The torturous warmth of the flames behind her, the smoldering gaze of the mistress before her. She turned her eyes down. "Thank you, Mistress Claudette."

"You're burning up," the mistress declared. "Come away from the fire and sit next to me here."

Sitting next to her, Mistress Claudette fussed over Zephyrine like a mother. She poured her a glass of water, straightened her heavy skirts as she sat. Secured to the waist of the mistress's gown was a gold chatelaine. Elaborate jeweled trinkets hung from the diamond-crusted brooch by delicate chains. They chimed across her lap as they rolled against one another. For women like Zephyrine's mother, a chatelaine was made of tarnished pewter and the chains attached to actual tools for house chores or sewing. The mistress's chatelaine was nothing of the kind—from it hung ornate baubles made to look useful: a pair of scissors with an amethyst connecting the blades, a letter opener like a pearl-handled dagger, a hairbrush made for a doll-size head.

The mistress reached to her chatelaine for a beguiling vessel the size of a large plum, covered in woven gold and punctuated with beads of bright turquoise. She uncorked the crown-shaped stopper and added drops of its amber liquid contents onto a linen soaked with water and patted behind Zephyrine's neck. The fragrance of muguet enveloped her. Those tiny white flowers, shaped like bells, that pop through the snow in early spring, so intoxicating, harbingers of warm days to come. The mistress's hands were smooth. Zephyrine's mother's touch had always brought her comfort, the rough nicks and calluses of her fingertips tickling her skin. The mistress's touch was different, though. An enticing caress.

"Do not grow accustomed to this, young Zephyrine. It is you who will cater to my needs soon enough. Has Sylvie explained to you your duties as my lady's maid?"

"Only a little, Mistress."

"You are my shadow. You will assist me with my bathing and appearance. Choose my clothing for each day. You will join me on all my errands and my social calls. You are my keeper of confidences and teller of gossip, maintaining a close ear on the goings-on around the house. Is that understood?"

Zephyrine looked out the window toward the front drive, where the doctor and a corpulent man she assumed was Master Auguste spoke. Looking at him, Zephyrine found it hard to picture how he and the mistress Claudette were a pair. He was as amorphous as a piece of bread soaked in milk. He might have been handsome once, before excess had gotten the best of him.

The master and the doctor stood near the carriage they had arrived in and exchanged words. Master Auguste retrieved a small pouch from his waistcoat and placed it in the doctor's hands. With the thick fingers that had explored Zephyrine's mouth, the doctor examined the gold coins inside the pouch. Had her arrival here with her brother been a transaction? Before the thought could take seed, the touch of her mistress's hand on top of hers brought Zephyrine back into the room.

"We will be the best of friends. Don't you feel it, Zephyrine?"

CHAPTER TWENTY

The floorboards creak as Zephyrine shifts her weight outside the master's bedroom. The naked man looks over from his position on the bed and he and Zephyrine lock eyes. The man smiles.

Zephyrine hurries away.

Both sister and brother are meant to join the master and mistress at tonight's dinner party alongside their degenerate friends. It's unheard of for the likes of Zephyrine and Gilbert to be invited to sup with the aristocracy. Zephyrine isn't sure if she should be honored or suspicious. The two unfortunates, rescued and on display—shiny baubles in a glass cabinet. They even had a suit made for Gilbert. The master and his friends have repulsive, boundless appetites for food, wine, ether, and everything else. The Revolution, no more than a feeble memory, occurred well before they were born, and the intemperate tastes and expenditures of the noble class returned like a cancer.

It's rare that Zephyrine and her brother are alone together. Their positions don't allow it. So she has little opportunity to discuss the situation. And what would she say? Other than the master's abhorrent proclivities, there's nothing actually wrong, is there? She should be grateful that she and Gilbert are being taken into the fold. Then she thinks of the master and how horrible it must be for her mistress to be wed to this animal, and the fire of her hate rekindles. Is the mistress aware of her husband's drug-addled sexual leanings?

Zephyrine hastens down the hall toward the mistress's room, fantasizing about ways to do away with the pig: smothering him with a pillow as he sleeps, pushing him down the dizzying staircase, tossing a match strike from a pyrogène onto his ether-soaked handkerchief, watching him burn.

Head down, she runs straight into Sylvie.

"There you are. The mistress sent me looking for you. She is waiting for her bath."

Sylvie grips Zephyrine's arm far tighter than necessary and leads her toward the door. Wresting free of her grasp, Zephyrine says, "I know the way, thank you, Sylvie."

Sylvie's face darkens.

"I am sure you do, Zephyrine."

Zephyrine draws the bath for her mistress. Should she share what she knows and feels with Mistress Claudette now? No, she needs time to gather her courage. If she is to say anything, it will be when they take their daily afternoon perambulation by the pond and across the bridge.

The lady's maid has never considered hurting another person. It's not what her parents taught her, yet if ever the absence of one human would make the world a better place, it would be the death of Master Auguste.

Stop entertaining these thoughts, silly girl.

Zephyrine's wishes are no more than those of a teenager blinded by infatuation. It was a scene much like this one—Zephyrine drawing her mistress a bath—when their relationship blossomed, a mere month after taking the position of Mistress Claudette's lady's maid.

As had become her custom, Zephyrine averted her eyes downward as the mistress untied her robe and lowered herself into the bathwater. Mistress Claudette had never instructed Zephyrine to look away; Zephyrine did so because when she did see her mistress's naked body, she felt an inexplicable stirring inside her. Only later, at night and alone in her bed, would she allow the image of the mistress's body to play along with her fingers, her cries of pleasure muffled into her pillow.

That day was different, though.

Zephyrine held the mistress's robe in her hands and looked down, waiting for her to enter the tub.

"Look at me, Zephyrine," the mistress said.

She turned her eyes and watched as Mistress Claudette ran her hand between her breasts, fingers trailing down the center of her abdomen and to the flare of her hips.

The mistress edged her feet into the tub, rested her buttocks on the side of the vessel, and spread her legs, hands running between her thighs, her clean nails lost in the thatch of hair there.

"Why don't you join me in my bath today?"

"Join you, Mistress?" Zephyrine said, the words trapped in her throat, a croak of sound.

The mistress rose and walked through the bathwater, displacing small waves onto the floor. Taking the robe from Zephyrine's clutching fingers, she unlaced her bodice. She leaned in and kissed Zephyrine's neck. The rounded scar on the mistress's upper lip pressed into her flesh and made its way down her sternum. For a month, Zephyrine had admired that scar, wondered what it would be like to touch it, to feel it on her own lips, and here it was snaking across her flesh like a living pearl.

Everything she'd hoped for.

Zephyrine would never forget those first moments, which changed her life. She tried to follow the mistress's lead, returning each kiss in kind, peeling away the layers of her clothing until they were no longer lady's maid and mistress, instead two synchronized bodies, their societal status left in a heap of garments soaking on the floor.

"You're preoccupied this morning, Zephyrine," the mistress says now, pulling Zephyrine from the memory of their first encounter. "Does something concern you? Do not allow your pretty thoughts to interfere with this time we have together." She reaches for Zephyrine's hand.

We. The word is honey from her lips. That Mistress Claudette thinks of what she and Zephyrine have together as a *we*. The two-letter word strengthens her resolve to share her worries.

This is the time to tell her what she's witnessed and the love she feels for the mistress. Mistress Claudette must be made to realize that Master Auguste is a philandering libertine. She couldn't ignore it if she knew, could she?

Zephyrine kisses the palm of Claudette's hand and takes a breath.

"Mistress, forgive me for being bold, but I must—"

There is a knock at the bath chamber door.

"Mistress?" It's Sylvie.

Mistress Claudette rolls her eyes at Zephyrine, annoyed by the spinster's interruption. Further proof to Zephyrine that she means as much to the mistress as the mistress does to her.

"Yes, Sylvie, what is it?"

Sylvie enters the room and Mistress Claudette stands, naked and dripping in the tub.

"Pardon me, I can come back, Mistress," Sylvie says, and attempts to leave.

"Don't be silly, Sylvie. I'm finishing my bath. The sight of my body is nothing new to you."

Did Sylvie flinch, burned by the mistress's comment?

"You look like a jealous old goat, Sylvie. Dry me off, Zephyrine," the mistress says.

Zephyrine does as she is told and pats the moisture from the mistress's skin. Uncomfortable with Sylvie in the room, she avoids the areas she worships most when they are alone.

"Be thorough, my girl. You're skipping the best parts," the mistress sneers.

It's a cruel streak Zephyrine has never seen before. Although she dislikes Sylvie, she can see how pained she is by her behavior. A jealous vapor fills the room. The mistress is humiliating the older woman. Zephyrine wonders why Sylvie would be jealous. Does she have affections for the mistress as well? Sylvie is a handsome woman, to be sure, but at least ten or fifteen years older than Mistress Claudette. The idea of there having been something between them makes Zephyrine's stomach twist.

"The kitchen staff has requested your approval of this evening's table setting," Sylvie says, jaw tight.

The mistress clasps her hand over Zephyrine's as she dries her breasts, massaging her own flesh with the help of Zephyrine's palm. She tries to remove herself from the mistress's grip, but it only makes her push down harder.

"What do *you* think, Sylvie? Is the table up to my standards?"

"I am sure I could not say, Mistress," Sylvie says.

"Ah, but I am sure you can," the mistress says.

What is happening here? Zephyrine is a pawn in a game that only the mistress and Sylvie know how to play. She doesn't like this side of her.

"Then, *yes*." The word hisses from Sylvie's lips. "Yes, the table setting will meet the high standards of Mistress Claudette."

"I'm glad to hear it. Was there anything else?"

"No, Mistress," Sylvie says.

"Then off you go," the mistress says.

Sylvie's gaze meets Zephyrine's. If Zephyrine expected daggers, she doesn't get them. The look isn't one of jealousy or hate; it's pity.

Sylvie leaves and closes the door behind her.

The mistress turns to face Zephyrine and presses her nude torso against her dress, kissing Zephyrine hard on the lips, tongue exploring, her round scar lifting to a smirk as it rolls across Zephyrine's teeth like a pebble.

CHAPTER TWENTY-ONE

Before that fateful day when she and the mistress shared their first kiss, the initial weeks at Château de Barbitière had been like a dream.

Both Zephyrine and Gilbert adjusted well to their new roles. Her brother felt at home with the stable of horses. The stable master was a widower and showed Gilbert how to clean and prepare the stable in the mornings, how to brush and feed the horses.

He was a happy young boy, and that was something Zephyrine cherished. After losing both parents in rapid succession, both their fates hanging on the precipice above the hungry mouth of Paris, that they'd landed here at Château de Barbitière had been a blessing. There was open sky and green gardens, the beautiful pond where she and her mistress would take a daily constitutional. They had food to eat, clean clothes. It was all thanks to the doctor who had delivered them here.

Zephyrine pushed away the memory of Master Auguste placing a sack of coins into the doctor's palm. At first, there was nothing untoward she could see—that she wanted to see. Both siblings blended into the fabric of a humming château staff in the countryside.

There were, however, moments that gave Zephyrine pause: Sylvie's disapproving gaze whenever she and the mistress giggled like schoolgirls; the first time she saw the master's late-night visitors to the château from her window when she should have been sleeping. The nagging question was always in the back of her mind: Where had the mistress's other lady's maid gone?

Zephyrine had been so caught up in her new life, in the warmth that grew with each interaction with the mistress, that she put aside any concerns and tallied them up to the newness of her role. At first, she could not define her feelings for her mistress.

She was her employer, but it didn't feel like work: tending to the mistress's toilet and dress, accompanying her on social visits to other ladies of high society and watching as they had tea and frivolous sandwiches that were more art than sustenance. Zephyrine listened while the ladies spoke of attending the opera and the latest fashions, gossiped about other friends who weren't in the room. Zephyrine absorbed the foreign language of their conversations.

One day, as they strolled the winding path that led to the pond, the mistress had said, "You do realize you're beautiful, do you not?" The comment made Zephyrine blush.

"If it pleases the mistress to say so, then yes," Zephyrine said.

"Your formality makes you all the more adorable."

"I only want to behave as expected," Zephyrine said.

"It is no accident that you ended up here at Château de Barbitière. The doctor is a family friend of Master Auguste and he has a keen understanding of my needs. You're doing a fine job and are a breath of fresh air, compared to the last one."

The last one. There it was, finally, a mention of the existence of the previous lady's maid.

They stood on the bank of the pond. The charms of Mistress Claudette's chatelaine rang like chimes as she leaned to lift a stone off the ground, throwing it into the rusty water. Concentric circles spread across the pond. The disruption attracted a frog. Its dome-shaped eyes popped above the surface.

"If I may, Mistress, what happened with your previous lady's maid, so I'll be sure not to repeat her mistakes?" The mistress's expression suggested that Zephyrine should tread with caution. "I apologize if the question is intrusive. Forgive me."

"Not at all. You are inquisitive and intelligent, a good thing to be as a woman. One morning, she was gone. Must have snuck out in the middle of the night with a stable hand." She winked at Zephyrine. "Good riddance to her. I have you now, don't I?"

Mistress Claudette plucked a reed frond from the water's edge. They walked arm in arm onto the arched bridge that crossed over the pond. It was an imposing feat of architecture, stone and wood that rose like a sea serpent from one side of the water to the other. They stopped in the middle, the clouds reflecting in the cinnamon-colored water below. The pond appeared a bottomless chasm.

"Pull up your sleeve and close your eyes," the mistress said. Zephyrine looked confused. "I won't feed you to the alligators, my dear."

"Alligators?" Zephyrine stepped away from the railing.

Mistress Claudette laughed. What a beautiful thing to see. Her face lit up, her eyes shining. "Of course not, my girl. It was a jest."

She held the reed between her teeth and unbuttoned the sleeve of Zephyrine's blouse, rolling it up past her elbow. Her new mistress was a mesmerist, Zephyrine unable to take her eyes off her, the reed tucked between her lips, that beguiling scar.

"I said close your eyes, Zephyrine. Do as you're told," she teased.

Zephyrine shut her eyes as the sun sneaked through her lashes. She held her bare arm out in anticipation—of what, she was unsure.

Mistress Claudette swirled the whiskery frond on Zephyrine's wrist. "Does this tickle?" she said.

"A little." Zephyrine cheated and opened an eye.

"No peeking!"

Zephyrine closed her eyes tight. "No peeking, Mistress."

"Good girl," she said. "Tell me when I reach the crux of your elbow."

The mistress inched the frond up her arm, stopping to go back, swirling in one place before moving up to the next. Zephyrine's skin danced with excitement, an itch in need of scratching, the tickling frond a splendid tease. Zephyrine felt it land on the bend of her elbow, but didn't want the moment to end. Instead, she played dumb so the mistress would have to do it again, until Zephyrine guessed right.

Later, the two women had lain down in the warm grass looking up at what had turned into a cloudless sky. It was then that she'd fallen in love with Mistress Claudette, when she had become more than a girl's infatuation. Her mistress had been kind and funny, sharing stories that a woman of her stature would only share with a friend. Zephyrine knew in her heart that she was more than just a lady's maid to Mistress Claudette.

Lying in the grass that afternoon, the sky full of dandelion parachutes, loose filaments of larvae silk floating like threads of sugar, she felt the world was a bright and cherished thing. Soon after, Zephyrine and Mistress Claudette consummated that love.

CHAPTER TWENTY-TWO

"Zephyrine, there you are. Look at me!" Gilbert says, unable to hide his excitement over his new wardrobe.

The master's valet brushes off the shoulders of Gilbert's blue velvet waistcoat and steps away from him, avoiding eye contact with Zephyrine. She'd been walking toward the mistress's dressing room, on her way to set out her gown for this evening, when she heard Gilbert and the valet. He hugs his sister for a long time. Not long ago, Gilbert reached only to her waist. Now his head is nearly up to her bosom.

"All is well, little brother?" Zephyrine asks.

"Yes. Though I do miss Mother and Father. I've begun to forget their faces. Isn't that terrible?"

"I understand, Gilbert. I feel the same. They would be very proud of you." She pulls away from him. Gilbert looks like a proper little French gentleman. "You're still pleased with your horses?"

"Everyone has been kind, and I'm very happy. The horses have come to recognize me, too. They fuss and whinny when I come to feed them in the morning. We're friends, I think."

Her brother beams with anticipation over tonight's dinner party. Who is Zephyrine to spoil that for him? A young boy need not hear of the goings-on in the master's bedroom or his own sister's homicidal fancies.

"Good. I wish I could see you more. The mistress keeps me busy."

It isn't a lie. She *is* kept busy, and it affords little time for them to interact, but the truth of the matter is that she is so infatuated with Mistress Claudette that any free time she has is taken by their stolen trysts. She blushes thinking of such things with her brother present. A better sister would keep an eye on her young brother.

The sight of her dear Gilbert in such finery should bring Zephyrine joy, yet it fills her with an inexplicable dread. Her brother, handsome—his fine features and chestnut-red hair, framing dark green eyes with long fringes of lashes.

"Why are you crying?" Gilbert says.

Unaware that a tear has run down her cheek, Zephyrine lifts her hand and feels the droplet sting her skin. "Oh, I—I'm thinking of how happy Mother and Father would be to see you now."

It's true—to a degree. They would have been overjoyed to see how grown-up Gilbert looks, how poised, but for Zephyrine, they would feel shame that their daughter had taken comfort in the bed of a woman, and had not followed the path to finding a good husband and becoming a mother herself someday. Zephyrine is casting aspersions on the master's illicit behavior while she is herself guilty of sin. Her stomach is in knots. Why, she is no hapless observer in this degenerate château—she is an active participant.

If Gilbert is aware of how his sister has fallen for Mistress Claudette, he doesn't show it.

"Do you think so?" Gilbert says.

She's lost in thought and has forgotten what he is responding to. "Think what, Gilbert?"

"That they would have been happy to see me dressed like a proper young man?"

"Yes, of course they would have."

"You will be at dinner tonight, will you not? I'm afraid I won't know which utensil to use."

When the mistress told her she and her brother were to attend tonight's dinner party, it had seemed strange to her. Yet the idea is enthralling: to dine at a table with a class of people (however immoral) that, until a few months back, had been completely alien to her; to look across the table at the woman who had stoked within her a fire that consumed her entire being; and to hold that bewildering secret inside her while others ate and chatted nonsense? The danger of it is intoxicating.

"I will be at dinner tonight, yes. Don't worry, Gilbert. Do as I do, and you will be fine," Zephyrine says.

Though what will that dinner look like after Zephyrine declares to her mistress that she is in love with her, and that she has seen Master Auguste engaging in narcotized acts of congress on more than one occasion? The first answer is easy: The mistress loves Zephyrine as much as Zephyrine loves her, and she will reciprocate. Of course she will. The second is more complicated: Will the mistress be devastated by her husband's infidelities? What if she harbors the same murderous thoughts as Zephyrine? Now, that would be grand.

She kisses the top of Gilbert's head. "I must prepare the mistress's wardrobe for this evening. I will see you later, little brother."

Zephyrine's distraction is absolute.

Mistress Claudette consumes her every thought. With only hours left before guests arrive, she has little time to come up with a script for what she will say to her mistress. She lays out the gown the mistress will wear this evening, yet she can't help but think she is missing something.

Zephyrine's never been in love before, never experienced the pleasures that she and the mistress share when they are alone. Surely it must be love? Only true love can weigh like a stone on the heart. Two people can't be together as she and Mistress Claudette have been without calling it love. Yet it gnaws at Zephyrine that the mistress has never once uttered those words—*I love you*—nor does she seem to be aware of (or care about) her husband's repulsive dalliances.

It's unfair of Zephyrine to expect the mistress will tell her how she feels, or denounce the master. The risk for her is too great for such declarations. A woman of her stature in society can't be expected to make such pronouncements to her lady's maid. It is for Zephyrine to tell her. Once she opens her heart to the mistress, Mistress Claudette will walk right in.

The mistress's gown for this evening is a deep ocher. It was custom made for her at the atelier of the venerable Charles Frederick Worth. Any woman who is anyone in high society would travel far and wide to be groped and measured by the House of Worth. Mistress Claudette is one of his top clients, right below the new bride of Emperor Napoleon III, Empress Eugénie. Zephyrine and the mistress had traveled into Paris only weeks earlier for the fitting. It had been the first time that Zephyrine had returned to the city since that day riding in the Citadine with the doctor.

That day, she saw the city with fresh eyes. Instead of it being the open-mouthed monster that she and her brother had feared months before, she saw Paris as it must appear to women like Mistress Claudette. They rode through its dusty and rank streets, safe and detached in their carriage, trotting past the inconvenient poverty and misery that lay outside the doors. Zephyrine and her brother had been only days away from being tossed out and left to fend for themselves. Zephyrine imagined herself and Gilbert out on the street as the mistress and another lady's maid drove by. She shuddered at the thought, the razor-thin edge that had led her to a life *inside* the carriage instead of out. What would she and Gilbert have done to survive? Where would they be now?

Zephyrine recalls the visit to Paris and to Monsieur Worth. His halting French, an army of helpers there to translate, to fetch bolts of the finest tulle, and to offer tea. Even Zephyrine benefited from the visit. Tonight she would wear a gown of pale green. The dress had been intended for another young woman, who had died in childbirth. It was tragic, though not uncommon, and the dress fit her perfectly. The day in Paris had been a dream. Riding out of the city, as they headed northeast toward Château de Barbitière, Belleville was a mirage on a hill, merely a place where a different incarnation of herself had lived. The one that existed on the other side of the blade's edge.

As the city roads turned to countryside, Mistress Claudette lifted the turquoise-beaded bottle from her chatelaine and uncorked it. She dabbed the amber oil onto Zephyrine's throat, and her blood coursed under the mistress's fingertips. They kissed and pulled the curtains shut. The women's exhalations filled the carriage cabin like perfume.

CHAPTER TWENTY-THREE

Zephyrine hurries to get herself ready, late for her afternoon walk with Mistress Claudette, which is already truncated because of this evening's party. So much time and attention had gone into the care and dress of Mistress Claudette that it's left very little for herself, and even less time to think of what she will say to her once they get to the pond. Words swim in her mind, chasing one another's tails, unable to form a complete chain.

Zephyrine's hands shake as she tries to secure the last fastener to her gown.

"Let me finish that for you, Zephyrine," a voice says.

It's Sylvie. Zephyrine hadn't heard her enter the room. Sylvie's presence is unwelcome and interrupts any gains Zephyrine has made in the speech she plans for her mistress.

"No need, Sylvie. I almost have it."

Zephyrine's tone is meant to encourage Sylvie's departure. Instead, the stubborn head of the household takes a seat and watches as Zephyrine continues to struggle with the dress.

"Are you sure? You don't appear to *have* anything," Sylvie says through a smirk.

She's making the situation worse. Zephyrine relents, if for no other reason than to make the older woman shut up and leave her in peace.

"Fine. Yes, thank you, Sylvie."

Sylvie stands and secures the last hook and eye, smoothing her hands across Zephyrine's back as she finishes. Her touch reminds Zephyrine of that first day at the château, Sylvie's hand enclosing her ankle in the warm bathwater.

"You're not the first," Sylvie says, palms stretched around the curve of Zephyrine's hips. "You know that, don't you?"

Zephyrine pulls away from Sylvie and faces her. Her features are strong, but she can see how attractive Sylvie must have been once, before time pecked away at her youth.

"I'm not the first what?"

Sylvie disregards the question. "I like to think it was I who taught her everything she knows. How to love another woman."

Zephyrine's ears ring and her breathing becomes rapid. *Sylvie* taught the mistress everything she knows? It couldn't be. Sylvie is no more than a jealous old woman.

"I do not know of what you speak. It's inappropriate, and Mistress Claudette will be displeased that you're telling tales. Please get out of my way. My mistress awaits me."

"Oh dear. I see it now. It's written all over your face. You have fallen in love with Claudette."

Sylvie speaking so informally of the mistress angers Zephyrine. Has her love for her been that obvious? Sylvie uttered aloud the words that she herself was summoning the courage to say to the mistress. This is not going as Zephyrine planned. Not at all. And is Sylvie suggesting that there have been *others*? That Sylvie herself has been one of them? It can't be true. The mistress and she have found true love and it will prove Sylvie wrong.

Zephyrine is perspiring. She will ruin her beautiful dress before the party has even begun.

"I apologize, Zephyrine." Sylvie's words are insincere. "I knew you were lovers, but I hadn't realized how deeply you'd fallen.

I can see it in your eyes. To be sixteen and as beautiful as you are—and you are the *most* beautiful of Mistress Claudette's paramours, I can assure you of that. Well, I can see how you could have been fooled by the attentions of a woman like Claudette."

"Fooled? How dare you? I love the mistress, and she loves me."

There. She's said it out loud, and it's the most thrilling thing she's ever done. It gives her strength.

Zephyrine continues, "Now, step aside and let me pass. The mistress waits for me downstairs."

Sylvie does as Zephyrine asks, the look of pity that she saw after the mistress's bath the other day returning. To think Zephyrine felt bad for the way the mistress spoke to her and treated her that day. It's as Zephyrine thought: The older woman is jealous. If there ever was anything between them, it's long past. Sylvie can't accept that Zephyrine has stolen the mistress's heart and that she is no more than a spinster in her eyes. Her mention of *others* is nothing more than a poisonous wedge to tear the women apart.

It won't work. If that is what Sylvie is trying to do, it will only make their bond stronger. Buoyed by this certainty, she pushes past Sylvie and heads down to her mistress—sure now of what she will say to her.

Zephyrine's first reaction was panic and resentment that the mistress had taken other lovers. That's what Sylvie hoped for in her confrontation. It has had the opposite effect. Zephyrine isn't as naive as Sylvie suspects, and she is surer than ever that the mistress will not only reciprocate her love but listen to the truth about Master Auguste.

The château buzzes with preparations for tonight's festivities. Fragrant blossoms and birch branches festoon the staircase and entryway. Fresh candles are placed in sconces and candelabras.

A cacophony of voices issue from the bowels of the kitchen, the cook barking orders to the staff. Tonight's feast will be a celebration of the coming summer. And though their relationship will not change in the eyes of others, Zephyrine and the mistress will be forever linked by their soon-to-come proclamations of love.

Mistress Claudette is resplendent in her gown. She stands in the shade of a plane tree, running her fingers through the charms attached to her chatelaine as she awaits the arrival of Zephyrine.

"Apologies, Mistress. I had a terrible time with the last clasp of my gown," she says.

Zephyrine looks back up in time to see Sylvie duck behind a curtain in the dressing room where they just had their encounter.

"Let's not dally, then. I need a walk to clear my head and stomach before the evening's excesses," Mistress Claudette says.

The mistress's words are clipped, though that is not uncommon in front of the rest of the staff. Zephyrine understands she must keep up appearances. As they walk away, the employees of Château de Barbitière scurry in and out.

CHAPTER TWENTY-FOUR

The two women amble along the pebbled pathway that slices between two gardens, a low maze of hedges to the left and mounds of rosebushes and lavender to their right. The only sounds are those of their feet on the gravel, the trinkets jangling from the mistress's chatelaine, and nature around them—swallows in the sky and honeybees on blossoms. The late-afternoon sun is strong, but a breeze cools. Château de Barbitière dissolves into miniature behind them. For Zephyrine, the rest of the world shrinks into irrelevance.

The two exist within their own universe, strolling side by side. Zephyrine has calmed after her confrontation with Sylvie and she is thinking clearly. Her fears of confronting Mistress Claudette with her pledge of love and her misgivings about the master now feel unfounded. Sylvie's words were meant to flare her doubts, to divide the two lovers, but she has failed.

The pond extends before them, and Zephyrine returns to that first day exiting the Citadine carriage. A lifetime ago. Zephyrine has matured. She is no longer a girl of sixteen, but a woman.

Rays of sun bounce off the water ahead. Deep gold and copper, dotted by lily pads. The arched spine of the bridge bends like a cornered cat.

Mistress Claudette threads her arm through Zephyrine's as they round the bank.

"You are awfully quiet this afternoon, Zephyrine," she says.

Frothy dandelion chutes dance through the air and land on the water's surface.

This is Zephyrine's chance. They walk onto the bridge, the sound of their footfalls on the wooden planks a hollow *thrum* beneath them. The first time they walked across the bridge together, Zephyrine had been nervous—nothing but an old wood-and-stone bridge separating her from the deep water. The mistress joking of alligators. Today, she is without fear.

Stopping in the middle, Zephyrine turns to the mistress. Château de Barbitière is a thimble of stone in the distance, too far for anyone to see Zephyrine lean in and kiss Mistress Claudette and run her tongue across the firm round of her scar.

Mistress Claudette pulls away from her lady's maid. "You've become bold, Zephyrine. We've spent hours getting me ready for the evening. This is not the time to get . . . disheveled."

"I must speak with you, Mistress."

"It's difficult to speak when your lips are on mine, is it not?"

Was that meant to be a jest? Her voice still carries the terse tone from earlier. It seems unnecessary with no one else around.

"Mistress." Zephyrine pushes on, and takes a deep inhale. "I love you. No, I am in love with you."

If Mistress Claudette is surprised by Zephyrine's proclamation, she doesn't reveal it. The mistress looks away from Zephyrine and plays with her chatelaine, rolling the golden perfume bottle in her fingers.

"Yes, you have come to mean very much to me as well, Zephyrine." She is fidgeting. "Perhaps we should go back now? There is still much to do."

The mistress must not have heard her. She could never be so

dismissive of a statement that took incredible resolution to make.

"Did you not hear me? I said that I am in love with you . . . *Claudette*."

That gets the mistress's attention. Her eyebrows lift. "Not only have you become bold, but also brazen. It's time to go back."

Mistress Claudette turns to walk away from Zephyrine. The sight of her back is a slap to the face.

Now Zephyrine understands what's happening. Mistress Claudette can't be as forthcoming as Zephyrine in this situation. Her status won't allow it. It is for Zephyrine to lay it out for her. Only then can she let down her guard.

Zephyrine grabs the mistress's wrist to stop her. The act is too rough.

"How dare you handle me like that? Let go at once."

"I'm sorry, Mistress. It was not my intention. Please, listen to me."

She's lost the mistress—she must explain, must make her see.

"Return with me to the château at once, before you say something *else* that you'll regret."

Regret? How was announcing their love for one another a regret?

"Please wait, Mistress. This isn't coming out the way I had hoped. You are not understanding me. I'm unaccustomed to speaking so plainly and the words are falling from me like rocks."

"You're behaving like the other girl, Zephyrine. Clinging to me like an unruly vine. It's disappointing."

The other girl. Does she mean her previous lady's maid? The one who ran off with a stable hand in the middle of the night? Zephyrine is being lumped together with someone so insignificant that she has no name other than *Girl*.

"I don't . . . What you are saying, Mistress? You love me, too. I am certain. Two people can't be together as we have been without being in love. I've seen it in your eyes."

The mistress Claudette laughs. The sound is devastating. Zephyrine can scarcely breathe. This is no polite laugh, not a delicate chortle like the ones she shares with her society friends over tea. No, this laugh emanates from somewhere deeper. A long-standing amusement that she is only now privy to.

Zephyrine is the joke.

She is the jest that germinated four months ago. A vulnerable orphan of sixteen, her desire for members of her own sex coaxed out, exploited, exposed, and then nurtured for the entertainment of a woman who, until this moment, she was sure had reciprocated her feelings.

Zephyrine's chest caves in. Her insides collapse and her bones no longer support her limbs. She leans onto the wooden railing with her full weight. It creaks at the effort.

Through sobs, she says, "You love me. You do. You brought me here. I saw it in your face that very first day, the expression when you looked into my eyes for the first time. You felt it, too. We were connected. We *are* connected."

Mistress Claudette continues to laugh.

Zephyrine takes hold of her shoulders. "Stop it. Please. We can be together. Your husband is a terrible man. I have refrained from saying anything, but . . . but Master Auguste disrespects you terribly. I have seen him with another woman *and* a man in his bedchamber—not once, many times—breathing ether for pleasure as he watches them perform."

"And?" Mistress Claudette's laughter subsides. "Do you think I don't know that? That I care? Master Auguste indulges me in my every desire for clothing and jewelry, in trips to Paris for the opera. We attend and host parties for the finest people in society. He allows my dalliances with young girls like you and I grant him the freedom to do as he wishes and with whom. It is the ideal marriage."

"That's not true. I know it isn't," Zephyrine says.

She is desperate to make her understand. Zephyrine takes the mistress's face in her hands, kisses her again and again, as though she can kiss away her terrible words. She whispers, "No, please, you don't need to say that, to protect him. We can find a way to be together if he is gone. There are poisons. He could have an accident. Breathe in too much of his ether, perhaps? No one need know and then we could—"

The mistress pushes Zephyrine away and slaps her hard across the face. Pain fires across her cheek, stinging and numb. Blood trickles from her nose.

"What are you saying? How dare you even suggest such a thing? You and your brother will leave here today. Threatening to kill my husband? Are you mad? People hang for lesser things."

She turns to walk away.

Zephyrine's corset squeezes the air from her lungs. She cannot breathe, speak. It was a terrible misstep and declared all too fast. She must take it back, make things right.

She grabs the mistress's arm to stop her and rips a seam of Mistress Claudette's gown. The mistress's eyes are filled with hate, disgust. These can't be the same eyes that have gazed upon Zephyrine when they have been alone together. The ones that said that she loved her, too.

Mistress Claudette's voice is measured, calm.

"You will make me say it, then. I had hoped to spare you the truth: My darling Zephyrine, you and your piteous little brother did not come to Château de Barbitière out of charity after your wretched parents' deaths. No, the doctor saw an opportunity, and he seized upon it. And for that, he was rewarded. You have ruined it, girl. People of your ilk are so predictable; show them some kindness and they attach to you like a leech."

The satchel of coins placed in the doctor's fat palm on that first day. It had given Zephyrine pause then. She should have listened to her instincts. What could she have done? There was little possibility of a good life without the doctor's assistance. It would have been a meager existence on the cobbled streets of Paris, not knowing when the next meal might come, begging with legions of other orphaned or abandoned children, Zephyrine selling her body in order to feed them. Time and poverty eating away at what little life they could have, until there was nothing, until they were tossed into the ground without ceremony with others of their kind. Their *ilk*. Just like their parents. Their *wretched* parents.

How could Zephyrine have been so foolish? Is this the punishment for lusting after another woman? For believing that kind of love could be anything but a perversion? Could be anything but shame in the eyes of God?

Lost in her miserable thoughts, Zephyrine startles at a sound like burbling water. Her hands have wrapped themselves around the throat of her beautiful mistress. Her long neck fits well between her fingers. The pressure turns the round scar on the mistress's lip white, the firm tissue trying to escape like a cork from a bottle.

Mistress Claudette can't speak. Her hands claw at Zephyrine's. Those soft fingers, the ones that had caressed her that first day as she cooled Zephyrine's skin. The digits that have opened doors on Zephyrine's body that she never knew were there to be unlatched.

Zephyrine watches herself from the outside, observing as Mistress Claudette's face turns a deep red.

What is she doing? Who is this person strangling the life out of the woman she loves? *Loved*. After what Mistress Claudette has just said, that love is gone, obliterated, and hate has taken its place.

Zephyrine is not the tragic innocent who came to Château de Barbitière months ago, grateful that she and her brother had been saved. It was Mistress Claudette's own fault for being so beautiful, so attentive. Zephyrine could have stayed on the path of silent longing, never stepping over the line to a place where she had no birthright to be. It was the mistress who did this. All that is happening is her doing.

Zephyrine thinks of their stolen moments together—in the mistress's bed, the bath, in the tall grasses that lie beyond the end of the bridge they stand on now. None of this is happenstance. Zephyrine and her brother's presence here is transactional. Zephyrine, a conveyance of pleasure for the mistress, and nothing more, as disposable as the last lady's maid surely was. And the one before her? And Sylvie? Sylvie is made of stronger stuff than Zephyrine. She had endured being pushed aside, and understood her place—unlike Zephyrine—and that allowed her to rise in the ranks, to retain value in the mistress's eyes.

It's too late. There is no way out. Whatever happens next, Zephyrine is doomed: continue to squeeze the breath out of the mistress, or face the consequence of threatening the life of Master Auguste. Where does that leave Gilbert? Oblivious, dressing himself for the evening at this moment, thinking he has been taken into the fold of Château de Barbitière—when in reality he is a mere shiny ornament, one that will be cast aside from a château filled with the abandoned detritus of this world of excess, while the rest of civilization starves at their feet, while their *ilk* live in drab shades of gray beneath them.

Mistress Claudette makes the choice for her. The familiar song of the charms on her chatelaine plays beneath the mistress's struggle for air. Undetected by Zephyrine, the mistress Claudette's fingers have found the pearl-handled letter opener and pulled it free. The blade plunges into the side of Zephyrine's neck.

Stunned, Zephyrine releases her grasp around the mistress's throat and tends to her own. She pulls the handle from her neck and a gush of blood follows with it, flowing over her fingers, seeping into the pearlescent green of her sleeves—life itself emptying from her. Zephyrine can feel as it's siphoned away. She stumbles against the railing and it creaks with the impact. Mistress Claudette leans next to her, gasping for air, her breath raspy and strained.

Zephyrine loses her balance, and she takes hold of folds of orange silk, pulling the mistress into her. A bloody and breathless last embrace. Zephyrine's spine, no longer willing to keep her upright, bends backward, and she hangs over the rail. Her blood runs across her face and she watches it trickle into the water like viscous rain.

Alligators, she thinks.

As she falls, she loses her grip on the mistress's gown. She grabs for the mistress's chatelaine and grasps at the gold perfume bottle, studded with turquoise, each rounded lump of stone reminding her of the scar on her mistress's lip. Her tongue running across it. Her fingers.

The plum-size perfume bottle breaks free from its golden chain and Zephyrine holds on tight as she falls into the silky brown water below.

The water is warmer than expected. It has a heft to it. Heavy with algae, it wraps its liquid limbs around Zephyrine and pulls her down. Eyes open, her own blood clouds around her, joining the rusted brown of the pond. If there are alligators, they will find her now.

Of course, there are none. They were as much of a jest as Zephyrine has been. An elaborate joke. She grips the golden bottle in her hand, remembering Mistress Claudette painting drops of perfume on her neck as they fell to the floor of the carriage. The smell of muguet forever links her to Claudette, to their intertwined bodies, to those effervescent moments that she now knows were a lie, an amusement. She should fight against the water that pulls her down, but she can't. Or won't. She no longer has the will to do so.

Is death more a matter of the mind than the body? Is it acceptance? She thinks of her father and mother living their last days racked in pain, fighting for each breath and battling to stay alive for their children. The fear of death was in their eyes, the fear of what would happen to Zephyrine and Gilbert once they were gone. The uncertainty of where death would take them. Soon—very soon—Zephyrine will know the answer, too. Will they be reunited?

The water above her shimmers. A bronze blanket held in place by the sunlight. Above, Mistress Claudette leans over the bridge. Zephyrine feels the heat from the fireplace that first day, the moment that Mistress Claudette turned to face her. How something in her awakened in that instant. It's not the mistress's face she should think of as her body drifts downward. It should be that of Gilbert, of her mother and father. Of those that truly loved her in her brief life.

Her lungs fill with water. The worst is over. The pond has won. It's filled her lungs and taken her blood and there's no need to struggle. The velvety bottom catches her fall, cradles her. The pond is not as deep as she imagined when she and her love had stood on the bridge, looking down. The turquoise-beaded bottle rolls off her palm and sinks into the silt. A ray of sunlight catches the golden orb as it disappears and leaves a cloud of particles above it.

Mistress Claudette looms above.

Zephyrine is full. The water displaces any life that may remain inside her. She and Claudette are lying in the grass together, the sun above them, the sky full of dandelion parachutes. Loose filaments of larvae silk float past like threads of sugar. A primal part of her reaches out one last time, clawing for air. There is none.

A dark figure appears next to Mistress Claudette. A shadow that goes unnoticed. Zephyrine's quieting mind can't make sense of it, of who—or what—it is. The being rises in the air and then pierces the water, a great penumbra passing over her inert body. From the inky presence a sleeve of black unspools outward—an arm, digits made of something dark as night—as liquid as the water and her own blood around her. The being is indifferent to Zephyrine's lifeless body as it searches the ooze next to Zephyrine's open hand. From the murk, it retrieves the perfume bottle.

Before her world collapses in on itself, the monstrous shadow turns to her. The place where its face should be flaps like a mirrored black sail on the wind. Then it's gone.

Everything has disappeared.

CHAPTER TWENTY-FIVE

Greta Davenport gasps for air. Her joints throb, her body heavy under the weight of an invisible lead blanket. Struggling to sit up, she explores her neck with her hands. She searches for the wet of blood, an open wound. There is none.

Her mind isn't her own, and a stunning terror, so complete, overwhelms her. She writhes, thirsty for air. Splinters of images flash through her thoughts. They're disjointed and one won't connect to the other. Greta tries to answer the most basic questions: *What's my name? Who am I? Where am I?* The answers elude her. Her sense of self is lost in a turbulent sea of firing synapses.

"Oh my Dieu. Qu'est—qui—happening?" Her words are a gibberish of French and English. She coughs and gulps the air. The words are out in the open, no longer trapped in her head like before.

"Greta Davenport," a woman's voice says, but Greta can't see her. "Greta Davenport," the voice says again. Declarative. She is answering a question Greta doesn't even realize she's asked. *What is my name?*

Greta looks up, and a woman stands in front of her. She knows her. *How?*

The woman's hand massages Greta's shoulder. Each finger bedecked in a ring. On her thumb, a band shaped into an elaborate tree with golden branches, emeralds for leaves; its roots extend toward her wrist, the thickest in its center, dotted with saffron-colored topaz, forming an arrow.

Miranda.

"That's right, Greta. I'm Miranda," she says, her breathing oddly shallow and deliberate. Greta had only thought her name, hadn't she? Had she said it aloud? "Congratulations on returning from your first voyage. This is the hardest part. It will soon pass."

It seems hardly possible, but Miranda is more aglow, more vibrant than she was before Greta went on her voyage. The goddess is revivified. Profuse, jet hair, shiny to the point of blinding. Her fertile look is that of a woman who's about to share the secret of her pregnancy with her best friend. Suddenly, inner lids, like those of a shark before it feeds, flutter for a split second within Miranda's eyes—then vanish. Greta's hallucinating. She tries to reach out to Miranda, but her arm won't move. It's resting in a mold of quivering silver. The Obitus Mold. In her palm, there's a glass perfume bottle, covered in gold thread, and studded with turquoise beads. A greenish-brown slime drips from its surface. Greta's heart aches at a memory she can't identify.

"Mistress Claudette?" Greta says. As the name falls from her lips, Greta cries. She can't help it. The sumptuous pain doesn't belong to her, yet there it is.

"It's okay, Greta," Miranda says, a ringed finger stroking her own upper lip. "What you're experiencing is normal. Try to breathe."

Greta does as she's told. Miranda's hand traces down Greta's body, lingering a moment too long. Inhaling deeply, she then pulls out a pair of latex gloves and snaps them on. Using gold forceps, she extracts the dripping bottle from Greta's hand. She opens a wooden box and, after wiping the bottle, places it back in. Miranda lifts Greta's arm and the Obitus Mold recedes beneath the chaise. She helps Greta to sit up.

"There, there," she says. "These are someone else's tears, not yours. Deep breaths."

My name is Greta Davenport. This much she knows.

The rest falls into place: She's in the Found Object Society located in the South Street Seaport of Manhattan, beneath a building known as the Captain Joseph Rose House, and she's just experienced the magnificent, terrible death of a young woman named Zephyrine who lived in nineteenth-century France, and who was murdered at the hands of the woman she loved.

Horrifying. Wonderful.

Greta's body shudders, riding the tail end of a wanton wave that has only just crested, crashing and frothing across the sand. She tries to grasp the surf before it recedes. She can't let it go, won't, but it's gone again. Pupils dilated, sensitive to the light, Greta looks up at Miranda and says, "Let's go again."

"Alas, no, Greta," Miranda says as she stands her up and leads her out of the cabin. If Greta didn't know better, she'd think Miranda is as disappointed as she is.

The heavy door opens with that familiar drowsy sigh. Greta notes several of the other cabins' lights are illuminated blue. Others are having an experience like she just had. Greta feels some serious FOMO.

Like a kid being forced to go home after a day at Six Flags Great Adventure, she puts on the brakes and says, "Seriously, Miranda, now that I understand it, I'd like to go one more time. Please?"

"Rule number four, Greta: Under no circumstances can you take a voyage again so soon. For your *safety*, you must wait at least seventy-two hours," Miranda answers.

Greta half expects to be shoved into the back seat of a Volvo station wagon so she can pout on the ride home, but she's a thirty-seven-year-old woman and she has some dignity left. She's wide awake, electrified.

What the hell is she going to do with herself for the next seventy-two hours?

Big Daniel Craig is standing, expectant, as they enter the front welcoming area. He's holding a large glass of opaque coral-colored liquid, a wedge of cucumber resting on its edge. It's like *Fantasy Island*, only she's on her way out, not arriving on the dock via seaplane.

"Miss Davenport, this is for you. Drink up, lots of potassium. You'll need it," BDC says.

Miranda stands back by the velvet curtains, looking impatient. Greta wonders again who else is in there and if she knows any of them.

She reaches for the glass. A cocktail isn't what she needs. "Uh, thank you. What is it? I'm not in a boozy mood."

"It's not alcohol," Miranda says. Her answer is curt, maybe a bit too loud. "Pardon me, Greta, we're busy tonight. It's just guava nectar with added electrolytes. It will help you recover, rebalance."

"Got it," Greta says. She takes a small sip, and it sparkles over her tongue. It's only now that she realizes how thirsty she is. She gulps it all down in one swig.

BDC grabs a pitcher from a side table and refills her glass.

"Thank you," Greta says.

"Pleasure," he says.

Miranda pulls the gold chain from between her breasts and looks at it. What Greta'd thought was a pocket watch is maybe, in fact, a stopwatch, because she clicks a button on the top, then parts the curtains.

"Greta, my apologies, another client is returning from their voyage and I must attend to them. We look forward to seeing you again. We'll be in touch to schedule your next voyage before the seventy-two-hour window closes." She turns to BDC. "Will you please be sure that Ms. Davenport is in stable condition before she leaves?"

"Yes, of course, Miss Miranda," BDC says.

With that, the Oaxacan goddess and her murmurations of fabric and baubles are gone. With her departure, BDC's shoulders relax—Mommy's left the room.

Greta raises the glass to her lips again and before she can knock it back, BDC says, "Easy now, Greta. Take it slow. Take *everything* slow tonight."

Tonight?

Which night? It can't still be Thursday night, can it? How long has she been here? Hours? Days? Greta's voyage took her through the last days, weeks—maybe even months—of poor Zephyrine.

"What day is it? How many days have I been here?"

BDC smiles, then chuckles. "Your voyage lasted exactly fifty minutes, Miss."

Like when they say you're getting a one-hour massage, but it's really only fifty minutes to account for you getting undressed and dressed? Greta always thought that was bullshit. She paid for an hour massage, so that's what she expects. But this? To experience someone's last days so vividly and to suffer their exquisite death in less than an hour? It's a frickin' miracle.

"Seriously?" Greta says. "How?"

BDC beams with pride.

"Indeed, Miss Davenport," he says. "How is any of this"—he stretches his great wingspan wide, taking in the entirety of the Found Object Society, gathering it in his arms like he's

Papa Christmas, his resplendent suit shimmering against a dizzying backdrop of sumptuous fabrics and psychotropic-worthy wallpaper—"*any* of it, possible?"

It's the same phrase Eileen used at their office in Tribeca. Is it a slogan the Found Object Society is trying out? Is it in beta test mode?

"Right, right," Greta says, raising her glass to BDC. "Cheers to you and the Found Object Society." That pleases him. He blushes in a humblebrag kind of way.

The last ripples of Greta's high ebb away. Death's caresses—the ones that had brought her to a place of astounding pleasure—are replaced by a deafening void. She's losing steam. Fast.

She leans against the wallpaper. The images are fragmented and haphazard—Tupac's enchanting fringe of lashes; the swirl of Apollo 1's fire; a horse rearing up on its hind legs, an exaggerated shadow cast along the ground behind it. Her stomach lurches and she feels nauseous.

BDC rushes to a listing Greta and supports her with his plate-size hands. "Are you all right, Miss Davenport?"

She shakes off the queasiness, the ringing in her ears.

"I'm good. I think. I'm a little wiped out from, you know, the death and everything." Didn't that sound stupid? *The death and everything.* Idiot.

For a moment, BDC and Greta stand in awkward silence. This would be the time to ask some of her questions about the Found Object Society, but Greta's thoughts are too discombobulated. BDC fiddles with his ascot, brushes invisible lint from his waistcoat. He clears his throat.

"Feeling better, then, Miss Davenport?"

"I think so. Yes," she says, without meaning it. She's acutely aware that she's expected to wrap up her visit.

She finishes her second glass of guava nectar and bites into the wedge of cucumber. Its cold burst makes her teeth ache. Her mind is racing. She's uneasy. Like after a night of snorting coke, she's getting paranoid, entering that twitchy, downward spiral. The plummet from a great height.

The hollow that only knows one cure: more.

CHAPTER TWENTY-SIX

BDC unlocks the wallpaper-camouflaged safe and hands Greta her phone.

"Now, Miss Davenport, I'd like to remind you of the rules of the Found Object Society," BDC says, sounding stiff. He taps his finger on the framed sign on the wall for emphasis.

5. Do not loiter in the waiting area.

BDC's message is clear: *You don't have to go home, but you can't stay here.* They probably don't want members fraternizing. Who knows? They might talk.

To appease him, Greta nods and makes a show of reading the rules with interest. Truth is, she can't; she feels caged up and finds it hard to focus on the words. She's exhausted and restless all at once, though rule number three sticks with her, the one that says discussing the society with anyone who isn't a member is *strictly forbidden*. Greta knows *that* one—forbidden to the point of making a threat to that person's well-being. She recalls the photo of Lis holding the mug in her hand the other morning. The one that came with a seven-word warning: *We told you not to tell anyone.* The morning that seems like a lifetime ago, yet it's only been two days.

"Okeydoke, I got it. Thanks—" Greta's about to call him Big Daniel Craig when she realizes she doesn't know his name. "I'm sorry, what's your name?"

He smiles, his bright blue eyes crinkling, almost disappearing, "You can call me Daniel, Miss Davenport."

"Are you serious? Daniel?"

"Sure." He leans his mass closer to her and whispers, "Though my close friends call me *Big Daniel Craig*."

His proximity makes Greta tingle, burn red. Miranda must have told him. How embarrassing.

She stammers, "Ha, well . . . I–I meant it as, you know—? I didn't mean anything, just—"

He's unlocking the elaborate bank vault door, the air depressurizing with its passionate gasp as he pulls it open. "It's a compliment, Miss Davenport, and I rather like it."

"Oh, good. Good. Well, um, *Big Daniel Craig*, I'll see you soon."

"Indeed, you will. Careful home, now. Drink lots of fluids and get some rest. You've had quite a death, after all." He winks and starts to shut the vault behind her.

When Miranda's not around, Big Daniel Craig is more at ease, more willing to gab. Greta's not sure that she would sanction their flirtatious, witty repartee.

"Wait," Greta, forever the opportunist, says. It takes all of BDC's bulk to stop the closing of the vault door.

"Yes, miss?" he says.

"Is this place for real or what? I mean, my death . . . Seriously, you can tell me. How do you guys do it?"

A tic, barely discernible, crosses Big Daniel Craig's face. As he opens his mouth to speak, the old-fashioned phone rings and interrupts him. Miranda must be calling. "Excuse me, Miss Davenport. I have to get that. Please take care out there," he says, and closes the vault.

Cold water's been thrown on Greta's attempt to sweet-talk BDC for information. She's left standing in the all-black vestibule where she entered the Found Object Society a mere hour or so ago.

That's hard to process. Fifty minutes is all it took for the miserable, sensuous, and overwrought last sprint of Zephyrine's life to play out, her last memories now also Greta's. Her final scene, resting at the bottom of a silt-filled pond, blood leaking from her throat, her lungs full of stagnant water, and the gold-and-turquoise perfume bottle rolling off her palm like an activated grenade, and then . . . something else. In her dying moment, the actual instant where Zephyrine's life was extinguished, there'd been a passing shadow, a dreadful presence, and like the last bit of a dream upon waking, it's gone, elusive.

There was something there, though. She's certain of it.

Uneasy, Greta continues forward down the vestibule. The bare blue light bulb hangs at the end of the walkway. The shock of exiting the vibrant and otherworldly confines of the society leaves her vacant. Without the distraction of BDC, the wallpaper, the fetching Miranda, Greta transitions into a colorless world.

It's not a good place to be. She likens it to the comedown after molly or blow. Dark fills her mind, each thought teetering on a cliff above a canyon. No up, only down. Her stomach gurgles in revolt.

She's going to be sick.

Greta pitches up the stoop stairs, into the humdrum of the twenty-first century. She covers her mouth, not wanting to vomit at the doorstep of the Found Object Society. Wedging herself into the narrow alleyway between the brick Captain Joseph Rose House and the building next to it, she empties the bright pink contents of her stomach. Her retching continues until there's nothing left. Her legs shake and her ab muscles cramp up. For someone who just spent half a million dollars to experience a poor young woman's death, she's acting like a ten-dollar-a-hit crack addict. *Pure class.*

Greta leans her forehead against the cool, rough brick and catches her breath. She blinks her watering eyes. The alleyway ends with what must be heaps of garbage bags and trash cans. It's hard to discern at this distance. What the hell's she supposed to do now? How can life go on as it has before, after this? Or at least for another seventy-two hours until she can do it again. Until she can die again.

"You okay?"

The voice startles her, and Greta turns to see a stranger looming at the entrance of the alley.

CHAPTER TWENTY-SEVEN

Puking is a private venture. Greta prefers to do it alone, not in front of a stranger.

She holds up her hand to stop the man from moving toward her. "Yes, I'm fine, thanks. Just need a minute."

He doesn't take the hint and enters the narrow space, sidling toward her between brick walls. The man reaches into his pocket as he approaches. Greta's skin prickles with the instinct of fight or flight. There's nowhere to go, though. The dead-end alley is barely wide enough to accommodate a single body, let alone two bodies in a scrum, or one body that's going to make a run for it, and the only way to get out is over the second body. She was a fool to cram herself in here, and now she's stuck. Her street smarts have gone to shit.

"Really, sir," she says. "I'm fine. Please, go."

"I get it," he says, his voice deep and soothing. "A Black man coming down an alley toward a white woman puking up guava nectar? It's the white American nightmare."

He knows she's vomiting guava nectar? That must mean that he's—

"Look. See? I'm stopping a few feet away from you and I'm taking out a handkerchief. Okay?" he says.

He stretches out his hand and offers Greta a purple silk pocket square that's far too nice for her to wipe her pukey mouth with. Still leaning against the wall, Greta takes in his face. His head is bald and his skin is smooth and dark, eyes deep as honey. His lip curls up to one side, giving her a *What have you got to lose* twinkle. Greta drips with vomit in front of one of the sexiest men she's seen in a long time.

Fan-fucking-tastic.

"Are you sure?" Greta says, as she extends her hand to his.

"I'm sure. I'll send you the dry-cleaning bill."

Greta laughs. It hurts her stomach, so she stops. *Sexy as hell* and *funny, and here I am, dripping with pink puke.* Taking the violet square from his hands, she dabs at her chin and mouth. The material smells like a beach: salt and seagrass, warm sun. She pulls it away from her face. It's soaked, dotted with little chunks of cucumber.

"Want this back?" she says.

"Not so much. You keep it—to remember me by."

They laugh, and Greta's insides are calming. Standing there, stuck between two brick walls, he seems as unsure as she what comes next. She's reminded of the claustrophobic feeling that came moments after Miranda's injection: when she woke to darkness, the walls compressing around her, squeezing her out and into space, toward the eyes of Zephyrine.

There's scrabbling behind her at the dead-end part of the alley, clawed feet scritching across the concrete. Two rats squealing, duking it out. The shadow cast from the mountain of garbage takes the form of a distorted tree, and a prismatic slick of oil stretches out, rootlike, seeping into the foundation of 273 Water Street.

"Don't know about you, but I'd love not to be in here anymore," Handkerchief Man says.

He slides toward the street and Greta follows, careful to step over the pool of her own vomit. Leaving the rats to their fight club, the two emerge in front of the Found Object Society.

Standing on the sidewalk, Greta gets a better look at him. Have they met before? He's familiar, though she can't place why.

It's late, but the pulse of lower Manhattan continues in the background. Two strangers, standing in front of one of the oldest houses in the city, beneath which lies a secret society for the extraordinarily rich, the supremely bored. The numb. The ones who can only find life in someone else's death.

In short, two sickos, perfectly matched.

Handkerchief Man is dapper as hell. Maybe a tick less so, without the plum pocket square sticking out of his dark gray blazer. He wears a white collared shirt—pressed by a pro, not some schlub at home wielding a leaky iron—plus dark jeans, and navy suede Tom Ford sneakers.

The recognition must be the unspoken familiarity of wealth. Both of them are casually dressed rich people. Effortless casual that costs thousands of dollars.

For all his high-end styling, there's something off about him. Taking him in, it comes to her: His blazer is a smidge too big, his jeans need more help from his belt than they should, and his cheekbones are a little too concave. This gorgeous man is shrinking. It's a look she knows. It's one she's seen not only on random people on the subway or sidewalk, hollow husks of humans shuffling to the next fix, but in herself in these days since her visit with Eileen. A slow wasting, the body consuming itself because something else has superseded the need for survival.

It's the look of addiction.

They shift their diminishing weight back and forth, each waiting for the other to talk, for one of them to acknowledge where they both just came from. At least, Greta's fairly certain he's a member of the Found Object Society. He pointed out that she was puking up guava nectar and, unless he's a forensic analyst of human excretions, that's the only way he'd know.

Greta breaks the ice.

"Um, what time is it?"

He peeks at his wristwatch. It's a vintage Patek Philippe—no cheap Seiko for this man. No wedding band either. She notices that, too.

"Sure, it's just after midnight."

Greta absorbs that. "Wow. Okay. Friday. Just after midnight."

"Yeah . . . crazy."

They're playing chicken, both testing to see who will mention the basement of 273 Water Street first.

Handkerchief Man cocks his head toward the Captain Joseph Rose House and shrugs. "Right?" he says.

Greta's wondered about other members of the society—if there even *were* other members, or that maybe this wasn't real at all but a complete break in her sanity, a massive hallucination created by a head trauma she'd been unaware of after her near-crash of five days ago. This is her chance to talk to someone about it. Another person who just so happens to be very attractive and standing right in front of her.

He speaks for her.

"Should I say it?" he says. "Okay, look . . . I'm gonna say it. And if you turn and run, well, then you turn and run."

Greta raises her eyebrows in the affirmative. *Please talk about it. Please be like me. Please, please.*

"Unless I'm mistaken, you just came out of"—he gestures toward 273, and leans in, whispering, even though there's no one else around—"the Found Object Society. You just had your first *voyage*, I'm guessing, since I found you, uh, getting sick in the alley. Am I right?"

Relief washes over Greta and her body relaxes from its clench. She's not alone. She's not nuts (not completely).

"Yes. Oh, thank God, yes. You too? I mean, yes, duh, you too, or else you wouldn't be . . . I mean, you couldn't know about the whole . . . the whole . . . the guava nectar and—" Greta teeters; she's dizzy.

He puts a hand on her shoulder. Not the meaty paw of BDC, but a gentle, cradling palm.

"I remember feeling like you are after my first time. You won't be able to sleep for hours. Want to take a walk?"

He's right. Greta should be exhausted, but she's not. At least, her mind isn't. It's racing, and she needs to talk about what happened to her. To ask questions. To share this with someone where the sharing won't risk the other person's life.

As of this moment, Handkerchief Man is Greta Davenport's best friend. Her only friend in the world.

CHAPTER TWENTY-EIGHT

Greta has so many questions, she's unsure where to start. Getting Handkerchief Man's real name is foremost.

"Since you've already had the pleasure of watching me retch in an alley, I may as well introduce myself. I'm Greta Davenport. Pleased to meet you."

Greta reaches out but thinks better of it, what with the puking. Laughing, they offer elbows.

"I'm Ezra Somers. Nice to meet you, Greta."

They walk. The two weave through the cobbled streets, past landmark buildings hanging on for dear life next to chic restaurants and converted condo buildings.

"It gets better, you know. After the first one, I mean. Promise," he says. Then he adds, "Or maybe that's worse?"

Greta's mouth is as pasty as plaster of paris.

"I'm so thirsty. Mind if we get something to drink?" Greta says.

"You mean like a bar?"

No, not like a bar. The idea of being around other people who haven't gone through what she's gone through doesn't appeal. Anyone else is on the outside. Living on another plane. She and Ezra, they're in deep. They're at the core.

"I don't think I can handle seeing other people. You know—"

"Outsiders." Ezra finishes the sentence for her. "Yep. I know what you mean. From here on, you'll see that everyone—

everything—in your life is secondary to what goes on back there." He points back toward Water Street. Ezra's right, of course he is, because Greta's already counting down how long she'll have to wait until her next voyage. Her next death.

They enter a narrow vape shop, barely wider than the alley where they'd met. The walls on either side are lined with glassed-in shelves filled with every weed-smoking apparatus imaginable. Echoes of the Found Object Society are all around them. Greta sees the cubbies stretching for miles, filled with centuries-old objects, each diseased with the energy of a traumatic death.

Would one of these bongs end up in there one day? Imbued with the energy of a thirty-year-old perpetual college student who gets high all day before meeting some bizarrely tragic death? His bong delivered to the society and placed on a shelf, labeled *NEUSA21C-48912*.

Delivered. How, exactly—and by whom . . . or *what*?

"Coconut water?" Ezra says. He holds a quart-size box up to her, giving it a seductive shake.

Greta snaps out of it. "Yes. Oh yeah, that sounds good."

Ezra puts it on the boxed-in glass counter holding lottery tickets and scratch-offs. A handwritten (and misspelled) sign is taped on top: $2,500 WINER HERE!

The man behind the register tears himself from what looks like a Home Shopping Network show, but in a language Greta can't identify.

"Eight," the man says, and looks back at the TV.

Ezra takes a money clip from his front pocket and taps his card to pay.

"Thanks," Ezra says. There's no response.

They turn to leave. As Greta steps down to the sidewalk,

she narrowly misses crushing a colossal water bug as it scurries by. The kind of prehistoric beetle that will walk the Earth long after humanity's demise.

Ezra and Greta wind through the blocks that surround the Found Object Society, sipping coconut water, reluctant to leave the immediate environs, like the place may disappear if they travel too far. They meander onto Peck Slip, between South and Front Streets, the FDR vibrating behind them and the East River a black snake dotted with the reflected lights of the city.

Greta stops. Her mind is playing tricks on her. She's looking at a limestone building with a colonnade, clean and bright and with the word ARCADE etched in giant letters above the passageway that cuts through it. At the far end of the passageway, bright blue sky and the Brooklyn Bridge, and beyond that, the ghost of the Manhattan and Williamsburg Bridges. The problem is it's nighttime, and the real Brooklyn Bridge, with its flow of cars and an American flag that flaps high atop the stanchions, towers behind this mirage.

"Trippy, isn't it?" Ezra says.

Greta's standing in front of a massive trompe l'oeil mural painted on the windowless side of the otherwise block-shaped Con Edison substation.

"They almost painted over this in the nineties. Thank God they didn't. It's by a muralist named Richard Haas. It's been on that wall since 1978," Ezra says.

"I can't believe I've never seen this before. Or noticed it, rather," Greta says.

Though why should she have? The South Street Seaport always seemed like a total tourist trap. It wasn't the kind of place a woman like Greta Davenport would hang out.

"Haas hated what they did when they restored it. He said the colors were all off. It's so great, though. Look at the detail of the parted curtains in the windows. Each one's different, each drape and shadow individual," Ezra says.

Above the passageway are five windows, each with flowing white curtains in varying stages of closure. The one in the middle is shut. What did Haas envision was going on in that room? The mural continues to the left, with another perfect replica of a red-brick building, this one with a slanted copper roof that's oxidized green with age, the words LITHOGRAPHERS, PRINTING, and the name of the company, SWIFTSURE EXPRESS, across the facade. Greta imagines late-nineteenth-century New Yorkers going in and out. She half expects to see Miranda and BDC walk past.

"I'm seeing the Found Object Society in everything now. I can't shake it," Greta says. They continue, leaving the replica behind. "I have a million questions. I don't know where to start."

She downs the last of the coconut water and tosses the carton into an overstuffed garbage can.

"You're the first person I've talked to who's a member, too. At least as far as I know," Ezra says. "I guess there could be others in my day-to-day life, but it's not something that'd just come up. You know?"

"Yeah, I do. So, how long have you been a member? How many voyages have you had?" Greta says.

Ezra counts them off on his fingers. "Six. Well, after tonight, seven."

"Holy shit. That's a lot. Isn't it?"

"Maybe? But who can stop?"

"That's what I'm afraid of," Greta says.

They amble without purpose until they find themselves across from City Hall Park. Cars stream onto the Brooklyn Bridge.

The traffic never stops; it only thins out as the night wears on. The promenade from the Manhattan entrance to the Brooklyn side beckons.

"Should we cross?" Ezra says.

"Sure, let's do it," Greta says.

It's not like Greta to take up with a stranger, but Ezra Somers doesn't feel like one.

Over a mile of wooden walkway stretches before them. Vehicles a constant drone below. The bridge reverberates with traffic.

Greta grills Ezra on the basics: when and how he got his invitation; his first appointment, when he met Eileen. Their experiences aren't altogether dissimilar, though Ezra lives in a doorman building, and when the card slid under his door, he'd figured it was a delivery menu. Like Greta, he couldn't throw it away. He sensed there was more to it, its heft and sheen, the lack of writing. He too found the QR code by mistake with his phone camera.

"I wonder if anyone's thrown the invite away. You know, by accident?" Greta says.

"That would suck for them," Ezra says.

They reach the bridge's highest point, almost eleven stories above the churn of the East River. Flashes of memory cut into real life. Zephyrine and her mistress, standing on the little bridge. The young woman's declaration of love thwarted, mocked. Greta grabs at her throat and bends over in pain.

"What's wrong? Are you okay?" Ezra says.

In a panic, Greta's fingers fumble across her neck, looking for the source of her sudden agony. She finds none. The sharp spike of pain departs and a rapturous surge of heat momentarily takes its place. She leans on the metal railing and grips Ezra's wrist.

"Oh my God. I just felt it. I felt it again," she says.

"What? What did you feel?"

"Zephyrine. My first death. I just felt the letter opener go into her neck. *My* neck."

"I've had that, too—a sudden burning sensation, a rock to the head, the taste of poison, car tires crushing—" A black cloud crosses Ezra's face. For a moment, he freezes and looks down at the slither of the East River. He shakes his head, snapping himself out of whatever momentary trance he fell into. "You're okay, though, Greta. It's a phantom memory, like a lost limb," he says.

Maybe the experience is like reliving those best moments, the ones you replay over and over again in your memory so you can recapture each detail as it happened. Like a first kiss with someone you've gravitated toward for ages, longed for, and fantasized about, the first time you feel the warmth of their breath as they lean in and your lips connect. Greta's had those kinds of moments on repeat plenty of times in her life.

Except *this* moment is someone's death—their last gasps of life, the terror of knowing that the end is seconds away. Young Zephyrine stabbed in the neck by the woman she thought loved her back, before tumbling and sinking into the water. The recollection is succulent. It's unforgivable that Greta should take such pleasure in someone else's tragedy, but that's what this is all about, after all. Going to that place from which there is no return—or from which there *should* be no return, rather. Half a million dollars buys you that round-trip ticket and keeps you coming back for more.

The experience is fading, though, like fragments of a dream. It was vivid when she was in it, and now that she's out, pieces fall away. The pain she felt in her neck was real, exquisite. And yet, she's safe and sound, standing on the Brooklyn Bridge with a man named Ezra Somers.

Greta looks down and realizes he's holding her hand as they approach the Brooklyn side of the bridge. Her heart rate quickens. The waterfront park and the River Café are down to their right, dark and closed for the night. Only the line of decorative lights above the agitated water remains on. Ezra stares over to their left. His eyes latch onto the glassed-in masterpiece of Dumbo's Jane's Carousel, the gilded horses frozen in space, enclosed in their diorama. He takes a long inhale as they continue on.

"See that building by the park?" Ezra says, gesturing to a modern titan of a structure covered in glass and staggered terraces. "That's where I live."

He stops and faces Greta. Despite the growing concavity of his features, there's a warmth simmering beneath. She's drawn to him, another survivor found on her deserted island.

No longer alone, Greta says, "Are we going to have a sleepover?"

CHAPTER TWENTY-NINE

Maybe Greta's getting old, but for her, now tangled in the sheets next to a man she'd only met hours before, the sex was a letdown. In the past, these trysts had been electrifying wrestling matches of lips, limbs intertwined, dancing tongues, all the parts clicking together. Bodies hungry. Tonight, it wasn't that they weren't compatible, or that he didn't do everything right, or that she didn't get lost in the briny seagrass of him. No, it's that her entire being is elsewhere, focused on a craving that's far greater than a good lay.

Satisfying that ache is still over seventy hours away.

What just happened between them is filler. A way to while away and whittle down the time before they can go back and die again. Ezra's words play on repeat: *But who can stop?* What does Greta's life look like, swinging from a trapeze with seventy-two hours of air between leaps? How long can an existence like that go on?

Greta's in that darkest of places now. The one that comes out of hiding between three and four in the morning. The one that lives in the dull recesses of the mind before the rise of the sun, made only more malevolent because of outside influences like cocaine or molly—or someone else's death.

Ezra lives in the penthouse. Windows reach from floor to ceiling and stretch like a gaping mouth, ready to swallow Manhattan on the other side of the East River. The electric shades are open to the skyline and the bridge that they just crossed. No one to look in unless they have a telescope or powerful binoculars. Where Greta's old house in Litchfield is stone and beams, suffused by the energy of families who've lived and died there since the 1800s—haunted by the memory of Greta's parents—Ezra's place is stark, newborn, a blank, emotionless spread of glass and white. Modern art and sculptures are at home here, and if Greta had gone to more museums or paid attention in her art history classes, she'd be impressed. Instead, she lies next to a man, a stranger, in what feels like a floating capsule adrift in space, the dark notions of three in the morning filling the void.

Greta can't shake the feeling that there'd been another presence alongside Zephyrine on the pond's sludge floor. A malignant one. It was there, in Zephyrine's last flash of existence. That final instant of life is the orgasm of the Found Object Society experience—the payoff. And what was next to Zephyrine in that propulsive last gasp, as her body succumbed and released its being, keeps eluding her.

Ezra stirs next to her. He isn't asleep either. Light from the city perforates the topaz of his eyes. The sex hadn't been great, but at least they're together in this trough of night.

Greta unwinds herself from the sheet, freeing an arm. She reaches across Ezra's chest, his body a life raft, and pulls herself close. What has she gotten herself into?

There'll be no return to an idle life from here. No dull blade of day-to-day, no banal chat at parties or fundraisers. That's what she'd been searching for in that last treacherous country-road drive, wasn't it? The razor blade's edge. She's balancing on it now.

Her voice breaks through the abyss. "You know those shows about reincarnation?"

Ezra clears his throat and turns to her. "Like on the Discovery Channel? Sure. They used to have actual shows based on genuine science. Now it's all ghost hunters, or some assholes surviving naked in the Rockies."

"Right. The reincarnation people always claim to have been someone famous or historic in their past life. I mean, how many people could have been reincarnated from Joan of Arc?"

Ezra laughs. "Are you disappointed? Had you hoped to experience Joan of Arc's death instead of what's-her-name? Zephyrine?"

"No, it's not like that. I mean, why doesn't anyone ever claim to have been someone like her? A poor orphaned girl—" Something occurs to Greta. "Like me. I'm an orphan—minus the poor part. Miranda said the objects I had to choose from were based on the information gathered from the Obitus Mold with Eileen. Maybe it makes each death more relatable?"

"Yeah, maybe," Ezra says.

His answer is terse. Greta continues, wanting to understand. "Do you see echoes of *your* life in the deaths you've experienced?"

Ezra rolls over, turns his back to her without answering.

"Did I say something to upset you?" she says.

"No," he says. His voice is small, jagged. She's hit a nerve. She watches him in silhouette take a controlled breath in and out. He rolls toward her again, whatever disturbance her comment created defused. He strokes her arm. "I'm fine. Just tired."

They lie like that for a moment.

"How can this be happening, Ezra? Is it real? Who are these people that created the Found Object Society? I'm peppering you with questions, I know. I can't wrap my head around it. Is it just what it says it is, an amusement park for rich people like us, and nothing more?"

"You've done drugs before, right?"

Greta nods, and rolls her eyes. *Duh.*

"So, when you've done coke, do you think, *Hey, how does this work in my brain? What's it doing to my synapses to make me feel like I'm invincible?*" Ezra says.

"No," Greta says.

"No. Of course not. So instead of asking those questions and wondering about the science of your blow—the Colombians who gathered the coca leaves and processed your coke in a bunker in South America—instead of doing all of that, what do you do?"

Greta thinks. "You do more."

He slides on top of Greta, kisses her neck, her eyelids, his erection insistent against her thigh.

"That's right, Greta Davenport, you do more."

The second time is better. Greta and Ezra savor it, nourish one another with their bodies.

It's been a while for Greta. Since breaking up with Ryan she's had a dry spell. Yes, the second go-around is better, but she still has the sense that they're biding time until their next fix at 273 Water Street.

Exhausted—she's been awake for what feels like days—Greta yields to sleep as the sun reaches its fingers onto the horizon, pulling itself up and hurling light onto the skyscrapers of Manhattan across the river. The drift of dreams leans into her chest, her subconscious a pair of knees that hold her down. Abstract glimpses of other people's lives alternate with periods of pure black. Greta is an observer in her dream state, never the subject of the action. What appears to be a ball made of fluid black silk rolls past her line of vision. It comes to a stop. Two strips of the watery fabric extend out toward her, like arms. Uncoiling and elastic, the sphere takes on a near-human form. From the arms sprout willowy digits. The thing floats closer, covering Greta's face with its sticky hands, suffocating her like a hood.

Greta wakes alone in an unfamiliar bedroom to a half dozen missed calls and texts from Lis. She groans and shoves her cell phone beneath the sheets. The sun soars over the New York City harbor; helicopters flit low over the skyline. The ferry departs from the dock outside Brooklyn Bridge Park, disgorging New Yorkers and tourists alike.

Greta hears Ezra's voice in another part of his vast top-floor apartment. He's on the phone. The conversation sounds anything but cordial.

How long has she been asleep? What the hell day is it?

However long it's been, or whatever day it may be, she's that much closer to going back to the Found Object Society. And that's all that matters.

CHAPTER THIRTY

Dressed, Greta finds Ezra in his epic living room. His conversation (argument?) is over. The sunlight is harsh and sharpens the edges of what was soft only hours earlier. He's leaning on the glass of the floor-to-ceiling window, palms extended on either side, cell phone in one hand and legs akimbo. A parachuter in vertical free fall. She can't help but feel like she's an intruder, someone who doesn't belong here. Then she remembers that he's her only link to this parallel universe where she now exists.

Normally, she'd try to make a polite excuse as to why she has to go home, to leave, but she still has questions she wants answered, shared experiences that she needs corroborated. Plus, she likes him.

"Good morning?" she says.

Ezra turns and tucks his phone into his back pocket and steps back from the precipice.

"Hey, good afternoon, actually."

Barefoot and wearing a T-shirt and jeans, Ezra continues to waste away. He's being eaten alive by something deep inside of him. He's haunted, shrunken.

"Everything okay? I heard you on the phone," Greta says.

She notices a square white card at the end of the counter next to a pile of unopened mail. It's his invitation to the Found Object Society. It's only then, the sunlight revealing the naked truth hidden by the night, that she notices how dusty the apartment is, the greasiness of the kitchen sink—like the place hasn't been cleaned in weeks.

"Sorry about the mess, I haven't had my cleaner here in a while," Ezra says. He must have noticed her checking things out.

"No need to apologize to me," Greta answers.

The distance between them is awkward and strange. A glass partition in a prison visitor's booth. She sits on a barstool, a pit metastasizing in her very soul. This is bad. The canyon she's dragging herself through is deep and dry, and salvation is still nearly sixty hours away.

He pours them coffee from a coffee press.

"Milk?" he asks.

"Sure," Greta says.

He opens the refrigerator. It's bare, save for a couple of bottles of wine, some beers, and various food-delivery containers. There's no milk.

"Sorry, no milk. I may have some Parmalat somewhere," he says, and opens other cabinets.

"Black is fine," she says. "Please don't worry about it." There's something going on with him today. He's on edge.

He rushes over to her. His abrupt movement takes her by surprise. She doesn't have time to react, and if he plans to hurt her, she's in trouble. What he does instead surprises her even more.

He wraps his arms around her and buries his face in her neck. Ezra begins to cry.

"Ezra? Ezra, what is it? What's happened?"

He's wrapped himself around her, absorbing her. This man she's only just met is cracking open for her. She holds him tight. Strokes his muscled back. His neck is hot with emotion.

"Tell me. Talk to me, Ezra."

He unlocks his grasp and sits on a stool next to her. She

wipes tears from his face and grips his knees, willing him to talk to her. To tell her what's going on.

He slows his breathing. Whatever this grief is, it's chiseled away at his youth. They're about the same age, but this pain inside him has made him older. Ancient.

Ezra fights to get the words out. "Five years ago today, my son died."

"Oh my God. No. I'm so sorry."

He ducks his head down low, escaping an invisible punishment. "It was my fault."

The revelation is a blow to her gut. Hits hard as a two-by-four.

"Ezra. I—I can't even imagine. . . ."

She takes him in her arms again, and they stay like that. Speaking without words. Greta *can* imagine, though. Not because she's lost a child, but because of the guilt that's gnawed at her for twenty years. And as she takes in his glamorous Brooklyn apartment, the signs are all there if you know how to look for them. A dwelling unpolluted by sentiment. No personal photos, no knickknacks brought home from family vacations—snow globes, stray beach glass, and clean cockleshells—only dust-covered Roche Bobois furniture, abstract paintings the size of movie screens, and acres of glass.

And like Greta's house in Litchfield, Ezra's apartment is flayed clean. When she'd inherited the home fifty years too soon, she endeavored to clear the memories of her parents by getting rid of almost all there was to remember them by—everything but what's hidden inside a shoebox, tucked deep within the confines of her closet.

"Do you want to tell me about it? I can relate. My parents died because—" Greta can't finish her thought, because Ezra is kissing her now.

His lips feed on hers in desperate bites. She holds back at first, unsure this is what he needs. What *she* needs. But it is.

The complete collapse of one human into another. The necessity to share the skin of someone else. To crawl in and take cover from the world outside with the singular pursuit of the voiceless thing of love. They fall to the rug, trying on each other's bodies. The third time is nothing like the previous two. Unified in their tragedies, in their new addiction, Ezra and Greta unravel and rewind, tossed in violent waves upon jagged rocks, struggling their way back to shore.

After, they lie there gasping and Greta is reminded of last night when they met, of how she'd felt like she'd found another survivor on a deserted island—the only other person who could understand about the Found Object Society. From this moment on, the language they share is theirs and theirs alone. No one else, not even Lis, would understand. And even if she wanted to share it with her, she can't. The warning on her phone a few days ago made that clear.

The sun bounces off the iridescent invitation on Ezra's kitchen counter.

Why? That's the big question. Why can't she tell anyone? Why would they threaten someone's life if they were to know? And why—*why*—did they choose Greta and Ezra?

The answer lies there with them in the jumbled pile of clothes and the salt of their skin. Greta need only find it.

PART THREE

Found Object #2
Origin: North America, Western United States, Late 20th Century

CHAPTER THIRTY-ONE

Sex has kept the wolves of grief at bay. For now.

After Ezra revealed his tattoo of heartache, their trajectories changed. The first turn in Greta's life came when she walked through the door of the Found Object Society. The second, this afternoon, on the rug of Ezra's living-room floor. They are together, fused by their shared regrets.

Greta doesn't want to ask how his son died, or why it was his fault. He'll tell her when he's ready. She can relate. Greta will tell Ezra about the car crash with her parents when *she's* ready. Instead, they spend the next few hours exchanging stories of their deaths. At least, Greta tells him about Zephyrine. Ezra is vague about his voyages and speaks in general terms. He seems to prefer to listen to her recollection.

They walk through Brooklyn Bridge Park and along the river, passing under the bridge itself. It's one of those early spring days that hint of summer, bringing New Yorkers out in droves. The river is active with ferries and taxi boats taking people with newly signed leases to Ikea in Red Hook, the only place to go if you want to buy furniture and still afford to eat after paying rent. Concerns that neither Ezra nor Greta have ever had. Their wealth sets them apart from most of the population. Their addiction isolates them even further. A wedge carved from the 1 percent.

Standing under the thundering expanse of the bridge, they stop. Greta has read that by the time they finished construction in 1883 over twenty people had died while building it. Some from horrible tumbles off towers, others from falling debris, a sad handful from the agony of the bends. Most anonymous immigrants. Few given credit. The water seethes between concrete stanchions.

"Until Miranda explained it to me, I thought that my death voyage would be the actual *moment* of death, not the weeks leading up to it," Greta says. She adds, "All in a tidy fifty minutes."

"That'd be like sex with no foreplay. It wouldn't be as good, would it?" Ezra gives her a playful nudge with his hip.

"True, it wouldn't." Greta leans in and kisses him. At the Found Object Society, the death itself is the crescendo: Zephyrine at the bottom of the pond, seeing her ending, knowing her heart was taking its last beats. That moment is what makes Greta want more. *Need* more. The buildup, the drama, the heartache? That was heavy petting. "Mine was so dramatic, like some BBC period piece, heaving corsets and furtive glances, servants versus masters." She pauses, giving Ezra the opportunity to chime in about his experiences. He doesn't. Instead, his gaze travels past the bridge in front of them and lands on Jane's Carousel. His thoughts are somewhere far away. Ezra must be thinking of his son, of whatever real and terrible event that caused his death and made him feel responsible.

Greta's phone vibrates in her pocket of the jeans she's been wearing since yesterday. She'd showered after their floor sex and borrowed one of Ezra's oxford shirts—hers had spots of guava nectar on it. It's getting time for her to go back to her pad in SoHo. Her internal clock is off. It feels like late morning, but it's approaching four p.m.

"I should get back to Greene Street soon," Greta says.

"Hang out a little longer," Ezra says. "Please?"

For the past five years since his son's death, this day must have been the one he dreads most out of the year. Like the anniversary of Greta's parents' deaths the other night, it's a date that looms on the calendar until Ezra can hurdle past it and nose-dive the rest of the way, until the climb starts all over again on January 1. How can she say *no*?

"Sure, of course, yeah," Greta says.

Ezra says the details of voyages fade with time, like a dream, though specific details linger: the interior smell of an Edsel; the red of a velvet theater curtain as it's pulled back; a bloodied horseshoe, still attached to a hoof in a frozen trench in Russia in World War I. He doesn't talk about the people so much as these pointed details. In Ezra's eyes, Greta sees his longing to go back and get lost in someone else's mortality. Someone else's misfortune other than his own very personal one.

Greta feels it, too. Though last night had been her first, it won't be her last. How sustainable is this life of deaths? From the moment she came to after being behind the eyes of Zephyrine, she wanted more. It was gluttonous. She's kicked drugs before, slowed down the booze for a time. Is this how it would be with the Found Object Society? Die a few times and then take a break, rejoin the country club set until she can't take it anymore? Drop another five hundred grand and go for a while again?

That doesn't seem like the way it's gone for Ezra. He's taken seven voyages in under a month, and from the looks of it, his life has suffered for it. Unopened mail, a dirty apartment, his body thinning as the things that sustain us—food, water, contact with other humans—fall to the wayside. Greta and Ezra are together because of happenstance.

If Greta had never received the invitation and if Ezra had passed her on the sidewalk, would Greta have noticed the sharpness of his cheekbones, the flat, determined focus of his eyes—fixed on a thing that's seventy-two hours away and known only to himself—and thought, *That guy's an addict*?

Greta gets back to her apartment on Greene Street as the sun dips down: a ribbon of red lines on the horizon like a bloodshot eye.

She walks in and can no longer ignore her cell phone's insistent buzz.

"Hello," Greta says, tapping on speakerphone and putting her cell on the dining table.

"Finally. There you are. What the ever-living fuck, Greta?" Lis says. Her voice is ragged.

"Sorry, Lis. I know, I know. I've been, uh, preoccupied," Greta says. She lowers the shades and turns on a few lights. She undresses, leaving her clothes in a heap on the floor. The first hints of an addicted life appear in the sooty city grime on the windowsills, the dirty, caked-over dishes in the sink, the smell of stale, unoccupied air.

"No. Fuck that, Greta. That's not good enough. Ever since the gala, something's been up with you. I'm seriously worried. It's not like you to blow me off like this. Ryan? Sure. But not me."

"Ryan? I broke up with him. Why would he try to get in touch with me, too?" Greta says. She walks with the phone in her hand and stands in her bedroom, naked in front of the full-length mirror. *Mistress Claudette, easing onto the side of the tub, spreading her legs and inviting Zephyrine to join her.*

"—dated him two years, after all," Lis says. Greta missed what she said before that. Snippets of the last days of Zephyrine play in her mind, uninvited.

"Sorry, you dropped out for a second," Greta lies. "What did you say?"

Lis sounds exasperated. She repeats herself. "I *said*, since you weren't answering my texts or calls, I got worried. So I called Ryan. *I called Ryan*, Greta. You know how much of an asshole I think he is. That's how worried I've been. I thought maybe he'd heard from you—he hadn't. Then he called and texted you, too. You *were* dating him for two years, after all."

A different Greta had, it's true. She's not the woman standing here now, though. That was a lifetime ago. Greta wants to tell Lis the truth, to share everything about the Found Object Society, but she already knows the risk (or at least the implied risk) of that.

She tosses Lis the bone that she knows will throw her off Greta's scent. "Okay, the truth is I met someone. And he's great, really great. I'm kind of falling for him," Greta says.

When she says it, it *sounds* convincing, as if it's the truth. Hearing the words aloud, Greta realizes it is.

CHAPTER THIRTY-TWO

Lis buys Greta's story about having met someone. It appeases her—to a degree.

Greta tantalizes her with partial truths: running into him on the street, striking up a conversation, walking around the South Street Seaport and then across the Brooklyn Bridge. Lis asks what the hell Greta was doing in *that touristy shithole*. She avoids the question and tells her about the sex instead. Greta and Lis have always swapped stories about good and bad grope sessions, embarrassing queefs, and triumphant orgasms. That works. It plays. Lis lets it go. Greta promises to introduce her to Ezra if things get serious. They hang up.

The subterfuge will buy Greta some time.

Greta enters the walk-in shower and turns on both showerheads and the steam. A eucalyptus wood bench, big enough for four, is attached to the tile wall in the middle. A bathroom as big as some people's studio apartments.

At the start of her journey, right before she locked onto the two windows that were the eyes of Zephyrine, Greta had thought it was her body that was floating, but it had been her mind, not her physical being. At first, she'd felt corporeal, until she dissolved like a sugar cube into the life of Zephyrine. Greta's breathing deepens at the arousing memory. Eyes closed, she conjures as many moments as she can. It's like Ezra said. It's snippets: the hum of bees on mounds of fragrant lavender, the curve of Mistress Claudette's hip, the melodic *clink* of the golden bottle studded with turquoise on her chatelaine.

Pain shoots through her neck again. Greta paws at her throat, looking for the source. The agony is momentary, beautiful. She slides down in a rapture onto the wooden bench. Conjuring Zephyrine's last moments, Greta can feel her body sinking into the water, her arms enveloped by the silt as she hit the bottom. Her right hand clutching the perfume bottle . . . and then, a shadow. A dark presence appearing in the water, waiting.

Greta opens her eyes. The image ends there. It's gone. Steam shrouds Greta's trembling body.

"Fuck," she says. The reliving of Zephyrine's death will not be enough. It's something, but it won't sate her.

By Greta's accounting, she has a solid forty-eight-plus hours before she can go back to 273 Water Street—before both she and Ezra can. It feels like a fucking eternity. Patience has never been one of Greta's strong suits.

The titillating threat of money has always sped up life's minor annoyances for Greta. Jumping to the front of the line (any line) is easy when she can lube someone up with a wad of bills. Wealth makes you big, scary.

The Found Object Society is different. They already have her money—a shit-ton of it. So offering more will not get her in any sooner. Seventy-two hours is such an arbitrary number, though. Did the creators of the society conduct studies? Have they run tests? Maybe someone's head exploded because they had another voyage after only sixty hours, or twenty. Or, what if that person died because they couldn't handle another one so soon and then the last thing *they* touched was sitting in a cubby, waiting to get selected, and then a member like Greta or Ezra can experience *their* death? *So fucking meta.*

How long has the Found Object Society even existed?

Greta's working herself into a tizzy. She's got to keep her shit together and wait it out. Live her silly, reckless, regretful, and privileged life like she has for years and get through the next two days.

It's two days. Come on, dope!

Miranda said they'd be *in touch* when she could come back for her next voyage. Ezra confirmed that when you least expect it another little card will appear out of nowhere. He's even discovered one in a coat he was wearing, like reverse pickpocketing.

Christ, what if she misses it or throws it away?

Still wet, Greta throws on her robe and tears through the apartment. She rifles through and rips apart her stack of mail, shaking catalogs and magazines to make sure the next invitation hasn't gotten stuck in the pages, or between envelopes. Crawling on all fours, she lifts rug corners and pulls up sofa cushions. Opening the coat closet, she looks through jacket pockets, examines the insides of shoes and boots she hasn't worn in months—years.

A terrible thought occurs: The other two cards she's received came to her house in Litchfield. One hundred and eleven fucking miles away. *Jesus Christ*. It could be sitting in the entryway right at this moment. What if she doesn't open it in time and the QR code expires or something? That'd be a disaster.

Greta has to get home. *Home* home, not pied-à-terre home.

She calls her regular driver. It's nine thirty p.m. Carl will not be happy.

"Carl? Hey, it's Greta. I need to get back to Litchfield ASAP."

She was right. He isn't happy. "I'll pay you double the regular amount, Carl. I need to get home."

Her voice is pitching up, getting whiny. Carl's been her driver for years and he's all too familiar with her whims. He's also seen enough shit in that back seat that he could blackmail the crap out of her.

Once again, the lure of money works and poor Carl will be there as soon as he can. He just needs to kiss his wife and kids and say good night. This is meant to make Greta feel guilty. She's incapable of that at the moment. All she feels is relief, her hysteria put on hold as she awaits her next invitation to the Found Object Society.

In the back seat of Carl's Mercedes S-Class, Greta tries to decompress. She's left her loft on Greene Street in a state of disarray. It looks like someone broke in searching for a microfiche with the nuke codes. Who cares? She catches Carl looking at her in the rearview mirror.

"You okay, Ms. Davenport?" he says. He has an accent. Eastern European or something. Maybe it's Greek? Greta's never bothered to find out, or if he's told her, she sure wasn't listening. *Yes*, she thinks, remembering that drunken drive home after the gala, *I always* have *been this much of a douche.*

"Yes, Carl. Thanks. A lot on my mind. Busy. You know."

Carl doesn't know, that much she's sure of. He probably doesn't care as long as he gets paid for his troubles. That's unfair. She shouldn't paint Carl with her own brush. He's always been a good guy. He has a real life. A real family—even if he does live in stinking Queens.

It's close to midnight. They drive on the same road she nearly bought the farm on the other night. Was that almost a week ago? It was. That was the night this all started, and her life took a direction she could never have anticipated. They cruise past a gray mound on the road. It's a dead possum. Like, *really* dead. His head flattened, tongue hanging out, and teeth exposed in an Elvis-like snarl. One of his crossed eyes stares at Greta, ready to pop and roll away, like a Ping-Pong ball.

The dream returns to her: A ball of silk, unraveling and taking shape. Sticky hands covering her mouth, smothering her.

Greta's freaking out on the inside. This isn't tenable, this in-between state. She has to get it together, to figure out a way back to a semblance of normalcy.

At least for the next forty-plus hours.

CHAPTER THIRTY-THREE

A good person, a nice one, would ask Carl if he needs to use the bathroom or have something to drink before his drive back to Queens. Greta's not that good, not that nice.

She grabs her bag and, getting out of the car, says, "Thanks, Carl. I sent the money on the app."

"Take care, Ms.—"

Greta closes the door, cutting him off. The Mercedes idles as Carl waits for Greta to get inside her house, as he always does. The house where he can't pee or have a drink before driving another two hours to get back home. Back home, where he'll tell his wife what a bitch Greta is. Greta thinks they may even argue about her. *But the money—the money*, Carl will say. That settles any argument.

Alarm deactivated, Greta enters, and flicks on a light. She tosses her bag and scans the entryway floor—a cadaver dog sniffing out her next invitation to the Found Object Society. The same catalogs and magazines and other bullshit junk mail that she gets at Greene Street are piled on the floor here, too. So much wasted paper. She shakes it all out, just in case. No card, not yet. Maybe it's too soon? She's home now, so she can't miss it.

There's movement in her periphery. A tinkling of a little bell. Greta freezes, the sound all too familiar. A cat walks, tail up, past Greta and into the living room.

"Murphy Brown?" Greta says, croaking the words out, taut with terror.

That's impossible—of course it is. Murphy Brown is long gone. She enters the living room and looks around. She's the only living thing in here. *Shake it off.* Her brain juices are all sloshed around from her first voyage. That's what's happening here. Nothing else. That's why they say you have to wait seventy-two hours, so your mind can settle. At least that's what Greta tells herself. She did not just see the ghost of their old cat. No way.

Her phone vibrates. It's a 917 number—the area code for a cell phone in the city. Would the society call her? It's late. It must be Ezra. They've known each other for such a short period that she hasn't even entered his name into her contacts. Near strangers, yet he's the only person she'd answer the phone for.

"Hey," she says.

"Hey," Ezra answers.

He's so quiet, Greta thinks they may have gotten cut off. She looks at the phone. The call time is still ticking. They're still connected.

"Ezra? You there?"

He sighs. "Yeah, yeah, I'm here. I wanted to hear your voice."

Greta lies down on her couch, pulls a pillow to her chest. "I'm glad you called. Me too. I mean, I wanted to hear your voice, too."

"How's the loft?" he says.

"I'm not there. I lost it a little—well, a lot—and got worried I'd miss getting the next invitation, so I got my driver to take me back to Litchfield."

"Shit. And here I was going to invite myself over," he says.

It's after midnight. *It's now the day after the anniversary of his son's death*, Greta thinks. Ezra made it through another year. The

364-day countdown begins anew. Then it'll be six years since his son died. Then seven. Eight. Will it ever fade? When will the countdown stop? Greta knows it won't.

"You doing okay?" Greta says.

"Sure," he says, and, as if reading her mind, adds, "I made it through another one, another year. I'm glad you were there this time. Thank you."

"Me too. I feel like I've known you forever." Greta cringes at her sappy comment. "Is that cheesy?"

"I like cheesy." Ezra laughs. It's a nice laugh, a release valve.

Ezra's voice calms Greta, makes her feel less tweaky.

Like high school steadies, they talk on the phone until deep into the night. Greta wanders the house, phone to her ear. She finds her earbuds and puts them in, tucking the phone into her pocket.

The conversation meanders to places Greta wouldn't go face-to-face. It's more confessional than conversation. She unburdens herself of the sins that rattle around in her skull: those blurred first years after her parents died, her time at college, the *Whatshisnames*, the drugs and partying, the drunk driving. She shares things that even Lis doesn't know about. Her best friend, supplanted by this stranger in a mere twenty-four hours.

Ezra, her bestest junkie buddy.

He shares with her in equal measure. Their lives often parallel. Both had parents that lucked into wealth with the tech boom. Neither Ezra nor Greta come from old money, but new—*new* somehow *less* to the blue-blood kids they grew up with. Ezra lived his teenage years in Connecticut, too, before heading to Stanford for college; his parents also moved out West, to nearby Carmel-by-the-Sea.

Greta again wonders if she and Ezra crossed paths when they were younger without knowing it, some invisible thread linking them to one another, woven by future tragedies and secured with the knot of regret.

They both circle the epicenter of their personal devastations. Greta is the one who dives in first.

Greta drifts off midsentence.

She opens her eyes. Her earbuds remain in place and her cell rests on her chest, the battery power icon showing red, near dead. She's disoriented. From her vantage point on the couch in the living room, everything appears as it did twenty years ago: The original walls with their bookshelves and knickknacks closing off the space, separating it from the dining room. Spidering cracks in the plaster of the ceiling above her. Greta's feet stretched across the sofa cushions, her toes painted the bubblegum pink she always wore in high school. A color she hasn't worn since.

A hand touches her shoulder, gives her a little shake. The smell of Coco Chanel envelops her like a fog bank over her head.

"Greta. Honey?"

The voice of her mother.

Greta reaches for the hand and sits bolt upright. Instead of a hand, she grips the hoodie of her sweatshirt draped over her shoulder. Her toes are her normal shade of almost-black purple, Luxedo. A ghostly blue static dances across them. First, she thinks she saw Murphy Brown and now, her mother?

"Greta? You there?" Ezra's voice trickles from the white snails of her earbuds.

"Holy shit. Yeah, I'm here. I just had the most vivid—"

The metallic *clank* of the mail slot reverberates from the entryway of the house. Greta leaps off the couch, cell phone falling to the rug, and runs toward the front door. Her head rushes with blood and she lists to the right, catching herself on the doorjamb.

Sure enough, on the floor is a jet-black six-by-six card.

"Hey, you okay?" Ezra's still there and talking through her earbuds. "I got my next invitation for Sunday at ten thirty p.m."

She picks the blank card up off the tile floor. Greta's hands shake as she examines it.

Could it be a coincidence that the card arrived right after what must have been a dream a few moments ago? Her mother's hand on her shoulder, Coco Chanel evaporating off her wrist. No, it can't be. The Found Object Society's reach is far and deep.

"I got mine, too," she says.

He doesn't answer.

"Ezra?"

Going back in the living room to retrieve her cell from the floor, she sees that it's dead. *Dead* dead. She won't find the QR code without her phone camera.

"Goddammit!" she shouts.

She needs to chill the fuck out. The invitation is in her hands, and there's light at the end of the tunnel. She heads to the kitchen to find her charger so she can get enough power to turn the fucking phone on again. Pulling open drawer after drawer, she shuffles through their contents. She dumps flatware on the kitchen island. Stray bits of twine, buttons, old Post-its, menus of restaurants with grand openings that have since shuttered. Drawers hang open like lolling tongues, a vomit of thingamajigs strewn across the countertop. Then she sees the charger, already plugged in, mocking her, by the blender.

She remembers that the trail camera is outside and should be working. Maybe this time it captured something real and not the terrifying ghost of a license plate when the card was delivered. Once she has power, she'll check that, too. Greta plugs in her phone and waits. She's a helpless Weeble, unable to do anything on her own without the guidance of her phone.

Pathetic.

Last time she'd reviewed the footage, the seventh video had a glitch. A high-screeching sound and then cobalt video snow, followed by the stationary image of the license plate of her parked car. Only it *wasn't* her car—it was her parents'. Yet another in an ever-increasing line of hallucinations. Leaving the charging phone behind, Greta unlocks the door and steps outside into the humid, cool night air. All quiet. Her Mercedes is parked in front of the fading forsythias. The air is still, unmoving. The scene suspended in the liquid of night.

The resident mockingbird explodes into song, hopeful that Greta may be the answer to its lovelorn prayers. Poor guy, still looking for love in all the wrong places. The bottoms of her bare feet are damp from accumulated dew. Greta's footprints on the block of slate outside the front door vanish seconds after they appear, absorbed back into the atmosphere like the surf erasing imprints on a beach.

She goes back in and grabs her sufficiently charged phone. To her great relief, she finds out that—forty-five hours from now, Sunday at eleven p.m.—she'll have her second voyage. Her next death. Ezra's eighth will start thirty minutes before hers.

Who can wait? Not Ezra and Greta.

The throbbing need for her next death hasn't subsided, but the knowledge that it can (and will) happen soon softens the edge. Keep the members happy. Keep them coming back for more.

Greta's about to crawl into bed and under the covers when she remembers the trail cam.

She checks the app. This time there are only three clips. The third, right around when Greta woke and felt her mother's hand on her shoulder. She's tempted to delete it. She can't, of course she can't. Heart racing, she hits Play.

That familiar high-pitched screech, then the blizzard of indigo static. It's her driveway again. She follows the frame to the car parked in the background. Not her car. It's her parents', with the Connecticut plate starting with *T3R*. This time, a triangle of light appears across the pea gravel, flaring out the exposure before it settles again. It's light coming from the front door that's been opened. A cat, Murphy fricking Brown, runs into the pool of light. There's no sound. The cat stops suddenly and looks back toward the house, as though someone's called for her. Her eyes glow, and then the image disappears.

It's gone. Greta replays it. This time it's her car in the background, not her parents', as a field mouse scurries past the frame.

She's losing her mind. Lost it. *Lost, lost, lost.*

Shaken, Greta lies awake in bed. She needs rest to prepare for her next journey. The sun will start its ascent in a few hours. Greta's normal daily routine has gone to hell since the first card came: No more early-morning workouts followed by emails and phone calls with Lis or her various committees. No more calendar dates for luncheons or dinners. Her life is now a tenuous balancing act across a seventy-two-hour tightrope and the safety net of someone else's tragic demise below.

She's taken two Tylenol PMs to shut down her mind, to rid her of the image of Murphy Brown's glowing eyes looking back at her from the past. The past is intruding through a door left ajar by the Found Object Society. For what reason?

Greta gazes at the silhouette of her bedside lamp. The shape of it shifts, elongates, looks almost human in the dark. A thought lingers in her half consciousness—a question she wants to ask Ezra when she sees him next—but it's slippery. Why doesn't she keep a notepad on the nightstand? She should write this down. She'll remember, won't she? Of course she will. Her lids blink closed, curtains too heavy to lift.

Remember, Greta, remember to ask Ezra . . . remember, remember.

Has he ever seen anything else at the moment of death, a shadow that didn't belong?

CHAPTER THIRTY-FOUR

It's raining tonight.

Ezra and Greta huddle under an umbrella a few buildings down from 273 Water Street. In case there are security cameras at the society, they figure it's best they aren't seen together. It's not on the list of rules that society members shouldn't interact, but neither of them is willing to take the chance of getting kicked out.

Greta wasn't sure she'd get through the day and a half leading up to this evening, but she did. She'd busied herself with attempts at cleaning, responded to emails and texts—enough to get people off her back. Last night, Carl drove her down to Brooklyn so she could stay with Ezra. They had a lovely evening, their humor buoyed by the knowledge that the following day they'd be back at the Found Object Society.

Ezra had ordered dinner from an oh-so-Brooklyn restaurant that had been featured with a big photo spread in the *New York Times*: farm to table, with bespoke condiments or whatever the fuck, craft cocktails, a sea of bearded and tattooed staff preparing their meals for pickup, the name of the restaurant something unfathomably twee. Greta stayed in his penthouse while he went to get their food.

Naked, she wandered his apartment. She looked for clues about Ezra's history. There wasn't much to find. The place was stripped of personality, memories. In his office, she turned on the light. An enormous desk, covered in dust, looked south toward Governor's Island and the Statue of Liberty beyond. No family photos or trinkets. A wooden box with intricate inlay—the only dust-free item in the room—rested next to his laptop. She knew she shouldn't be so nosy, but she couldn't help herself. She turned the tiny brass key and opened it.

Inside was a stack of cards—eight, to be exact. Eight invitations from the Found Object Society in a box that should hold precious mementos or notes from loved ones. The society and his voyages were his only savored memories and keepsakes. Is this what Greta would become, too? She was already most of the way there. All she had at home—hidden in the recesses of her closet—was a nondescript box. It held memories of her parents, their life together as a family, a few heartbreaking objects from their last night on Earth. It's a box she only opened when she was desperate for punishment, drunk enough to bear the plummet. Greta hoped that her invitations from the Found Object Society won't someday push them out. An invading cuckoo come to usurp a foreign nest.

She turned off the light at the sound of Ezra's return at the opposite end of the apartment. In the dark, she noticed two luminous shapes on the wall by the large bookcase. She took a closer look. They were two glow-in-the-dark star-shaped decals adhered to the wall. It looked like someone had tried to peel them off and had failed—or given up. On the opposite side from the bookshelf was a couch, the logical place for a bed if this had been a bedroom. A child's bedroom. Greta pulled out a stack of books to get a better look at the wall behind it. A phantom pattern of leftover adhesive followed the trajectory of the two stars that remained. It was the Big Dipper. It *had been* the Big Dipper.

"Greta? Food delivery!" Ezra called out.

"Coming," she called back.

She jogged closer and then turned the jog to a saunter. She was naked, after all, and since she was no longer twenty, all her parts wouldn't look that good bouncing.

"Oh. Why, hello there," she said, as she turned the corner and into his view.

"A cash tip would've been fine, but I'm good with this," Ezra said.

He put the food down on the kitchen counter—the food they would later only make a show of eating, as if proving to one another that they weren't complete addicts. He walked over to her and she put her arms around his neck and kissed him. Jumping up, she wrapped her legs around his back and he held her in place by cupping her butt.

It was like a movie scene. The kind that's super sexy while being physically improbable. In real life, tendons would be strained, back muscles pulled, an unintentional fart released, but like the show of eating a dinner like regular people, this was just as much of a demonstration of normal. Greta and Ezra, conscious of it or not, tried to prove to one another that they were okay. That all was fine, and that they weren't hooked on a subterranean society that lurked across the East River awaiting their arrival.

"I'm going in," Ezra says.

"Lucky bastard. What am I gonna do for the next half hour?" Greta says.

Ezra shrugs. His eyes dart between her and 273 Water Street. Greta can see he's itching to get back in. She can't blame him. She's tweaking, too.

"Go on. Go have a good death," she says.

"I'll meet you later. Have a crazy one," he says, and gives her a quick kiss.

Then it comes back to her. A part of it, at least. She takes hold of his hand.

"Hey, I remembered something," she says.

"What? What is it? I gotta go," he says.

"I don't quite know, but . . . but it's—"

"It's what, Greta? Come on, I need to get in there." He's pulling away from her.

"Right, yeah. Go," she says. It's on the tip of her tongue, this *something*. She can't put her finger on it. "I guess . . . try to be on the lookout for anything weird while you're in there? You know, inside whoever's about to die."

"Uh, sure. Will do," he says. Ezra jogs through the rain, crossing the street. He disappears down the stairs that lead to the Found Object Society.

The rain pelts down harder. Its drumming on her umbrella blocks out all other sound. At home, two nights ago, she'd almost had it. The thing she wanted to remember, that she'd been too tired to write down.

CHAPTER THIRTY-FIVE

"Welcome back, Miss Davenport," Big Daniel Craig says, as the behemoth vault door gasps behind her.

Greta shakes off her trench coat and BDC holds out his hand to take it from her.

"Sorry, pretty rainy out there," she says.

He disappears into a closet, its door hidden by the wallpaper.

"Your cell phone, please?" he says, without making eye contact.

This time, Greta hands it over without hesitation. She wonders where Ezra is now. Which era, and whose death he will experience. She hopes he tells her about this one. An unexpected pang of jealousy surges through her.

Let it be my turn already.

The room is as vibrant and disorienting as she remembers. Greta could swear that some of the images in the wallpaper have changed, shifted. Tupac's face is several feet from where she thought it'd been last time. An image she hadn't noticed before takes his place: a log cabin next to a roiling river, an axe resting half in the water, half out.

BDC isn't chatty tonight. He's looking at a screen on a pad and swiping through. Occasionally, he looks up at her and then back down again. Did Greta get him into trouble with their banter last time?

Greta shivers.

"Are you cold, Miss Davenport?" BDC says.

She's not. Greta's shakes come from nerves of anticipation. She's more anxious now than she was even before her first voyage. If only Miranda would get out here so she can start. It's this last stretch that's killing her.

"A little wound up, I guess," she says.

"Miss Miranda will be out any moment."

Greta sits in one of the plush chairs, shifting back and forth, unable to relax. Her right knee bounces up and down, a Geiger counter of nervous energy. She's always hated this tic in others.

"How have you been, Daniel?" she asks. Greta's ready to burst, to scream, unable to think of any form of release other than idle chitchat.

"Very well, thank you. Kind of you to ask," he says. "And yourself?"

"Good, good, you know, just . . . *this*."

BDC is judging her, she can feel it. She's a tweaker like all the other rich turds that come through that Orgasmatron of a front door.

"Sure, of course," he says.

The velvet drapes part and Miranda emerges, somehow more regal than the first time. Instead of a dress of copious folds of blood orange, this one looks made of gunmetal, her neck wrapped in a garnet-stoned necklace, the chain with her pocket watch tucked as before between her breasts. Whoever does the costume design for this place deserves an Oscar.

"Good evening, Greta. Nice to have you back," Miranda says. Her fingers sparkle with her myriad rings. Greta's taken aback by the tree-shaped one on her thumb. It appears alive, the roots boring into Miranda's flesh. It's grotesque.

"Doesn't that hurt?" Greta says, pointing to Miranda's thumb.

"Doesn't what hurt?" Miranda says.

"Your thumb ring, it looks like it's—" Greta looks back at Miranda's hand. It's normal. The skin unbroken, the bejeweled root system resting cozy on her knuckle. "Never mind, it was a trick of the light. Uh, yes, it's great to be back. Thank you for having me."

Thank you for having me. Sure, *thanks for having me after I handed you half a million dollars*. Very generous.

Miranda leads Greta through the curtains as BDC utters his trademark phrase.

"Enjoy your death, Miss Davenport."

Entering the bowels of the Found Object Society, Greta feels like Violet Beauregarde in front of a river of chocolate in *Willy Wonka and the Chocolate Factory*. Greta wants to dive in, to swim in the objects, gulp them down and all the deaths that come with them. Get washed away.

She follows the susurration of Miranda's floor-length gown into the Collection Room. Does she even have feet? It takes time for Greta's eyes to adjust to the dimness. The near black of Miranda's dress renders her bodiless, her head floating in the air.

"Welcome back to the Collection Room, Greta. I covered a lot of ground last time you were here," Miranda says.

Last time? Like seventy-hours ago, last time?

"You did, yes," Greta says.

"Is there anything you'd like me to go over again? Any lingering questions?"

Greta laughs and Miranda gives her a curious look.

"I don't mean to laugh. It's just that *all* I have are lingering questions. Like, how does this even work or exist? Who are you, and when was this invented? Who collects these objects?"

That last question acts as a stoplight. Miranda blinks hard. That jogs a memory: the strange inner eyelids Greta had imagined when she came out of her first voyage.

"No one wants to see the sausage getting made, Greta. They only want to eat it," Miranda says.

Miranda's right. Greta wants to know, *and* she doesn't want to know. She really just wants to do it again. And again.

Miranda's pulled out her tablet from her pocket and starts to swipe and tap. Greta watches as, with the chimes of a tinkling bell, pin lights turn on, then cut through the dark into seven different cubbies.

"Your selections for this evening's voyage, Greta," Miranda says. "Please, take your time. Wave your hand at the front of an aisle shelf to see the region and era."

"Got it, thanks."

Greta walks back and forth and waves her hand in front of the aisles with illuminated cubbies.

Australia/New Zealand 1875–1940

Western Europe 1750–1850

Greta peruses her menu of deaths, tonight's chef recommendations. Last time was Western Europe, so maybe something else? *United States 1950–2000*. Closer to home could be cool.

Miranda puts her finger to her ear. Greta spots a tiny earpiece tucked inside. Someone's talking to her.

"Would you excuse me for a moment, please?"

Not waiting for an answer, Miranda shuffles away, back toward where the cabins are located.

"Sure, no problem," Greta says.

What's that about?

Eyes on the prize, Greta heads down the United States aisle from 1950 to 2000 and toward a lit-up cubbyhole. What she sees makes her laugh: a pair of clear plastic sunglasses with windshield wipers and a AA battery in each arm, an orange light bulb above each lens.

It's too ridiculous, right? Her first death had been dramatic and overwrought, a period piece—très French. Maybe this one is funny. Is that even a thing? A comedic death? Miranda hasn't returned, and Greta is unsure what to do. She's been instructed not to touch the objects, and she doesn't want to screw anything up or break something. The surrounding cubbies are dark. There are silhouettes inside each one, but not enough light to see the contents. She remembers last time, when she reached toward the perfume bottle, how the cubbyhole's murk had reacted to the proximity of her hand.

Would it be that bad if Greta reached in for a wee peek?

Still no Miranda. Greta takes her chances. She reaches her right hand up toward a blackened box. The dark appears solid, gelatinous. Her fingertips hover a mere inch from the opening. Easing ever closer, Greta senses resistance. An invisible set of fingers mirror her movements, press back, fingertip to fingertip. She waves her hand to the left and the other hand follows. She pushes into the cubbyhole and she's shoved back, hard. A familiar crackle of blue static jolts her, giving her an electric shock.

"Jesus Christ!" Greta shouts, shaking her hand from the pain.

Shrouded in shadow, Miranda appears right next to her. "Greta, what are you doing?"

"I was just curious. I wanted to see what was there. I just—" Her fingertips are numb; blue flashes of light, of energy, scatter across her nail beds.

A hint of perspiration licks Miranda's hairline. "Please don't do that again. There are many things you don't understand—don't need to. You must follow the rules. Understood?"

Cowed, Greta hangs her head. "Yes. Totally. I apologize. Won't happen again."

"Good. Let's move on, then. Have you made your choice?"

Greta's still freaked out over what just happened. It's her own fault. She doesn't understand a goddamned thing about this place, it's true, other than she *needs* it. If she fucks this up, and gets kicked out, then what? That can't happen. This beats any drug she's ever done before, any daredevil late-night drive while under the influence. With the Found Object Society she can die over and over again, and live to tell the tale.

"I have," Greta answers. Pointing up to the absurd windshield-wiper sunglasses, she says, "This one."

Miranda leads her toward a cabin at the end of the hallway with the other cabins. She's holding the box containing her 1970s novelty sunglasses, its interior matching the exact size and shape of the object—like they knew it was the one Greta was going to select.

Most of the cabins are lit up blue—members actively on their voyages. Ezra's in one of them. He must be close to dying, if Greta has her timing right. The door of one berth is ajar, none of the lights above illuminated. Greta slows and cranes her head to look in. The door is cracked open enough for her to see a man's shoe lying on the floor, like it was kicked off in haste. Before she can see all the way inside, the room floods with white light and the door closes on its own.

Startled, Greta says, "What's up in there?"

"Maintenance," Miranda says as she guides Greta forward again.

They enter Greta's cabin for the evening, its green light on. Miranda shuts the door. The image of the shoe without a foot dissipates as Greta's focus shifts to her upcoming voyage. The one she's been jonesing for seventy-two hours. The interior of the cabin is identical to the other from three days ago. A plush womb ready to birth Greta into someone else's death. This isn't quite old hat, but Greta makes herself comfortable on the chaise as Miranda prepares. Uncovering the rolling cart, Miranda offers Greta the taffy on the saucer.

Rolling the tart chew on her tongue, the calming effect is instantaneous. The tang of the berry, the smells and sounds of the boardwalk, her father's and mother's hands warm and comforting around hers. The weight of her body sinks into the chaise.

Miranda hits the hidden switch and the Obitus Mold extends from the side of the chaise longue. Greta rests her right arm in it as it grows around her skin. Latex gloves on, Miranda retrieves the glasses and places them into Greta's open palm.

Any perspiration that was on Miranda's brow is gone, her tawny skin flawless—poreless—once more. She prepares the needle and swabs Greta's forearm.

"You're in for a treat with this one. Ready?" Miranda says.

In for a *treat*? Has Miranda tried all these objects on for size? Too weighted down to ask more questions, Greta nods in the affirmative.

Miranda pushes the hypodermic into Greta's forearm, depressing its silvery contents into her bloodstream. Greta's drifting off; blue light ripples across her fingertips like distant lightning.

"Time to set sail, Greta. Bon voyage."

Entombed in darkness, Greta opens her eyes. She's disoriented. It's like waking in a hotel room, unsure of your surroundings. Then she remembers she's about to go on her second voyage.

The membrane enclosure constricts around her and lifts her head above her feet. She sails forward, feetfirst, and exits into a pocket of nothing. She's floating, drifting again toward two windows.

Somewhere, an unknown control room, born from an incomprehensible science, plugs in coordinates and maneuvers her ever closer to the target. Greta connects with a dull *thud*.

CHAPTER THIRTY-SIX

Twenty-eight-year-old Lassiter Evans isn't handsome, not like Ted Bundy, the smug headline-hogging bastard.

Standing in front of his bedroom mirror, he decides that he's definitely better-looking than that chunky Son of Sam, though. Somewhere between the two. That ain't bad.

Thunk.

Something hits his second-story window. Correction: his *mom's* second-story window. Yes, he still lives at home. He sure as shit doesn't want to, but he has to. Lassiter walks to the window, and clinging to the glass is a patch of little feathers. Down below, on the concrete patio, lies a dead house finch.

Birds whacking into windows are endemic to their subdivision on the outskirts of Fresno, California, stuck inland between the right-angled bend of the San Joaquin River to the east and the Pacific Ocean of Monterey Bay to the west. The birds have nowhere to go. There are no actual trees to speak of—not since the enormous machines made way for the houses. No place to roost or build their nests. They fly in any direction they can, hoping to find somewhere to exist, somewhere habitable, and the windows of this faceless subdivision keep impeding their salvation.

Thunk.

Lass and Mom moved in soon after the rows of identical houses started popping up. Zits across the useless landscape.

The tract had been built to support the produce workers and farmworkers in the valley. What they didn't expect was the devastating drought from 1976 through 1977. The rivers shrank and the lakes all but disappeared, and by the time Lassiter and Mrs. Yvonne Evans carried in their last box in September 1977, the few trees that had been left were gone. They replaced them with saplings that soon choked and died, and now their corpses dot the landscape, dried-up spinal cords jutting from the ground.

With the storms of '78, things got better, yet the damage has been done. During the big rains Lass's mom contracted some mysterious illness the doctors couldn't identify. They declared it a *woman's issue*. To Lass, she's just fat and old and feeling sorry for herself. And since she's bedridden, he's the only one to take care of her. His real father left years ago and any boyfriends since have fled like the birds of the San Joaquin Valley.

He opens the window and leans out to clean off the feathers. The early-evening heat bakes his skin, the air full of dust and dried soil. The feathers detach, swept away with the hot wind. The rear of their property has a reasonably sized yard, like all the rest. From this height, the rows of houses form a dizzying pattern, a matrix of beige siding and driveways woven through with sidewalks. Streets with innocuous names speak only to their inorganic nature—East First Street, East Second Street, East Third Street, and so on. Main Street is the artery that divides the east streets from the west. Visitors, when there are any, get lost, and since almost half of the homes are still unoccupied, there's no one around to ask for directions.

At 211 East Seventeenth Street, Lassiter and his mother share their cul-de-sac with two other families. Their street is the easternmost one and also the one where the developers gave up, packed it in. Stretching beyond their yard are acres of bald earth, abandoned tractors, and a deep trough filled with the recent stormwaters and rimmed with rotting logs.

"Lassie? What the heck are you doing? I told you I need the bathroom," his mom calls from down the hallway.

Calling him Lassie was okay until he was eight. Since then, it's an embarrassment, like everything else. *Lass* is borderline, but he accepts it.

"Yep, coming, Mom," he says.

He tucks his newest disco shirt into his off-white pants. It's a flashy, button-down polyester number with a graphic of overlapping clouds in various shades of blue. The money he makes at the local electronics store isn't bad, but it's not where he belongs. He has a degree from UC Santa Cruz, so he's no dummy. And since his mom has no one else, well, he has to bide his time until she croaks and he can get out of here.

In the meantime, though, he's going to give that Ted Bundy a run for his money—starting tonight.

"Lassie!"

He storms down the shag-covered hall to his mom's bedroom. An invalid shouldn't live on the second floor, what with the inability to run down the stairs in case of fire. When they moved in, she'd been pretty okay and then—the "illness." So tough luck, Mom. Besides, it's not like there's a good place for a bed on the first floor.

Her shades are down, as usual. The sunlight etched around the rectangle of window is a grim reminder of the world she's closed herself off from. Lassiter turns on her bedside lamp. Prescription bottles and empty cans of Tab soda litter its surface. An open bag of Doritos is tucked next to her propped-up and ever-expanding body.

"Mom, you know you can do this by yourself. You go to the bathroom when I'm at work or when I go out," he says.

"You aren't *at work*, though, and you aren't *out*, so you should help your mother," she says.

He maneuvers her walker near the bedside and crams his hands under her steaming armpits. He can't help but see down the gaping front of her housedress. Her threadbare bra barely contains the roaming blobs of her breasts. There's a Dorito chip wedged in one of the bra cups, sticking out like a third nipple. He's about to remove it, then stops.

Let's see how long she takes to notice it's there.

Getting himself clean and dressed this early to go out had been a mistake. Mom is getting her stink all over him and he'll have to wash up again, scrub away her rotting skin cells and sorrow. That means he'll be late to Club Alonso. That also means his plans for Janine may get screwed up. All because Mom wants him to help her go take a piss when she's capable of doing it on her own.

"Ow, Lassie! Watch what you're doing. You're pinching my skin," she says.

He's surprised she can feel anything beneath all her insulating layers of goo.

"Sorry, Mom, but you've got to help out a little. Push yourself up, you're getting too—" Lassiter almost says *fat*, almost says, *You're getting too fucking fat for me to help you out of bed.* Thankfully, he stops himself.

"Push yourself up, Ma."

With a great heave and grunt, the once attractive Mrs. Yvonne Evans slings her legs over the side of the bed and sits up.

"Okay, okay," she says.

Lassiter corrals her dangling legs with the frame of the walker and holds on to either side, bracing for the impact of her girth.

She places her hands on the rails and pulls herself up. Her slick face is close to his, her giant pores an infestation around her nose. She leans in and kisses his cheek.

"That's my baby Lassie, helping his mama."

The vinegary black cherry of Tab, mingled with the nacho cheese of the Doritos, invades his nostrils. He wipes his face with the back of his hand.

"Mom, Jesus Christ."

She makes her way, one creaking step after another, toward her en suite bathroom. The door is ajar and as she walks in, she pulls up her tent of a housedress, revealing her sagging underpants and what appear to be a growing number of bedsores on the backs of her thighs.

Lassiter shuts his eyes and waits for the bathroom door to close. Once he hears her repertoire of grunts and fumbling with the toilet seat, he turns and pulls up the shade to look down into their backyard.

He smiles.

Their backyard is like the rest, save for the shed that Lassiter built in his spare time—the one with a twin-size bed with fresh bedding, a drawer with rope, a hammer, a mouth gag, and newspaper clippings, and the door with a heavy padlock.

Lass has never committed a crime, nothing substantial. A little shoplifting, some underage drinking. Big whoop. If he's going to be a criminal, he may as well go big. He's smart enough. He'll figure it out. As his mother relishes in reminding him, he has a history of impulsive career choices he's never followed through with: marine biologist (he took one course at UC Santa Cruz until he discovered his fear of the ocean); actor (that was embarrassing); airline pilot (that was a no-go on so many fronts it's not worth mentioning). Being a *serial killer* isn't a job per se, but it is headline grabbing.

Bundy had already killed who knows how many women by the time he was Lass's age. Here in June 1979, Ted Bundy is thirty-two and defending himself in his own murder trial in Miami. Crazy bastard. He'd gone on his killing spree at the Chi Omega sorority house the year before and here he is in the papers and on TV, smiling for cameras, dressed in a corduroy sports jacket and looking like a college professor—the kind all the coeds go bonkers for. Lassiter will not be a skull-crushing, nipple-biting, garrote-using murderer. No, that's a bit much. He doesn't have the stomach for it. To be honest, he hasn't thought the whole thing through, but, yeah, once again, he'll figure it out.

He started building the shed in his spare time. It began as a space to call his own, where he could hide away from his mother's incessant complaints. Maybe he'd find a hobby or at least have a private spot to look at porno mags, drink beer, and jerk off. Life's simple pleasures. Then this Bundy stuff started coming out on the news. The man was everywhere, still is. That's when the light bulb turned on.

One day, shed almost done, Lassiter smashed his finger with a hammer. He watched as his nail bed turned from white to pink and then filled with blood, tingeing purple. It hurt like a motherfucker.

He looked up at his mom's bedroom, shades drawn, then over to the winding writhe of beige intestines that is their subdivision. It was hot. It was dry. He realized he didn't even know what season it was. The sun was always scorching. The soil, dust. Other than an occasional rainstorm, there was nothing to differentiate one day from another.

There was a newspaper by his feet, on it Ted Bundy's smiling face. The headline read: *All-American Boy on Trial*. Lass thought to himself, *I want that*.

That day, he decided to make the shed a love snare. A place he could take a girl—one like Janine, whom he's meeting at Club Alonso tonight. The pad would look nice, inviting. The girl wouldn't be scared. They'd get comfortable, share a bottle of Blue Nun, mess around, and then he'd tie her up, gag her, and . . . and then what? Use the hammer in the drawer?

He can't get past the *and then* part, but he has given himself a name. One that will look great in newspapers. There's Son of Sam, the Zodiac Killer, the All-American Boy . . .

And next, Lassiter Evans would be dubbed *Classy Lassie*.

CHAPTER THIRTY-SEVEN

"What are you gonna do with that thing?" Lassiter's mom says as she exits the bathroom and points to Lassiter's crotch.

He didn't hear her flush the toilet or open the door. He also didn't realize that he has a hard-on as he looks at his shed and thinks of his half-baked plans for Janine. Lassiter pulls the shade down and plunges the bedroom back into darkness, save for the bedside lamp. Mrs. Yvonne Evans plods her way back to her bed like a circus bear with a walker.

"Jesus, Mom," Lassiter says.

He helps her back onto the bed and she grunts him away.

"Don't you come near me with your thing all pointy like that," she says.

Kill me now, Jesus.

No need to worry. The sight of her made his *thing* collapse, retreating as far away as possible into his body.

"Shut up, would you, Ma?"

She plunks down with a great creak. He moves the walker out of the way to a spot he knows she can't get to without a lot of effort. She may even fall off the bed, reaching for it. *That'd be rich*.

They wrestle her body into its standard position, two pillows propped behind her.

"I'm serious, Lassie. That thing of yours gets men into trouble. Who pays for it, though? I'll tell you. Us women, that's who.

You be careful where you put that or else some poor young girl will end up like me someday," she says.

He's heard this before, over and over. How his father wronged her, got her pregnant, stuck around for a time, and then split because she started getting fat and old. Whatever the fuck happened, she had some control of her own life. She didn't have to end up like this. Yet here she is, spreading like a bucket of dough across the bedspread, sitting in the dark with a Dorito for a third nipple.

He cracks open a Tab and puts it on the table. It's warm, but Mom doesn't care. Neither does Lass. He collects her empties and used tissues and tosses them into a bag.

"I suppose you have nothing to say about that? You're ignoring me, as usual. I have life experience, you know. I may look like this, but I'm a person on the inside. Not just your fat, sad mama," she says, tears welling up in her eyes.

He hates when she does this, makes him feel bad. Her situation is not his fault. Somewhere inside this thing on the bed is the woman he remembers coming down the stairs in a red dress one Christmas a million years ago. She was pretty then. She took his little face in her hands and kissed him. "Merry Christmas, Lassie," she'd said, and led him to the living room. The air smelled of pine and he caught his reflection in the mirror, the imprint of his mother's red lips etched on his forehead.

"I know, Mom. I know," he says.

He should hug her. He should. It's what she wants. He can't bear the idea of feeling her width against him again, her sweat seeping into his brand-new shirt. Instead, he pats her hand and gives it a squeeze.

"I'm going out soon. To see friends. I'll bring your dinner before I leave, okay?" he says.

She's turned away from him, her gaze falling somewhere far away.

"Sounds fine, Lassie."

Back in his room, Lassiter opens the brown paper bag from Spencer Gifts. He loves that stupid store. It's where kids go to buy fart pillows and fake puke splats, plastic dog poo and Coal Mine Naughty Nugget Bubble Gum, which tastes fruity but turns your mouth black. Hilarious. Right next to the kid stuff is the *adult* section, nothing to keep away the innocent eyes of the dog poo buyers other than a sign that reads ADULTS ONLY. Instead of acting as a warning, it's a magnet for curious boys and girls who have realized their private parts are made for more than just taking a piss.

Earlier today, Lassiter didn't go in to buy a hand-crocheted penis warmer or latex replicas of human excretions; no, he was at Spencer Gifts for the clear plastic sunglasses with battery-operated windshield wipers and an orange headlight above each lens, exactly like the ones Elton John wore.

They're funny and cool and sure to enchant Janine when he sees her at Club Alonso. Lass opens the rainbow-striped box and pulls out the glasses. He pops a battery into each of the arms and puts them on in front of the mirror. The frames are round with apricot-tinted lenses. The guts of the machine are tucked into the bridge and visible, making the whole thing that much cooler. He rotates the black switch on the right arm and turns them on.

Whir-whir-whir-whir. Whir-whir-whir-whir.

They're noisy as hell and the orange headlights aren't bright, but who cares? Lassiter Evans is going to be the most happening guy at Club Alonso tonight. Hands down.

Lassiter doesn't feel like taking another shower, but he's skeeved out by his mom's depressing funk. Leaving his novelty glasses on the dresser, he removes his cloud-covered shirt and goes to his bathroom. The sink basin is caked with toothpaste smears, and pubic hairs surround the drain. His mom never comes in here, so she can't complain about the filth or the dog-eared *Penthouse* and *Playboy* magazines strewn about. Living with an invalid mother has its advantages.

He takes a birdbath, splashing his face and chest with water, and dries off with a towel long overdue for a date with the washing machine. Lass dabs Pierre Cardin for Men onto his neck, chest, and wrists. The cologne smells fine, but it's the bottle that does it for him. It's shaped like a cock—a silver ball on top and a clear glass shaft below. So obvious, yet they still advertised it on TV and in magazines. The subtext: *cock, cock, cock*. Boy, that Pierre Cardin guy knows what he's doing.

Unlike Mr. Cardin, Lassiter has no real clue what he's doing or how to do it. Planning a murder is a big deal and he should be giving it more thought, *a lot* more. He's being glib. Bundy was a planner—removing the passenger seat of his VW so he could hide his victims, luring them in with his fake arm cast, asking the girls for help with his schoolbooks. *Genius.*

Lassiter *has* planned, kind of. He built the shed, right? Made it look nice and inviting on the inside. He's stocked it with all the accoutrements of a seasoned serial killer. What's left to figure out is the whole how-to-kill-her and what-to-do-with-her-body stuff, which has him stymied. It makes him queasy. He'll work through it when the time comes. Wing it.

Here's the worst-case scenario: He gets Janine into the shed and they do *it* on the little bed. Sex, that is. One hundred percent worst case. That's not bad.

CHAPTER THIRTY-EIGHT

D*ing* goes the toaster oven. The Stouffer's chicken potpie for his mom is done. Lass is too worked up about tonight to eat anything substantial himself. He puts the steaming tin of gelatinous chicken, potato, and carrots encased in a glob of processed white-flour goo onto Mom's plate and brings it upstairs.

He doesn't bother knocking anymore. It's not like she's doing anything more than lying there watching TV or reading a magazine.

"Dinner, Mom," he says.

Lassiter used his employee discount at the electronics store to get Mom the TV with a remote-control box. She'd thought he'd splurged and done it as something nice for her. The truth is, it makes his life easier, no more changing the channels for her or turning the damned thing off or on. If it earns him some brownie points, all the better.

He puts the plate on the tray table by her bedside and swings it over. Not long ago, he could rotate the table across her lap. Now she's so mountainous he has to tuck it next to her side.

"It's still hot. Poke some holes in it so you don't burn your tongue . . . again," he says.

"It's not my first chicken potpie rodeo, Lassie," she says. She grips the fork and stabs it in and out of the underdone piecrust. An Old Faithful geyser of steam shoots out.

Well, excuse me for acting like I give a shit.

She's watching the national news on ABC. After that, she'll drool over Richard Hatch in *Battlestar Galactica*, followed by *The Love Boat* (which will most likely have big-titted Barbi Benton costarring for the millionth time), and then Mr. Roarke and Tattoo making dreams come true on *Fantasy Island*.

"Can you believe this sicko?" she says.

Lassiter knows who she's talking about without facing the television set. It's Ted Bundy—of course it is. She shovels a piping forkful of potpie into her mouth. His mom doesn't chew, but leaves her mouth open, the peas and carrots glued to the chunks of chicken with cornstarch, and unhinges her jaw back and forth, trying to cool the mound of food. It's burning her tongue. Her eyes are watering and her cheeks are bright red. Either she doesn't care or her mouth is lined with asbestos.

Mouth full, she says something. He knows what she said but doesn't want to give her the satisfaction. If she's going to chew her chicken potpie like cud and assume her son can comprehend her, well, that's on her and she's going to have to work for it. He's not going to just lie down and go along with it.

"Mom, I can't understand you when you talk with your mouth full like that," Lassiter says.

She makes a big show of chewing and swallowing, choking down the molten bite, and turns to Lassiter.

"I said"—she takes a swig of Tab—"he's so handsome. Ted Bundy, that sicko. No wonder those girls went along with him."

Lassiter doesn't think the two Chi Omega sorority sisters he killed on January 15 of last year, or the two others he beat within an inch of their lives that same night, went along with anything.

"Being handsome isn't everything," he says.

"No, but it helps," she says.

"He shouldn't be getting all this attention. It's not like he's Burt Reynolds," he says.

"You sound jealous," she says, heaping in another bite. "I bet if you stopped being such a busybody about other people, you could do more with your life." She gulps.

Lassiter balls up his fists, knuckles white.

"You have no stick-to-itiveness, Lassie," she continues. "*That's* your problem."

Oh, is that my problem? Maybe my problem is that I have a mother who's given up on her life and feeds the beast of her sadness with chicken potpie and Doritos and who insisted we move into a shit-ass subdivision where no one else wants to live, amid a dying valley, when all I wanted to do was get away and go anywhere else—anywhere—as long as it was away from her. So, what did she do? She got "sick," in fucking quotes, but she's not "sick," she's feeling sorry for herself and can't bear to be alone and wants me to be as miserable as she is, so she's handcuffed me, her only son, to her side for the ride down to hell with her.

He doesn't say any of that. Instead, he says, "I'm going to do plenty. You wait and see, Mom."

"Mm-hmm. Well, don't go writing your acceptance speech before you've even done anything, Lassie," she says.

Sure, he's having a hard time coming up with how to kill Janine, but his mom? That'd be easy. That'd be a joy. He chokes down his fury and tries to channel it into when he gets Janine into the shed later tonight.

Maybe he can kill his mother another time? That's reassuring.

"Right, well, I'm going to go now, Mom. Have a good night and I'll see you later," he says.

Despite the cruel things she's just said, that she often says, Mrs. Yvonne Evans leans her cheek toward Lassiter, inviting him to kiss it. By reflex he obliges and sees the Dorito chip is still poking out of her bra. She hasn't noticed it. The woman hasn't noticed a goddamned three-pointed corn chip covered in cheese dust and salt, half in and half out of her bra and stabbing her drooping booby.

Repulsed, he leaves without kissing his mother's cheek.

"Night, Ma," he says, and slams the door to her bedroom, leaving the fat old bag alone with her potpie and her chip for a nipple.

"Love you, Lassie!" she calls back, oblivious to the venom in her son's words.

Should he walk into Club Alonso wearing the windshield-wiper glasses? Or should he bust them out at the bar with Janine, maximizing the wow factor? Something to think about on the twelve-mile drive into town. For now, he leaves them propped on top of his head.

Lassiter shakes off the unpleasant encounter with his mom—the omnipresence of Ted Bundy—and checks on his backyard shed. His *sex shed*? His *murder shed*? This is the last time he can check everything before he comes back with Janine later. The last time before he becomes *Classy Lassie, the Dashing Lady Slayer* (or something or other).

Normal subdivisions would be full of the sounds of summer on an evening like this one: kids jumping through sprinklers in their yards or biking down the street, playing cards *clack-clacking* in their spokes, and the fringe on the handlebars *swooshing* as they pick up speed; grown-ups hosting barbecues for friends, plumes of charcoal smoke tinged with lighter fluid filling the air. This isn't a normal subdivision, though. This one's dead, shriveled, and abandoned. Not *abandoned*; that's the wrong word—never *inhabited* is what it is. Never filled with life.

Lassiter and Mrs. Yvonne Evans's yard is the end of the line. To Lass, it looks like the end of the world. Their rug of sod ends in a hard slash. Where there should be a fence to delineate it from the house that was meant to be built behind it, it simply stops. A border of yellowing grass and then dirt. Dried dirt for as far as the eye can see, dipping down into a deep trough filled with fetid water and the remains of the last few trees circling it, rhinos frozen in time at a watering hole. Lass's shed sits on the border between this facsimile of lawn and the expanse of barren death beyond.

Even while building the thing, Lassiter was reluctant to step over into that other dimension beyond their yard. It was like playing the game poison at the beach: Whoever let the frothing surf touch their feet at the ocean's edge is a goner. Dead. It's irrational. It's just dirt. But to Lassiter it feels like death.

Looking up to his mother's window, he sees the blue of the television pulsing along the edges of the drawn shades. She's not going to get up and look out here, so why worry? He's being smart, practical. That's why. A future murderer must be aware of his surroundings, of potential witnesses. There are no neighbors on either side of the house and the wide expanse of nothingness in the back. He'll be fine.

He takes out his keys and finds the one that fits the shiny new padlock on the door. There's enough light coming from the kitchen downstairs so he can see what he's doing. He's been very clever, though. He's *planned* for later. When he comes back with Janine, it'll be dark and turning on the houselights may wake his mother, so he has a mini squeezable flashlight as a key chain.

On the ground, a reddish ant marches from the dried soil landscape and up to his left shoe. It rears up on its legs, ready to attack his loafer. Lassiter stomps on it without a second thought.

"Take that, you nasty bastard," he says.

He examines the interior of the shed with his flashlight. The bed is small, but it'll do. He's salvaged some bedding from their linen closet, left over from when he was a kid. They're cute, harmless, not at all murder-y looking. There's a rug woven out of colorful rags on the floor, and by the one window, a plate full of candles. Romantic. He's pinned up a couple of pleasant posters: a beach sunset and one with a basketful of puppies. *So* unmurder-y. He opens the nightstand drawer. Coiled inside is the length of rope, ball gag, hammer, condoms, and all the Bundy newspaper clippings he's cut out.

Pleased, Lassiter steps out and locks the padlock.

"See you in a few hours," he says.

Despite the sun dropping below the horizon, it's still hot. Lassiter notices a shape in his periphery. A pile of dirt rises a couple of feet into the dead tract of soil behind, outlined by the remaining light of the day.

A pyramid of earth, tiny figures running up and down its sides building it higher.

CHAPTER THIRTY-NINE

The guy who sold Lassiter his Datsun 510 ripped him off. The dude insisted it was a great deal. Lass's mom warned him it was too good to be true. He hates it when she's right. The driver's-side door is a bitch to open, the hinge and door misaligned enough to produce a deafening metallic screech every time he opens it. The avocado-green paint flakes off a little more with each opening and closing. Lassiter's car screams: *The owner of this car is a chump*. But it's the only car he has, so he's stuck with it.

Imprisoned inside Lassiter's piece-of-shit Datsun is the stifling valley air. He lets the interior breathe for a minute, the hot inside mingling with the fractionally less hot outside. The vinyl seat is *this* close to melting. No sense making a broth of his balls before he even hits the dance floor at Club Alonso, so he leans against the car and puts on his Elton John sunglasses.

Whir-whir-whir-whir. Whir-whir-whir-whir.

The sunglass wipers create a View-Master effect of images as his eyes scan the abandoned neighboring houses. Streetlamps amplify the postapocalyptic-ness of their cul-de-sac on East Seventeenth Street. The cloned houses, lined up like bassinets awaiting newborns, all dark, save for their place and two others. Lassiter doesn't even know the neighbors' names. Three anonymous households relegated to this central California purgatory.

Whir-whir-whir-whir. Whir-whir-whir-whir.

He's startled by his own Future Man–looking reflection in the side mirror. His cloud-adorned shirt is open just enough to reveal a few chest hairs, the glasses wiping away phantom raindrops, two dim orange bulbs above the lenses. Could this be the reflection of a murderer? A soon-to-be murderer? Maybe this is a bad idea. Janine is nice enough. In fact, she's *very* nice and looks all right to boot. Has he got this all wrong? Killing a stranger makes more sense, if he thinks about it. There are too many people who can identify Lass who'll see him dancing with Janine at the club.

You have no stick-to-itiveness. That's your problem, Lassie.

Once again, his mom is right. He *doesn't* have stick-to-itiveness, gumption, moxie, whatever the fuck it takes to become something in this idiotic world he lives in, one where a *handsome* guy like Ted Bundy gets showered with attention for murdering women who were dumb enough to fall for his smile and fake arm cast. Is murderer the next logical stop after failed marine biologist, actor, or airline pilot?

I'm a hemmer and a hawer.

Lassiter Evans is not cut out for anything worthwhile. Never will be. Maybe he's destined to only be a salesman in a Harry's Electronics store in downtown Shitville, suburb of Fresno, who cohabitates with his ever-expanding mother in a nameless house, on an abandoned cul-de-sac, in a ghost town of a subdivision abutting the dusty, dirty end of the world.

And that's all.

Lassiter's right arm suddenly twitches and thrashes away from his side. What's happening? His arm flails, lifts above his shoulder, and freezes. Then it waves like there's someone to wave to. Lass isn't doing that. Well, his body is, but his brain isn't. It's as though an unseen puppeteer is manipulating his arm.

Great, on top of everything else, he's having a stroke or an epileptic fit or something. The action stops as abruptly as it started, and his arm falls back down to his side. The switch that was turned on shuts off.

That was weird. Super-duper weird.

He pinches his right arm to see if it's numb. It isn't. Everything seems normal, as far as he can tell. He turns the glasses off and silences the *whir-whir-whir-whir* of the wipers. Could the glasses be the culprit of his involuntary fit? Did he get a shock from them? Is that even a thing? Can you get electrocuted by a couple of AA batteries? That's dumb.

Nerves. He's anxious about tonight and it manifested itself in his right arm wigging out on its own. Other than a catastrophic brain event, that's what makes sense. Lassiter's body and mind now seem to be operating normally.

He shrugs it off and gets into the car, pulling the door closed with great effort and a metallic shriek. Lassiter pictures Janine and her very fine ass in the passenger seat next to him. He can and will go through with this, this *thing*. This . . .

Say it, asshole!

"This murder," he says to his reflection in the rearview.

He drives off toward Club Alonso and Janine. Lass can't shake the feeling he hadn't been alone in that moment, his arm shaking and waving, that there'd been someone else in control. Someone else inside his head.

The parking lot of Club Alonso is already packed when Lassiter pulls up at eight thirty p.m. on a summer Saturday night. People come from all around to dance here, to drink, party, do coke in the bathrooms, get blow jobs in back seats of cars. Unless you want to drive all the way to Fresno (and who the fuck wants to do that?), this is your only option. The lot teems with every shape and color of human, checking out each other's disco duds, smoking, and laughing.

It's a relief to hear voices other than his mom's, sounds beyond the dull throb of her TV set, the creak of her mattress. Lassiter twists the rearview mirror so it faces him. What's best? Wiper glasses on or resting on his head? Maybe tucking them into his open shirt? That's it: Novelty glasses hanging from his shirt, casual-like, real cool, then whipping them off and putting them on in one smooth movement. Yeah. A Kojak kind of thing.

He practices a few times to get the choreography down. He's almost got it, when someone presses their bare ass against his driver's side window. Dark hairs splinter out of the crack and spread across the pimpled cheeks. *Brad.*

Lassiter bangs his fist on the window and yells, "Get your greasy ass off my window, Brad!"

Brad obliges and pulls up his pants, an oily butt cheek imprinted across Lassiter's window. Brad leans in front of the windshield, smiles wide, and gives him the finger.

"Nice car, *Lassie*," Brad says. He walks away, zipping up his pants and tucking in his shirt.

"Asshole!" Lassiter gives him the finger back.

Brad's another viable candidate for murder. They work on the sales floor together at Harry's and it's like going back to high school. The taunts of *Laaaa-ssssie*, the inexplicable need to moon him every chance he gets—in the break room, the stockroom. Sometimes even when Lass is talking to a customer, Brad will pull his pants down in Lass's line of vision, trying to fuck up a sale. Lass lets it get to him every time. Every. Single. Time. No wonder he keeps doing it.

He pushes open the car door with his foot. A great crunching squeak of metal-on-metal issues forth and he steps out. In the reflection, he checks the placement of his glasses in his shirtfront. His right hand is normal and that unnerving sense of not being alone has passed, the feeling of someone else huddled inside his brain. It's agitation, that's all. He could shit fiery gravel now, he's so nervous. He is not going to do that, man. No way, José.

Classy Lassie makes his way toward the entrance of Club Alonso, where his first murder victim awaits him by the bar.

CHAPTER FORTY

The nondescript building that houses Club Alonso could be anything. It's been a bowling alley, a supermarket, a Knights of Columbus. An unremarkable single-level concrete bunker with a neon sign in orange cursive that reads CLUB ALONSO. It isn't the biggest disco, not like you'd find in Fresno, but it doesn't have to be.

Janine works in town at a women's boutique. Lassiter first noticed her in the shop when he'd walk past for his lunch break. They'd not spoken, though, until two weeks ago at the club. Janine admitted she'd never noticed Lass. That's not unusual; lots of people don't notice him. He's had girlfriends before, nothing serious. It was right around when they first met that Lassiter had seen the *All-American Boy on Trial* headline. Then the light bulb went off. It's not Janine's fault she's going to be his first. Timing, timing, timing.

His intestines gurgle. Lass needs to knock back a few if he's going to go through with this. If he has to run to the bathroom while trying to sweet-talk Janine, he'll never get her home. Not for murder—not even for sex. Goose egg.

He pushes through the crowd and spots her at the opposite end of the long bar. She's gabbing with a couple of her shop friends, so she hasn't seen him yet. He sidles up to the service area and grabs a draft beer off a waitress's tray as she turns to deliver drinks. Lass has disrupted the balance of her carefully placed beverages.

"What the hell, man?" the waitress says.

"Sorry, super thirsty." Lass drops two wadded-up singles onto her tray.

She rolls her eyes and walks away.

Lassiter chugs down the beer. It settles his stomach. He belches, and it goes unnoticed under the moans of Donna Summer's "Love to Love You Baby."

Janine and company are deep in conversation. Lassiter tries to will her friends away before he gets there.

Go away. Go. Away. You want to dance. You want to leave Janine and go dance.

The throngs of steamy bodies slow his approach. It's an obstacle course of sweaty flesh, Danskin leotards and wrap skirts, tequila sunrises and Slow Screws, and Shaun Cassidy and Farrah hairdos. Lassiter is about to break through and get in Janine's line of vision when her two friends join hands and head to the reverberating dance floor. It worked. He'd willed them to leave, and they did. Maybe Lassiter has more power than he gives himself credit for. Maybe this entire plan isn't so crazy after all.

He reaches for his windshield-wiper sunglasses hanging from his shirtfront and—like he'd practiced—whips them open and onto his face in one smooth motion and turns them on.

Just like Kojak, motherfuckers.

"Lassiter? Is that you?" Janine yells over the music. She's smiling a big, beautiful smile and they head toward each other. The sea of humanity parts for this moment.

Whir-whir-whir-whir. Whir-whir-whir-whir.

The wipers hum a lullaby in Lass's ears. Janine isn't the only one impressed. Some club goers have stopped their conversations to take in Lassiter's approach. They nod their approval and step out of his way. He catches his reflection in the wall of marbled mirrors behind Janine.

Damn, these glasses make him look cool. A real badass. Cloud shirt open, revealing a snarl of chest hair, an unconscious strut taking over his gait. This is the single best purchase he's ever made.

God bless Spencer Gifts.

"It's me," Lassiter says.

"Oh my God. Oh. My. God! Those glasses. Those are the Elton John ones, right?" Janine says.

Before he can answer, she wraps her arms around him and kisses him on the cheek with her sticky lips. They've never hugged before and she's certainly never kissed him. This evening is starting out better than he could ever have imagined.

The motion of the wipers is making him dizzy. A carousel of photographic slides of Club Alonso flash by with each swipe. He has to turn these off soon, but for now, he can deal. He wants to bask in the boozy Midori of Janine's breath, her tight brown curls nestling against his neck, her boobs squishing up against him through her tank top. Janine must not be wearing a bra, because he feels the raised bumps of her nipples through his polyester shirt. His crotch tingles. He wants to keep this hug going, to keep squeezing her into him, but getting a boner at this point in the evening might blow the deal.

Don't you come near me with your thing all pointy like that.

The sound of his mother's voice in his head is all it takes to curtail the flow of blood to his penis. Mission accomplished. He puts his hands on Janine's shoulders and separates their bodies.

"Yeah, these *are* the Elton John ones. I got them at Spencer Gifts," he says.

"I love that store," Janine says. "Can I try them?"

He switches them off, grateful for the break from the noise and the strobe effect. He's about to hand them to her and realizes the cooler thing to do, the sexier thing, is to put them on for her. Sliding them onto her face, he puts the sunglass arms behind her ears and untucks her curls from behind them. Her hair is soft, not coarse and greasy like his mom's.

"How do I turn them on?" Janine says.

"It's that little knob on the right side. Give it a twist," he says.

The wipers spring to action—*Whir-whir-whir-whir. Whir-whir-whir-whir*—and the orange lights turn on.

"Far out, Lass," she says.

She's grooving to the beat of the music, bopping her head from side to side. Her neck is long and pretty. Strangulation? Lassiter could fit his hands around her throat. That would mean he'd have to look her in the eye while he's killing her. He can't do that. Man, this is not going to be easy.

"Let's dance," she says, and grabs his hand, pulling him to the dance floor.

She's being so nice, so friendly. Janine must actually like him. Go figure? Chic's "Le Freak" comes on as they make their way to the illuminated dance floor. No, it's not like the one in *Saturday Night Fever*; still, it's not bad for a bunker disco in the suburbs of Fresno. Everyone is packed in tight. Strangers' butts and arms brush up against him while they dance. He's not a bad dancer—not a great one either. Right down the middle, boring, safe.

Janine's dancing style is . . . *bouncy*. Lassiter's okay with that, especially without her bra. Her curls bop along with her, the novelty sunglasses still resting on her face and *whir-whir-whirring* away. This is starting to feel like a real, actual date.

Here it is, Saturday night, and they're dancing. Lassiter trying to come up with a way to kill this woman who likes him just so he can make a name for himself. All because Ted Bundy's omnipresence in the news makes poor loser Lassiter feel like he has to emulate him, one-up him. As if that's the only way he'll matter in this world. The only way Lassiter's life will matter a single, stupid lick.

CHAPTER FORTY-ONE

Lassiter is flummoxed. The evening has surpassed his expectations. He'd counted on Janine playing hard to get or going off and dancing with other guys or hanging out with her friends and being only half interested in him. The opposite is true. They've danced and laughed, had drinks, and swapped wearing the Elton John glasses. And right now, Janine's got her hands on Lass's knees and is leaning into him as they sit at the bar.

If she'd been a bitch or a bore, it would make trying to kill her easier. He likes her, though. He really likes her. Lassiter can feel his ambition to become *Classy Lassie, the serial killer* ebbing away. Once again, he's lacking stick-to-itiveness. Lass should feel happy that a normal, pretty woman like Janine is taking an interest in him. Instead, he feels depressed, like he's failing at something he'd been determined to do, like all the other things he'd been determined to do in his life.

Whir-whir-whir-whir. Whir-whir-whir-whir. The wipers are a thrumming heartbeat in his ears.

"It's getting late, Lass," Janine says, leaning ever closer to him. She sinks her fingertips farther into his thighs, dropping a hint the size of an anvil.

This is what he's wanted: Get Janine home, have some sex, and then possibly (*maybe?*) kill her.

"Do you want to, um, I mean, how would you feel about, you know, coming home with me?" he says. He braces for rejection even though she's not indicated that she wants to do anything other than fool around.

She reaches up and pulls his sunglasses off. They *whir* in her hands like a captured insect. She kisses him firm on the mouth, her tongue brushing across his teeth, the grenadine and orange juice of tequila sunrises escaping from between her lips.

"What do *you* think, Lassie?" she says.

Coming from her pink, juicy lips, the name Lassie sounds sexy, like it belongs in the air around them.

Lass shouldn't drive. He'll be okay, though, if he keeps the windows down.

Janine sits in the passenger seat, and she didn't make a single nasty comment when he had to fight to get his driver's-side door of his piece-of-shit Datsun open. The screech of the grinding metal echoes across the emptying parking lot, and the valley fog creeps in as it does in the wee hours of the morning. The Elton John glasses rest on her lap and stare forward like another passenger. Wipers and lights off. Lassiter goes to roll down his window when he notices Brad's greasy ass print on the glass. *What a dick*.

His hands shake and for a nauseating moment Lassiter worries that the invisible puppeteer will return and botch his chances with Janine. It's only nerves. The natural excitement of getting naked with the person next to him for the very first time. Will he do it right? Will she be turned off by the slight left list of his penis? Will he come too soon? (Not to mention the whole *he may still try to murder her* thing.)

"It's like we're driving into another dimension," Janine says, as they creep through the fog and off the main strip and into the vast nothingness of the valley.

If it weren't for the center lines of highway that take them the twelve miles to his ghost of a subdivision, he'd drive off the road and into the lakes of dusty dirt that surround them. The Datsun is cocooned in the valley's miasma, propelled forward by a force greater than its firing pistons. Between his drunkenness and the building apprehension of being alone with Janine in his shed (and what the hell he's going to do when he gets her there), it's a wonder Lass can drive at all.

Janine fiddles with the radio, stabbing at the buttons to no avail. Lassiter is so fixed on keeping them on the road that he hasn't spoken since they left town.

"It doesn't work," he says. The words come out sharper than he intended.

"Oh, okay," she says, sounding hurt.

"Sorry about that. Focusing on the road," he says, placing a hand on her knee as an apology.

The gesture soothes and Janine lifts the glasses from her lap and puts them on, flipping the switch. *Whir-whir-whir-whir, whir-whir-whir-whir.* The sound is annoying, but he needs to keep her happy.

Janine starts to sing the lyrics from David Bowie's "Space Oddity." *"This is Major Tom to Ground Control."*

Her outburst (and tone deafness) take him by surprise. Lass glances over. The sight of this bouncy-curled woman sitting in his miserable car, wearing his prized glasses from Spencer Gifts, and willingly going home with him on an eternally depressing and foggy central Californian night warms him in a way he can't identify. They're passengers together in this rickety capsule, hurtling alone through space and time. They could be anywhere. The dense fog cloaks any recognizable landmarks; distant house lights pulse like faraway solar systems, unexplored planets housing unknown civilizations.

If only they could stay like this, suspended above the fray of planet Earth in late June 1979 with its incessant media buzz surrounding a killer named Ted Bundy, if they could stay right here, in this Datsun, away from everything, everyone, away from a haunted subdivision strewn across a dead valley, like the unearthed skeleton of a dinosaur, and a mountain of a mother with a Dorito stuck in her bra, if time could stop and Lassiter Evans and Janine could soar through the fog of time forever, maybe none of what's about to happen would happen. Maybe Lassiter could embrace the warm thing he can now name: happiness. For the first time in a long time, Lassiter Evans is happy.

Radio dead, Lass and Janine join in a rousing a cappella version of the demise of astronaut Major Tom. The entrance to the subdivision springs from the haze and Lassiter turns in.

"This is where you live?" Janine says.

The question doesn't warrant a response.

Yes, this is where I live. This is where I live with my mother.

Even thinking it sounds depressing, let alone uttering the words out loud to a woman Lassiter is hoping to bed (among other things). The fog has lifted a bit, revealing the bottom halves of the identical houses as they drive deeper toward East Seventeenth Street.

"Geez, I didn't think anyone lived out here," Janine says, as she cranes her neck looking for signs of life. "It looks so . . . abandoned."

The tone of her voice has shifted. Moments ago, it was playful and upbeat—she was singing, for God's sake—now it's tinged with anxiety. Who could blame her? This place *is* pretty creepy. House after house, empty, unlived in. Here she is with a guy she barely knows, in his piece-of-shit car, being driven to his home in a tract that looks like it's part of a dystopian movie set. She may even be getting the idea that Lassiter wants to do her harm, and he can't have that, even if it's true (or at least was true until a little while ago). In all honesty, Lassiter doesn't know what the fuck he's doing. He needs her to relax again.

"Yeah, it's not so bad. We got a good deal, though." The moment the word *we* comes out of his mouth, he regrets it. Now, he has to explain who *we* is.

"*We?* Who's *we*? Lassiter, if you're married and want some kind of skanky ménage à trois, you've got the wrong girl." Janine crosses her arms tight over her chest. "This was a bad idea. Maybe you should take me back."

Lass has to turn things around before his entire plan blows up. Then there'll be no sex and certainly no murder (if that's even on the docket anymore).

"You've got it all wrong," he says, and pulls the car over so he can look her in the eye.

She's still wearing the glasses. The wipers are going and he can see her concern growing with every back-and-forth swipe. He reaches over, removes them from her face, and turns them off.

"Honestly, it's embarrassing, Janine. *We* is me and my mom," he says with a sigh.

Saying it out loud makes his voice crack, and the truth makes him want to cry. The *patheticness* of Lass: still living with his mother, bound to her by whatever malady she suffers from, manacled to this pointless existence where he's unable to follow through with anything, to do anything of value, where the very best idea he's come up with is trying to become a murderer of women. A murderer of a sweet and pretty woman like Janine, who until a minute ago was sold on the idea of Lassiter Evans.

"My mom is sick and I'm the only one she has to take care of her. Pathetic, right?" Janine is looking at him, sizing him up. He resigns himself to failure. "You're right, Janine. I'll take you back."

He's about to put the car in drive, when Janine leans over and kisses him. Her lips warm, soft. Small fingers of electricity flow from her and into him.

She puts her hand on his cheek. "No, Lassie. It's not pathetic. You're sweet. In fact, you may be the sweetest man I've ever met. Take me to your place." She kisses him again. "Please."

Lassiter cuts the lights before turning into the driveway.

It's unnecessary, since his mom's bedroom is at the back of the house. Plus, she's probably in a near coma from painkillers. Janine looks out the windshield. The curtain of fog has dropped again, skirting just above the ground.

"It looks nice," she says. She's lying. Lass appreciates the effort.

"It looks like all the rest. If there wasn't a number on it, I wouldn't know which driveway to turn into."

He hangs the novelty glasses on his shirtfront and forces his door open with a kick. The screech peals into the fog. He hurries to Janine's side and opens her door. What a gentleman. Janine is unsteady and leans into him.

"Sorry," she says. "I got out too fast. I guess I'm tipsy. Is your mom awake? I mean, do we need to whisper, or what?"

"No, she's passed out. She takes pills to help her sleep. Besides," he says, leading her along the side of the house toward the back. "We're not going inside. We have our very own little bungalow in the backyard."

They stand on the carpet of yellowed sod in the backyard. Lassiter's handmade murder shed looms before them in the mist.

He fumbles with the keys and unlocks the padlock. Lass should've taken the lock off before he left. It would be less creepy. A long row of ants marches from the sea of dirt off the back and past the side of the shed. Erupting from the ground is the ever-growing mound, the fog resting atop its miniature mountain peak. The shape he'd noticed earlier is an enormous anthill. He makes a mental note to destroy the thing tomorrow.

Before stepping in, he sees the flickering blue of the television screen peeking around his mother's shades. She's fallen asleep with the TV on again.

He opens the door and leads Janine in. Taking a pack of matches from the windowsill, he lights the plate of candles.

"Wow, Lassie. You built this?" Janine says.

"Yeah, I did," he says.

"It's pretty rad."

It is, isn't it? Lassiter built this, and it's not falling down. It's not crooked. It's not half finished—like everything else he's ever attempted to do. That's too generous. He's never gotten half finished with anything. More like a quarter finished. The shed is 100 percent done, and it's rad. Maybe he should be a carpenter?

Janine kicks off her shoes and steps closer to Lassiter. She's a good three inches shorter now. The top of her head only reaches his shoulders. She runs her hands across his cloud-covered shirt, traces the frames of the glasses with her fingers.

"I like this shirt. It makes me think of that Joni Mitchell song. You know? The one about the clouds," she says, her voice deep and sultry.

"Oh, right? Yeah, 'Both Sides Now.' I hadn't thought of that," Lassiter says. He's nervous. Really nervous. When's the last time he's been alone with a woman like this?

Lass can't believe this is happening. That Janine is here. Actually here in this shed with him. In the place that he built and hoped to murder her in, to christen his big serial-killer career. Who was that guy? What'd he been thinking? He can't conceive of a single reason why he'd want to kill her. Why, of all the people that may be worth ending—like Brad, his mom, even—how could Janine end up on that list?

His stomach sinks at the sight of the nightstand. Inside its drawer are the instruments of murder—the rope, the ball gag, the hammer. Worse still are the newspaper clippings about Ted Bundy. As long as Janine doesn't open the drawer, he can leave all this murder stuff behind him.

CHAPTER FORTY-TWO

Before he has time to let what's happening sink in, to savor Janine's kisses and her roaming hands, they're on the little bed. Lassiter leans his back against the wall. Janine straddles him, unbuttons his shirt. She threads an arm of the novelty glasses into one of his buttonholes. He grips the blanket and sheet on either side of him—holding on for dear life.

Janine pairs each unbuttoning with licks of tongue across his neck, her pink manicured nails inching a little farther down his torso. Lass feels the heat, the wet, of her crotch pressing against his hard-on. Her miniskirt has slid up to her waist, revealing the black lace of her panties in the candlelight, a sheer veil covering her pubic hair. He rocks his pelvis up to press himself closer to her. Closer to where he wants—*needs*—to go. His pants are unbearably constrictive. He knows she's working her way down there. His desire for her to touch him, put her mouth on him, or to get inside of that wonderful hidden tangle of hair and moist is almost too much to take. He groans.

"You're so sexy, Janine. You're killing me," he says.

"I can feel that," she says, grinding her way into his pants. Teasing, tantalizing.

Pulling off her tank top, Janine confirms Lassiter's suspicions she was braless. Her breasts are miraculous, defying gravity like champs. Lass's mind drifts to the Dorito stuck in his mother's bra. He wonders if it's still there.

Stop it!

This is not the time to be thinking about his mother's body. To break the train of thought, he puts his hands on her beautiful boobs, runs his fingers across her nipples, squeezes her springy flesh. She moans in appreciation and he leans in to kiss them, lick them. Her skin is salty and smells of coconut.

She maneuvers a hand between her crotch and his and kneads him to a point nearing no return. His brain has shut off. Lassiter fumbles with his belt and pulls at the buckle the wrong way.

"Ready to come out and play?" she says.

Janine pushes his useless hands aside and pulls the end of the belt hard, squeezing him tighter, taunting.

"Oh God, Janine. Please," he says.

She pops the two prongs from the buckle and releases the pressure. Drops of precome seep through the polyester of his pants.

"Ooh," she says, pressing her thumb into the damp, stroking him.

He's not going to make it. Maybe he should go back to thinking about the chip in his mother's bra? That's it: the way her gown hangs around the acreage of her skin, a collapsing circus tent; the creak of her bed frame as she adjusts her body; the enormity of the pores bordering her nostrils. These ugly thoughts help stem the tide. He better not go too far, though; Lassiter doesn't want to lose it altogether, for fuck's sake.

His eyes roll back in his head as Janine unzips his trousers. She's unleashed him and he wants in. All the way into the marvelous musk of where his hand has found its way. Fingers tucked into the black lace, searching for a pink pearl and lost in her silky brine.

"You have a rubber, Lassie?" she says. Her hand finding his skin beneath his jockey briefs.

Without thinking, *without fucking thinking*, he points to the nightstand.

"In that drawer," he says.

She swaps her right hand for her left and continues to caress him as she reaches for the drawer. His senses have gone kablooey, now focused solely on points south. If even part of his brain was on, functional, he'd realize what she's about to see when she opens that drawer. He'd be able to anticipate her reaction when she sees the length of rope, the ball gag, the newspaper clippings of Ted Bundy's escapades—the hammer. Then he could at least try to come up with an excuse that doesn't make it sound like he built this shed to be a murder site. To somehow make it seem like any other goddamned thing but the truth. To make Janine believe she is most definitely not his first intended murder victim.

Rather, *was* his intended first victim. That's changed now, hasn't it? His grand plan chipped away with each passing minute he's spent with the woman who has her hand on his erect penis. Janine has been fun, attentive, and kind. Not to mention being understanding (even touched) when she learned Lassiter lived with and took care of his ailing mother. Sure, he hadn't told her everything, like how Mom disgusts him, how she's ruined herself and her life by investing everything she has in her own self-pity. How her choices have isolated them from normal society. How her subtle (and not-so-subtle) denigrations of her only child, her only son, have brought him to a place where the very pinnacle of what he felt he could achieve was to emulate a serial killer. It's about to be too late to explain all of that, to backtrack.

She reaches to the table and picks up the newspaper with a smiling Ted Bundy emblazoned on the front page. Tossing it to the floor, she says, "Yuck, this guy gives me the creeps, Lassie. Why would you have that in your little love—" She stops short as she pulls open the drawer for a rubber, its contents exposed. "What the fuck?"

She retracts her hand from the drawer. Its handle a hot stovetop that's burned her fingers. Her sudden motion has dislodged the drawer from the table. Hammer, rope, ball gag drop to the rug on the floor; paper clippings and condoms rain down like a burst piñata.

Lassiter's brain is only now catching up with what's going on, with what she's seeing and how she's interpreting it. The irony is that she's 100 percent right. Whatever she's thinking, the alarm bells that ring in her head, they're sounding for all the right reasons. Janine falls off the bed, hitting her head against the wall.

She starts to scream.

"No, Janine, no, please. *Shh-shh.* I can explain," Lass says. But can he? Can he explain?

He gets up from the bed, shirt hanging open, Elton John glasses secured to his shirt like a boutonniere. His pants slide down his hips, his softening penis bobbing in defeat. Lassiter looms over her on the floor. The square footage of the shed hampers his mobility. Below him, Janine's screaming escalates. He needs her to stop or else his mother will wake up. The few neighbors they have will call the police. Life as he's known it, however deplorable, will be over.

"Please stop screaming. I know how this looks. It's not what you think," he says.

It's exactly what you think, Janine. You're smart and right, but I changed my mind. Can't that count for something?

Lassiter reaches his hand down to help her off the ground.

Still topless, her lovely breasts droop off to either side, her skirt pulled up high to her waist, panties askew, showing the thicketed forest that only moments ago he was preparing to explore. Between the implements of murder, the booze, and the claustrophobia of the shed, Janine is losing her shit. Lassiter is trying to calm her but, panicked, Janine swats his hands away.

"Get away from me! Don't touch me. *What kind of sicko are you?*"

She gets to her knees and lunges for the hammer. Swinging it wildly, it connects to his knee with a sickening crack.

"Goddammit!" Lassiter clutches at his patella. Spots of white pain cloud his vision. "Jesus, stop. I'm not a murderer. You have to listen to me."

Janine gets to her feet and grabs at the doorknob. It flies open, and she tumbles out onto their patch of lawn, shrouded in fog.

"Help!" she screams. "He's trying to kill me!"

Lass can't let this continue. He needs to control her, bring her back inside, and quiet her down so he can explain. His plan has gone off the rails. The flickering blue light of the TV rimming the shades in his mom's room changes to a steady white.

Shit, she's awake.

Janine tries to get up from the mist-soaked ground and Lassiter tackles her harder than he intended. He's not trying to hurt her, yet this needs to stop—now. The situation is so fucked up, out of control. There has to be a way to right the ship, to get her back inside and calm her down. It's a big misunderstanding . . . sort of.

A sharp pain flares across his ankle. It burns like a match to his skin. Then it happens again on his Achilles. Searing, excruciating. Janine is beneath him on the ground, sobbing. She's not doing anything to cause this pain. What is? The hot poker hits him again, higher on his leg. That's three times. Then four, five . . .

There's something on Lassiter's leg and he kicks his feet in terror, trying to shake whatever it is off. He forgets about Janine underneath him and rolls off her, swatting at the invisible fire on his leg.

"What the fuck is this? Get off me. Get it off me!"

Is it his pants? A burning candle could've fallen off the windowsill in the scuffle and ignited his polyester pants. There's no flame, though, and the stinging pain accelerates. A volley of artillery, flaming arrows, crawling up his leg. Janine scrambles to her feet and runs. She's holding her top against her bare breasts and Lassiter watches her disappear through the fog and around the side of the house. She's gone. His throat tightens as he battles an invisible foe on the wet lawn.

He's writhing on the grass when he sees them. Row after row of red ants surging across the battlefield from their triangular mound only six feet away. Crossing over the border from the barren valley of soil and into the territory of Lass's backyard, charging forward across his shoes and into his pants leg.

Ants? He's being attacked by ants?

A memory comes to him, a small column in the newspaper overshadowed by the hoopla about Ted Bundy: Central Californians were told to be on the lookout for the imported fire ant, which had become a menace to livestock and fieldworkers. They were highly aggressive.

The swatting makes it worse, heightening the tiny bugs' agitation. Lass has to get his pants off. The pain of each bite is a thunderclap on his skin. Lassiter kicks off his shoes in desperation and wriggles out of his pants. His hands are wrong, though. They don't look like his. Fingers, swollen red party balloons. His skin expands, filling with water from an invisible spigot. He's having a severe allergic reaction to the bites.

Anaphylactic shock.

Gone are his concerns about Janine running away and calling the police. He hopes she *does* call for them and that they get here soon and get these fucking evil bugs off him. He can't breathe. God, his throat is constricting. His legs bare, pants kicked off to the side, a minor impediment to the ants' incessant progress. There are hundreds of them—thousands. The mound of dirt is alive with motion. When he was building his shed, he'd thought of the soil beyond the yard as another dimension, one to fear. Stepping into it had felt like death. At the time, it was irrational; now the death is coming to him.

Lass stands. *Get to the house. Get inside and safe.*

His legs are numb and bending his knees is near impossible. He can no longer see his patellas, his legs swelling beyond recognition as the ants continue their attack, moving higher. Stumbling like Frankenstein, wearing only his briefs, his socks, and his cloud-covered shirt with the Elton John glasses still attached, Lassiter collapses into the back door of the house. He wraps his bloated hands around the knob and pushes it open.

His line of vision is shrinking into slits. A scraping sound, like tearing sandpaper, fills his ears. It's his breathing, what's left of it, rasping in and out of the shrunken capillary of his throat.

"Maaa-gghhh-uuh. Maaa-gghhh-uuh." Tongue swollen, he tries to call for his mother. His invalid mother, who hasn't come downstairs of her own volition in months.

He flounders past the kitchen, falling more than walking.

The ants have reached his balls. He can't feel it. His entire body is aflame and numb all at once. Reaching the stair landing, he crumples to the floor and lands on his back.

"Maaa-gghhh. Maaa-gghhh."

The Elton John glasses dislodge from his shirt and land by his distended hand. He flexes his swollen fingers around them as the impact turns them on. *Whir-whir-whir-whir. Whir-whir-whir-whir.* His line of sight narrows to a thin horizontal line. All he can see now are a few of the stairs that lead up to their bedrooms and the two orange lights from the glasses, the wipers moving back and forth. There's a muffled explosion—or is it thunder? If it is, that's good, they could use rain. It's so dry, so dry. Dusty, dusty, dry, dry. The thunder is louder, closer. Crashing. Falling.

Falling.

Lassiter's mother is tumbling down the stairs, trying to get to her son. To save her son.

"Maaa-gghhh."

Vision narrowed, he can only see bits of her expansive body. An ant stands on the thin aperture of his right eye and bites. *Blink*. Down to one eye, one slit. Ma, panting, in pain. Picking ants off her son and wailing. He can't hear her, not really. Out of his left eye he notices a shadow, out of place, moving down the stairs like a waterfall of black. A Slinky of darkness.

"Lassie, my Lassie," his mother cries.

Sirens sound in the distance. How will they find them? How will the police find their house that looks like all the others in this dead and anonymous landscape?

The shadow moves again. An arm unfolds and flows toward the Elton John novelty glasses from Spencer Gifts. The single best purchase Lassiter's ever made.

The vacant black shimmers and turns to him. *The queen. Is this the queen of the ants?*

His mother doesn't notice it—this sable Slinky thing lifting the glasses from her son's hand. How can't she see it?

Mrs. Yvonne Evans leans over Lassie. Her housedress hangs open. *It's still there*. It's the last thing Lassiter Evans sees before his life is snuffed out. The goddamned Dorito chip lodged in his mother's bra.

CHAPTER FORTY-THREE

"Get them off me! Mom, get them off."

Greta Davenport is back—part of her, anyway. She's thrashing on the chaise, trying to shake her body free from invisible ants. Her eyes blink open. She's caught between the intoxicating death of creepy, deplorable Lassiter Evans and whoever the hell she is. *Wherever* the hell she is.

It's a ship's cabin. Above her a rectangular window with no ocean view. Greta peers down at this stranger's body. It's a woman. Her limbs aren't swollen and she can breathe. Her mind belongs to two people and they're having a duel. To hell with her mind, though. Her insides and skin quake with the glorious aftershock of pleasure from Lassiter's gruesome last moment on this planet. His agony is her ecstasy.

"Greta. Greta Davenport," another woman says. A gorgeous woman in a Victorian-era dress, so glistening gunmetal that it's almost a shadow, stands with her arms crossed. Her bosom rises and falls, her breathing accelerated. She's talking to someone named Greta. That's familiar.

"Focus your eyes on me. You're at the Found Object Society and you've just come back from a voyage. Your name is Greta Davenport."

Greta's mind is a settling snow globe. The flakes drift down to the bottom, revealing the plastic castle in the middle. *Greta*

Davenport. That's my name. I'm back from a voyage at the Found Object Society.

"Miranda," Greta says.

"Good, yes. My name is Miranda. Welcome back." She sits next to her on the chaise and picks up Greta's wrist, checking her pulse. Miranda's touch is warm, almost burning, as her eyes scan Greta's face. Her stare a wordless interrogation. A white membrane nudges a fraction out of the corner of her eye, then retreats. Miranda cocks her head, finding an answer to something within Greta's features. She swallows. "Yes, I knew that would be an exciting one. Your pulse is high."

Exciting? Had it been? Lassiter Evans's and Greta Davenport's minds part ways. Greta is alone again. Herself.

"I need a minute before I get up," Greta says.

"Of course, get your bearings. Let me collect this so you can relax your other arm," Miranda says.

Greta forgot about her other arm, the one that's extended to her right and entombed in a glowing, metallic mold. Resting in her palm are the sunglasses with the wipers and the orange lights. The best purchase Lassiter Evans ever made (the last one, too). Latex gloves on, Miranda removes the glasses from Greta's hand. She's about to put them in the wooden box when she notices an ant crawling across the frames. Miranda flicks it away and stomps on it when it lands on the floor.

"I brought an ant back with me? That's possible?" Greta says. A similar thing happened when she returned from the death of Zephyrine—slimy pond water dripping off the perfume bottle.

"It's only temporary," Miranda says. "Like how the light of a flashbulb sticks around when you close your eyes. You open them and it's gone. See?"

Miranda points to where she squashed the ant on the floor.

There's nothing there. If it wasn't there to begin with, why did Miranda feel the need to crush it with her foot?

This idea puts something to work in the background of Greta's thoughts. A theory forming in the recesses of her consciousness.

Then a gear clicks into place.

Greta remembers a point during her voyage to 1979 where she'd become aware, lucid. She'd taken control of Lassiter's right hand and moved it, made it wave. Greta had *interfered* with her vessel—hijacked Lassiter—a big no-no. Before Greta's first voyage, Miranda made it sound like such a feat wasn't even possible. What she'd really meant was that it was *verboten*.

And Greta just did. She fucking did.

For a quick moment, she and Lassiter shared the same space. He'd felt her there with him. This is important. There's something to it. Greta need only find out what it is.

Greta steadies herself and follows Miranda's shushing dress as she leaves her cabin. The door exhales behind her. Greta's intentionally lagging. It allows her to take in the other cabins as she walks past. The one with the shoe is still closed, no lights on above it.

Maintenance. That's what Miranda had said. She clearly didn't want Greta to see in there. Whose shoe was it? And what was with the bright white light?

Ezra must have died already. Will he share with her more than vague details this time? As planned, he'll be waiting for her by the Haas mural.

Ahead of her, Miranda slides the box containing Lassiter's glasses into a pneumatic tube of sorts and latches the little door shut. That must have been the clanging and *whoosh* that Greta mistook for heating pipes during her first visit. An engine comes to life as the box gets sucked away. Greta assumes it'll get reshelved and used again for another member's voyage. Miranda then turns out of sight toward the society's front waiting area.

The stupor of Greta's post-voyage high slips away like water down a drain. Her stomach drops and that hollowed-out feeling returns with a vengeance. It scoops out her insides, fills the chasm with soot. Emotions flailing like amputated stubs. The down after a voyage is deep. Worse than any other comedown she's had. The high is also higher than any conventional drug. Which is why, with each step away from the plush sanctuary of her cabin, Greta can think of one thing, and one thing alone: counting down the seventy-two hours before she can come back and find entertainment and pleasure in the death of another human being.

Greta's walking unsupervised through the Collection Room. A clatter sounds in the distance. At first, Greta figures it's the pneumatic tube system. It's not that, though. Something's fallen onto the floor in an aisle to her right. Greta adjusts her eyes and sees at the far end a tall figure bending over to pick something up. The aisle is dark, but the form is even darker, blacker. A living void. A memory shakes free. Two: The thing in the pond with Zephyrine lifting the perfume bottle from the silt. And the black Queen of the Ants cascading like water down the staircase and picking up Lassiter's glasses.

Greta's heart pounds at the realization of what she must be seeing—at the end of the aisle stands the Collector.

Greta blinks hard. Whatever she saw (or thought she saw) has morphed into the darkness surrounding it. There's nothing there, just the pitch at the end of the aisle. She's certain she saw it, though. There's no doubt she heard the noise of something falling to the floor. A clatter. Was what she saw after a hallucination? Her brain piecing together a kind of post-voyage logic to make sense of a sound that didn't belong? The memories from the last seconds of her deaths, those were real—or as real as these experiences are. After her first voyage, Greta strained to recall what she'd sensed as Zephyrine lay at the bottom of the pond—that there'd been a presence down there with them. She couldn't identify it then. Now, so soon after her death with Lassiter, the experience is fresh.

This time she remembers: At the end of each of these people's lives, an entity lurks nearby, waiting. It takes the last object they touched and brings it here, to the Found Object Society.

Miranda returns, looking perturbed. "Greta, please stay close."

"Coming," Greta says, and walks toward her. Miranda holds the velvet curtain open to the waiting area. Greta tucks past her. "A little groggy still, I guess."

She's anything but groggy. She's sharp, alert, her body electric. Greta knows what she saw.

Like the first time, Big Daniel Craig hands Greta a glass of guava nectar.

"Welcome back from your voyage, Miss Davenport," he says.

Greta reaches for the glass, ready to chug it down; then she remembers vomiting her guts out in the alleyway after her first voyage. The first time she met Ezra. How is that only three days ago? She wants to ask BDC about what she saw, but feels like she can't with Miranda still here.

"Thank you," she says, and takes reasonable, small sips of the sweet liquid.

"That's it, take it slow this time," BDC says.

Miranda stands behind Greta. Though she can't see her face, Greta gets the sneaking suspicion that she and BDC are having a silent communication. BDC looks past Greta and nods.

Then Miranda speaks: "If you'll excuse me, Greta, I have to get back inside to attend to other members."

Greta turns around and says, "Sure, no problem."

Miranda extends her elegant ring-bedecked hand. Greta resists the impulse to bow and kiss it, and instead gives her an awkward shake. Miranda squeezes tight, too tight. The golden tree ring on her thumb is warm. The roots squirm against Greta's skin. She extracts her hand. The ring is inert, unmoving. She's seeing things again. Miranda turns and disappears through the curtain.

Greta and BDC are alone. Greta sips on her guava nectar, taking in the wallpaper, trying to look casual and relaxed when she's anything but.

BDC goes to open the wall safe for Greta's phone.

"So, only you and Miranda work here? In this huge place?" Greta says, hoping to take BDC by surprise with her question.

"What?" His hand freezes for a moment before continuing to unlock the safe.

"I asked if it was just you and Miranda here. It seems like a lot to handle for two people."

Enveloping her phone with both hands, he says, "Well, there's the Eileens—" He comes to a stop and corrects himself. "I mean, *Eileen*, of course. You met her."

The Eileens?

"Sure, yeah. But I mean *here*, though." She gulps down the last of the juice. "Eileen is in Tribeca."

"Why do you ask?" he says.

"Because I swear I saw someone else in the aisle of the Collection Room."

Regaining his composure, he says matter-of-factly, "The light in here plays tricks on you. Especially after a voyage."

Greta keeps eye contact with him. He doesn't flinch. Yes, that's what Greta had thought at first, too. It had felt so real. *Looked* so real. She can't help but feel that BDC is evading the question.

"Here's your phone, Miss Davenport," Big Daniel Craig says.

"Thank you, um, Daniel."

She checks the time on her phone. It's minutes before midnight. She's been here just under an hour, like clockwork.

BDC unlocks the elaborate apparatus of the vault door; cogs and gears shift and clack. His action indicating that their conversation is over. The door opens with its usual lusty intake of air and the atmosphere shifts. Her thoughts are moving at light speed. She steps into the darkened hallway beyond the interior waiting room.

Her stomach is less jumpy this time. Now it's her brain that's overloading. There are so many things she doesn't understand, so many questions that BDC can't answer—or won't. Greta needs to compare notes with Ezra to see if they're experiencing the same things. Foremost in her mind is the Collector. This terrifying presence looming at the moment of death, the one she's sure she saw in the Collection Room. How can it be? How can any of this be?

Just then, BDC leans in close, his mass a celestial body pulling her into his orbit. He whispers, "Miss Davenport, please be careful what you do in there next time. They can see everything, you know."

He closes the vault door before she can respond. The bare blue light bulb at the end of the hallway beckoning her to the exit and out to civilization.

CHAPTER FORTY-FOUR

"There's something going on in there," Greta says, amped up and breathless, as she approaches Ezra.

He's leaning against the trompe l'oeil mural a couple of blocks away from 273 Water Street. The one with the limestone building and the word ARCADE chiseled into the archway above the painted passageway. Their designated meeting spot.

The rain has stopped. Greta's startled by Ezra's appearance. Like when they first met, only a few nights ago, he seems to be shrinking. The puddles of rain near his feet make it look as though he's melting. This thing they're doing, experiencing the deaths of other people, it's a monster. A big, hungry monster. Ezra and Greta feed it with their personal tragedies. This beast of death is famished and will eat until they're gone. Ezra's been a part of her life for mere days, but Greta has the terrible feeling that he's coming to the end of his line. This man, who she's fallen for, soon will be gone.

If only they'd met sooner.

"What's going on? What do you mean?"

He takes her in his arms and Greta sinks into him, both exhausted and energized. She thinks of BDC's parting words, his last salvo as the vault to the Found Object Society shut. Was he warning her about asking too many questions? Trying to reach into the cubbyhole? Or was it something else?

"A million things. I can't sort them out yet. Can we walk a bit? Head to my place in SoHo this time?" she says.

"Sure. I'll slum it," he says. "What have I got to go home for?"

There's so much weight to those words, yet Greta still doesn't know the full story behind them. She has to let him tell her about his son in his own time. Pushing it would be a mistake.

"Ta-da," he says, and presents her with a carton of coconut water. "Hope you don't mind. I already had some."

"You're a saint," she says, and unscrews the cap.

She takes a swig as they wend their way through the haphazard pattern of blocks in southernmost Manhattan, still turning BDC's words in her mind. After a few blocks of silence, she comes to a sudden stop. There are people around—there always are, no matter the time of day. Strangers flow past Ezra and Greta, rapids surging around two rocks in a river.

"Okay, first off, I think Big Daniel Craig threatened me, or gave me a warning or something when I left," Greta says. Ezra laughs, not the reaction she was expecting. "What? That's funny?"

"No, sorry. Definitely not funny. That name cracks me up every time you say it. *Big Daniel Craig*. It's so apt. That's messed up. What did he say?"

"He opened the vault door for me to leave and then leaned in real close and whispered, 'Be careful what you do in there next time. They can see everything, you know.'" Ezra stops, stunned. "Right? That's crazy, isn't it?" Greta says.

"What's he even talking about? In where? Like during your voyage? Is that it?" Ezra says.

"BDC wasn't specific, but . . ."

"But what? Did you do something in your vessel?" Ezra says.

She did. She *had* done something to her vessel.

That was BDC's warning: She'd broken rule number one of the Found Object Society. She'd manipulated the body of Lassiter Evans.

She looks up at Ezra, her blood effervescing with excitement. "I did. I made him move."

"Are you kidding me? I mean, how? How could you even do that?" Ezra says.

They continue to walk.

"I guess the best way to describe it was like lucid dreaming. Have you ever tried it? You know, if you're being chased by some rabid dog in your dream, try to acknowledge that it isn't real and turn and face the dog and it'll disappear—"

A young couple, laughing and drunk, walk between them, like Ezra and Greta aren't even there.

Ezra rolls his eyes. "Bread and butter," he says to Greta.

She continues. "Right? Anyway, as I was saying, I didn't do anything major, I just became . . . aware? It was like my very being slipped into a glove and the glove was Lassiter Evans. That's the guy who was my vessel. It wasn't much. I kind of jerked his right hand around and made him wave. That was it."

"How did the guy, Lassiter, react?" Ezra asks.

"It wigged him out a bit," Greta says.

"Holy shit. That's crazy. It's never crossed my mind. I mean, I know it's one of the rules to not interfere, that you're a passenger in your voyage, nothing else. I never gave it much thought. Never thought you could do it. Wow."

"Yeah. I mean, it's cool in itself and has me thinking of all the other kinds of things that I can't put into words yet. That's not the main point, though," Greta says, vibrating with exhilaration as they turn onto her block on Greene Street.

"What is, then?" Ezra says.

"The point is what BDC said. He warned me to be careful and that *they* can see everything you do in there. That's what he said." Greta looks for her fob as they stand outside the door to her building.

"So . . . who are *they*?" Ezra says, arriving at the place where Greta's thoughts have gone.

"Exactly," she says. The door clicks open. "Who are *they*?"

CHAPTER FORTY-FIVE

They ride the elevator up to Greta's place in silence, both contemplating the weight of Big Daniel Craig's warning. She unlocks her front door and tosses the keys onto a console table. She never pulled the shades down or bothered to tidy before she rushed out to meet Carl the other night. Greta'd forgotten about her panicked state at the time: ripping her place apart, looking for the invitation for her next death, afraid she'd missed it.

"Shit. Okay, before I turn on the lights, I have to advise you it's kind of a mess in here," she says.

Greta taps up a dimmer, the rough terrain of overturned couch and throw pillows coming into focus like a sunrise.

"Jesus. And I thought I'd let things go," Ezra says.

"I know, I know," she says as she attempts to tidy up the pillows and strewn junk mail. "I kinda lost it when I got back here after, well, you know, after your place. I was worried I'd missed my next invitation, so I tossed the apartment."

"A junkie searching for her spoon. I hear you," Ezra says. He sounds exhausted. "How do you lower the blinds?"

Greta points to a remote on the wall and he activates them with a touch. They slide down, giving them privacy, something that doesn't matter at Ezra's place, where the only possible voyeurs are seagulls and pigeons.

"What's the point of waiting for an invitation, anyway?" Greta says. "It's so much pomp. I mean, we *know* we can come back in three days, right? Can't they pull up the calendar on their iPad or whatever, save someone the hassle of delivering the invitation? Skip the drama?"

"I guess that's not how it works," Ezra says.

"It pisses me off. I mean, come on."

Ezra doesn't respond.

Greta shrugs and opens the fridge, scanning without really looking. She's winding herself up and she shouldn't, but she's paid five hundred thousand goddamned dollars for this and she expects an opening every three days, as promised. Is that so hard? Money gets you to the front of the line, period. Why a mysterious invitation every time? She gets the first couple. *Fine*. They were part of the whole spectacle. Sure, it's super clever and cool—congratulations—but to have to wait days for another square to float through her door when she knows damned well that it'll be in seventy-two hours seems like a lot of unnecessary pageantry.

Greta's all tweaky again. She needs to relax. Forces are at work at the Found Object Society that go way beyond her understanding. If it makes them feel good to deliver a secretive, coded card to her before each voyage, so be it—whatever. The society isn't a nightclub or top-rated restaurant she can bully her way into. *Just breathe.*

She leans away from the fridge. There's not much in there: a few half-consumed bottles of wine; a wedge of cheese that may or may not have started off as moldy; a couple of cartons of leftover Chinese food from the last time she was here.

"I don't have much to offer you, Ezra. Sorry. Want me to order anything in or what?"

Ezra doesn't answer. He's standing in front of the windows and staring straight out—but the shades are down. His eyes are vacant, as though there's a view in the opaque blinds only he can see.

"Ezra?"

"I'm not hungry," he says, eyes fixed forward. "I'm never hungry anymore. Not since this all started."

Closing the refrigerator, Greta navigates around the strewn detritus of her apartment and puts her arms around him from behind, leaning her body into his. "You okay?" she says.

He turns around and faces her, reciprocating her embrace. "Nope. I am one hundred percent *not* okay. How about you?"

"Completely fucked, yeah. What've we gotten ourselves into?"

They lie facing each other on her messy bed, fully clothed. Neither of them sleeping. Tired beyond belief, yet the engine of addiction fires on autopilot in the background.

Ezra is her partner—her enabler—in this madness. Well, that's unfair. She's enabling him, too. With each voyage he takes, each death he experiences, he's being whittled away to nothing. Maybe that's what they both want: to carve themselves down until all that remains is the space they once occupied. To float. To find their way back to those they've lost. This is their punishment for the deaths of those closest to them. Greta's parents. Ezra's son.

Greta's always taken chances with her reckless lifestyle, and now, every three days, the Found Object Society has given her the opportunity to die—over and over. Both of her deaths have been so . . . pathetic. The torment of unrequited love for Zephyrine. Lassiter's existential loneliness and need for attention. The deaths of other people, not her own. And what about Ezra? His body count is what? Eight? Nine? When does it end?

Will either of them say *enough*? Once more, she wishes they'd met sooner, under different circumstances.

There's something else happening here that Greta needs to identify. The Found Object Society is more than a rich person's amusement—at least for her. She wants to find out who's behind it, who *they* are, who the unearthly figure is at the moment of death. The same one she's positive she saw in the Collection Room tonight.

Greta traces Ezra's hand with her index finger, runs along the deep lines of his palm. His skin so dark next to her pale, translucent hand, blue veins running beneath the surface.

"I think I've seen who *they* are. Or one of *them*, anyway. Well, I mean, maybe. It's a bit insane," she says.

"Who?" Ezra says, drowsy, eyes glassy.

"I sensed it after my first voyage. It wasn't until this second one that I was more sure. At the point of death, have you ever noticed anything in there with you? Someone, some*thing* that didn't belong?"

"Like an anachronism?"

"In a way? But not like a laptop in eighteenth-century Scotland kind of way. More of a presence," Greta says.

Ezra closes his eyes. She can't tell if he's thinking or drifting off to sleep. He opens them again and says, "No. I mean, that's kind of like asking me to do the multiplication table at the moment of orgasm. The moment my vessel dies, that's the . . ." Ezra swallows hard. He seems reluctant to follow his train of thought.

"The what?" Greta says.

Ezra exhales. "The rush. It's the rush. The pinnacle. Anything else, I don't see. Can't see. And then when I'm out, those three days? Well, that's biding my time until the next voyage."

The comment stings and Greta lets go of his hand. He reaches back, touches her face.

"That's not what I meant, Greta. It came out wrong. Being with you is not biding my time between voyages. Not at all. In fact, you're what keeps me going. Most of the time I wish all that was left of me were in one of those objects on the Found Object Society shelves. My life a carnival ride for rich assholes like us, so they can see how miserable my last days were. The only thing I'm living for out here is you. Please know that. Please."

He kisses her. She knows. She does. Because it's the same for her, this feeling of being lost and without worth, awash in regret for twenty years.

"I do. I promise," she says.

"You were saying? That you've seen something in your death that doesn't fit?"

"I have. I saw it again tonight, not only at the end of my voyage, but in one of the aisles of the Collection Room. I'm almost positive."

Greta tells Ezra about the arm unspooling in the pond, reaching into the silt for the perfume bottle in Zephyrine's inert hand; of the lanky figure following Lassiter's mom as she tumbled down the stairs to help her son, how it lifted the Elton John glasses from him. She talks about tonight, the crash of an object deep in the bowels of the Collection Room, and how a tall shadow bent over to pick it up before fading into the black. BDC's odd slip when he said *the Eileens.*

"So . . . the Found Object Society is run by phantoms? Wraiths? Tolkien?" Ezra says. "Several women named Eileen?"

"That does sound bananas. No, I'm not saying that. Not exactly, anyway. Shit, I don't know, Ezra. I'm just saying that's what I've seen—a shadowy, almost fluid black being waiting at the end for the person to die so they can collect the object and bring it back to the society. And that I'm almost sure that I saw one of them drop an object as it was *restocking* the shelves," Greta says. "Then it disappeared."

"Well, someone—or some*thing*—has to collect the objects, right? There needs to be *the Collector*, as you put it—or many of them. They don't just buy the stuff on Amazon. So, sure, why not a phantasm or gang of them dispersed across the Earth, waiting for people to die, instructed by humans—or vice versa, even? Who knows?"

Greta's not sure if he's mocking her. He looks deep into her eyes and continues.

"I get that's what you've seen, Greta, and it's as possible as any of the rest of this. Does it matter, though? Do you really care who or what's involved?"

Greta thinks about that. Does she?

"I suppose I do. Maybe there's a reason that I'm seeing *it*, or *them*. Maybe there's a good reason I was able to become lucid in my last death."

The cogs shift in the engine room of Greta's subconscious again: getting closer to locking into place and giving the Found Object Society a meaning beyond pure entertainment and an unquenchable high. She wades through the morass of dopamine and serotonin, searching for clarity.

Then it comes to her, a stark bell ringing on a clear and still night: She was able to break through and control Lassiter's body, at one point. What if she takes it further? What if she defies the rules and goes beyond being a passenger in her voyages, and takes the wheel instead? Changing the outcome of a person's death.

What if she could go back and stop what happened to her parents?

PART FOUR

Found Object #3
Origin: North America, Central United States,
Early 20th Century

CHAPTER FORTY-SIX

"I don't know what happened to Jake, my son. Not exactly." Ezra's voice startles Greta back from the place of half sleep.

It's the middle of the night—the abyss that waits in the dark, orbiting and landing in the mind when all else is still. They're lying on their sides, face-to-face, and fully clothed. Sex is way on the back burner of their voyage-depleted bodies. Greta had been trying to work through the idea of controlling the outcome of a person's death, and if it's something she's even capable of. If she is, can she use that ability to change what happened on that night twenty years ago? What would be the consequences of doing that? She'd drifted toward sleep before she could get very far, the bits of thoughts elusive, slipping away.

Ezra's comment has taken her by surprise. Greta's treaded carefully with Ezra about his son. This is the first time he's uttered his name.

"Jake," she says. "Your son's name was Jake?"

He nods. She adjusts her body and rests a hand on his warm forearm. Greta wants him to know she's awake, present—listening to whatever it is Ezra needs to tell her.

"I'd always loved being on the water, near the water. I grew up by the Jersey Shore, and my dad would take me fishing, but always from a dock or pier, lakeside or casting into the surf—never a boat. Neither of my parents could swim, so getting onto a boat was not an option. My father feared the water. I wasn't about to inherit that trait. There weren't many Black kids at my school and I wanted to fit in with the cool crowd, which was mostly white. I was not going to be the Black kid who couldn't swim. I took swim classes on the sly and became a good swimmer, a really good one. I was even on the swim team in high school and at Stanford."

He pauses and looks at Greta. She encourages him with a slight nod.

"In the summer, I'd visit frat brothers on the Cape or in the Hamptons. They grew up with sailing in their blood and taught me the ropes: jibing, tacking, taking the helm. I belonged. It was exhilarating. The older we got, the more successful we all got. We had fancy cars, second homes. *They* also had boats—sailboats, fishing boats. The logical next step was for me to get one. By then, I was married and Jake was a toddler. I trained for my captain's license. I was careful, diligent. A responsible sailor. We had a house in Sag Harbor and went for family outings on Long Island Sound. It was everything I'd dreamed of being—becoming—as a kid. I'd not only overcome my parents' fear of the water, I'd learned to conquer it.

"We were coming up on Jake's sixth birthday and he wanted to have an overnight sailing trip just with me. His daddy. Teresa—my now ex-wife—was against it. The idea of us on the water alone at night scared her. Finally, she caved. She knew I was cautious, and I promised we wouldn't go out into the open sea, that we'd stay close to shore on the Sound. We'd anchor somewhere safe and calm. And that's what we did."

Ezra's words freeze in his throat. Greta squeezes his arm, lets him know he's safe.

"It was the perfect spring day, the right amount of wind, clear skies, no threat of bad weather. Jake was so excited. We packed up all our supplies, and I snuck a bottle of wine into my bag since we'd be anchored and I wouldn't have to sail again until morning. On the dock, Teresa secured Jake's life vest and gave him a last hug. She trusted me, but I could still see she was worried. I told her we'd be fine."

Ezra stops talking and rolls onto his back, staring up at Greta's bedroom ceiling. Should she say something? She anticipates the terrible place where this story will land, because hers has the same ending.

"You know where this is going," Ezra says.

"I think I do. You don't have to tell me more if you don't want to."

A tear rolls from his eye, reflecting the bits of streetlight sneaking in through the shades.

"I haven't repeated this for a long time. Not since the police questioned me—over and over." Ezra takes a deep breath.

"We'd had a great day and evening. I taught Jake how to tack and steer with both our hands on the helm. In the lower cabin we had a dining area, a kitchenette, and two sleeping berths, one across from the other. I anchored us in a protected cove. A couple of other boats were overnighting not far from us. It was safe. Jake had his life vest on at all times—even during dinner. We played checkers before bed and Jake fell asleep with a checker piece clutched in his hand. When it was time to sleep, we took the vest off so he'd be comfortable. Besides, the only place he'd go was the bathroom in the cabin. There was nothing for me to worry about.

"I tucked him in and took my then half-empty bottle of wine up to the deck. The stars were out. There was no moon. An hour later, I was tipsy and exhausted and went down to bed. I latched the cabin door behind me—I was positive. Jake was asleep, and I leaned in and gave my son a kiss on the forehead. His breath was sweet like grass. That's the last time I saw him."

Ezra had looked familiar to Greta when they first met, and now she understands why. It wasn't just because they were both filthy rich, no. Five years ago, Ezra Somers had been headline news.

"I woke with a start a couple of hours later. Not sure why, but I had to pee. I came back from the tiny bathroom and lay back down. Through my wine and sleep fog, I noticed light coming down into the cabin. The cabin door was ajar, which was weird. I got up to relatch it, when a stab of panic hit my gut. I rushed back to Jake's bed and saw he wasn't in it. I called his name—no answer. I ran up to the deck and he wasn't there. I looked out at the Sound and it was flat—a stretch of black linoleum from the boat to the shore. I called his name again and grabbed a flashlight. I shone it all around the deck and ran back into the cabin, turning on the lights. Jake was nowhere.

"His life vest was where we had left it on the dining chair. His bed was still a little warm and the checker piece was under his pillow. This couldn't be happening. Jake would never just get up and go out on the deck alone. He'd sleepwalked a couple of times before, no big deal. Yet, he was gone. Panicked, I started yelling his name. I sent out a Mayday call on the ship-to-ship radio saying that I feared my son had fallen overboard. I called 9-1-1 on my cell phone and dove into the icy Sound. I kept diving into the frigid, black water. I followed the chain of the anchor as far down as I could until I thought my lungs would burst. Hypothermia was setting in. I could barely move my arms and legs. Someone pulled me from the water and back onto the deck of my boat. If Jake was in the water, how long could his tiny body last? Where was he? What was happening to him?

"By that time, other boats had heard my distress call and approached—floodlights shone into the water all around us. A flotilla of coast guards and boaters surrounded our sailboat trying to help. Helicopters flew overheard, searchlights arcing across the water. Jake was gone without a trace. Crowds gathered on the shore. After a few hours, I was being towed back to the dock. I couldn't think or talk, let alone operate the boat. Teresa was waiting there, in the same spot where we'd left her twelve hours earlier. I was the only one disembarking. Jake was gone."

Five years ago, Ezra's story was all over the news. Greta recalls the details now, the heartbreaking photos. One in particular of Ezra on his knees on the dock, staring out across the water. A coast guard boat blurred in the distance. Thinking about the photographer who dared take that picture at Ezra's darkest moment infuriates her now that she knows him. Now that she's falling for him. The tabloids had been filled with salacious headlines. A father-and-son trip at sea gone wrong. Suspicions swirled around Ezra: the negligent father; some witnesses claiming to have smelled alcohol on his breath; not-so-subtle allusions that Jake's disappearance was related to this successful businessman's *Blackness*. Ultimately, it was determined to have been no more than a tragic accident. The story faded, like they all do. Jake's body was never recovered.

Ezra's son truly was *lost*. Lost at sea. Greta used the same word to apply to the deaths of her parents. It's the word that dances around what you really mean—*dead*, *died*. Jake was *lost* in the truest sense.

Which is worse? Greta's grisly memory of coming to in the back seat of her parents' car, being showered with broken glass and blood, her parents' bodies contorted and pressed into the windshield? Or Ezra, not knowing what happened to little Jake? Jake's fate was left to Ezra's imagination: his son, floating in the water, sinking to the sandy floor of the Long Island Sound, the parental tide rocking him back and forth, blue crabs and bottom-feeders having their way with him. It's unbearable to think about.

Ezra's experience is a transfusion from his veins into Greta's. Part of her is angry with him for sharing it. There's a finite amount of space inside of her for heartache and loss. Their shared tragedies are a contagion that consumes them. The Found Object Society is the pathogen that feeds the spread of their terminal illness. Ezra's shrinking with each voyage makes sense now. Layers of him sloughing away, until soon, there'll be nothing left.

Greta's always walked past the skeletal people with substance-use disorders in front of the methadone clinics with disdain: thought of them as inhuman, vapid creatures, skin wrapped tight around their bones, cheekbones threatening to break through as they lurch to a stop in the middle of the sidewalk, a soda can in hand as they drift forward in a trance, their batteries drained on the busy sidewalk as people like Greta hurry past them.

The erosion of Ezra isn't all that different from those sidewalk drifters. Like Ezra, they once had lives, too, people who loved them. Greta's lying to herself if she thinks she's much different. With every voyage, Greta's eroding, too.

"I'm so sorry, Ezra," Greta says. "When we first met, you looked familiar, but I didn't make the connection. I can't even . . . I don't know what to say."

It's true. What words can soothe him at this point?

"Nothing to say. You're the only person I could—I wanted to—tell this to in five years," he says. He sits up, propping himself with pillows. "This time of night is the worst, you know?"

"Oh, I know. Dark thoughts crawling out of the woodwork," she says.

He scoops his arm under her back and pulls Greta close. She maneuvers herself and straddles him, stroking his face with her hands.

He leans forward to kiss her. "Can we make it go away? I need it to go away . . . at least for a little while."

Drunk with exhaustion, they peel away each other's clothes and, for as long as they can, get lost in one another's bodies. They unearth something other than pain, the one thing long unfamiliar to either of them, the only salve for this barren night: a thing close to love.

CHAPTER FORTY-SEVEN

B*uzz-buzz. Buzz-buzz.*

Greta blinks life into her desiccated eyeballs. It feels like all her bodily fluids have been sucked out of her. The ache in her joints suggests the waking moments of a much older woman.

Buzz-buzz. Buzz-buzz.

The sound doesn't register at first. Her brain can't make the connection. *My cell phone.* Her phone vibrates across the nightstand like a beetle. They must've fallen asleep. Who the hell knows what time it is now? Since the Found Object Society came into her life, Greta's habits have devolved—up all hours of the night, sleeping through the day. A general fuckup.

Buzz-buzz. Buzz-buzz.

She sits up, woozy. Ezra's no longer beside her. She hears the shower running. Picking up the phone, she sees that it's Lis calling. She can't keep blowing her off. She wants to, but she can't.

Greta clears her throat, tries to make it sound like she isn't just waking up at one o'clock in the afternoon. "Hey, Lis. I was about to call you."

"Sure, I bet you were. What's up with your voice? You sound like my grandmother."

Greta reaches for the glass of water next to the bed. It's empty. "Dry, that's all. Let me get some water."

She walks from the bedroom to the kitchen and hears Ezra shut off the shower. Greta cradles the phone in the crook of her neck and fills her glass from the faucet. She chugs it down and fills it again.

"Sorry about that," Greta says.

"Oh, no problemo. I could listen to you gulping water in my ear all day. You wanna eat a sandwich while you're at it? Or open up a bag of chips? Chomp an apple, maybe?" Lis says. Sarcastic Lis, in full effect.

"You're hilarious. What's up?" Greta says.

"Don't *what's up* me. You know damn well I've texted and called you. You've disappeared again. Is it that guy? *Whatshisname?*" Lis says.

It's the joke they've used for years. Whenever there's a new guy in the picture, they call him Whatshisname. The boyfriends have always been disposable, not worth naming, but Greta and Lis? They're BFFs. This is different. Ezra is different.

"His *name* is Ezra, Lis."

"Right, Ezra. You told me that last time we talked. Nice name. Everything okay with you?"

Last time they spoke, Greta knew the details she gave about Ezra—his apartment, the sex—could only appease Lis for so long. The fuel from her story is down to vapors and Greta has to tank her friend up again.

An ant crawls across Greta's kitchen island and stops to test the air. Greta's thrust back into Lassiter's mind, the last minutes of his life: chasing after Janine, trying to explain that things weren't what they seemed—even though they were; how he'd wanted to tell her he wasn't going to kill her after all, that he liked her and would never hurt her; the little fires exploding over his body, the electric shocks he felt with each toxic ant bite; the entity that followed Lassiter's mother down the stairs—the same one that was in the water at the bottom of the pond with Zephyrine.

Greta smashes the ant with her palm and flicks it into the garbage disposal.

"Are you there?" Lis says.

"Yeah, I'm here. Uh, I'm fine. Yes, everything is A-OK with me."

"Perfect. Then you'll have no problem meeting me at Balthazar for dinner tonight. In fact, let's invite Ezra. I'd love to meet him. You're in the city, right? I assume you are, since you weren't at home when I went by this morning."

"You went by my house?" Greta says.

It's a perfectly acceptable thing for Lis to have done. No reason to get riled up. The two of them pop by each other's places unannounced all the time, have for years, no invitation needed. This time, though, it feels like a violation. Lis is getting clingy, annoying. Why won't she just let her live her life?

"You could have called first," Greta says.

"That's a joke, right? What's wrong with you, G? Since when do I—or *you*, for that matter—need to call before we come over?"

Greta's ragged. "Maybe it's time we start acting like grown-ups and not *show up* unannounced. How would that be?"

"Where's this coming from? Look, I've tried to call you. Repeatedly. I've called, texted, and you haven't bothered to respond. Ever since the gala, you've been acting crazy. I haven't wanted to say anything, but when I came over to your house last time and we had coffee—sorry, *tea*—it was like you'd become a different person. Don't play dumb, Greta. I know when you're lying. I know you better than anyone. Something's going on here, and it's not good. Is it Ezra? Are you doing blow again? Is that it?"

Greta snaps. "Why? Because he's Black? Is that why you think I'm doing coke again?" As soon as she says it, she realizes how unhinged her comment must sound.

"What the fuck are you even talking about? *I've never met him*. Remember? I don't know what he looks like. I don't give a shit what color he is. I can't believe you'd accuse me of something like that."

Greta can't take back what she said. This conversation is spiraling out of control, like everything else in Greta's life. She's accusing her best friend in the world of being a racist? Lis hasn't even met him. It's absurd. Embarrassing.

"Right. Right. I'm sorry, I know that. I can't talk anymore. I just . . . give me some time to work some things out. Okay?"

Lis is silent.

"Okay, Lis?"

"Fine. Whatever," Lis says.

"We okay, Lis? Lis?"

Greta looks at her phone screen. Lis is gone. She's hung up on her.

"Goddammit," Greta says.

She tosses the phone onto the kitchen island. Two more ants are exploring the marble landscape. Greta smashes them both, bludgeoning them more violently than necessary. Ezra is standing in the doorway to Greta's bedroom, a towel around his waist.

"Uh . . . did I miss something?" he says.

Greta startles.

"It sounds like you were discussing my . . . *Blackness*?"

Greta tightens the belt of her robe. One of the ant carcasses is stuck to her palm. She wipes it off on a dishcloth. "No, I'm just an under-caffeinated asshole, that's all. I was talking to my best friend, Lis. She *was* my best friend, at least, until she hung up on me. I should never have answered the phone."

"I'm sorry," Ezra says.

He pulls Greta close. Drops of water are peppered across his eucalyptus-tinged skin, the towel around his waist, damp. Their bodies connect against cloth. An insistent tingle pushes her farther into him. Having a physical need beyond waiting for her next voyage is a pleasant change of pace.

Entwined, they make their way back to Greta's bedroom. Ezra's towel falls to the floor and Greta unwraps herself from her silk robe. Who cares if it's one o'clock in the afternoon on a Monday? Calls can wait—texts and emails. Any responsibilities can be delayed, canceled, put on hold. All that matters is Ezra and her need for him.

This is Greta's life now: Ezra and death. Ezra and death. Rinse, repeat.

So why waste her time placating the likes of Lis, or anyone else?

CHAPTER FORTY-EIGHT

Greta's been hunched over her laptop for hours.

The falling-out with Lis has set wheels in motion. She can't tell Lis the truth about the Found Object Society. It's not an option. Severing ties is the only way to keep her friend safe if the threat to Lis that day in the kitchen is to be taken seriously. If Greta's theory that she can alter the outcome of a voyage is right, then what's happening now is bigger than friendship. It could change everything. It's insane.

The Found Object Society has been the most addictive, mysterious, and immersive experience of her life. That's all that's mattered. That is, until her voyage with Lassiter. Now that Greta believes it may be a means to an end, neither the delectable high nor the *what* and *who* of the society matter so much anymore. If she could alter the outcome of her parents' accident? Well, that would eclipse everything.

Greta's always had excellent dream recall. Lucid dreaming had come up in a lecture at college once and it stuck with her. Her psych textbooks are long gone, but with the magic of Google, Greta's devouring as much information about dream awareness as she can. Lucid dreaming used to be thought of as hokey, lumped together with the healing powers of crystals. Books about it were few and stacked beneath macramé dream catchers in shops that reeked of patchouli.

Of course, the Found Object Society isn't about dreaming; it's about dying. Even so, Greta hopes to apply the same principles of becoming lucid in a dream to becoming aware within the mind of the person who's about to die, and then to play with the outcome. It's far-fetched, sure, but the society's very existence defies explanation. Why not take it further? Game the system?

Lucid dreaming doesn't come naturally—you need to train for it. And today, Greta's discovered several methods for lucidity in the sleep state. The one that makes the most sense is the MILD technique, which stands for *mnemonic induction of lucid dreams*. It requires you to wake after five or six hours of sleep and repeat this mantra before falling back asleep: *Next time I'm dreaming, I will remember I'm dreaming.* Greta has to pee at least once a night, so this could work. Sleep's been anything but regular lately. She'll just have to figure it out. If she can at least have a trial run before her next voyage, that should be enough.

Ezra went home to leave her to her studies. They promised they'd both attempt to eat some real food, to take care of themselves. Greta's not holding up her end of the bargain. Her stomach growls in protest.

Greta could tell the conversation they'd had before he left had rattled Ezra. He'd been skeptical of Greta's plan to take control on her next voyage.

"Are you sure you want to mess with this? What if it's dangerous? Big Daniel Craig said *they* see everything. What if you get kicked out?" he'd said.

"I know. I've thought of that. It's a big risk. Bribe my way back in? I haven't gotten that far. It's all hypothetical. I can't get it out of my mind, Ezra. I'm going to do some more research, but if I can become lucid, and play with the outcome of my next voyage, I mean, the implications of that . . ."

She sat on the edge of the bed and Ezra knelt down on the floor in front of her.

"Look at me," he said. He took her hands in his, imploring her to focus on him. "I know what you're thinking: You want to see if you can change what happened in the crash with your parents. I get it. I want nothing more than to go back to that night on the boat, to throw that bottle of wine overboard and make sure I latched the door of the cabin, to make sure that Jake was safe. God, to even know *what* happened to my son, where he went. To know more, beyond the fact that he simply disappeared without a trace. As far as I know, I can't do that. Even if you can become lucid, Greta, how can that be applied in your parents' accident? The Found Object Society is sick entertainment for rich jerks like us. It's the closest I can come to the realm of where my son might be. So maybe, when the time comes for me to actually die, I'll be ready."

Death is what they're barreling toward, isn't it? The living world no longer holds appeal for either of them. Death is the thing. It's what they crave. Death is the addiction.

"How do you plan to even go on their voyage? It's not like they'll just have an object from the crash on the shelf in the Collection Room, right?" he said.

That's what Greta'd been thinking about. The gears that had been grinding in the back of her subconscious for days had finally locked together. It was then that the big picture appeared to her, the solution.

"They won't," she said, thinking of the shoebox hidden in the bowels of her closet. The one that held mementos of her parents and their life together—and one thing in particular from that awful night. "You're right. That's why I'm going to bring the object to them."

CHAPTER FORTY-NINE

Greta's lucid-dream training has been a blessing. Unlike the last time, her gnawing anticipation of receiving her next invitation from the Found Object Society has taken a back seat to her research and attempts at reaching awareness during REM sleep.

And when the invitation arrives under her door that Tuesday night at the Greene Street loft, she's ready. Readyish. Ezra had assured her that the society will find her to deliver the invitation no matter where she is, and that she needn't go back to Litchfield and wait. The Found Object Society never ceases to defy logic.

So, instead, she's stayed put in SoHo. She feels like Sarah Connor getting jacked up, working her guns in *Terminator 2*, preparing for battle with the machines. Only instead of doing sets of pull-ups she's getting out of bed at four o'clock in the morning and muttering to herself, "Next time I'm dreaming, I will remember I'm dreaming. Next time I'm dreaming, I will remember I'm dreaming."

Glowering on the dining table next to her sits the square-shaped invite for her third voyage at the Found Object Society. Like the rest, its QR code hides in the textured pulp of the otherworldly black paper. The scan of her camera phone connects with the Bitly link, then hurtles her through a pulse-pounding animation, traveling past stars and galaxies and coming to a stop in the vacuum of space, followed by the AI voice welcoming her back to the basement of Water Street on Wednesday night at ten thirty.

She strokes the card's surface and continues her incantation: *Next time I'm dreaming, I will remember I'm dreaming. Next time I'm dreaming, I will remember I'm dreaming.*

Tonight, Greta's alone; both she and Ezra are gathering their collective strength for their return to the Found Object Society. Ezra still thinks Greta should leave well enough alone and not mess with a technology they don't understand. Even though they've been together for less than a week, he knows not to impede her plan, however implausible.

Greta pushes back the memory of BDC's warning from when she left after her second voyage. The one where she first tinkered with this idea of being the puppeteer, a hijacker: *Be careful what you do in there next time. They can see everything, you know.* Tomorrow night, she'll not only disregard his veiled threat—she'll take it a step further. Damn the consequences.

It's a risk. But not trying? That's worse. Ezra may be content to keep going back for voyage after voyage until there's nothing left of him, but not Greta. This is an opportunity she won't back away from. She needs to give it a shot. What does she have to lose?

If she finds she can control the person—the *vessel*—of her voyage, then what? Is she altering the outcome of history? Or are these voyages simply isolated spools of cerebral film that feel realer-than-real? Replayed like Netflix for any rich schmuck who drops half a mil to watch them, their outcome a fait accompli. Greta had messed with Lassiter. She *had*. She heard his thoughts when she made his hand twitch and wave. It scared him. Lassiter had been afraid it might happen again. Had Greta's actions tweaked the outcome of her voyage? Of his death?

There are so many questions. In all likelihood, there are no specific answers. Maybe each voyage has tangents, parallels of possible lives and versions of everyone.

Damn, Greta's going too deep. She needs to keep her eyes on the lucid-dream prize and stop asking questions at four in the morning about things there are no answers for. Not unless she's Stephen Hawking—or maybe God. Her mind is running, and she's not only jittery and craving her next voyage; she's also trying to figure out the meaning of life—death. She's in way over her pay grade.

Greta needs to do this, to try. Her mother and father deserve at least that much. If nothing else, she needs to do this for her own sanity.

"Next time I'm dreaming, I will remember I'm dreaming. Next time I'm dreaming, I will remember I'm dreaming," she says.

Greta kicks off her slippers and they land on the floor. An image comes back to her: the man's shoe in the cabin, the door ajar, the flare of white light, Miranda calling it *maintenance*.

"Stop it, Greta. Stay focused," she says.

She crawls back into her bed and closes her eyes. The mantra is the thing. It's the only thing.

Her training and repeated refrain of *Next time I'm dreaming, I will remember I'm dreaming* is paying off. It's working. Greta's pushed out all her other worries and concerns. She's dreaming and lucid.

She's in a vape shop like the one she and Ezra walked into the first night they met. The space is tight, glassed-in shelves with tiny cubbyholes containing bongs and pipes of every shape, size, and color. A man is behind the counter, protected by plexiglass. He's seated, but she can see he's wearing one of BDC's suits: a jacket of ornate paisley silk with a matching vest. Underneath, a yellow-stained *I ♥ NY* T-shirt peeks out. He's watching TV. She can't tell what.

Greta catches her reflection in the glass case.

She stops cold. It's the version of herself that she saw in the security footage from her driveway when she first set up the trail cam. The gaunt woman who faced the camera, mouthing a phrase over and over that Greta couldn't decipher. It's clear now. Obvious.

Her reflection is saying, *Next time I'm dreaming, I will remember I'm dreaming.*

A quaking starts in her chest and lungs as the words spill from her own mouth. The Greta who is standing in the vape shop is saying it out loud.

"Next time I'm dreaming, I will remember I'm dreaming."

"What did you say?" the guy behind the counter asks.

Greta's dreaming. She's aware that she's in a dream. She's done it. The thread holding her between the dream world and consciousness is delicate as spun sugar. She has to tread carefully, to will herself to stay here as long as possible so she can test her abilities.

She turns to face the man behind the plexiglass panel and says, "I'm dreaming. You're in my dream right now."

"Fuck off. You're drunk," he says, and goes back to the TV.

Greta walks over to him and puts her hands against the plastic wall that separates them. "You're not real, dude. What're you watching?"

"If I'm not real, why are you talking to me? Buy something or get out," he says.

Greta's in control. This is her mind, *hers*. She hesitates for a moment, then reaches through the plexiglass, as if it were air, and toward the man's TV. On-screen is an ancient tree next to a brick house. It glows from within, its anaconda-like roots twisted and piercing the ground and into the foundation, rats scurrying past. In the background, the sound of horse hooves on cobblestones. It's 273 Water Street as it must have appeared when Kit Burns lived there.

"Whoa, whoa! You can't do that, lady." He switches off the TV. "You're batshit. I'm calling the cops."

Then he's gone. The entire vape shop has disappeared and Greta is standing barefoot on her driveway, holding her phone. The app for her security cam is open.

This is weird. Greta didn't will *this* to happen, but at least she's lucid and knows this isn't reality, that she's asleep. She'll be ready for tomorrow.

She looks back at her phone and a video is playing. There's a high-pitched screech and a momentary, grainy blue static. It's nighttime. In the frame is the rear of a car, a partial license plate visible. Greta looks up with a start. Is she in the video?

Parked in front of her is her parents' car. The one from the crash. An older Connecticut license plate, the first three symbols are *T3R*, the rest *6614*. A triangle of light splashes onto the gravel, flaring out the image until it settles. Murphy Brown runs out and turns around as if someone is calling to her. The cat's eyes glow in the night vision. Two shadows etch across the light. One moves forward, toward the cat.

Greta closes her eyes tight and shouts, "I will remember I'm dreaming! I will remember I'm dreaming!"

CHAPTER FIFTY

"Promise me you'll be careful in there tonight," Ezra says.

They're standing at their spot in front of the trompe l'oeil mural in the South Street Seaport; the fake Brooklyn Bridge is placid behind them, while the real one roars with cars and buses in the distance.

"I will, Ezra. I've got this," Greta says.

She sounds confident, but inside she's freaking out over her dream last night. It was like a fun-house mirror: that ghastly tree outside of nineteenth-century 273 Water Street; the reflection of herself from the video of a week ago, mouthing words that she couldn't decipher at the time, a mantra that she didn't discover until *two days ago*; then back home in her driveway, her parents' car on a video screen, and then, right in front of her, Murphy Brown, the silhouettes, one of them walking forward.

It's too overwhelming to contemplate.

Her plan to become lucid is solid, though. Kind of. What the fuck does she have to lose, anyway?

Greta reaches her arms under Ezra's blazer and around his waist, pulling him close. She can't get enough of the smell of him. It's as addictive as her voyages—*almost*.

"Aren't you even a little curious about what you could do in there instead of being a passenger?" she says.

Ezra presses his cheek against hers and squeezes her back hard, whispering, "No, Greta. I'm okay with being along for the ride."

"Okay," she says. "I just think—"

His kiss stops the words from coming out of her mouth.

"I'll see you here when you come back, okay?" he says. He pulls away and looks at her, through her. Greta gets the chilling sense that this is the end of something, that they're up against a wall.

"What is it?" she says.

He sighs. "Nothing. Nothing. I was . . . I was just thinking that if I was a different me, well, *that* me would be telling you 'I love you' right now."

Him *not* telling her says more than anyone else has ever said before. Him not saying *I love you* is the most love she's felt from a person who wasn't her parent. She knows exactly what he means.

He points to the mural, to the Brooklyn side of the river painted on it. "That version of me would invite you to Jane's Carousel with me and Jake. It was his favorite."

Wouldn't that Ezra still be married? Does it matter? She knows what he's trying to say. Greta thinks back to the first night they met, walking across the bridge, and the pall that passed over his face as he looked down at the darkened carousel below.

"A different me is saying 'I love you, too,' Ezra. And I'd be honored to join you both there. I would."

He kisses her again, long, hard. "Okay then. It's a date. I hope we're all very happy together," he says.

"Me too," Greta says.

Ezra walks toward his next voyage at the Found Object Society. As Greta waits her turn for her third death, she scans the intricate illusion of the Richard Haas mural. For the first time, she notices in the detailed folds of one of the curtained windows a hand, pulling it open.

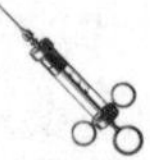

Greta watches Big Daniel Craig place her phone in the hidden wall safe.

The Found Object Society's whole cachet is their secrecy. Membership is only offered to the wealthy and elite. What's *cachet* if no one knows about you? This isn't velvet-rope stuff, though. There are underlying forces within this subterranean acid trip that can't be legal. Add the phantomlike Collector into the mix and you've got some real *Ghost Hunters* shit going on.

And here Greta is, in the midst of it, preparing to break the rules. Like when driving drunk, she's testing the boundaries. Only with this, the outcome isn't as predictable as wrapping her car around a tree.

As if reading her mind, BDC clears his throat to get her attention. She looks over at him.

He says with a smile, "And how have you been, Miss Davenport?"

While he's smiling and talking, he's also tapping one of his giant sausage fingers onto rule number one on the placard of House Rules:

Interfering or tampering with the vessel of your voyage is strictly prohibited. You are a passenger ONLY. This rule will be enforced to its full extent.

He gives her a subtle nod, emphasizing his actions, not his words. Greta tries not to look as rattled as his gesture and subsequent nod have made her feel. Does the Found Object Society know what she's planning?

She hurries over to him and puts her hand on his thigh-size forearm, whispering, "What are you trying to tell me?"

The menthol of his breath burns her cheek, he's so close. "Leave well enough alone, miss. It could be dangerous. You're not the—"

Before he can finish his sentence, Miranda sweeps through the velvet curtains. Greta and Big Daniel Craig step apart, acting nonchalant.

If Miranda saw them conspiring, she's not letting it show. She's a chiaroscuro of satiny crimson, bosom, and cheekbones. With every meeting, she takes Greta's breath away. It's hard to picture Miranda anywhere but here in this opulent basement, doling out death like Halloween candy, sending the entitled rich off into the ether to die. *Bon voyage, dickheads.* What does Miranda's apartment look like? Does she ever scamper off to Equinox in her yoga leggings? Men and women alike collapsing around her, poisoned by her beauty.

Like the Found Object Society itself, Miranda's too much. A genetic improbability.

"Good evening, Ms. Davenport. Welcome back," she says. There's a chill in her voice Greta can't help but notice. Maybe she did see them talking? Still, she extends her elegant, multi-ringed hand to shake Greta's unmanicured one. The tree on Miranda's thumb is glowing, alive—like the one on the TV screen in her lucid dream.

Greta's so gobsmacked by Miranda's appearance that she could address Greta as *bitch* and she wouldn't bat an eyelash. "Thank you, Miranda. It's a pleasure as always," Greta says, and blushes like a pubescent eighth-grade boy.

Miranda pulls the curtain aside to let Greta pass and her eyes track and land on BDC. "After you, please," she says.

Greta passes through and enters the Collection Room.

CHAPTER FIFTY-ONE

"I think you'll be pleased with your selection of voyages this evening," Miranda says.

There's a wary undertone to Miranda's words that hasn't been there before. Maybe Greta's reading into it too much, but she doesn't think so. Between both BDC's warning of three days ago, and what he just tried to tell her in the waiting area, Greta is walking on thin ice. She doesn't care, though. She needs to try to at least give it a shot. Tonight's voyage is a test run for her theory.

Her big, cuckoo, *I've lost my mind* theory.

Yes, it's a far-fetched notion she may be able to go back and change what happened in the car with her parents twenty years ago, but if you told her the night of the gala that there's a place called the Found Object Society that allows you to experience the death of another person simply by holding the object they'd last touched before they died, well, Greta would've thought you were nuts.

Miranda's taken out her tablet and swipes and pecks the screen seven times. A delicate tinkle sounds for each tap and a corresponding spotlight slices through the weighty dark of the aisles and shines into a cubbyhole. Greta hasn't thought this part through all the way. Does it matter what object she chooses for her voyage to conduct her experiment? Is one era or locale more conducive to having a successful lucid experience?

"Greta? Would you care to take a look at our offerings?" Miranda says.

"I'm just trying to think what I'm in the mood for today," Greta says.

She sounds glib, like she's pondering ice-cream flavors and not the dramatic and gruesome death of another actual human being.

Which region or era should Greta choose? It should be irrelevant, since she's a passenger inside the vessel, and whatever language the person speaks, or the era they live in, feels natural while she's inside their minds. There'd been something more relatable about Lassiter's time period. Even though Greta hadn't even been born when Lassiter died, there was comfort in the familiarity of being in the United States and in a decade not so foreign to her.

"I'll take a minute and look around," Greta says.

"Of course, Ms. Davenport. We want you to be pleased with your selection."

Greta walks past the aisles, waving a hand in front of each one to illuminate the plaques identifying the specific region and period. This is the third time she's been to the society, and each time, the stock of the aisles and shelves changes. How do they do it? The selection is limitless: *Southeast Asia 1720–1773*; *Western Canada 1850–1885*; *Saharan Africa 1920–1947*.

Unlike her last voyage, when Miranda had run off to attend to something while Greta perused the aisles, this time she is watching her like a hawk. If she wasn't, Greta would try to test the dark of a cubby again. She recalls the sticky sensation of fingertips pressing back against hers; an electric field pushing her away; blue capillaries of lightning sparking off her hand—the azure static that's been a consistent theme ever since her first visit with Eileen and the introduction to the Obitus Mold.

Greta has to make a choice.

She gets to the aisle where the seventh pin light shines: *Central United States of America, 1900–1930.*

Bingo.

Miranda walks ahead of Greta, holding the box containing item number CUSA20C-39211 and leads her to her cabin for the evening.

It's a slow night at the Found Object Society. Six of the cabin lights show as green (available), four others as blue (occupied). Ezra is in one of the blue ones. The cabin with the errant shoe, the one that was undergoing *maintenance* last time, looks to be operational again, a blue light on above its door. Who fixed it? BDC? Other than the sighting last time of who Greta believes to be *the Collector*, the only people that seem to work here are BDC and Miranda. And *the Eileens*, of course. Ha.

Miranda gives the brass handle of the cabin a tug. It opens with a drowsy moan. Greta jumps at the sound, even though she's heard it before. She's on edge. Nervous not only about what she's going to attempt, but the fact that the Found Object Society seems to be onto her. What if she gets kicked out? She's playing with fire. Of course she is. Her checkbook has always extinguished any inferno she's created. It should work here too, right? She's getting ahead of herself.

Concentrate, dummy.

She has to shake it off, stay on track. Greta follows her in. When Miranda turns her back to prepare the room, Greta mouths her lucid dream mantra to herself: *Next time I'm dreaming, I will remember I'm dreaming. Next time I'm dreaming, I will remember I'm dreaming.*

"Did you say something, Greta?"

"Uh, no, just humming a song that's stuck in my head. You know how that can be. An earworm or whatever," Greta says. She's anxious, saying dumb things. She shoves her shaking hands into her jeans pockets.

"Yes, those *are* annoying," Miranda says. She holds out her hand toward the chaise, indicating Greta should lie down. "Please, get comfortable. You'll be setting sail in no time."

Greta lies down and Miranda hands her the pre-voyage taffy. Her body sinks into the plush green velvet. The curve of the chaise cups her spine and elevates her knees. Her body is in the perfect neutral posture, weightless. Greta's eyes grow heavy and the caw of phantom seagulls emanates from behind the glowing cabin window. She has to hold on, to remember what she's come here to do tonight.

During her voyage, Greta will become conscious, she will. Hands on the helm, she'll steer her vessel.

Miranda extends the Obitus Mold from beneath the chaise. Without being told, Greta slides her right arm into it. The warming metal adds to her grogginess. It's heavy, comforting, like one of those thunder vests for dogs. Latex gloves on, Miranda extracts found object number CUSA20C-39211 from the box.

Tonight's selection is a remarkable cigarette lighter: a square art deco triumph of inlaid black-and-eggshell enamel. The body is mostly black with jags of creamy white forming mountain peaks at the top and the bottom. The inside of each peak is filled with flakes of diamonds. At the lighter's center, a rhomboid is outlined with the same vanilla-colored enamel. Inside that, a monogram: the letter *C*, followed by a multi-spiked star, and then the letter *D*. The object is so stunning, it makes Greta want to be a smoker.

People really knew how to make shit back then.

Miranda places the lighter in Greta's open palm. It's cool and smooth, the silver lighting mechanism colder than the rest. Steampunk brass hypodermic in hand, Miranda lowers the fiber-optic-thin needle onto Greta's forearm.

"Another fine choice. This voyage is a doozy. Are you ready?" she says.

A doozy?

Greta can't answer. Her tongue is an immobile stone in her mouth. She nods instead. Miranda depresses the plunger, sending the opaque metallic liquid into her bloodstream.

"Bon voyage, Greta."

Greta awakens, blind and disoriented. It's dark and she can't move her arms or legs, body vacuum-sealed by a membrane of night. Her mind clears, and she recalls that she's on a voyage. Greta's third voyage at the Found Object Society. The enclosure constricts around her and tilts downward. She descends, feetfirst, extruded into a void like a squirt of toothpaste.

Ahead, two windows.

Greta drifts without sound, tethered, guided by an unseen hand toward the light. As she approaches, Greta has the sinking feeling that she's forgotten something, that there's something very important for her to remember. She flails her arms to slow her forward motion. The effort is in vain. Greta needs time to extract this memory from her mind, to remember. To remember . . .

Wait, that's it: *To remember*. To remember that . . . what? *Next time. Next time she's* . . .

Greta docks against the windows. A flash of orange and a deafening *POP!* startles her.

Whatever she's trying to recall evaporates.

CHAPTER FIFTY-TWO

The one and only Colleen Davies, silent movie star (and now, in 1930, flop of the talkies), just shot her husband dead.

There's a black hole where his left eye used to be. She didn't shoot her beloved Harold Stark—who happened to be the head of the small but mighty film studio Stark Pictures, in Chicago—because he was a homosexual and didn't love her, *not like that, Colleen*; no, she shot him because he dared tell her the truth. *Show* her the truth.

As long as she's been Harold's number-one box-office star, there's been one hard-and-fast rule: *Never tell Colleen Davies the truth, not if it's bad.* This last particular truth was a crackerjack. It had to have been, since she used her dainty German .25-caliber pocket pistol like a melon baller to his eye socket.

"You just bumped off Harold Stark! You're crazy, Colleen," Tyrone says.

Colleen has forgotten about her young lover hiding in the bedroom of her top floor suite at the Edgewater Beach Hotel overlooking godforsaken Lake Michigan. It's January, but even in June the wind lashes across the surreal blue water and threatens to rip the tower where her suite is right off. Yet here he is, twenty years her junior, naked as a jaybird under the brocade smoking jacket she got him this past Christmas. Great, now he's turning on the waterworks, too.

"Dry up and pipe down, Tyrone. I gotta think," Colleen says, her body shaking.

What is there to think about? Chances are good someone heard the *pop* of her petite beanshooter and they're calling the cops. If she's lucky, they might believe the sound came from a contraband champagne bottle. The brief argument leading up to the *pop* hadn't been very celebratory. In fact, Harold and Colleen had been screaming at each other. Tyrone had run for the hills when Harold knocked on the door, cowering like a Chihuahua.

Colleen picks up the cigarette lighter Harold gave her when their tenth silent picture, *Eager as Dawn*, broke box office records. The lighter's a real beaut, inlaid with spikes of black-and-cream-colored enamel, encrusted with bits of diamond. In the center, Colleen's initials bookend a star.

"Butt me, would you?" she says to Tyrone.

Remembering the headlines, Colleen grimaces at the sound of her own voice. *Bleating Goat of the Silver Screen*; *Car Horn Colleen* . . . the unflattering list of puns reviewing her and Harold's first talkie went on and on. She turns her back to Harold, who's still sitting in the club chair across from her. He looks like he's taking a nap, except one eye is open and the other is, well, gone.

She didn't mean to kill him, not exactly. These little Fritz pistols are notoriously inaccurate, and Colleen kept it in her purse for show. She'd fired it only once before. It was after a long day on set at Stark Pictures on West Argyle Street, a short hop from the Edgewater Beach Hotel. Colleen had gotten good and ossified with a bottle of hooch she'd hidden in her changing room and she wobbled into the parking lot. She put the dead soldier on the hood of a car and shot twice. She missed both times. In an ironic twist, she managed to shoot a couple of holes into the windshield of the Rolls of the great Western actor Broncho Billy Anderson. She never told anyone about it and the mystery of whodunnit remained unsolved.

Tyrone bends down to pick up the matching cigarette case for her lighter from the coffee table. His smoking jacket falls open and his penis hangdogs, useless and vulnerable. Realizing his proximity to the dead Harold, Tyrone closes his eyes as he searches the surface of the table for the case. He knocks down the stack of newspapers that Harold brought featuring Colleen's stinkin' reviews. *Garbo Talks, Davies Squawks* falls by her feet.

"Open your goddamn eyes, Tyrone," she says.

He does as he's told and locates the case, jumping away from the table like it tried to bite him. His hands shake as he offers her a cigarette. The man who was supposed to be his golden ticket lies dead, murdered, three feet away. *Poor kid.* This isn't what he signed up for when he hitched his star to Colleen Davies's wagon.

Colleen steadies his hand with hers and takes out a smoke. She lights it herself and pulls deep into her lungs.

"Attaboy, it'll be okay. Don't you worry," she says, patting his cheek.

She tucks the lighter into her dressing gown pocket and reties the belt to Tyrone's smoking jacket, shielding a penis that looks as terrified as he does. Twenty-two years old and gorgeous, black hair and goo-goo baby blues. Right now he looks about ten. For the first time in their relationship, Colleen feels old, feels like his mom. His lousy forty-three-year-old mom.

It won't be okay, of course. How could it be? He falls sobbing into her arms, and she holds him with one arm and uses the other one to smoke. Smoking helps her think, keeps her a spooky kind of calm.

"Why'd you do it, Coll? Why?" Tyrone says.

"I didn't mean to. Honest, I didn't. Who knew I'd hit him so bull's-eye, anyway?" she says.

Tyrone pulls away from her. "That's what we'll tell the cops when they get here. Right? They'll understand, won't they? It was an accident. The gun went off. It was dumb luck. I mean, you're Colleen Davies."

"Yeah, I am," she says. "But he's Harold Stark."

"*Was* Harold Stark," Tyrone says.

"Was," she repeats.

CHAPTER FIFTY-THREE

This whole talkie business started for her a few months ago.

Colleen Davies, like most of the silent movie stars, had thought little of them. They'd shrugged it off like the malarkey it was. A flash in the pan. After all, the audiences didn't come to hear them talk; that's what the title cards were for, stupid. Had audiences become so dumb that they needed to hear Charlie Chaplin's voice? The thought of that made Colleen cringe. It was blasphemy. Charlie said so himself: "Talkies are spoiling the oldest art in the world—the art of pantomime. They are ruining the great beauty of silence."

Amen to that, brother.

Then Harold walked into Colleen's dressing room one day, full of ideas. He knocked and entered without waiting for an answer. It'd been the last day of a long shoot and Colleen had her feet on her new boyfriend Tyrone's lap. He was rubbing her bunions. He was a real swell.

"I wish you two would be more discreet," Harold said, blushing as he looked at Tyrone. Pretty, pretty Tyrone with his shirt unbuttoned, a lock of jet hair hanging past his cheek.

His implication wasn't that people would know she was having an affair—it was the *why* of it that made Harold nervous. The *why* of him being hunky-dory about it. His marriage to Colleen was one of convenience and respect. Colleen knew Harold liked men, of course she did, but the rest of the world couldn't know that one of the biggest studio heads in show business liked to play with other men's tallywhackers. She was fine with that. Colleen Davies did what she wanted.

To the silent picture–loving public, though, theirs was the ideal marriage of glamour and power. Colleen was at the top of her game—even if she had already squeaked past forty. Fans recognized her wherever she went, and if they didn't, she'd be sure to make a grand entrance to set them straight. Most times, Harold Stark was right there next to her. Smiling. His arm linked through hers, happy to give her the spotlight while the bulbs of the press flashed and rabid fans asked for an autograph. They'd paint the town and stay visible for only as long as was necessary to perpetuate the saga of the power couple, then go their separate ways: Harold to a club more secretive than a speakeasy; Colleen back to the Edgewater, where some tasty boy they'd call a *nephew* to anyone askin' awaited her arrival.

"We *were* being discreet, my darling husband. The door was closed. You're the one that barged right in." Colleen winked at him.

"Tyrone, could I have a minute with my wife, please?"

Obedient Tyrone lifted Colleen's swollen feet from his lap and helped her into her ostrich-feathered slippers. He buttoned up his shirt, tucking it back into his pants.

"I'll see you later?" Tyrone asked.

"Eight o'clock at the Edgewater. We'll have a celebration in the Marine Dining Room, the three of us. Husband, wife, and nephew," Colleen said, not a care in the world.

Tyrone walked out and closed the door. Colleen watched as Harold's eyes followed him as he left.

"He's mine. You can't have him," she said.

"I don't want him, Coll," he said, and sat in the chair Tyrone had vacated.

"You look serious, Harold. You know I hate serious."

Harold inhaled, girding himself for something. He straightened Colleen's dressing gown and smoothed the silk across her knees, leaving his hands there. Harold Stark was a handsome man, a powerhouse. If he hadn't been a fairy, Colleen still would've married him. This setup was better, however; it offered variety.

"Whether you like it or not—whether *I* like it or not—Colleen, talkies are here to stay, and we have to get on the bandwagon or get lost in the prairie."

Colleen protested. Harold held up his hand. "Let me finish. It's Pandora's box. It's been opened, and it's out. It's here, Coll. Everyone's saying in a few years silent pictures will have gone the way of the dinosaurs. We have to get ahead of it. *We*, Colleen. Stark and Davies. Husband and wife. I'm looking at scripts now and I've got one—"

Colleen pushed Harold's hands off her and jumped up. Grabbing her silver-plated hairbrush, she threw it at his head and it connected with a *thunk*. *Never tell Colleen Davies the truth, not if it's bad.*

"Jesus Christ, Colleen! That hurt. That really hurt. You can't do that to me."

Colleen wasn't sorry, though. She was steaming, hopping mad.

"Listen to me, Harold. We've been over this. My audience does not want to hear me talk. What if they don't like what they hear? And how am I supposed to act when I have to worry about saying *lines*? How's the director going to give me direction while I'm talking? Or how about when someone drops something, and it makes a loud noise? Is everyone on a set supposed to be quiet? It's so ridiculous. I can't believe you're falling for this talkie hoopla. I won't do it, Harold. I won't."

Harold reached up and touched where Colleen's brush had connected with his blond head. He looked at his fingers and saw that she'd drawn blood.

"Jesus, Colleen. You're gonna kill somebody one day with that temper of yours. You gotta do this, Coll. If I didn't believe it, I wouldn't be asking. Trust me or it's going to be over for you, for both of us. We have to keep up."

Colleen's ability to shift from rage to kindness and back to rage was legendary, terrifying. She dipped a handkerchief in a glass of water and dabbed the cut on her husband's skull.

Cooling down, she said, "No, Harold. I don't *gotta* do nothing."

He took her hand in his and stood up, squeezing harder than Colleen had expected.

"I didn't want to tell you this, but . . ."

"But what, Harold?"

"Garbo's doing it." Harold braced himself for another body blow. "Greta Garbo is doing a talkie."

That Swedish bitch.

Colleen fell back into her chair, lightheaded.

"That's a joke, right? Tell me it is, Harold."

"No can do. It's the truth. They're shooting later this year. They're adapting O'Neill's *Anna Christie*. But we can get ahead of it. We can. I have a script and it's good. It is, Coll," he said. "If we get to work now, we can beat Garbo. Trust me on this, please."

Beat Garbo? Colleen and Garbo's relationship has always been *precarious.* They belonged to different studios but ran in similar circles. The two went to many of the same premieres, grinned through awkward photo opportunities together—Garbo often muttering something in Swedish under her breath as she gave that annoying, blue-eyed sideways glance of hers. She wasn't even an American, for God's sake. Colleen pictured audiences booing when they heard that ridiculous accent of hers for the first time. That warmed her heart. Garbo was gorgeous, but what did that matter if she sounded like a foreign country bumpkin? Colleen could slay Garbo without having to lift a finger. Sure, she'd have to talk on-camera herself. Was that really such a big deal? Colleen Davies would have a long, gorgeous gam up.

Beat Garbo? Yes, that she could get behind.

"Okay, Harold. I trust you," she said. "You're a real bastard of a fairy, you know that?"

Harold kissed Colleen on the forehead. "That's my girl. We'll get started with some vocal coaches right away, only the best. You can do this. You are Colleen Davies. Never forget that."

Colleen stood and hugged her husband tight, too tight, and whispered in his ear, "No, *you* never forget that. And if this doesn't work, Harold, I will kill you. So help me God, I will." Then she laughed to let him know she wasn't serious. Not entirely.

A drop of coagulating blood fell from his earlobe and onto her dressing gown. And like Thomas Edison harnessing electricity, there was no coming back from the dark. The talkie age was coming, and Colleen Davies was in. Come hell or high water, she was in.

CHAPTER FIFTY-FOUR

Colleen had a scant couple of weeks to get into vocal shape before shooting started, and she hadn't taken it seriously. Cameras would roll in less than a week, and the dread was taking hold.

Give Us the Night was a decent script, more than decent in fact, and the emotional subtleties, the highs and lows that were required of Colleen, not only vocally but as an actress, kept her up at night. Never before had she doubted herself. Now she was losing sleep, thinking she'd bitten off more than she could chew. Going from silent-movie acting to talkies was like learning a new language, or being told you had to play the piano when you've only played the banjo, or being asked to become a painter when all you've ever known was sculpting. And at the ripe old age of forty-three, to boot.

It was two in the morning and Colleen was chain-smoking. Tyrone was fast asleep, naked and sprawled on the velvet covers. The light from the moon bounced across Lake Michigan through the balcony windows. In the glow, Colleen could swear he was transforming—the deep sleep of youth maturing Tyrone's body, his cells replicating before her eyes. Colleen's cells were going in reverse. Cracked, broken, irreparable. Tyrone's trajectory was forward and up. Colleen had crested and was on her way down.

The wind groaned across the water, smacking up against the penthouse suite before making its way into the streets of Chicago. Inside it was cozy, yet Colleen shivered nonetheless.

She stamped out her smoke and opened the enameled cigarette case for another. Popping it open, she put a butt between her lips. Her mouth was dry and the coffin nail stuck to her thinning pout like flypaper. She rolled the enameled lighter in her fingers. It was smooth and warm, and the diamond flakes tickled against the pads of her fingers. She could read the letters *C* and *D* within the rhomboid with her fingertips. Harold gave the best gifts.

Lighting the cigarette, she pulled in deep and approached the window, watching her reflection as she got closer. She looked tired, older. Another middle-aged dame awake in the middle of the night. She exhaled the plume of smoke on the glass, hoping to scare the old bag away. As the smoke dissipated over the flat surface, what Colleen saw looking back at her in the glass stopped her heart cold.

Superimposed over her own reflection was someone else. Another woman. At least, Colleen thought it was another woman. Her clothes were screwy. She wore what looked to be a man's undershirt and a pair of dungarees, a leather belt with two metal *C*s interlocked as a buckle. Her hair hung loose around her shoulders. The reflection wasn't from someone standing behind Colleen, but of someone *overlapping* her, like they were inside her and trying to get out.

Colleen lurched back from the glass door and ran into the bedframe, losing her balance. Tyrone stirred, shifted his nude body, and then lay still again. Who the hell was that?

Coll steadied herself. She looked behind her, though she knew full well that there was no one there other than Tyrone. Someone else—a woman—had existed within her own reflection. Ciggie in mouth, she approached the glass again. In the distance, a freighter stitched its way across the lake, heading for points north. She refocused her eyes on the window, drew in hard on the butt and exhaled onto the glass, thinking maybe she could make the genie reappear. The smoke billowed across the window in all directions. When it was gone, that same old sack of a silent film star was all that stared back at her, wide-eyed and losing her marbles.

Goose pimples covered her arms and her heart pounded a mile a minute. Was it the hooch? It could've been a bad batch. That happened from time to time. Other than the apparition, Colleen felt right as rain and straight as an arrow. It must have been a figment of her imagination. A manifestation that emerges in the middle of the night when the world is at its darkest.

She closed her eyes and leaned her forehead onto the glass. What Coll needed was some air. She opened the balcony door and stepped outside. The wind charged past her at a mighty gallop, and toward the sleeping Tyrone. Why the Edgewater bothered having balconies that faced the rage of Lake Michigan was beyond her. There were only a few days a year when you could sit out here without being tossed around like a twister in Kansas. The view sure was something, though. The faraway lights of Milwaukee way north, to the hazy firefly of Grand Rapids across the lake to the east. In the deep of the night, the sky was the arched roof of a fearsome maw, the expanse of beach below a tongue coming to lap you up and gulp you down.

Colleen's dressing gown flapped behind her. She rested her forearms on the icy metal railing and looked the sixteen stories down. That's a long way. Poor Tyrone hated heights and usually he wouldn't set foot out here. Sometimes Tyrone could be jumpy as a cat.

"When you're a star, you get the penthouse, Tyrone," she'd said that first night she brought him up here. "The two-bit hacks get the lower floors. You don't want to be a two-bit hack, do you, Tyrone?"

The promise of him being pulled up from whatever little Podunk town he'd crawled his way out of had quashed his fear. He'd shaken his head and then she'd kissed him, hard and long. And here they were, a little over a year later, Colleen seeing ghosts in the glass and Tyrone sleeping the sleep of a well-suckled babe.

She tossed her ciggie off the edge and watched as a gust picked it up and smacked it into the peach melba exterior of the hotel. Her eyes watered from the cold and wind. Blinking them shut, she conjured the woman's face again: eyes big and vacant, cheekbones sharp, hair hanging loose, and those strange clothes. It wasn't just that she saw her; it was more like they saw each other. She was looking at Colleen as much as Coll was looking back at her. Colleen felt as though she'd been dreaming and wanted to wake up, but she already was—awake, that is. That face gave her the heebie-jeebies.

"Coll, what gives?" Tyrone had opened the balcony door and was standing with a pink velvet pillow covering his goods.

Tyrone had come a long way from the days where he wouldn't even stand by the window, and here he was talking to Colleen on the balcony. He must've been worried.

Colleen walked over to him and guided him back inside, shutting the door behind them. It was only then that she felt the cold of her skin. She pulled Tyrone in close and he dropped the pillow. He was half asleep. Parts south were not. Gotta give it to these young ones—middle of the night, acrophobia, bitter cold—it didn't matter. When it came to grinding the corn, anytime was the right time.

"Couldn't sleep is all," Colleen said, and wrapped her robe around his naked back. "You're nice and warm," she said, pushing up against him. His hair smelled of soap and cigarettes, his neck baby sour.

"And you're cold. Come back to bed," Tyrone said.

"You think I'm good, don't you, Tyrone? I mean, that I can do this talkie business?"

Like she had with Harold, Colleen had trained Tyrone to tell her what she wanted to hear. So what was the point of asking?

"You're Colleen Davies and you're gonna show 'em. You're doing great. Hittin' on all sixes."

"You think so, Tyrone?"

"Of course, I do. You okay? You're white as a sheet," he said.

"Sure I am. Everything is ducky. Promise," she said.

Everything wasn't ducky, not by a long shot. And as Colleen led Tyrone back to bed and let him peel off her dressing gown, the silk falling to the floor in a puddle, his young lips warm and exploring her body, she thought of that woman again. That ghost.

Whoever that phantom was, she didn't feel like a ghost from the past, but from the future. And that felt worse—far worse.

CHAPTER FIFTY-FIVE

Colleen stopped tossing her cookies long enough to hear the insistent knock on her dressing room door.

"Coll? Baby? You doing all right? We're ready for you."

It was Harold knocking, and today was the day. The first day of shooting Colleen Davies's debut talkie, *Give Us the Night*. The first time Colleen would speak into one of those microphones that hung over you like a carrot on a stick. It was unnatural. How many balls was a gal expected to keep in the air at once? She had to memorize her lines and make sure she was facing the camera right so her nose didn't look too big; she was supposed to remain as still as possible since these new giant cameras couldn't move, and remember the director's instructions from before they started rolling, because it would wreck the recording if he yelled them; she had to conjure up whatever goddamned emotions she was supposed to be feeling, interact with her fellow actors, oh, and *Don't mind that thing on a stick that's hanging above your head like a piano on a wire*, and *Stop shouting, Colleen! The microphone can hear you. You're still shouting. Quieter!*

Coll dry heaved again into the toilet. She had to pull herself together. It didn't help that for the past five weeks of coaching and getting used to a set built for recording sound, Colleen had noticed that the entire crew had looked away, looked anywhere but at Colleen after she rehearsed her lines. Like they were all of a sudden busy with their pencils and clipboards and couldn't make eye contact with her. Sure, Colleen Davies's number one rule was *Never tell Colleen Davies the truth, not if it's bad*, but the silence? The silence from the costume designer, the makeup girl, the carrot-stick operator said more to Colleen about her performance than anything. Harold's and Tyrone's placating comments of *You're aces, Coll* and *Every day you're getting better and better* weren't cutting it.

The unease and angst she felt grew like a ball of yarn, wrapping around itself tighter and tighter. Here she was, on the very first day of shooting, and that ball took up all the room inside her. Pushed everything else out until she no longer felt like the one and only Colleen Davies who'd taken the silver screen by storm but more like the young kid who had showed up at Stark Pictures twenty years earlier, poor and scared with a pocketful of hopes and dreams. Now that pocket had a big hole in it and those hopes and dreams rolled on the floor like bad pennies.

Damn, she needed a drink. A drop or two of courage. She kept a bottle in the false-backed flower vase one of the set designers had made for her. The Volstead Act was nonsense, but it did make you clever about your hooch and how to hide it. Getting lit when she didn't have to say words out loud was one thing; doing it when she had to enunciate was another. *Stop shouting, Colleen!*

"Coming, Harold. Hold your horses," Colleen called back.

Harold was getting desperate. She could tell by the way he was tapping like a woodpecker on her door. His career was on the line, too, if Colleen didn't come through. She'd kicked Tyrone out of her dressing room an hour ago. His incessant pacing was giving her fits. Who knows where he was now?

Colleen soaked a washcloth in cold water, twisted it out, and patted her face and neck, careful not to mess with her makeup.

She'd need a good touch-up after pulling a Daniel Boone into the toilet for the past twenty minutes.

She straightened herself and left the bathroom. Took a deep breath and unlocked the door to let Harold in.

"There she is, ladies and gentlemen, Colleen Davies. My gorgeous star." Harold was all smiles. The sweat lining his forehead told a different story, as did his twitching jaw muscle.

Colleen wanted a ciggie. That would set her straight. Her vanity was more cluttered than usual with flowers and cards wishing her well on her first day of filming a talkie. To anyone else, the scene would look celebratory, ebullient. To Colleen, it felt like she was getting dolled up for the gallows. She rifled through the compacts and hairbrushes and thought about throwing the silver-plated one at Harold's head again, like she had five weeks ago. He'd gotten her into this mess, but Colleen was going to get herself out of it. She had to if she was going to beat Garbo. Goddammit to hell, she was going to pulverize that Swedish tomato if it was the last thing she did.

She opened her cigarette case and stuck one on her lip. Her lip rouge was crimson and sticky, and the coffin nail clung to it like glue. A smoke would make her feel better. It always did.

Harold stood behind her, both facing the vanity mirror. The round bulbs were like clementines of light that bounced off their faces, shrouding them in an idyllic glow.

"Well, aren't we a pair?" Colleen said, allowing herself a smile. And they were. They were one hell of a pair.

Harold picked up the lighter he'd given her and pressed down, igniting the flame. He held it at the end of her cigarette and she cupped her hand around his, shielding from a breeze that wasn't there.

"Indeed we are. Stark and Davies. Davies and Stark. It's

going to be great. It is, Coll. You're aces," he said, wrapping her shoulders in the white fox stole she'd be wearing for her first talkie scene.

You're aces.

She filled her lungs with the sweet tobacco and blew out into the mirror. The smoke detonated across the glass. For a halting moment, Colleen thought she saw that scooped-out tomboy face again, the one who came from another time and place. But it was only Colleen Davies and Harold Stark who looked back at her. Coll splendid in her glamorous on-screen finery; Harold dignified, powerful, the moving picture–loving public in the palm of his hand.

Squish Garbo like the tomato she is.

She stamped out her cigarette in the full ashtray, then stroked her husband's cheek.

"What are we waiting for? Let's go make a talkie, Mr. Stark."

For once in her life, Colleen wished everyone wasn't fussing over her. Acting like she was the cat's meow. Of course she was, the cat's meow, that is, and they better never forget it, but for the next hour, while she got herself situated and had her first few takes, she wouldn't mind being a big, fat nobody. A zero. That wasn't gonna happen, though, because every pair of eyes on that stage—that *sound*stage—was fixed on her. Were they hoping she'd fall on her face? Or did they really want her to succeed?

Coll had pissed off most of the rubes in the room at one time or another. That's what you do when you're a star. You high-hat all the little people. Then when they turn into a big shot themselves, they'll do the same to someone else. So it was hard to tell if all those grinning mugs, those encouraging calls of *Go get 'em,*

Colleen, were the real McCoy or something more sinister . . . like schadenfreude. That was the word: reveling in other people's misfortunes. Great word—even if it was German—unless, of course, it was being applied to her.

Someone was talking to her. Colleen was so caught up in the swirl of activity around her, she hadn't noticed her costar, Tighe McClellan, standing right there. How long had he been yapping for?

"—historic moment. It's a real honor for me, Ms. Davies, to be working with you again. Here in this remarkable circumstance, on the cusp of the future. The times we live in—"

You'd think he was standing on a soapbox or in front of a podium. If you let him, Tighe would keep talking until he sucked all the air out of the room, leaving no oxygen for anybody else.

"Go soak your head, Tighe," Colleen said. That shut him up. It always did. He stood there and played with his tux and tails, his mustache dyed black, covering his grays, waiting for someone else to tell him what to do.

Colleen scanned the room. She and Tighe stood in the middle of a posh living-room set. The makeup girl and the foreign wardrobe lady had already been by and smoothed, powdered, and tucked. The scene was as familiar as waking up in her Edgewater penthouse, but it was also different. Like thinking a dream is real because everything looks normal, then something weird happens and you realize it's not real. You're dreaming.

Today, the *weird thing* was the giant box where the camera usually sits. That, and the goddamned carrot-on-a-stick hanging over their heads. The box was a kind of soundproof armor they put around the camera so the carrot-on-the-stick wouldn't pick up the sound of the *clackity-clack* of the film reel when it rolled. If Colleen could place a bet on how long the camera operator would last in that hotbox before expiring, she would. Ridiculous, right? It was enormous, like something out of the war. The camera and its box were so heavy that it couldn't be moved. And if it couldn't move, well, neither could she and Mr. Hot Air McClellan. So they were just going to have to stand there, like a couple of stiffs, and say words to each other.

Off to the side was a new guy. The *sound operator*, they called him and, next to Colleen, he was the most pampered of anyone in the room. You'd think he was made of gold. Sitting there at his little table with all those buttons and knobs, turning them this way and that, wearing a set of headphones and giving people the thumbs-up. The sound table looked like a prop out of a science fiction picture. If Colleen could place another bet, she'd say the sound operator had no idea what he was doing and all those round, colorful geegaws were fakes. But today he was the king (or so they said).

Stop shouting, Colleen!

Colleen regretted not having that drink.

Harold stood, hand on hips, just outside the stage lights, half in shadow. His icy blues were fixed on her, but another person, fully in the dark, whispered in his ear. Harold's blond head bobbed up and down, listening to whatever the person was saying. Was he agreeing with them? Colleen couldn't tell. He wasn't smiling, that much was clear. When he smiled, delicate crinkles formed around the edges of his eyes. Colleen loved him, she did. He was her best friend, her savior, as much as she was his. They had taken his little picture studio and made it big. Big enough to compete with the muckety-mucks of Hollywood. The same ones that were getting ready to roll on Greta Garbo's first talkie, *Anna Christie*.

Squish that Swedish tomato.

Where was Tyrone? The stage door opened and light spilled in from the outside world. Colleen glimpsed her hotsy-totsy boy, standing in the back. He'd been nervous as hell for the past couple of weeks, worrying about today like Coll was due to give birth or something. Would the baby come out cockeyed? Sideways? A bearded sideshow baby? The door swung shut again and Colleen saw Tyrone wasn't alone. Sidling close to him was some young Jane. Colleen had seen her around a couple of times before and hadn't thought much of it, just another pretty dragonfly out in the field. There she was alone with Tyrone in the dark. Colleen should've been mad, jealous even. Instead, she felt a kind of beaming pride. *Motherly* pride.

Something surged through Coll in that moment. A certainty of purpose, an unflappable confidence that she could do this. All the people in that room—no matter what she'd done or said to them, or what they'd done or said about her behind her back—they were depending on Colleen to get this right. Harold was depending on her. Tyrone. Silent movies were already on their way out. The truth was in the tea leaves. And for Colleen Davies to remain *the one and only Colleen Davies*, she had to adapt. Think of where she'd come from to get to where she was now? It was a kind of alchemy—turning dirt to gold.

She could do it again. She *would* do it again. If this went to hell, it wasn't going to be because she hadn't tried hard enough, hadn't believed. Colleen would not be the one left holding the bag if things went south. No sir.

With that, Colleen and Tighe took their places. Coll ran her lines in her head as the director shouted his directions into a megaphone and someone else called out for the first time, "Quiet on the set!"

CHAPTER FIFTY-SIX

Considering the novelty of the shoot, Colleen's anxiety, and the technical shenanigans, the first day of filming had gone well.

Give Us the Night started rolling on October 7, 1929. One entire week before Garbo's *Anna Christie*. It was going to be a race to the finish line. Garbo had the muscle of MGM behind her, sure, but she was also Garbo. Prone to finicking and delays. Harold and Colleen worked together like hand and glove, and even though Harold wasn't the director, he was there for each take, and they both kept things moving. *Give Us the Night* had a twenty-eight-day shoot schedule. Ambitious, though doable. There was a lot of chatter out there about the stock market, but that was another world. They had a picture to make, and this was show business, not Wall Street.

Colleen, Tighe, and the rest of the cast and crew were tuckered out. By midday, Coll had almost forgotten that the carrot-on-a-stick was there, and the camera operator emerged from his box from time to time, basting in his own juices. He may have gone in chunky, but he was going to come out like a string bean. The King fiddled with his knobs and, as far as Colleen could tell, seemed satisfied with how things were going.

Most of the crew had packed it up and left for the day. Colleen, Tighe, and Harold were taking a load off in their director's chairs. They'd survived their first day on the battlefield. Tighe was going on about some play he had done and his grand reviews. Colleen gave him a good long dead-eyed stare. Not waiting for her to say *Go soak your head, Tighe*, he stood up to excuse himself.

"I bid you both a good evening and I will see you on the morrow," Tighe said, unable to talk like normal folk and always putting on airs. It was maddening. He took Colleen's hand and kissed it, and gave them both a bow before leaving.

"We weren't applauding, Tighe," Coll said. Tighe made a beeline for his dressing room.

"Take it easy, Coll. He's all right. You look good together," Harold said.

"Sure, that's the easy part. But how do we sound?" Colleen said.

"You want to hear it?" The voice from behind Colleen and Harold took them by surprise.

It was the King, sitting there at his console, guiding a ship of sound with his dials and buttons. Colleen and Harold slid off their chairs and walked over to him. His question had been loud enough for the remaining crew to hear. They all moved toward him like he was getting ready to open Tutankhamun's tomb—no one sure if an ancient Egyptian curse was about to be released into the atmosphere.

"You can do that? Now?" Colleen said. Her throat tightened as she took a drag off her cigarette.

"Ab-so-lute-ly. Sure can, Ms. Davies," the King said, pleased with himself. That made Coll nervous.

"It's up to you, Colleen," Harold said.

All eyes were on her, eager. They'd heard her say the lines out loud, but what did she sound like recorded on film? Was it different? What Colleen heard in her own ears seemed peachy. But what if it wasn't? What if this crazy console and the carrot-on-the-stick changed things? Made her someone else. What if she hated that someone?

What if everyone else hated her, too?

Saying *no* to the offer would be an admission of fear, self-doubt. Saying *yes*? That meant she was the confident, *one-and-only Colleen Davies* everyone had come to expect. So why did she feel like someone was about to read her diary out loud? It seemed like a private thing. That was absurd. She was making a film, for Pete's sake, the most *un*private thing in the world.

Everyone was waiting. Everyone except for Tyrone, who was nowhere to be seen. Coll thought of that little Jane again, leaning in close to her boy.

Colleen straightened her back, cocked her head to the side, and gave the King her famous arched-eyebrow look and said, "What are you waiting for, Captain? Play us the goods."

She smiled for the crowd, film star on the outside, skinny, broke nobody on the inside. Harold rested a hand on her shoulder and gave her a squeeze. The King fiddled with a couple of wires and dials, plugging into a loudspeaker that sat on a cart next to him. All eyes were on the big cube on the table. It was a real odd-bird moment. She reached for Harold's hand on her shoulder and squeezed back, hard.

"It's going to be ducky, Coll," Harold whispered, keeping his smile high and tight for the rest of the crew.

"Ladies and gents, here's a scene from this morning," the King said, flipping a switch and turning what Colleen was sure was a fake knob.

There was a second of crackling silence, then a voice rang out—no, *clanged* out. The lines were familiar, but it wasn't Colleen saying them—couldn't be. Whoever was talking sounded like a cornered goose spitting words through its beak. The loudspeaker was turned up too high, and those who were left, those who were listening, took a step back to escape the racket. The King adjusted the volume, but that didn't change the nasal timbre of Colleen Davies squawking out her lines.

Harold still had a smile plastered on his face. Colleen saw his jaw twitch, the twitch he got when he was nervous.

"My God. Is that . . . is that my voice? Is that what I sound like? Honestly?" Colleen said, trying to remain calm. *Never tell Colleen Davies the truth, not if it's bad.*

"Oh, that's you, all right," the King said. It was a snide remark, and the implication of his words didn't go unnoticed by either Colleen or Harold. Harold stared him down and the King redoubled his focus on the control panel, fiddling with the levers as if his life depended on it.

"You sound fine, Colleen. Fine and dandy. Doesn't she, everybody?" Harold said, eyeing and nodding to the crew, encouraging them with his glare to say something positive. "It'll take some time for you to get used to it, is all. Isn't that right?"

Murmurs—*Right as rain, Coll; Aces, Ms. Davies; Attagirl, Colleen; You bet, Mr. Stark*—punctuated the air. Colleen shuffled back to her chair and sat down. She was dizzy. She pulled from her smoke, trying to right her brain. The world was off-kilter, and her ears were ringing. Colleen envied the deaf. What did they care about talkies? What she'd give to be deaf right now.

The King looked up again, grinned, and gave her a half-hearted thumbs-up.

The only thing to do was to carry on. And carry on she did, for twenty-seven more days of filming.

Hook, line, and sinker, Colleen believed every positive word Harold said about her vocal performance. She bought every false compliment and morsel of encouragement from Tighe and the rest of the crew, even the bit players who laid it on thick as molasses.

The King, though, he kept his trap shut most of the time after that first day. *Oh, that's you, all right.*

That night, lying awake next to Tyrone in the wee hours, it wasn't the next day's script that she went over in her head. No, it was that tendril of doubt that came from those five words, *Oh, that's you, all right.* But by the time the sun rose, she'd tucked that uncertainty away and into a dark corner.

The positive reinforcement kept the engine of Colleen's ego chugging. All the way through the shoots and the editing. *Chugga-chugga.* The publicity shots with Tighe and Harold. *Chugga-chugga-chug*. The adoring fans and the autographs. *Chugga-chuggga-chugging* up through the night of the premiere in January of '30, which, much to Colleen's chagrin, also coincided with Garbo's premiere of *Anna Christie*.

That's the night the steam ran out. The theater was full of expectant fans. Then began the sniggers, the smattering of boos. The *one and only Colleen Davies* train stalled before it reached the station.

Harold Stark, her own husband, was responsible for this. Harold Stark was to blame.

So, when Harold came into her suite thirty minutes ago—tail between his legs—with two icy-blue eyeballs still bouncing in his head and carrying a pile of newspapers with the evening's cruel headlines, Colleen Davies cracked.

In two.

Colleen and Tyrone had skedaddled out of the theater even before the lights came up. Harold said he'd meet her back at the

Edgewater later. She knew he'd wait for the presses to churn out their late editions. He always did after a premiere. Past reviews of Stark Pictures (especially the ones where Colleen was the star) had been positive. Tonight wouldn't be the same. Couldn't be. It felt like waiting for the confirmation of the end of the world, and she'd been right.

Coll should've listened to her gut after the King had uttered those words, *Oh, that's you, all right.* But she didn't. Instead, she bought into Harold and everyone else's baloney. Then, tonight, he'd handed her the papers, and she saw the headline—*Garbo Talks, Davies Squawks*—and that was it.

The argument was short, punctuated by some shouting. Then the same animal impulse that'd driven her to chuck the silver hairbrush at her husband's head made her reach for her cute little German beanshooter sticking out of her purse. She aimed and pulled the trigger without so much as a by-your-leave. *So long, eyeball. Goodbye, Harold. Sayonara, career!*

—There's a knock at the door.

"Ms. Davies? Is everything all right in there?"

It's one of the Edgewater bellhops. *Dammit.*

Tyrone rushes to Colleen, grabs her shoulder, and shakes her hard. "What are we gonna do, Coll? What're we gonna do?"

Time is moving too fast. She needs it to slow down so she can think. Tyrone shaking her like a rag doll isn't helping. She wriggles out of his grasp and slaps him across the face.

You're gonna kill somebody one day with that temper of yours. What has she done? Her Harold. Her sweet Harold.

"Everything is right as rain," Colleen calls to the bellhop.

Poor baby Tyrone is stunned. He's going to pieces, a million little pieces.

"Ms. Davies, Mr. Stark? Some guests have said they heard a gunshot." The night manager is outside the suite, too. Both of them knocking. A skinny door, all that separates Colleen and Tyrone from the apocalypse.

Colleen can't breathe. She needs air. Without responding to the imploring knocks, Coll rushes to the balcony door and throws it open. Frigid Lake Michigan wind charges in, blowing the newspapers off the table. She careens into the January night and grasps the railing. The cold metal fuses to her skin. Acrophobic Tyrone bolts out with her, his back glued to the glass.

"Coll! We gotta let 'em in. Tell them what happened. That it was an accident," Tyrone brays against the howl of the wind.

Colleen looks down at the crescent of beach below. Whoever thought a beach belongs here in Chicago? The sand is white as snow, the frothy chop of the lake crashing onto the shore. She dislodges her hands from the steel and tucks them into her pockets. The lighter—the one Harold gave her, the one with the inlay and diamond flakes, her initials sandwiched around a sparkling star, the one celebrating their tenth picture together—is warm to the touch. She rubs her thumb across the letters *C* and *D*. The one and only Colleen Davies, about to go down for the murder of her husband.

That's when she makes the decision. To jump. And that'll be the end of that. Tyrone will survive, maybe even become the big star he always dreamed of being. Colleen doesn't dare look back at him one last time. If she sees that sweet boy's face, she'll lose her mettle. She grips the railing again and lifts one of her legendary gams up and over.

Next time I'm dreaming, I will remember I'm dreaming.

Whose voice is that? Someone is talking to Colleen. Someone inside her head. She turns to face the windows and there she is in the reflection—the future ghost. Her mouth is moving. And every time it moves, she can hear the words, clear as a bell. She's saying them over and over: *Next time I'm dreaming, I will remember I'm dreaming.*

There's someone else here, too. Some*thing*. Colleen senses it more than sees it. The shadow in the far corner of the balcony is dark, too dark. It has mass. It moves. Two levers unfold from the pitch. No, not levers, but . . . arms?

The words are here again. The tomboy's mouth is moving, frantic: *Next time I'm dreaming, I will remember I'm dreaming.* Startled, the shadowy abyss retracts back into the corner.

"Colleen, no!" Tyrone shouts. She'd forgotten about him, forgotten about her leg draped over the railing.

Then Tyrone with the devastating fear of heights rushes to Colleen. In the glass, the tomboy jumps aside, and as she moves, so does Colleen. Colleen is her puppet, and her body shifts enough so that when Tyrone reaches and lunges for her, she's no longer there. Instead of Colleen, Tyrone hurtles into the heartless chill of Lake Michigan air.

Colleen's world shudders, tilts sideways. It blazes with light, then fades. A roaring waterfall of noise pulls her and everything around her into it. Sucks her in. The one and only Colleen Davies is absorbed into a deafening hollow of nothing.

CHAPTER FIFTY-SEVEN

"Greta, what do you think you're doing? Greta Davenport."

The voice is far away, angry. Greta is careening through a tunnel. Instead of falling down, though, she's falling up. Head and limbs, bumper cars against a black conduit that's extracting her from wherever she's been.

When Greta stops moving, it's like coming out of anesthesia. *Who am I? What am I?*

Whatever just happened wasn't supposed to happen. Her body shouldn't be here. Not yet. She's lying flat and strains to open her eyes, but can't. The effort to lift them is beyond her strength. Finally, one eye opens, and then the other.

Greta's in an anteroom. Piss-soaked hay covers the dirt floor. The stench and noise are overwhelming. Voices screaming and cheering emanate from just outside. Dogs bark. And all the while the shrieks of another, smaller animal pepper beneath the surface. An ancient woman with chiseled features stands over her, pupils dilated to the point of obscuring the irises. The woman's skin appears depleted, leathery. Her latex-gloved right hand trembles. In it, she's holding something.

The woman is angry.

Terrified, Greta closes her eyes tight. When she reopens them, the scene has changed. She's in an opulent cabin, and plush velvet cradles her body. Her right arm is extended out to her side, suspended by a shimmering cast of metal.

Who am I? What am I?

"Greta Davenport. Come all the way back."

Miranda.

Well, almost Miranda.

Still out of it, Greta could swear that Miranda's usual near-black hair is spiked with silver, that her previously curvaceous body now swims in her Victorian-era gown of blood silk. Greta blinks. Eyes open again: Miranda has transformed back to her voluptuous, sensual self.

The fog lifts. A fragment of an image of a gruesome scene flashes in Greta's mind. Then it's gone, like the wisp of a dream upon waking. Greta's in her cabin. She was on a voyage at the Found Object Society and has been extracted before reaching her final destination: the death of her vessel. Greta notices a pulse of diffuse red light coming from the cabin window. The same one that glowed green when Greta last heard the words *Bon voyage, Greta.*

Red.

In Miranda's now steady hand is an enameled cigarette lighter. The initials *C* and *D* flank a star made of diamonds. *The one and only Colleen Davies.*

The end rushes back to her. Greta's done it. Hasn't she? At least she thinks she has. She became lucid during her voyage and . . . and what? Has she altered its outcome? She doesn't know. Colleen didn't die, and she was the vessel Greta had been traveling in. It *should*'ve been her, but her voyage came to an abrupt halt. Miranda shut it down. *Too soon.* Pulled up too soon—it's like the bends.

Colleen had seen Greta on the balcony, and Greta had seen her. They'd acknowledged their mutual existence on separate planes, tracks. Greta *had* controlled her. She'd manipulated her body for long enough to move Colleen away from the edge. Had she saved her? She thinks so. What about Tyrone? Because of Greta, Colleen Davies lived. Had Tyrone fallen to his death instead? And Colleen and Greta had both seen it, in the darkened corner of the balcony: the Collector.

A latex hand is patting her cheek. "All the way back, come on," Miranda says.

Greta's surroundings and mind sharpen as her senses flood back, in pieces. BDC is here now, too. A tidal wave of a man, looming behind Miranda.

"Big Daniel Craig," Greta says. "Miranda. What happened?"

She looks at the grim faces of Miranda and BDC, and the question answers itself. They found out Greta was tinkering within her voyage. *Tinkering?* How about completely *fucking* with?

"I tried to warn you, Miss Davenport. I did," BDC says.

Miranda holds up the lighter between her thumb and index finger for Greta to see. "Rule number one, Greta: 'Interfering or tampering with the vessel of your voyage is strictly prohibited. You are a passenger ONLY. This rule will be enforced to its full extent.'"

Greta suspects she's about to find out what the enforcement part entails.

"Daniel, would you please assist Ms. Davenport in getting up?" Miranda says.

They wouldn't physically hurt her, would they? Of course not. That's absurd. Members of the society were too rich, too powerful. Though the only other member she's seen is Ezra, they must all be like them.

BDC shovels his giant mitts under Greta's armpits and pulls her up. When she extracts her right arm from the Obitus Mold, her head spins. "There, there, now, Miss Davenport. Upsy-daisy."

Greta's a toddler in his arms. She swings her legs down off the chaise. Her limbs heavy, useless. For a split second the room flips again—the reek of urine, shouts of men and dogs barking, animals squealing. Then she's back. Being plucked early from her voyage has messed with Greta's head. Her brain sauce is all shook up. Miranda drops Colleen Davies's lighter into the wooden box and shuts it with a bang. She's pissed.

"Look, I'm sorry, you guys. It won't happen again. I had to see if I could do it. You know? Not a big deal," Greta says.

She's trying to slough it off, to make them believe she doesn't have a grander plan in mind, but she's still too weirded out by her hallucination to be convincing. It's the song and dance routine that rich little Greta has performed all her life when she's taken something too far, been too elastic with the rules. It's in her DNA.

"The Found Object Society begs to differ," Miranda says, as she tugs open the cabin door, the air escaping with a surprised gasp.

BDC guides Greta to her feet, steadying her. She lists to one side, then self-corrects, finding the ground beneath her. One foot in front of the other, she gets used to this walking thing again. What are they going to do? Slap her with a fine or something? Greta's okay with that. *Whatever, mea culpa.*

She walks out to the corridor of cabins. Several bulbs are illuminated blue above the doors. The one above hers is red, as she suspected it would be. Naughty, naughty Greta made her light turn red. They plucked her from her voyage early. Ezra must still be on his. She resists the temptation to knock on all the doors, yelling, *Ezra! You in there?*

Up ahead, Miranda comes to a stop. She takes a small note card and pen from her copious dress pockets and scribbles something onto it. She opens the box holding the lighter from Prohibition-era Chicago and tucks the card inside. Then she opens the pneumatic tube hatch and drops it in. An engine churns to life and the box clatters away. Then silence.

The aisles of the Collection Room are to her and BDC's right. Is the Collector restocking out there somewhere? She looks up at Big Daniel Craig and their eyes connect. His gaze shifts away from hers and he shakes his head.

Miranda crosses her arms and faces Greta and BDC as they walk toward her. Greta's reminded of going to the principal's office for some infraction or another when she was in high school. Out of nowhere, she lurches back to that night twenty years ago at Todd Daehler's house. Greta and her friends around a table, half naked and playing strip quarters, as the headlights of Greta's parents' car swept over them. Everyone scrambling to find their clothes. Her mother walking in. Her father cornering Todd and his hard-on in the kitchen. Greta's shame and embarrassment as she walked out of the house and followed her mom and dad into their car, into their last minutes on Earth.

Greta stumbles, dizzy. The wall to her left catches her. When it does, it's as though Greta flipped a switch. The aisles of objects are gone, and she finds herself in a pit. Dozens of men line the perimeter, sweaty and hollering as they wave bills in the air. At her feet, a blood-soaked dog shakes a rat in its jaws. Dead rodents litter the red dirt floor.

"Steady, Miss Davenport," BDC says. He guides her away from the wall.

The switch flips again and the Collection Room is back to being the Collection Room—not a den of horrors. Miranda hitting the eject button on Greta's voyage has screwed her up.

Big-time. Her eyes dart across the floor—no men, no dogs, no vivisected rodents.

The trio enter the front room waiting area.

The wallpaper, the colors, the improvisational jazz of the furniture aren't helping Greta clear the cobwebs. What are these scraps of revolting images she's seeing? Could it be glimpses of Kit Burns's rat pit? Her imagination run amok? What she sees before her now, however trippy and impossible, is real. That's the reality of what she's been experiencing ever since she got the first mysterious invitation that glided across her floor, landing by her feet. A lifetime ago. But it's only been eleven days.

"Sit for a moment, Greta," Miranda says. She's calling her by her first name. That's a good sign, right?

Greta collapses into a purple brocade Edwardian number. Being seated anchors her to the ground, keeps her from floating away again.

Miranda walks toward the front desk, leaving BDC by Greta's side. The old-fashioned phone rings as she arrives, as though she was expecting it to. Miranda picks up the earpiece. She remains silent, only listens. Her stunning features give nothing away. After a moment, she simply says, "Agreed."

After hanging up, she returns. Who was on the other end of the line? Eileen? Miranda's superior, if she has one? Miranda and BDC loom above her. In her oversize chair, Greta feels like Alice in Wonderland sent to detention.

Big Daniel Craig hands her a glass of guava nectar. "This will help," he says.

Miranda's arms are crossed. She's thrumming her elegant fingers against her silk-covered biceps. Stacks of rings clink together with every motion. Her face shifts. She's made a decision and metes it out. "We have to ask you to leave," she says.

Greta gulps down the juice.

"*Leave for tonight* leave, right? I am sorry. Really, I am. I promise it won't happen again." *Liar, rich little liar.*

"You misunderstand me, Ms. Davenport." Uh-oh, Miranda's being formal again, no first name. Bad sign. "As of tonight, your membership to the Found Object Society is suspended . . . indefinitely."

It's a gut punch. Not entirely unexpected, but still.

A ridiculous ultimatum that another wad of money—wired into whatever the fuck illegal account belongs to the Found Object Society—can quell. It's always worked before. It's gotten her out of a DUI, given her the best tables, put her at the front of the line, secured her a first-class seat when there had been none available. Money fixes all. Heals all. It never *doesn't* work.

"How much will it take? Seriously. Give me a number and it's yours," Greta says.

"I'm afraid not, Ms. Davenport," Miranda says.

Greta protests. Raises a ruckus. The louder her voice gets, the more she threatens, the deeper Miranda digs in her invisible Victorian heels.

"It's best you leave now, Miss Davenport. Before you make things worse," BDC says.

Miranda gives Big Daniel Craig a look that could knock the cute off a kitten.

"We will reevaluate your membership in the future. For now, though, we ask—respectfully—that you leave and speak of this to no one. We will contact you," Miranda says.

Always the concern for privacy.

BDC hands Greta her phone but doesn't make eye contact. If Greta thought she had an ally in him, she was wrong. He's there to do Miranda's bidding, the society's. As they usher her to the vault-door exit, Greta tries to take it all in. Is this the last time? Greta's eyes dart around the room: Tupac's lacy eyelashes, the bloody axe on the riverbed, the pyre of Apollo 1, Miranda's regal bone structure, the rustle of her dress, roided-up Daniel Craig. This can't happen. There's too much at stake. *No, no, no.*

And with a resonant *thunk*, the vault shuts behind her and Greta is alone, standing in the darkened corridor that leads to the drab outside world. The world where her parents are forever gone and nothing else compares to experiencing the death of another human being. Greta and the blue light bulb. The dull of the city that never sleeps outside the door.

A lost opportunity. The end of the line.

CHAPTER FIFTY-EIGHT

Greta stands dumbfounded outside 273 Water Street. A wreck. She wants to go back down the steps and bang on the door, insist that they let her back in so they can talk this through. According to her phone, she should still have had another twenty minutes in there.

Goddamned Miranda. Goddamned BDC.

She's paid half a million bucks to be a member and they dare to give her the boot? Greta's not used to being told *no*. It's a total fucking outrage. The clichéd phrase *Don't they know who I am?* comes to mind. The answer is: *They do, Greta. Boy, do they.*

The Found Object Society knows who Greta Davenport is, and that's why her sad ass is standing on the sidewalk after being shown the way out. They know everything about her. They know that there's one giant, blistering boil of regret that's shaped her entire life and that she would do anything—*anything*—to go back and change it.

Agreed. Who was Miranda agreeing with? But what was she agreeing to? Kicking Greta out?

Her error was in having a dress rehearsal. But what other choice had there been?

Greta thinks of the box hidden in her closet at home in Connecticut. The one with keepsakes from her parents and their life together, items from that last night. The box she can only open on the rarest, drunkest, highest of occasions. If she's going to go on a voyage to alter the outcome of her parents' accident, she's going to have to return home and open that box. She's going to have to choose an object—*the* object—and bring it down here to Water Street. Then she's going to *make* them let her in. Force Miranda and BDC into allowing her to take a voyage of her own making.

But how? How on earth will she do that?

Greta walks (more like sleepwalks) the few blocks to their designated post-voyage meeting spot in front of the trompe l'oeil mural. Tonight, Greta's the one who arrives first.

People funnel past her as she plods forward. Pedestrians adjust around her. She stops at the mural and gazes up. The word ARCADE chiseled above the nonexistent passageway that looks so real; the window with a hand reaching out, pulling the curtain aside. Greta presses her cheek against the brick, half expecting to fall forward into the corridor, the vaulted limestone ceiling echoing above her. But it's solid brick, cool to the touch.

A single thought rises to the top of the million others that swarm in her head. She turns around and takes out her phone. Opening Safari, she types the name *Colleen Davies* into the search bar. A row of images load onto her rectangular screen. There she is, the *one and only*. Greta had never heard of Colleen Davies before. She was a real, flesh-and-blood human, and she'd been Greta's vessel. The arched eyebrow, the painted pout, arm in arm with Harold Stark at a glitzy supper club, both of them posing in the dining room of the Edgewater with a gorgeous young man Greta knew as Tyrone. The photos are black and white, but Greta had lived Colleen in color.

She clicks onto her Wikipedia page and scrolls down past *Early Life*, *Career*, and *Filmography*, until she finds what she's looking for: *Death*.

> *Colleen Davies's career took a nosedive after the eviscerating reviews of her first talkie movie in January 1930. The night of the premiere, and in a jealous rage, her lover (the bit player Tyrone Andisi) murdered Ms. Davies's film mogul husband Harold Stark, and then died by suicide, leaping off the balcony of her suite at the long since demolished Edgewater Beach Hotel on the shore of Lake Michigan.*
>
> *Ms. Davies, who experienced psychotic episodes and dealt with alcoholism, lived a reclusive life in a cabin near Lake Tahoe before her death in 1954.*

Greta's done it. Colleen hadn't killed herself. Greta had stopped her, and Tyrone died instead. Colleen had lived. It hadn't been a good life, but she'd survived that night.

If Greta could alter the history of a silent film star, surely she could change her own.

Greta can see the look of surprise on Ezra's face as he approaches her. She's not supposed to be here. Ezra should be waiting for her. Only an hour earlier, they'd said *I love you*—different versions of them had. The better ones. Since that time, they'd experienced the deaths of two more people. Well, Ezra had. Hers had been short-circuited by Miranda.

A thought pokes at her: Never once has Ezra told her about his deaths. She's regaled him with the sad tale of Zephyrine and the pathetic end of Lassiter. Any mentions of his voyages have been vague, offering descriptions of locales but not the person, his vessel. He's always turned the subject back to Greta's voyages.

"You're here already? What happened?" Ezra says.

"I'll tell you later," she says.

They embrace. Ezra's hair smells of smoke, burned wood.

"Why do you smell like smoke?"

"Fire. A house fire," he says. End of subject. Like the pond water and the ant, a part of Ezra's voyage has followed him out here.

"I did it, Ezra," she says. "I became lucid during my voyage."

If he's impressed, he doesn't show it. If he's surprised, he hides that as well. His response is neutral, matter-of-fact. With every passing voyage, the will, the life, is leaking from this man Greta loves.

"Did you?"

"Yes, I did. It was . . . it was amazing. Here, look." Greta shows Ezra the Wikipedia page describing Colleen.

"Colleen Davies? Never heard of her," he says. "She was your vessel?"

"Yes. I was almost at the end of my voyage when I became lucid. I'd tried a few other times but hadn't gotten all the way there. And then, when she was putting her leg over the balcony railing, getting ready to jump, to kill herself, I came to. I stopped her. She lived because of me."

Ezra studies the page. "This says nothing about her killing herself."

"That's what I'm trying to tell you. I was there. That night, *in* the hotel room. It was Colleen who shot her husband, not Tyrone. She couldn't stand the guilt, the fact that her career was ruined, so she figured the best thing to do was end it all. Tyrone rushed over to pull her from the railing because Colleen was *going* to jump. She was going to. I stopped her. *Me*. Not Tyrone. Poor guy went over the edge instead of her. I changed the outcome. *I* did."

Ezra takes that in. Greta can see his mental gymnastics. He absorbs her words and spins them around, looking for the pattern. Trying to solve the Rubik's Cube. He's most of the way there. She watches the colors match up—*click, click, click*—then fall into place.

"Oh my God," Ezra says.

"No shit, *oh my God*."

PART FIVE

Found Object #4
Origin: Unknown

CHAPTER FIFTY-NINE

Greta and Ezra are back at her still-disheveled SoHo loft. Plotting. Hypothesizing.

The ability to alter the outcome of a voyage, to keep a vessel from dying, cuts to the heart of their deepest desires, the remorse that has shaped them both. If Greta could go back and change what happened in the accident twenty years ago, if Ezra could return to the sailboat the night Jake disappeared, keep him safe, if they could find those they've lost . . . well, they'd be different people now, wouldn't they?

Greta neglected to mention that her membership to the Found Object Society has been suspended indefinitely—*revoked*—because of her interference. One step at a time. Her first hurdle is to make him understand the implications of her actions—that they can work the system to their advantage.

Her second hurdle: how to get them back in, when she's no longer welcome.

They sit cross-legged on her couch in the dark, two cartons of coconut water between them. The lights are off except for the one above Greta's stovetop. Flecks of dust and Manhattan street filth dance in a cone of light.

"Let me play devil's advocate here for a second," Ezra says. "I get you *believe* you altered the outcome of Colleen's life, but how can we be sure that what we read on Wikipedia isn't exactly what happened before you even went on your voyage?

That whether you chose the cigarette lighter or not, she really did die a recluse."

"Then that begs the question, why would Colleen's cigarette lighter have been collected in the first place? We can't be sure. Not one hundred percent. And that would mean that our fate, or whatever you want to call it, is just that. *Fate*. Written in stone and unalterable. Do you believe that?" Greta says.

"I'm not sure what I believe. It's hard to wrap my head around," he says.

"When we select an object for our voyage, we experience the death of the last person who touched it—who died right after they made contact with it. That's the whole raison d'être of the society. After the injection, we float, travel back in time, and connect with the mind of that person in their last hours, days, weeks, until we live through their death. There's no one else's point of view—ever. Right?"

Ezra sinks into the couch, his silhouette indistinguishable from the cushions. Exhaustion is taking hold. His head bobs in agreement. He yawns.

She continues. "I wasn't experiencing Tyrone's life, or Harold's. It was *Colleen's*. Therefore, it was Colleen who was *supposed* to die. Not Tyrone. I changed the outcome. Fate is *fluid*."

Greta's skin and mind crackle with electricity: the same sparking blue static that was on her fingertips after she'd reached into the cubbyhole at the Found Object Society, the same one that appears on the trail cam with the videos peeking into the past. Only this electricity is invisible. It's powering her forward toward something impossible.

"Ezra, isn't this why we've been doing this? Taking voyages at the Found Object Society? It's thrilling, sure, gluttonous, sick entertainment—"

Ezra emits a pained groan.

"What's wrong?" Greta says.

"Nothing. Nothing, I just . . ." He rubs his hands on his head, massaging away whatever agony her words have deposited there. "Never mind, I'm good. All good. You were saying?"

"If you could go back, change the worst day of your life, make it go away, wouldn't you? That night on the sailboat altered the entire course of your existence. Wouldn't you at least try?"

Greta waits for an answer. Ezra is quiet, unmoving in the shadows. Has he fallen asleep?

"Of course I would," he says. A fragile silence stretches between them. "That would mean something else, too. It would mean that you and I never met."

They've dragged their bodies to Greta's bedroom, lying next to each other, awake. Two seals on a rock.

Greta and Ezra's relationship only exists during the in-between. The seventy-two-hour bridge that takes them from voyage to voyage. Fix to fix. Death to death. Without the Found Object Society, there is no *them*. They would never have met. And if they had, would they have been a normal couple? Going off to brunches. Having friends over for cocktails. Taking vacations.

Theirs is a relationship forged from sorrow and loss.

Greta tries to picture them together in the future: Ezra and Greta. A couple growing old together, their bodies slowing down as the rest of the world speeds up around them, passes them by. Leaves them behind. Even so, they'd have each other. What would they look like? Where would they live?

Try as she might, Greta can't see it. The future is blank.

Each time she attempts to look forward to a viable life together, she hits the same wall. What she sees is this moment, together again in the middle of the night. She can also see their past. Ezra, five years ago on his sailboat, waking with a start from a drunken stupor, aware something was wrong, desperately searching the cabin for Jake. Going above deck and seeing nothing more than stars in the sky and the mirrored surface of the ocean, boats and land in the distance. No Jake. No sign of him. Not a splash, not a cry. Gone. Lost and never to be found.

Greta's past is clear, too: Stumbling out of Todd's house, her jacket hanging off her shoulder, her mother on her right, her father on her left, pulling her to their car, pushing her into the back seat like a perp. Greta's head spinning, swimming in cheap beer. Her parents saying words to her she can't remember. The anesthesia of the alcohol knocking her out cold as she lay across the leather-upholstered back seat. A maple tree looming over the hood of the car like an ogre. The metallic rhythm of a hubcap as it rolled down the road and came to a stop. The glass, the blood. Then her screams. An unharmed, seventeen-year-old girl screaming in the night as her parents lay dead through the windshield. The minutes alone with them before help came felt like hours. They were right there in front of her, yet they were lost, too.

That's all Greta can see, both Ezra's and her life-altering moments that led up to this one. The right now. It's like the future doesn't exist, can't.

The inky, deep trench that only reveals itself in the middle of the night has returned. Inviting the spiky, desperate thoughts and questions, the ones without solutions, while all the light in the world sleeps. There's no worse place to be.

"Something else happened tonight," she says.

He turns on his side to face her. "Something *else*?"

"Yeah . . . they discovered I was messing with the outcome of my voyage and Miranda pulled me out early," Greta says. "And then they kicked me out. Revoked my membership."

No longer being a member of the Found Object Society—no, worse; not being allowed to return to the Found Object Society—is a significant blockade to Greta's already shaky plan. There's no getting around it. Ezra hadn't acted surprised when she told him, and being presented with a problem that requires a solution is just the distraction their dopamine-depleted brains need.

"I have an idea. Kind of," Ezra says. "What's the first thing they do when we enter through the vault?"

Greta yawns, thinks for a moment. "They take our phones and put them in the safe."

"Right. And they do that because they want to ensure their privacy. To see that no one draws attention to them in any way or posts on social media," he says.

"Right. So, you're suggesting what?" Greta says. Her mind is weary.

"Publicity, or talking about the society to anyone who isn't a member, is one of their biggest fears. And according to what you told me about when your friend Lis came over, and the subsequent threat they sent you, they're dead serious about it. No pun intended." Ezra rolls onto his back. He's fighting to keep his eyes open.

Lisbeth. Greta hasn't been in touch with her best friend since she hung up on Greta a few days ago. They'd been playing a game of chicken, waiting to see who'd break first and contact the other. Greta won because Lis had texted and called her several times yesterday and she still hasn't responded.

"Blackmail them, then. Cause a general ruckus," Greta says, understanding where Ezra's suggestion is leading her. "Stand outside the door of 273 Water Street and get loud, threaten them with social media posts divulging the location and purpose of the Found Object Society unless they let me back in. Is that it?"

"That's pretty much it. I'm not saying it's genius or that it'll work. It might?"

"I like it. I mean, I think I do," Greta says. A wave of exhaustion rolls over her. "I can't think anymore, Ezra. I need sleep."

"I hear you," he says. "We'll figure it out when we wake up."

Their bodies migrate toward one another and they spoon, too tired to undress, sex completely out of the question. Ezra's arm is around her. The approaching dawn scares away the dark place and the emptiness recedes. Greta's about to drift off when the smell of woodsmoke from Ezra's hair snakes into her nostrils. *House fire*, he'd said.

A sickening fragment of thought comes to her, then. And as Greta falls asleep, she hopes it'll be gone by morning.

CHAPTER SIXTY

B*uzz-buzz-buzz. Ring-ring-ring. Buzz-buzz-buzz.*

Greta lurches out from the depths of sleep, trying to make sense of the cacophony of sounds all around her. Ezra's passed out next to her on the bed, oblivious. There's drool running down the corners of her mouth. The phone is on vibrate and she watches it dance across her nightstand, the name *Lis* blazing across the screen. That doesn't explain the other sound she's hearing. They're happening simultaneously, and Greta's only half awake.

"What the fuck?" she says.

Buzz-buzz-buzz. Ring-ring-ring. Buzz-buzz-buzz.

She halts the scuttle of Lis's call and sends her to voicemail. *Ring-ring-ring. What is that?* Regaining her senses, Greta realizes it's the video intercom in her apartment. That's rude. Who'd call up this early in the morning? Checking the time, Greta sees it's not morning at all. In fact, it's nearly one o'clock in the afternoon.

The intercom is insistent. Once someone calls up your apartment number, it keeps going for a good fifteen seconds. Whoever's out there isn't buying that no one's home. Greta gets out of bed wearing her bra and panties. She grabs her robe from the floor and throws it on, fumbling with the belt. She stumbles into the doorjamb with her shoulder. The pain shoots through her, the final blow to her grogginess.

"Goddammit. Coming!"

Her living room is only slightly neater than when she and Ezra walked in last night. It must be sunny out, because light slices at the edges of her drawn shades. The phone in her hand vibrates again. It's Lis. Greta's pretty sure she knows whose face she's going to see as she approaches the video screen of the intercom. Indeed, Lis's face fills the space. The fish-eye lens distorts her features, making her look grotesque, an agitated witch.

Greta takes a deep breath and girds herself for what's coming.

"Hello?" Greta answers, activating the talk-back and trying to sound as natural as possible.

"Jesus. I thought you were dead. Let me up. Now," Lis says.

Lis is pissed. Really pissed. Greta can't deal with her right now, and she certainly doesn't want her to meet Ezra. Not like this. Not today.

"Now's not a good time, Lis."

"Fuck that. I can't believe you haven't called me since our stupid argument. I had to be the one to reach out—again—and still you don't respond. We need to talk. I don't care what's going on, whatever it is, I'm your friend. Your *best* friend."

You were *my best friend*, Greta thinks, instantly regretting the thought. Lis is a stranger now. She wouldn't understand the Found Object Society. The way it's sunk its claws into her. Lis hasn't experienced a loss like Greta and Ezra have. And if Lis found out what she and Ezra were about to attempt, she'd try to stop her. Greta can't let that happen. Even if Greta wanted to tell her about it, she still couldn't. She recalls the image of the coffee mug Lis was touching appearing on her phone, a not-too-subtle hint to keep her mouth shut.

"I know, Lis. I'll call you later, I promise. Now's not—"

Lis interrupts her by waving a copy of the security fob to her building along with the apartment key Greta gave her years ago. *Shit.*

"I didn't want to do this, but I'm coming up, whether you like it or not."

Lis steps away from the screen and Greta hears the click of the lobby door as Lis waves the fob in front of the building entrance.

Then, much to her horror, she sees Ryan following her.

What the hell is Ryan doing with her?

Greta panics. What should she do? She considers blocking the doorknob with a chair, but that's dumb. That kind of thing never works, especially if Lis and Ryan are hell-bent on coming in—which they apparently are. She rushes over to her bedroom and looks in. Thank God Ezra's a deep sleeper. She pulls the door shut and hopes he stays that way. With any luck, Greta can convince them everything is fine before they even set foot inside.

She tightens the belt on her robe and checks her face in a mirror. She looks like holy hell. What had Colleen said? *A future ghost.* Seeing the apartment in the daylight, really seeing it, makes her stomach drop. It's a mess. For Lis, this scene will only confirm her worst fears: Greta's life has spiraled out of control since the gala. She's developed a drug problem that's anything but casual, and she's fallen for a guy who's an addict. They're enabling each other, like in *Leaving Las Vegas*. The real humdinger is that it's true. It describes Greta's situation to a *T*. Only the drug isn't coke or heroin—it's death. They can't come in, that's all there is to it.

The door chain.

Greta rushes to the front door and grabs at the dangling security chain she never uses, and fumbles to slide the end into the latch. Before she can get it to catch, the key has made its way into her Medeco lock and the dead bolt opens with a *chuck*.

Greta steps back as the door opens.

"Trying to keep us out?" Lis says, pushing past her and into the living room.

Ryan stands at the threshold, taking Greta in. She must be quite the sight.

"Jesus, Greta. What's happened to you?"

Lis patrols Greta's living room. A narcotic K-9, sniffing the place out. Lis takes the remote and opens all the shades, looks under cushions. She's looking for evidence of this drug addiction she's so sure Greta has: a smooth surface with cocaine residue, a spoon with burn marks, an empty bottle of oxy, anything to prove her suspicions.

Ryan enters Greta's home with more reluctance. He stands, arms crossed, staring at her. Anyone else would think that he's smirking at her. He's not. That's just his face. It's the way he's always looked. Smug, like he has all the answers. He came out of the womb that way—Greta's sure of it. He smirked his way through high school, college. Always Mr. Popular, the casually gorgeous lacrosse dude, tucking his chin-length hair behind an ear while the girls swooned, but he was smart. A nerd inserted into the body of a Hemsworth brother.

Greta hates herself for ever having been attracted to him, drawn in by his glad-handing charms, the upside-down triangle of his torso. Who was that woman?

"Last time I saw you, Greta, you'd just taekwandoed a tray of champagne at me and Raquel," Ryan says.

Greta gets in his face. "What are you even doing here? I broke up with you, jerk." Lis never liked Ryan, so why she's brought him along with her speaks to the desperation and concern she must have for Greta.

"Okay, okay. Shut up, Ryan," Lis, says. "We talked about this. We're here to help Greta, not lay blame. Try not to be a dick for once, okay?"

"Yes, ma'am," he says, sticking his tongue out at Greta as he hops onto a side chair. He swings his legs over the armrest, makes himself at home. Forever casual.

"Lis, can we not talk about me in the third person, please? I'm right here. Oh, and *no*, Ryan, don't make yourself at home," Greta says, pushing his legs off the chair.

"Will you sit down, G? We need to talk. I need *you* to talk to me. Tell me what's going on. Whatever it is, I can help. *We* can help. Isn't that right, Ryan?"

"One hundred percent. I know some great rehab places. Diss-creet," he says, winking with that smug-ass face of his and making the okay sign with his right hand.

Greta glares at Lis. "I can't believe you brought James Spader from *Pretty in Pink* over here with you. You thought he'd be helpful?"

"We both care about you. We're worried," Lis says.

Greta wants to yell, scream, throw things at them, but Ezra's in the bedroom. She needs to stay calm and get them out. She sits down next to Lisbeth, who's straightened out the cushions and taken a seat on the couch.

"I. Am. Fine. There is no drug addiction," Greta says, looking Lis straight in the eye. As long as she uses the modifier *drug*, it's not a lie—there's no narcotic involved. For emphasis, and to drive the point home, she takes Lis's hands into hers. "I am not addicted to drugs. Promise."

Lis knows when Greta's lying. They've been best friends for a long time, and she can always tell. *Always*. It's maddening. Greta needs her to buy her story and get out. This is not the time for outside interference. She and Ezra are close to something. It's the stuff sci-fi movies are made of, but it's real, and after what Greta was able to do, to manipulate with Colleen Davies's voyage, she has to go through with this—has to at least try.

"Look, I'll even piss in a cup if that'd make you happy," Greta says.

Lis reaches into her shoulder bag and pulls out a box. "Well, hello there! What's this? Nothing would make me happier than to have you do just that for me. Right now."

Ryan laughs and stands up. He shuffles through the mail piled high on Greta's kitchen counter, opens the fridge and scowls.

"Hey! Ryan, you don't get to do that anymore," Greta says.

He continues, undaunted. He's found something. Greta can't see from her vantage point, and when he holds it up and says "This is weird. What is it?" her heart stops.

In his hand is a card, square and black, opalescent. One of her invitations to the Found Object Society.

Greta snatches it out of his hands.

"Nothing. It's nothing. Just a new stationery I might use for an upcoming charity event," Greta says. She opens a drawer and shoves it back in.

"Pretty depressing-looking for a charity event, if you ask me. Looks more like a funeral invitation." Ryan's closer to the truth than he realizes.

"Please stop snooping around," she says. "Stop touching everything. Jesus, Ryan."

He shrugs and walks back over to the same chair. Ryan swings his legs over the arm again, then thinks better of it and places his feet on the floor. His right leg bounces up and down with excess energy. How Greta always hated that.

Lis holds up the at-home urine drug test. "Shall we take a piss?"

This is a fucking nightmare: the poking, the prodding. Ryan acting like he still belongs here, finding the invitation—*touching* it. Lis bringing a goddamned drug test, insisting Greta pee into a cup. Ezra asleep (God, she hopes he's asleep) behind the closed door to her bedroom.

Please don't come out. Please, please, please.

"If I do this, if I pass this stupid drug test, then will you leave? Will you back off?"

Lis considers it. "Maybe."

"No, Lis. Not *maybe*. This isn't cute. I'm serious. This is an incredible violation. For you, I'll do it. I'll pee in the cup to prove my point. But then you need to give me space. Okay?"

Lis is hurt. Greta sees it in her face. What other choice does she have? Lis and Ryan need to get out of here, not only so she and Ezra can figure out how to get her back into the Found Object Society, but for their own protection. The threat could all be smoke and mirrors. Or maybe not. She remembers the picture of Lis holding the coffee mug. Greta can't take that chance.

"If that's what you want, Greta. Okay. I'll give you space."

Their friendship teeters, hangs in the balance. Greta wants nothing more than to hug her best friend, tell her about what's happening to her, the Found Object Society, Ezra. To tell her she's going to try to go back and change the outcome of that night twenty years ago—the result of which could mean that she and Lis never even met. Thinking about it with regular people around, someone other than Ezra, makes it sound that much more insane, absurd.

"Thank you, Lis," Greta says, walking over to her sullen friend. "I'm assuming you want to be there to watch me pee?"

"Yep," Lis says. She heads toward Greta's bedroom door.

"Where are you going?" Greta says.

"The bathroom. Duh," Lis says, and her hand hovers at the doorknob.

"No, let's use the one out here. It's . . . cleaner."

"Whatever. It's your pee party," Lis says.

Greta sits on the toilet, holding the specimen cup beneath her, ready to catch the flow. No matter how many times she's done this at a doctor's office, she always manages to pee on her hand. Lisbeth leans against the vanity, facing the mirror so she can watch Greta do the deed without facing her directly. Lis is crying.

The pee flows and Greta pulls out the cup and places it on the vanity next to Lis. Sure enough, she's gotten some on her hands. She wipes and flushes, retying her robe. Lis is standing in front of the sink, blocking Greta from the faucet.

Greta holds up her wet fingers. "Do you mind?" She smiles, wiggling her fingers, trying to lighten the mood.

Lis slides over. "You're so gross."

Greta washes her hands and dries them on a hand towel. "You love me that way."

Lis follows the drug test directions, wiping tears from her cheeks. Lis sets the timer on her phone. "Okay, five minutes."

The two best friends stand in silence, watching each other in the mirror. Over the years, Greta and Lis have had their fights, but none like this. What's happening here isn't even a fight, not really. Greta has changed. In the blink of an eye, Greta's entire existence changed direction, purpose. What used to matter—Lis, her charities, her social calendar—are no longer of use to her.

If that drug test could pick up the dopamine-inducing rush of experiencing the death of another person, then Greta's in trouble. But it won't. Besides, the Found Object Society has surpassed the rush, the need. After her first voyage it's progressed and given Greta the opportunity to change things. To alter the past. However implausible that is, she has to see it through.

The pleasant wind chime of Lis's timer sounds. She checks the strips, one by one. And as each strip comes up negative, Lisbeth's tears come faster, until she's gulping for air.

"Happy? You're clean, you asshole. Just like you said you'd be."

Greta's heart hurts watching her friend's suffering. Lis is only trying to help. She can't, though. There's nothing she can do. Greta tries to put her arms around her, but Lis pushes her away.

"I don't know what's going on with you. I don't. And I don't know why you won't talk to me about it. I mean, look at you," Lis says, pointing to Greta's reflection in the mirror. "You're strung out. You certainly look like a user, even if you aren't one. You're shutting me out. We've always told each other everything and I don't understand what's changed."

"I'm sorry, Lis. I am. It's not . . . I will tell you someday. I will. Promise."

Lis, broken, is having none of it and opens the bathroom door.

When they walk back into the living room, Ryan stands there waiting for them, a shit-eating grin plastered on his face; to his left, Ezra, groggy and confused, wearing the clothes he fell asleep in and looking like he crawled out of the same cave as Greta.

"Look who I just met, everybody! Lis, *this* is Ezra. Ezra, this is Lis." He smiles again. "Fun, right?"

CHAPTER SIXTY-ONE

"You look familiar to me. Why is that?" Ryan says. "Doesn't he look familiar, Lis? Greta's boyfriend, *Ezz-raaa*? Cool name, bro."

Greta's body tenses, twists at the sight of Ryan and Ezra standing next to one another. Ezra looks familiar to Ryan for the same reason that he'd looked familiar to her when they first met: the newspaper headlines about the disappearance of his son. Ryan is provoking, taunting. She can't let this escalate, can't let Ryan's clever, stupid brain put the pieces together and realize who Ezra is. That'd be a whole other kettle of fish. They can't go there.

Lis, Ryan. Ezra, Greta. Two worlds colliding. *Crash-boom-bang.*

"I'm not sure, *bro*. It's funny, because you don't look familiar to me, though I know your type," Ezra says.

Oh boy.

"You do? Oh, I'm so interested to hear, *Ezz-raaa*, what type is that?"

They're both getting their hackles up. Testing each other. Greta half expects them to start circling one another—spiky collars of flesh fanning out from either side of their necks, like an Australian frilled lizard—then charge forward, rising up on their hind legs. A territorial-bullshit dance. Lis and Greta recognize it at once. They've seen it before. If you're a woman who's ever gone to a bar, a frat party, a gym, any goddamned place where men might interact and feel threatened by some invisible, biological nonsense—you've seen it. Despite the fragility, the near finality, of their friendship, Lis and Greta unify to defuse the situation (as women inevitably do).

Lis takes Ryan by the elbow, breaking his testosterone spell. "Okeydoke, Ryan. Let's take it down a notch. Greta did what we needed her to do, so let's go. Let's respect her space. Her and Ezra's space."

If Ryan was a dog, he'd be pulling on his leash now, craning his head to look back at his perceived threat as Lis leads him to the front door. Ezra hasn't budged. He holds his ground, eyes focused on Ryan. After standing next to Lis in front of the mirror, and now seeing how Ezra looks in the daylight alongside Ryan, Greta realizes how desiccated they must appear in comparison. Lis and Ryan, skin plump and hydrated with life. She and Ezra, shriveling up, the deaths of others visibly draining the vitality out of them. Is it any wonder that her best friend is concerned, intervening?

Greta's next to Ezra, her hand on his elbow (as if that could stop him from lashing out, if that's what he chose to do). It has the desired effect, though. The pin stays in the grenade. She can feel his body relax.

Lis opens the door to lead Ryan out. "I'm gonna remember where I know you from, *Ezz-raaa*. I am." Greta can feel Ezra's body tensing up again, the pin working its way out. She tightens her grip on his elbow.

"You do that, man," Ezra says.

Ryan stops their forward momentum out the door. Greta thinks he's about to bust back in. *Let the lizard wars begin.* Instead, he looks down at the floor by Greta's coat closet. What's he looking at?

"We're leaving," Lis says, insistent, yanking at Ryan. "*Now*, Ryan. Nice to meet you, Ezra, I guess."

"You too, Lis," Ezra says, ready to pounce as needed.

"G . . . you know how to find me if you decide you need me. Bye."

"I do, Lis. I do," Greta says.

As Lis starts to shut the door behind them, she glances down at the same spot on the floor where Ryan's looking.

The door almost shut, Ryan sends out his final salvo: "Hey, I think you have an ant problem."

Thunk.

Lis and Ryan are gone. What a horrible, stinking nightmare. Still, it could've been worse. Like two atomic detonations instead of one. After the first, can you really tell the difference?

Greta secures the chain latch on her front door for the first time ever. She's not taking any chances. In fact, she should've asked for her keys back, but that would've been so final, such a slap in the face. Looking down, Greta now sees what Ryan and Lis saw. A train of ants, one after the other, traveling with purpose alongside the floor molding. The image of Lassiter assaults her: him lying near the bottom of the stairs, eyes swollen shut, throat closing.

Greta snatches a sneaker from the coat closet and smashes the invaders. A few escape under the doorjamb, following the path of Lis and Ryan out into the hallway.

"Fucking ants!" Greta says.

"Not a Buddhist, then, huh?" Ezra says, watching her.

She throws down the sneaker and walks over to him. Wraps her arms around his narrowing waist, sinks her face into his chest. Any good the sleep did for her is gone. She's spent. Ragged. The interaction with Lis and Ryan was a total energy suck.

"Great guy, by the way, Ryan. I can see why you were attracted to him," Ezra says.

"I know, I know. Sorry. That was awful. I tried to get them out before you woke up. I did."

Ezra stamps the top of her head with a kiss. "It's okay. At least you have people who still care about you. Even if one of them is a total asshole. You've got me beat."

Such a lonely thing to say. Everyone who cared about Ezra disappeared along with his son. Abandoned him, assuming Jake's going missing was his fault—or worse.

"I don't know what to say to that," Greta says.

"Nothing to say. It's just a fact. That's all."

Greta and Ezra shield their eyes from the sun that's dipped in through the windows. Lis opening all the shades has the vampires off-kilter.

Ezra picks up the remote for the window treatments and taps them down again. "Do you mind?"

"Be my guest," Greta says. She tucks her body into the side chair that Ryan so maddeningly draped himself over only minutes ago.

The interaction with Ryan and Lis has her shaken. She's all but destroyed the relationship with her best friend of almost twenty years. Ryan? Who cares? Seeing him and Ezra perform their masculine Kabuki has upset her apple cart. Thoughts like a quiver of arrows pierce her consciousness.

There's the Lis situation: irreparable.

Greta's ejection from the Found Object Society: insurmountable?

Her plan to break back in, change the past: improbable.

Then there's the little thing of life as she's known it being obliterated in less than two weeks. She's living in a fever dream. Believing in the unbelievable—the stuff of fiction. That silken black presence, hiding in the shadows, waiting for someone to die to collect the last object they touched and catalog it, file it away like the motherfucking Dewey decimal system in an epic basement with a hideous past in the South Street Seaport.

And Ezra, Ezra, *Ezz-raaa*. The thought she'd hoped to forget as she fell asleep last night reappears, bright-eyed and bushy-tailed.

Greta lifts her head. "Why haven't you ever told me about any of your voyages, Ezra?"

CHAPTER SIXTY-TWO

"What?" Ezra says, even though Greta knows he heard her.

She watches as he busies himself with the crap that's piled up on her kitchen counter. Making each pile of crap neater, rearranging salt and pepper shakers.

"I've told you about all my voyages—who they were, what happened—but other than minor details, you've never once told me about yours. Why is that?"

"I like to hear you talk about yours. They're more interesting. That's all," he says, not looking her in the eye.

"I'll be the judge of that. I want to hear about them," she says.

"You don't," he says. "Trust me."

"Why? Why *don't* I want to hear about them?" She's pushing him. She should quit poking, but she can't help herself. She needs to know, has to.

"Because I said so, Greta. Okay?"

The stitches are unraveling and she can't stop it.

"Who died in the house fire last night? Who was it?"

Ezra tucks in his shirt, straightens himself out. He turns his back to her and goes into the bedroom. Greta follows him. He's getting ready to leave, shutting this conversation down. She can't let him. They haven't formulated their plan yet, how to get back into the Found Object Society, to blackmail them. How to create drafts of social media posts and schedule them to be released. Right now, Greta doesn't care about that. She needs to know. She needs for her suspicions to be wrong. They have to be.

"Tell me, Ezra. Who was your vessel last night?"

Fury returns to his eyes. The same anger she saw when he and Ryan had their face-off. A split second later, it pivots. His expression transforms into the one she saw the night he told her about Jake. This time, there are no tears, only an interior collapse. His face is an open canyon.

"Her name was Susannah Knowlton," he says, exhaling her name like a poisonous gas. "She lived in a Hooverville shack in Washington State, 1933. It was winter and she and her family were freezing. They broke their last chair into pieces to start a fire and it caught on to some bedding. It moved fast. She couldn't get out. None of her family could."

The unbearable thought that came to Greta last night rises to the surface. "How *old* was she?"

The canyon expands, tectonic plates collide, stretching it wider.

"She was ten years old. Susannah Knowlton was ten when she died a horrible death in a fire."

The truth is a mallet to the head.

Children. Why? Why would Ezra want to experience the deaths of children at the Found Object Society and pay extra for the privilege? Miranda said children's deaths were one of the society's *specialty* voyages.

"That's repulsive. How could you do that? Miranda told me some members paid extra to live the death of a child. I thought they must be real sickos, anyone who'd want that." Greta's backing Ezra into the wall, using her hands to push against his chest with each step. "But you? It makes no sense.

It's so fucking warped. After what you've been through. Losing Jake—"

She's unhinged with disgust and Ezra doesn't fight back. He's not responding or defending himself. He takes her rage, head down. She wants to rip at him, tear away this monster's mask she hasn't been able—been willing—to see until now.

"Why, Ezra? Why? Please tell me you don't get off on it? Please."

Greta pounds her fists against his chest, flails at his face. It's falling apart. The world is closing in. This thing, the Found Object Society, has been the ultimate high, the greatest rush in a life that'd gone numb, that'd careened off track ever since she lost her parents. *Lost, lost, lost.*

Here she thought she'd found a way back, discovered the path to the Lost Parents booth, and her partner, the person who'd help her get there, the man she's come to love is a . . . what? Sicko? Pervert?

A chill comes over her and she steps away from him. Ezra's up against the wall, battered, empty. Quiet.

"Did you do it?" she says. He looks up at her, eyes like glass. Her legs weaken beneath her, the effort from what she's about to say draining her. "Did you? Did you kill your own son?"

The words are a shiv to his abdomen. "What? How dare you say that? You don't get to say that to me."

Now it's Ezra who approaches her and Greta who's backing away. His hands are out, reaching for her. Her back is against the wall. His eyes are wild with fury, desperation. Before he can touch her, his body surrenders to the weight of her accusation.

His voice, barely a whisper: "You know me, Greta. You *know* me. Like no one else has. Jake was my world. I'd never do anything to hurt him, ever. Please, please believe me."

"If that's true, why, then? Jesus fucking Christ, Ezra. Why would you want to experience a child dying? Why?"

"This is why I never told you about my voyages. Because I get how it sounds. How sick it must seem."

"So *tell me*. If you didn't harm your son, why do you get off on the deaths of children?"

"Stop saying that. That's not why I do it. Nothing could be further from the truth."

She can't look at him anymore. They can no longer occupy the same space.

"You need to leave. I want you to go," she says.

"Please, no. You're all I have, Greta. I love you. This version of me, any version of me, loves you. Don't kick me out. I beg of you." He's grasping for her, trying to hold on as he loses his grip, falls off the side of the cliff.

"I can't think anymore. I need you to go," she says, wriggling away from him.

"I don't get off on it, okay? God, of course not. I could never."

"Then what? What is it? Why would you do something so depraved? And not just once, but over and over again. Why?"

"I didn't want to tell you, because I was afraid this is how you'd react. And when I became a member of the Found Object Society, I hadn't met you yet. I never thought I'd need to tell anyone—*have* anyone to talk to about it. It's not what you think. It isn't."

Greta sits down on the bed, hands over her head, face in her lap, assuming the crash position. "Then what is it, Ezra?"

He sits next to her without touching her.

"Not knowing what happened to Jake, no body ever being found, is worse than knowing he was dead. But I do believe he's lost, that he died that night. Drowned. Thinking about how scared he must have been, how he was all alone in the end, how I was too drunk and passed out to hear him sneak away, that I could've done something. It haunts me. It's ruined me and destroyed everything. You understand that kind of guilt, Greta. Of all people. I'm positive that's why we found each other. We both suffer from the debilitating pain of *what if*."

The *what if* is the golden rope that binds them together. Ezra is right. Greta so wants him to be the Ezra she thinks she's known. The one she's fallen in love with.

Ezra continues. "I've lived on the hope that his death was like everything else for a kid—that it was innocent, something not to be feared, because he hadn't lived long enough to even understand what mortality was. What a dark and terrifying place death and the idea of *nothing* becomes as you get older, as you realize that there is an end in sight, that it's only a matter of when. And then I got the invitation to the society, and discovered what it was, what it could do, and I wanted—needed—to see that a child's death was what I'd hoped it would be. That the vessel in my voyage was unaware of what was coming, unafraid. That the approaching end wasn't a thing a child feared in the way an adult would."

The choke hold of her disgust loosens its grip.

"Was it different?" Greta says. "Was there less fear?"

Ezra is shaking his head. "No. It's just as bad. Just as terrifying and painful."

"Why keep doing it, then? I mean, I know it's addictive. After my initial visit with Eileen, it was already in there. I was hooked from the start. Why didn't you switch to adults?"

"I was hooked, too, and I *was* going to switch. But after the first couple, when I realized it was no better for children than for adults, I decided this was my penance. My negligence killed my son and experiencing the cruelty of the last moments of other children has been my punishment. I don't know what happened to Jake, but I am responsible for it. Me. His father. For that, I have to pay. The suffering of children is my life's sentence."

Though Greta can't fully comprehend it, she no longer sees the monster mask. Ezra took each death of a child like a body blow, a form of self-harm, because he felt he deserved it. Is it any wonder that he's disappearing in front of her eyes? That they both are? For Greta, her voyages have been a rush, a high like no other. And then she found she could play with a voyage's outcome. She didn't receive her first invitation just so she could have a good time. There'd been a greater meaning to it, one she's unearthed on her own. The Found Object Society's has purpose. It's more than a drug. It's a way out.

It's a way back.

CHAPTER SIXTY-THREE

There isn't an actual clock ticking, but Greta can hear it nonetheless. Whatever she and Ezra are going to do, they've decided it's going to have to be soon. Tonight.

Greta's in an Uber on her way back to Litchfield County and she's not thrilled about it. Carl wasn't available on such short notice. His wife is sick, and he needs to stay home in their semi-detached little clapboard house (at least that's what she imagines it is) in wherever-the-fuck Queens and look after her and the kids. It ticks her off. Carl is a good guy. He cares about his wife, his children, and Greta is riled up about it because she loathes Ubers—loathes that every Uber driver pulls up in a goddamned black Toyota Camry, loathes the occasional dented eight-ounce Poland Spring water jammed into the netting pocket behind the passenger seat, loathes the stupid chime and the *add a tip* and the *rate your driver* of the app. Now Greta loathes herself for being rude to her longtime driver Carl, whose only sin is wanting to take care of his sick wife.

Ezra's back in Brooklyn and they've agreed to meet in front of the trompe l'oeil mural at ten thirty tonight. That means Greta has six and a half hours to get home to Connecticut, collect the object she hasn't been able to look at in over a year, and then get back to the city. It's tight. Doable, though, as long as Kirk the Uber driver isn't too picky about speed limits.

"I'm tipping you one hundred percent of the fare if you get me to my house and back to the Seaport by ten thirty. Right? We good, Kirk?" Greta says.

Kirk nods. He's not a talker. Greta is growing fond of Kirk, the non-talker.

She cracks open the dented Poland Spring bottle and chugs it down. Greta wishes there were more. Reading her mind, Kirk's hand appears holding two more, waving them like bait. She takes them.

"Thanks," she says.

Kirk nods. Greta is definitely growing fond of water-bottle-giving Kirk.

Ezra and Greta had been raw with emotion, exhausted from all that had happened earlier this afternoon, like frayed electrical wires. Ezra going on voyages to experience the deaths of children had shaken her to the core. She couldn't understand it—yet she could. He was punishing himself with each death. Other than it not endangering others, was it so dissimilar from Greta driving drunk at high speed? Taking her life to the very edge because dropping into that chasm is what she deserves? She's never been able to take the plunge, no matter how many times she's tried.

Tonight will be different. Greta's unafraid. She's going to do this, tonight, while she still has the mettle to go through with this. If she doesn't act now, who knows what the future will bring? Time isn't a luxury that she—either of them—has. That's assuming they can even get her back into the Found Object Society; she's become persona non grata there. Even if they can, the outcome is, of course, uncertain, and Greta's only tested this once with anything resembling success. So tonight is her shot. And it's a long one.

Ezra and Greta's plan—if you can call it that—involves the threat of exposing the society in any way possible. Will that be enough to gain her reentry? So much has to go right. And when they get to the door at 273 Water Street and make a scene, holding a cell phone up to the camera for Miranda and BDC (and whoever the hell else is watching) and threatening expository social media posts, there's no guarantee that they'll let them in. Maybe they won't care? Maybe the Found Object Society owns the internet, too?

Greta can't think this way, because this plan is all she's got. It's the first time in her life that she's had real purpose. A goal beyond getting the best table in the restaurant, forcing her way to a first-class ticket when there was none, getting that dress that no one else would see before it hit the runway in June. This time it's not more money that's going to get her in—it's not caring what may happen to her, as long as she can go back and change the past. If she accomplishes that, what will it even look like? Will she be here to see it?

And Ezra. What becomes of him? Them? He's going to help her in, and then what? What happens to Ezra?

Before he'd left, they discussed wording for hypothetical social media posts they'd use to blackmail the Found Object Society. Their hope was that simply causing a commotion in front of 273 Water Street would be enough without getting to that point. Hey, it's as rock-solid a plan for two death junkies as any.

Talking about their scheme, the society, in the light of day, makes it all seem preposterous. In the dark, at night, in bed together or on the sofa, the Found Object Society is so much more real, tangible. Crazy exists at night, thrives. It belongs there.

Speaking about their plan, daylight streaming in, has made Greta nervous. Who's to say that they aren't being monitored?

They must be. The Found Object Society somehow has eyes and ears on them. Is the society also aware that Ezra and Greta are together?

If they are aware, are they in danger before things even get started?

"Is this it?" Kirk says.

Greta hasn't noticed that they've arrived at her house. She's been so absorbed in her thoughts that she didn't see them pull through the stone arch entrance, hear the tires roll across the pebble drive.

"Yes. You can go all the way down the driveway and up to the house," she says.

"Sure. Just wanted to check, since you never know out here, you know? Pull into the wrong driveway and some MAGA dude comes out with a shotgun."

Now it's Greta's turn to nod.

"True, true," she says. She prefers Kirk the non-talker, Kirk the water-bottle giver.

Her vintage Merc is parked where she left it. How long has it been since she's been home? It feels like months, years.

She steps out of the running Toyota Camry. "I need about an hour. Will that give us enough time to get back by ten thirty?"

Kirk leans to look at the time on one of his three phones. All attached to the dashboard with an array of bendy arms and grips, the cockpit of his banal Camry a MacGyvered control panel for a rickety spacecraft.

"It'll be close. But I can do it. An hour, right?"

"That's all I need," Greta says. All she needs to prepare for one last voyage at the Found Object Society, a final Hail Mary to right her tragic wrong. She needs to clean herself up and collect the object she came home for. The one that'll take her back.

"You mind if I go grab some food? We passed a place a few miles back," Kirk says.

"Knock yourself out. See you in an hour."

Ghosts are everywhere.

They snake out with each footstep across the pea gravel driveway, the smell of May lilacs, the chill and dew on the jack-o'-lanterns of Octobers past. They lurk in the living room where her parents used to sit having cocktails after work, on the staircase where Murphy Brown would zoom up and down, propelled by an indefinable feline joy. In the kitchen, where her mom and dad would cook for guests, young Greta (pre-rebellious Greta) hovering nearby, eavesdropping on the foreign language of adult-speak. The phantoms of teen Greta, sneaking out at night to party with friends, knowing all the quiet spots to walk through the house so as not to wake anyone. Even in the dark, the map of the buried land mines that dotted the house were visible in her mind: where to step over an old floorboard, the exact way to turn a doorknob to avoid the squeak, walking with socked feet on the gravel driveway.

Later, lying had become easier. She was more adept. Greta could look her parents right in the eye without flinching, no tells, and say, *I'm staying over at Bridget's house tonight.* Arms crossed, defiant, daring them to say no. She knew they wouldn't. It was easier for them to say yes. Anything to avoid another argument. Their daughter ready to lash out at nearly every word they'd say. Their young Greta who'd held their hands on the boardwalk in Mystic, her tongue awash in blackberry saltwater taffy as the seagulls cawed and the funnel cakes fried. That Greta? She'd all but disappeared. It was Greta the child who'd gone missing, well before her parents did.

And why was that? It was a reflex for Greta back then—the anger, the talking back, believing that everything Mom and Dad said was dumb, wrong. Thinking back now, phantoms all around her, she can't remember why she acted out like that. Her parents weren't bad people. They weren't cruel. They loved her and provided for her. They tolerated her tantrums. Maybe she wanted freedom? Independence? To shake off the shackles of childhood?

Well, teenage Greta had gotten what she wanted. What she *thought* she wanted before the night of the crash. The night of her biggest lie. And even though she's had the walls torn down, the kitchen renovated, the ghosts are still here, all around her. Reminding her that twenty years ago, she was expelled from childhood and had landed headfirst as an adult. An orphan.

CHAPTER SIXTY-FOUR

Greta's only been away five days, but the house smells musty, like she's coming back from a long summer vacation. After deactivating the alarm, she switches on a few lights and heads upstairs to the bathroom. Since she and Ezra parted ways, she's been checking her phone obsessively, looking for any sign of trouble. So far, no warnings from the Found Object Society, no texts from Ezra saying he's had second thoughts. All quiet.

No news is good news, right?

She sits down to pee, and looks at her feet. Her toenails are bubblegum pink. *Bubblegum pink?*

The bathroom appears as it did twenty years ago, the year she turned seventeen. Makeup is strewn across the bathroom vanity, wads of toilet paper covered in that evening's lip gloss contestants, eyeliner worn down to a nub. Outside the door, voices stream up from downstairs. She hears her mother say *Peter!* (her dad's name) and then laugh. Greta's ears roar with blood. She looks down again. Her toenails are back to the near-black of Luxedo of thirty-seven.

What the hell is happening?

Whenever she's back home, snippets of her seventeen-year-old self break through. Since her first visit with Eileen, it's like the blue current from the Obitus Mold that danced across her fingers has followed her—created fissures in her consciousness, cracks in time. The same spark that pushed her hand out of the cubbyhole when she reached in. The same sizzling blue static from the videos on the trail cam, galvanizing the past into the present. These fissures need to stay sealed, at least a little while longer. Greta has to keep it together. Her self-imposed deadline of an hour doesn't give her much time, and she can't afford the luxury of hallucinations.

Greta showers and steps out, looks at her naked and *un*seventeen-year-old body in the mirror. She's shrinking, too, like Ezra. Her wet hair hangs around her shoulders. She leans forward and examines her features in the mirror. She runs her fingers around her sunken eye sockets and her sharpening jawline. Underneath that skin, her human wrapping, is a skull—like anyone else's. With each passing year, the vitality and elasticity ebbs away. One day she'll be bones, like Zephyrine, Lassiter, Colleen—her parents.

She shakes off that train of thought.

If there's a positive takeaway from the past almost twenty-four hours since they expelled her from the Found Object Society, it's that this plan, all this scheming, has distracted her from her usual tweaking and restlessness between voyages. Normally, she'd be bouncing off the walls right now. Jonesing for her next fix.

Now her mind is on one thing, and one thing alone—the box that holds her most precious objects, tucked in the recesses of her closet.

You'd think it'd be a fancy box, a special one carved out of an exotic wood, engraved, something worthy of its contents. It's not. It's an orange Nike shoebox hidden behind some purses. A box meant to be invisible, to not attract the eye every time Greta goes into her closet. Tucked way in the back of her walk-in, which is larger than some New York City apartments. The entire back wall lined with cubbies, each able to hold two shoeboxes.

The one she's looking for is in the farthest lower corner on the right, obscured by handbags. Greta stands there, facing the wall of designer shoes, and is struck by its resemblance to the Collection Room at the Found Object Society. She runs her hands across each cubby, half expecting to connect with a black membrane that pushes back and sends a jolt of blue electricity through her fingertips.

How long has it been since she last pulled the box out that holds the memories of her mother and father? Their family mementos? A year? More. It makes her heart pound every time. Glass falling like sleet, a shower of warm blood, the rhythmic roll of a hubcap harmonizing with Greta's screams.

She can't draw this out. Like pulling a Band-Aid, she needs to yank this off quick.

She crouches down, pushes purses to the side, and pulls the orange Nike box out of its place of safety. Picking it up—contents rattling, coming to life—she sits down on the cushioned dressing bench in the middle of the closet. Her hands shake, her entire body reverberating with the memories of her parents resting on her lap. She runs her fingers around the lid, down its sides. It's not that heavy. The weight comes from what the contents represent, not what they're made of. She tries to control her breathing, taking deep breaths in and out. Her fingertips tuck beneath the lid, the slogan *Just Do It!* egging her on. Mouth dry, eyes closed, she pries the top off.

It's all as she's left it before, a jumble of objects: shells collected from years of beach trips; a photo of Greta—maybe ten years old—on the floor by the Christmas tree, surrounded by wrapping paper and boxes, her mother next to her, a giant bow stuck onto the side of each of their heads, both of them laughing as kittenish Murphy Brown dive-bombs an ornament, her body a blur of motion; the three of them holding up carved pumpkins; coins from around the world, collected on their family voyages; Dad's favorite belt, coiled like a resting snake; postcards; cocktail napkins; movie ticket stubs. These are all mementos from before—before the crash. There's only one object in here that can take her back.

Only one that's infused with death.

Greta pulls out the plastic baggie from the coroner's office that hasn't been opened since they handed it to her the morning after the crash. It's the bracelet her mother wore on the night of the accident. The one Mom used to wear every day without fail ever since a young Greta had made it for her. Beads on an elastic string that had snapped many times, each time the beads threaded back into their proper order by her mother. Six balls of glass: blue, yellow, red, blue, yellow, red, followed by white and black beads, shaped like dice, each with a letter, G-R-E-T-A, then another bead with a red heart on it, followed by M-O-M, and then another blue, yellow, red, blue, yellow, red.

No matter how obnoxious teenage Greta got, no matter how much she rebelled, or cursed her mom out, she would always wear the bracelet. Greta wants to cry, scream, tear her hair out. What good would that do? What can be said about unconditional love? Nothing. Not a goddamned thing.

Nothing to say. Only one thing to do.

As Greta goes to put the lid back on the box, her eye catches something out of place at the bottom. It's pink. *Bubblegum pink*. The corner of a card. Greta's stopped breathing. She takes hold of its edge and pulls it out slowly, shells and coins clacking against one another as she extracts it.

It's a perfect square, blank and heavy in weight. A peculiar sheen ripples across it.

CHAPTER SIXTY-FIVE

Greta rushes down the stairs, almost falling.

She'd gotten dressed in a hurry, the hour up as she heard the wheels of the Uber crunching along the driveway, the beams of the headlights flashing across her bedroom walls. The baggie with her mom's bracelet is tucked into her shoulder bag along with the bubblegum-pink card.

So much for Greta and Ezra taking the Found Object Society by surprise.

She hasn't checked the card, but she knows she'll find a QR code. Where will it lead this time? Will it be another threat? And how the hell did the card get into that box? Greta's the only one who knows where it's hidden, that it even exists. How did someone get in without setting off the alarm? *You may ask yourself, Greta, how is any of this possible?*

Almost at the bottom of the stairs, Greta catches Murphy Brown in her periphery, trotting alongside her. She will not look down. Greta will not acknowledge that she sees her. Kirk's black Toyota Camry idles in the driveway, lights on. He honks. The sound rushes her mind back to that night twenty years ago. Her friend Bridget Bower honking in the driveway. Beckoning her to come out.

Dizzy, Greta walks out and closes the door without looking back to see the ghost of her cat, sorry to see her leave. She stops.

The trail cam. There's a video on it. There has to be. Each time an invitation has arrived, there's been a corresponding clip. One that progresses forward from a moment in time in the past. A moment unfamiliar to her. Kirk honks again and Greta holds up her hand, asking him to be patient. Opening the app, she finds the camera was activated within the past hour, while she was in the shower. She hits Play.

The screech, the jagged, transportive blue static. Once again, the license plate of her parents' car. The slab of light from a door opening and Murphy Brown running into the driveway, stopping and turning around, eyes aglow. Someone calls to her. Two silhouettes appear and one moves forward. A pair of arms reach down to lift the cat. A woman's arms, and on her right wrist a bracelet. G-R-E-T-A ❤ M-O-M—

Greta deactivates the phone and opens the door to the Camry.

She doesn't bother to turn off the houselights or to activate the alarm. She leaves it and its phantoms behind. Greta gets in the car as the mockingbird sings its lovelorn song.

Kirk is back to being Kirk the non-talker. *Thank you, Kirk.* His eyes are on the prize and he's driving fast. He has to, to get Greta back to the South Street Seaport by ten thirty.

After hours of silence, her phone chirps with a text. It's from Ezra.

Did you get one, too?

Of course he got one. Of course the Found Object Society knows they're in cahoots. It was dumb to think otherwise. Greta types.

Yes

Rolling dots. Rolling dots.

WTF?

Greta responds.

Have you checked?

Rolling dots. Rolling dots.

No. You?

Greta types.

Not yet

More rolling dots.

Let's

Greta sees Kirk look back at her in the rearview. She types in a thumbs-up emoji and a clenched-teeth emoji. She pulls the card from her bag and places it on her lap, her heart beating so hard she can feel it in her throat, hear it in her ears. Greta looks up. Kirk's eyes are back on the road.

She opens the camera on her phone and hovers it over the card. Nothing happens. She flips it over and it locks; yellow corners form a square, honed in on its Bitly target. She clicks the link. The screen goes black. There are none of the usual special effects. Only black. Then three words appear, one after the other.

See

you

soon.

CHAPTER SIXTY-SIX

The traffic builds like water behind a dam as the Uber approaches the city.

See you soon.

The Found Object Society is expecting them. Ezra's invitation had linked him to the same message: *See you soon.* They're waiting. Greta was put on some kind of probation only yesterday and now they've invited her back? Both of them? Well, sort of. *See you soon.* It's not a warm homecoming. Nor is it a direct threat. It's a statement of fact. We know you're coming. You and Ezra are coming and we will see you. *Soon.*

The FDR Drive is a blocked artery of cars. Vehicles tightly packed into its narrow lanes, built when all automobiles weren't Secret Service–size SUVs. Greta's muttering her lucid-dreaming mantra: *Next time I'm dreaming, I will remember I'm dreaming. Next time I'm dreaming, I will remember I'm dreaming*. Kirk must think she's deranged. Well, she kind of is, isn't she?

The car to their right is so close that if Greta wanted, she could roll down her window and reach out to slap the face of the infuriated dude driving next to her. Instead, she stares ahead, muttering to herself, pretending thousands of humans aren't crammed together alongside her, surging downstream.

The FDR ejects them onto Exit 3, South Street. She's almost there. Greta grips her bag tight to her chest. Its contents precious. The reality of what she's doing takes hold. This is dangerous. The society knows they're coming. What do they plan to do to her? Greta doesn't care anymore. She's going to go back to that night, whatever the threat. She's both chilled and perspiring, heart racing. Up ahead, standing in front of the mural, is Ezra. He's pacing. Greta exhales. She can breathe again. He's here, waiting for her.

Kirk's Toyota Camry has barely come to a stop as Greta climbs out.

"Thanks, Kirk. I've got you covered," she says, waving her phone with the open Uber app on it. Greta's already plugged in the 100 percent gratuity and she taps Submit.

Kirk is saying something to her, holding out his business card. She doesn't bother to listen and closes the door. She runs, practically falls, into Ezra's arms.

"Holy shit, Ezra. Holy shit," she says. "We're doing this, aren't we?"

"You're shaking," he says.

"Of course I'm fucking shaking. I'm terrified."

She puts her arms around his neck and kisses him. It's a needy, selfish kiss. His lips ground her, secure her to this reality they've created. The one they're about to embark upon. They pull apart, the trompe l'oeil mural rising behind them. One version of Brooklyn Bridge layered in front of the other, a passageway with no exit, windows with no rooms behind them, a hand with no body attached to it, pulling back a curtain.

"So, they know, then, right?" Greta says.

Ezra runs his hands through her hair, tucking one side behind an ear. "It would seem so. I guess we shouldn't be surprised."

"I mean, 'See you soon' means they're expecting us. That maybe we don't need to blackmail them to let me in. Right?"

Ezra shrugs.

The two walk, their internal clocks and compasses in sync, leading them to their destination.

"We'll just have to find out, won't we?" Ezra says.

They stand, hand in hand, across from 273 Water Street. Until recently, this building was as anonymous and unremarkable to Greta as the hundreds of others she walks past and takes little notice of. Just another old New York City building, a place where people sleep or work, go about their mundane lives. But beneath this one a secretive society sprawls. Are there others? How long has it existed? The Found Object Society defies logic and the laws of . . . well, the laws of everything, anything.

"If this works . . ." Greta says, without knowing what that might mean, without knowing how to finish the sentence.

Greta squeezes Ezra's hand. He squeezes back.

"I know," he says.

They cross the cobbled street. There are no cars or pedestrians. All is eerily quiet and feels abandoned for ten forty on a Thursday night. They walk down the steps and stand in front of the Cyclops eye of the security camera. Without touching anything or uttering a single word, the camera activates. A dim blue light illuminates Ezra's and Greta's gaunt faces.

"Miss Davenport, Mr. Somers, we've been expecting you." It's the voice of Big Daniel Craig.

The door to the Found Object Society clicks open.

Greta and Ezra stand in the dim corridor that leads to the vault door. Beyond that, the interior of the Found Object Society. It'd been easy—too easy. All the planning, the sweating over how to get Greta back in, has been for naught. So far, at least. Why is that? The question adds to Greta's unease. She tries to shake it off. The goal was to get in, and get in they have. *Almost.*

The blue tinge of the light bulb exsanguinates them. Greta and Ezra appear corpse-like, waiting for their cue to enter.

"That's it? We're in? We didn't even have to say anything," Greta says.

"No questions. No threats. They just buzzed us in," Ezra says.

This voyage is Greta's cross to bear, not Ezra's. He's gotten her in and it's time for him to go. She puts her arms around him again.

"You should leave, Ezra. There's no sense in you getting dragged down with me. This is my plan and I'm going to see it through. Try to, at least. You still have another forty-eight hours before your next voyage. I'm the scofflaw here, not you."

Ezra pulls away from her. A bemused expression on his face. "What are you talking about? Why would I leave?"

"Well . . . wait, what do you mean? This was my idea—to go back and change what happened to my parents." She pulls the coroner's baggie containing her mother's bracelet out of her purse as evidence. "I'm the one who's been practicing, the one who's tried it, at least. They're going to kick you out, and then what? Don't go down for my crime."

Greta sees it now. Before he answers her, she sees it in the concavity of his eyes. She's seen it ever since they met in the narrow alleyway. Since their first night together in the dusty vast anonymity of his glass apartment, and the breakdown over the loss of Jake. The crushing heartache of how he's never known what happened to his only child and the peeling away of life as he'd known it. Alone, suffering without purpose until the Found Object Society contacted him. Punishing himself with the deaths of other children. Ezra's only companions are Greta and his sorrow, and if she . . . if she what? Loses her mind? Disappears? After this, her last voyage, that torturous regret will be his only friend.

Before he even answers her, she knows what he's going to say.

He reaches into his jacket pocket and pulls out his own baggie. Inside it, a round disc, which the indigo of the bulb renders colorless.

"I can't be sure, but right before I tucked Jake into bed that night on the boat, we'd been playing checkers. I found this under his pillow after he disappeared." It's a checker piece. "It's all I've got. I have to try. Like you said the other night, if I had the chance to go back and change what happened, why wouldn't I?"

The mechanism of the vault's locks turns at the end of the darkened corridor. Toothy gears rotate and grind as bolts clack open, one after the other.

"You've never tried this before, Ezra. I'm no expert, but at least I've done it."

"I'll figure it out," he says. He puts his hands on her cheeks and looks into her eyes, through her. "Or I won't. Or maybe I won't." He shrugs.

The massive, ornate vault door gapes open.

"The mantra. Remember the mantra: *Next time I'm dreaming—*"

"*I will remember I'm dreaming.* I know, Greta." He takes her hand as they hurry to the end of the hallway and to the door, the lush glow of the Found Object Society just beyond.

Greta steals one last kiss. *Bon voyage*, she thinks.

CHAPTER SIXTY-SEVEN

The shift from the blue and black of the hallway into the technicolor of the Found Object Society's welcome area is a sugar rush. Everything, from the furniture to the wallpaper to Miranda's and BDC's clothing, erupts with saturated intensity.

Greta isn't sure what she expected when she walked in—when *they* walked in—but it wasn't Miranda and BDC acting normal. Like none of the night before happened. In Greta's previous visits, it'd only been BDC greeting her. Miranda always came in later. Not tonight. Greta gets the discomforting feeling that they're the only ones here, that they are the only clients in the catacombs of the Found Object Society.

Miranda's dress is an intense violet. The design is the same as all the others—tight, low-cut bodice, copious skirts. Her Victorian wardrobe is a mood ring of sorts, the colors alternating dependent on the situation. If so, what does purple mean? Bright, dizzying purple. Even BDC's vest and tie radiate with emerald green.

It's odd being in here with Ezra. The society is always cautious about clients not crossing paths, and here they are, breaking at least half of the rules listed on the wall placard in one fell swoop, standing side by side. Miranda looking like the cat who ate the canary; Big Daniel Craig resigned and slouching beside her.

As if all is as it was *intended* to be.

"And here you both are," Miranda says. Her statement making it clear they've known about them the entire time. Her arms are relaxed, ringed fingers intertwined and resting on the front of her skirt.

Just because they know about them and are standing here talking doesn't mean they'll let Greta and Ezra all the way in. Maybe they've only allowed them to enter so they wouldn't make a scene on the sidewalk? Calling attention to themselves and 273 Water Street, threatening them with social media posts and outing the society. Could that be the reason they're inside and chatting right now? Is that why it was so damned easy to get in? Because maybe letting them in was cleaner than the messy alternative.

Ezra speaks first. "You know why we're here," he says. It's a statement, not a question.

"Alas, we do, Mr. Somers," BDC says. "Please reconsider. You both seem like good people—"

Miranda shoots Big Daniel Craig a glance that stops him in his tracks.

"I believe their minds are made up, Daniel. If so, who are we to stop them?" Miranda says.

"Yes, Miranda. I've made up my mind. We both have," Greta says. Her eyes move to Ezra, who nods in agreement. "But why the sudden change? Only yesterday you kicked me out because I tinkered with my vessel, with Colleen Davies's fate. And now?"

No answer Miranda can give will change Greta's plan for what she's about to do. Still, alarms sound in her head. The saying goes, *You catch more flies with honey.* Is that what they're doing? Trying to trap Greta and Ezra somehow? If so, into what?

"You aren't the first to try this, Miss Davenport," BDC blurts out.

Miranda plants her hand on Big Daniel Craig's shoulder. She's a ferocious porcelain doll, taming Godzilla. Her voice penetrating, she says, "Daniel." The simple utterance of his name a retribution.

Miranda's thumb ring writhes. The roots reach toward BDC before retreating again.

"What does he mean by that? *Not the first*?" Ezra says.

Miranda keeps her grasp on BDC. "Regret. Tragedy. That's what brings our clients here to the Found Object Society—"

"So, of course, we're not the only ones who've ever wanted to change the past," Greta says.

"No. You aren't," Miranda says.

"And has it worked? Does it?" Greta says.

"It's what you both want, isn't it? More than anything?" Miranda says, without answering Greta's question. "To at least try?"

Looking over at Ezra, Greta realizes she loves him. It's a truth as real and immovable as a mountain. Greta loves Ezra—this version and any others of her that may exist. It's so *Romeo and Juliet*, *Thelma & Louise*, *Bonnie and Clyde*. . . . Greta knows how those stories end.

"Yes," Greta says. "Yes, it is."

Greta looks to BDC. His gaze drops and he shakes his head. He's not happy about this. It's Miranda's show, though. She's the ringmaster.

"Well then, let's get started." Miranda pulls the curtain aside to let them pass through. The roots of the gold-and-emerald tree ring on Miranda's thumb reawaken, burying themselves bloodlessly into her flesh.

Greta thinks of the Haas mural on Peck Slip: the spectral hand pulling aside the curtain as the person hidden from view looks out. What if the body beyond the hand *wasn't* trying to look out? What if it was trying to give the outside observer a better view *in*?

Miranda leads the way through the Collection Room. Ezra and Greta behind her, holding hands (why try to pretend?), with Big Daniel Craig bringing up the rear. They walk straight through this time, none of the usual pageantry. No tapping of the tablet, no pin lights coming on with the pleasant tinkle of a bell, illuminating a cubbyhole with an object inside specially selected for Greta. Chosen for Greta to journey back and experience the drama, the ecstasy, of a human being's last moments.

Theirs is a slow march. A troop of four heading to the front line. Greta hears Miranda's heels clicking with each step, but she can't see her feet under the violet dress. Miranda didn't answer Greta's question. Had it worked? Have the others who've tried this been able to go back and change the wrongs of the past? If so (or if not), where are those people now?

To their left, row after row of shelves stretch from floor to ceiling. The only light a faint glow toward the far end of each aisle. Greta spots something moving in the distance. A dark mass rolling toward them. A ball of pure black picking up speed, on a collision course, its movement silent. Is Greta the only one that sees it? Hypnotized, she watches as it unfurls across the floor, elongates, and halts with a splash at Miranda's feet.

It's Miranda's shadow. Yet another trick of the eye.

They continue past the shelves whose shadows form a cartilage of darkness, a black rib cage arcing over their heads like the inside of a giant whale, or the carcass of a dinosaur.

Trembling, Greta reaches her free hand into her satchel and finds her mother's bracelet in its baggie, gives it a squeeze. Her head buzzes as the room tilts. For a second, she's back in the pit—the metallic smell of blood, the cries of dying rats. She feels Ezra's arm slip around her waist and pull her close.

He leans down and whispers, "Are you okay? You sure about this?"

She shucks off the grisly scene and returns to the present. "Yes, I'm sure."

They turn down the hallway that leads to the cabins. As Greta suspected, each door is illuminated green. Ten vacancies. There's no one else here. Tonight, she and Ezra are the Found Object Society's only customers. The thought gives her no comfort. None at all.

Miranda stops in front of the third hatch in. "Daniel, I'll take Ms. Davenport into her cabin. Please escort Mr. Somers to his."

BDC nods and moves past them. Ezra doesn't follow. He stops to face Greta. Both Miranda and Big Daniel Craig look away, granting them a moment of privacy.

"I'm not sure what we're supposed to say now. *See you later*? *Good luck*?" Ezra says.

Greta hugs him close to her. Is this the last time she'll see him? Or is the Found Object Society what she suspected it to be from the first time she set foot inside: a bit of theater, a special effects extravaganza injected straight into their cerebral cortexes? It feels genuine enough. Ezra is real.

She inhales the briny sea air of him. The one that lulled her to sleep that very first night.

"I hope you find him," she says, whispering in his ear.

"And I hope you find your mother and father."

"Remember, *Next time I'm dreaming*—"

"*I will remember I'm dreaming.* Got it."

Ezra's gone down to his cabin, and Greta and Miranda stand inside hers. The hatch shuts with its seductive sigh.

"Make yourself comfortable, Greta," Miranda says.

Greta sits on the chaise and runs her palms across its velvety landscape. She opens her shoulder bag and only then realizes that BDC never asked for their cell phones. Could he have forgotten? That doesn't seem likely. Was the confiscating of their phones part of this whole trippy charade? Or maybe they didn't collect their cell phones tonight because they'd no longer be needing them.

Not where we're going.

Greta pulls out the baggie containing her mother's bracelet and holds it up to Miranda, who's been prepping the table along with the hypodermic. Latex gloves on, she takes it from her and scrutinizes the contents.

"Sweet," Miranda says. "Very sweet." Greta can't tell if she's being sincere or not. "Lie back, please."

Greta leans her body back, the curves cupping her spine and beneath her knees. She tries to control her shallow and rapid breathing. This is what she's wanted. For twenty years, she's lived her life to distraction, tested the boundaries of her humanity, wondered how—*why*—she survived the crash when her parents didn't, why she deserved to live on without them. The crash was her fault. *Hers.* This is her chance to change things, to right her wrong. It's far-fetched as hell, but it's something, at least. It's the only thing.

The Obitus Mold extends from beneath the chaise and Greta rests her right arm into it. The metal reacts and welcomes Greta with a squeeze. The weight and pressure are a comfort. The tension slips from her body and she closes her eyes. She hasn't been given the taffy, but she still feels the texture of it on her tongue, the sour tang of the blackberry. Seagulls caw. The sugar and oil of funnel cakes fill her nostrils, the warmth of her parents' hands holding on to hers.

"Amazing, isn't it? Your mind remembers the taffy. You only needed it once. We helped you remember. The rest you did yourself," Miranda says.

Greta's hand rests, palm up. She watches Miranda open the coroner's bag and expose its contents to oxygen for the first time in twenty years. She places the bracelet in Greta's hand with surprising reverence. Greta remembers making it, picking the glass beads and stringing them together with care, alternating the colors, being sure she had the spelling right. She'd been so proud when she gave it to her mother. And years later, the opposite was true: Her teenage self, embarrassed every time she looked at it on her mom's wrist. How she'd wished she'd take it off from time to time so that Greta wouldn't be reminded of the girl she'd been. The way her mother would rub it whenever they'd argue, as if that could bring little Greta back, like a genie. The daughter who had been so proud when she gave it to her. So full of love.

Greta's heavy, as if being pulled down into a warm bath. Words struggle to form in her mouth. "The first taffy . . . making my Obitus Mold . . . You've known what I was going to do all along?"

Miranda taps at the hypodermic, removing the air bubbles so all that remains is the mercurial liquid. She pushes it into Greta's skin. She feels nothing more than a tickle.

"All along, Greta," she says, and empties the contents into Greta's vein.

CHAPTER SIXTY-EIGHT

The hand of darkness slaps Greta awake. Her newfound consciousness is abrupt, thorny. The black wraps around her like a bandage, immobilizes her, renders her limbs useless. She's jostled back and forth before being put into motion, feet first, and sloping downward.

She's on a voyage. That much she knows. Her mind is dense clay, and she tries to find clarity in her thoughts. A hidden force thrusts her body forward in violent bursts, trying to dislodge her like a fish bone in the throat. This thing she's inside is choking, choking on Greta. With each movement her head and body knock into hard and unforgiving corners and edges.

This isn't how it's been before. Her past three voyages were languid journeys, her sense of self adrift. Her being floating until docking. Not now. Not this. Greta is a foreign body in need of extraction. Taking blow after blow, she sails down until she's ejected into a cavernous space. Greta's been expelled. The power of it has her careening forward, out of control. Greta's somersaulting through the air. Each time she tries to control the motion, it serves only to increase her speed.

Up ahead, two windows. Greta knows where she's going now. She braces for impact.

Greta's sailing into the mind of her mother and she has no brakes.

CHAPTER SIXTY-NINE

Lainie Davenport's head swims. She loses her balance and falls forward, the entryway wall catching her before she hits the ground.

What the hell was that about?

Moments ago, she and Greta had another argument. A big one. Her teenage hellion of a daughter stormed out and slammed the door in her face. Lainie got dizzy, like someone kicked her from the inside of her skull. Then she fell.

"Lainie!" her husband, Peter, says, rushing over to her. "Are you okay?"

Lainie shuts her eyes, regains her breath. The surge of blood that roared like a thousand voices in her ears subsides. "Yeah. I think so. Wow, that was . . . that was weird. I got dizzy suddenly, like I was pushed from the inside."

The beams from Bridget Bower's (teenage hellion number two) car headlights scan past them as she pulls out of the driveway. Peter and Lainie's seventeen-year-old daughter is in the passenger seat, probably giving her and Peter the finger—probably the double bird—as they drive off. Probably laughing their asses off as they light a doobie. *Probably.* They're up to no good. Greta and Bridget are always up to no good.

It's not like Lainie grew up a prude. She was a child of the sixties, a teen in the seventies. Sex, pot, booze—all were standard fare for a teenager growing up in her time. But this? This reflexive anger that Greta can't control, or refuses to, where did it come from? Had Lainie been this angry at her parents all the time? *All the fucking time?*

It's the money, has to be. Lainie wasn't poor as a kid, but what she and Peter have now? What Greta is accustomed to and surrounded by, with her equally rich and entitled friends, like Bridget Bower? It poisons you, skews your worldview. When Lainie and Peter went public on their dot-com startup in the late nineties, the money they got was *sick* money.

In grad school, they brainstormed about creating the company over long nights of bong hits, munchies, and sex (not necessarily in that order). The money that came from that brainchild was more than they'd ever dreamt of. More than they ever needed (than anyone ever does). And now?

Being Greta Davenport's mother is a little slice of hell.

Peter leads Lainie to the couch in the living room. He's guiding her over like she's an old lady.

"I'm not broken, Peter. I don't have the vapors or anything," she says.

He's trying to help. She knows that. But she can't stand the elbow cupping, the hand on her lower back, guiding her forward. A delicate doll. A frail butterfly. It feels so . . . Victorian.

"Christ, Lainie. I know that. Please sit your very strong, ferociously independent, gorgeous ass down for a minute."

She laughs. He can always crack her up, call her on her own shit. Lainie does the same for him. Always has, always will. Till death do us part, motherfucker. She means that in the best, most loving and in-love way imaginable.

The living room is the heart of their nineteenth-century stone house in Litchfield County. For other people, it's the kitchen. The kitchen's great, don't get her wrong, but the living room? An enormous stone fireplace anchors at its center, a fire burning in it now, softening the chill of an April evening. On either side are walls of bookshelves, artwork, and mementos from their travels. The travel is the best thing about the money.

Teenage Greta is the worst thing about it.

A long couch rests under the windows that face the fireplace. It's Greta's favorite place to nap, to hang out with their cat, Murphy Brown. At least, it had been until she started locking herself in her room, talking on her cell phone and playing around with her AOL account on her tangerine iMac, coming out only long enough to eat dinner with them in annoyed silence.

"She'll grow out of this phase, right?" Lainie fidgets with her beaded bracelet, the one Greta made for her about a hundred years ago. *Greta Hearts Mom*. She won't take it off. She'll keep restringing it every time it breaks and wear it until her dying day. Lainie's not dumb. She knows that childlike love doesn't last forever. It morphs, shifts. Each time Greta gets angry or they have a fight or she sits there silent, pissed off at some unseeable injustice, touching the bracelet reminds her of what Greta can be, what she's been. So, Lainie will wait for that Greta to come back, for that part of her daughter that loved her mother more than she hates her now.

"I hope so, Lainie. You grew out of it, right?"

"I was never this bad. I don't think," she says.

"We could call your mom right now. Conduct a survey? *Hey, Margaret, it's Pete calling. We'd like to know, on a scale of one to ten, how shitty would you say your relationship with Lainie was when she was a teenager? Oh, an eight? That's pretty rough.*"

Lainie punches Peter in the shoulder. His bad one from too much tennis, played too poorly. Pete sucks at tennis.

"Ow!" he says. Serves him right.

"I doubt I was an eight. Maybe a six. Six and a half."

Murphy Brown jumps onto Lainie's lap. Their cat's getting older, rounder, a feline dumpling. Most of her front fangs have been removed to preserve her dental health, so her love nibbles are no longer a threat to your hand. Now it's polite gumming. Lainie leans over and kisses the triangle of her head, the waft of Lainie's own perfume still embedded in her fur.

"Seriously, this Greta situation sucks. I'm not sure what we're supposed to do," she says.

"Me neither."

"Grounding her does nothing, she just finds a work-around. Talking to her is pointless, since she won't listen, won't talk back unless she's telling me how stupid I am, how I need to shut up and let her live her life." A memory returns. A good one. "Remember the Mystic boardwalk?"

"Yeah, we were heroes then," he says.

Heroes.

They'd walked hand in hand, the three of them. Greta eating blackberry taffy, seagulls swooping down for morsels of clam strips and funnel cakes dropped onto the ground, the smell of the sea.

"Heroes then, villains now. How does that happen?" she says.

"Damn if I know," he says.

"So, what do we do? Bridget's a nightmare. Greta's always staying over at her place. What do you think they do all night?" Lainie says. It's a rhetorical question. "Curl each other's hair and giggle about boys while looking through the yearbook?"

"I prefer to draw a blank. Do we really want to know what they're up to? As long as she comes home in one piece and we don't have to get her out on bail, that's a victory," Peter says.

"That's a crap way to think," she says.

"I'm kidding. Kind of," he says.

"It's not just you. It's me, too. It's easier to do nothing. Tonight, though, they're up to something. I know it."

Lainie rolls her bracelet under her fingers like worry beads. Greta driving away with Bridget into the night to do God knows what. There has to be a happy medium between dictatorship and doing bubkes. Has to be.

Tonight, Lainie, mother to a teenage hellion, is determined to find the in-between.

Lainie isn't sure what she's looking for in Greta's bathroom. Birth control? Drug paraphernalia?

Snooping around her teenage daughter's stuff is a violation. One that would've enraged Lainie when she was Greta's age. *Oh, how the tide does turn.* It looks like a tornado hit a Maybelline factory in here: opened tubes of mascara, uncapped eyeliners, little wads of toilet paper covered in different shades of lip gloss strewn across the vanity, tumbleweeds of sticky pink goo. Lainie picks up a bottle of Essie nail polish. It's the bright pink, the bubblegum pink that Greta always wears on her toes. Flipping it over, she tries to read the name of the color. *Tries.* Deny as she might, Lainie needs her glasses to read.

When did this impostor come and take over Lainie's body? The one who prowls through her adolescent daughter's bathroom; who needs glasses to read the menu when she and her husband go out on a date; the one who looks an awful lot like her mother, Margaret, when she looks in the mirror. The mirror smeared with her daughter's fingerprints and toothpaste from when she leans in too close when she's brushing. Her daughter cleaning her teeth so she can have fresh breath to . . . make out with boys? Of course Greta makes out with boys. *Look at her.* She probably does more than that. *Of course she does, stupid.*

An image of Greta out there in the night, some jock's hand up her shirt, flashes through her mind. The transformation of Greta's body from gangly tween to sinuous teenager had been abrupt. Auburn hair shining in the sun as she storms off to school in the mornings. Full lips begging for gloss. Skin uninterrupted by the fissures of time. Everything about her daughter's youthful body screams *Look at me, touch me.* Lainie remembers that time herself. The realization of the power she wielded from a simple walk down the street. Men's eyes following her every move. How the tilt of her chin, the lift of an eyelid, or the gentle rotation of her foot as she sat on a diner stool, reaching to touch her anklet, could change the air in a room. Electrify it.

Lainie remembers.

Older Lainie, Mother Lainie, extends her arm as far as she can until she can make out the name of the color underneath the nail polish bottle.

"You've got to be kidding me," she says to the old lady looking back at her in the mirror.

It's so on the nose, it's ridiculous. *Sleepover Squad.*

CHAPTER SEVENTY

Three hours have passed since the kick inside her skull. Three hours since her daughter stormed out, with Bridget Bower waiting in her car.

Lainie's been distracted all evening. She and Peter share a bottle of wine on the couch. Peter's had most of it. She's had a glass—tops. Her legs are stretched out, her feet resting on Peter's lap. Every once in a while, he'll give her arches a squish as he turns the page of his book. Murphy Brown is pressed against Lainie's hip, her fur absorbing the heat from the fire like blacktop. Lainie's fidgety, restless.

She's thinking of her fall after Greta slammed the door in her face, like someone collided with her from the inside. Lainie can't let go of the image of a jock with his hand up Greta's shirt.

Sleepover Squad.

"What if they're up to something?" Lainie says.

Peter, head down, deep into his book, grunts.

"Peter," she says, tapping her feet into the book cover, snapping him out of it.

"What? Sorry, what are you saying?"

"Greta. Bridget. I feel like they're up to something," she says.

"That's not breaking news. You're probably right."

She swings her feet off him and puts them on the floor. Murphy Brown pours herself from the couch and trundles closer to the fire, the bell on her collar a lazy tinkle.

"So, what? We sit here and do nothing?" she says.

Peter closes his book and puts it aside. *Peter doesn't need reading glasses.* The thought irks her.

"Okay. What do *you* think we should do?" Peter says. His eyes are glassy from the wine, his cheeks flushed by the warmth of alcohol and fire.

"I can't get rid of this image of some lacrosse jock making out with her and feeling her up," she says.

Peter slaps his hands onto his ears, closes his eyes tight. "Lainie! Why do that to me? Jesus, don't say that about our daughter."

"You don't think she's . . . you know, *active*? Do you?"

He pats his ears like he's putting out flames. "No, no, no. Why are we having this conversation? No, correction: Why are *you* having this conversation?"

"Because I get a bad feeling that Greta, *our* daughter Greta, isn't sleeping over at Bridget's house like she said she was."

"What are we supposed to do about it?"

"Be parents, for starters. Make sure our daughter is safe. You know, that kind of thing?" Lainie's getting sarcastic. Her mother is crawling around inside her, making her say things she never thought she'd say. Plus, why *doesn't* Peter need reading glasses?

Lainie can see she's killed his buzz, his chill. She's kind of glad.

"Okay, Lainie. Okay. Agreed. What do you propose we do?"

Lainie thinks about it. Bridget Bower is a piece of work, sure, but her mom is a whole construction site.

"We should call and check on them. We should call Harper Bower."

Communicating with Harper Bower in any kind of human way is a challenge. Most of the time she's either recovering from a cosmetic procedure or awash in gin, ranting about some intensely first-world problem. She's a delight.

So, it isn't without a fair bit of humility that Lainie picks up the phone and dials her number. She and Peter are in the kitchen and Lainie has her green address book of contacts open to *B*. Peter leans into the countertop, pouring himself the last of the wine. He's not thrilled with this turn of events. Lainie doesn't care. Murphy Brown takes their entrance into the kitchen—the room where all the cat food magic happens—as an invitation to another meal. She weaves back and forth between their legs, headbutting their shins with her hard skull.

"It's almost eleven o'clock," Peter says. "Harper's probably passed out on martinis and Vicodin, anyway."

She doesn't answer. It wasn't a question. It was a statement of fact. One that won't keep her from dialing Harper's number.

The phone is ringing. Three rings. Four. Five. Peter looks at her, expectant. Lainie shrugs.

Seven.

The sound of hard plastic scraping against hard plastic makes Lainie pull the receiver away from her ear.

"What? Fuck! What?" Harper's words come out like she's pushing them through a sieve.

"Um, Harper? Hi, it's Greta's mom. Lainie Davenport."

On the other end, Harper drops the receiver, or clutches it to her body, it's hard to tell what's going on. Then there's a crash and a persistent rustling of cloth—or is it plastic? A bag of chips?—followed by splashing and a faraway moan, as though Harper's made her way across the room with a blade in her ribs, crawling out of a flooded dumpster, bleeding.

"Hello. Harper? Everything okay?"

Lainie looks over at Peter, eyes wide. He mouths, *What the fuck?* She shakes her head.

All the sounds repeat, but in reverse: the faraway moan, the splashing, a crinkling and a rustle, and finally a crash.

"I'm here." Her speech is strangled, near unintelligible, like her jaw's wired shut. "I just ad eye wips done. I'm in the ath." *I just had my lips done. I'm in the bath.*

Oh, okay, these are normal things to say.

"Right, Harper. Um, sorry . . . I guess."

"What did idget oo now?" Harper says. *What did Bridget do now?* "I can't come ick her up now, if zats what yer asking." *I can't come pick her up, if that's what you're asking.*

"No, why would you . . . I mean, Greta's staying over at your place tonight. *With* Bridget. Um, your daughter. I'm checking in to make sure everything is okay? That the girls are fine?"

Peter's walked over to Lainie. He's leaning in, trying to hear what Harper is saying through the earpiece. It's hard enough for Lainie to understand Harper as it is, so she pushes him back.

"Dare at yer house. Not mine."

"No, Harper. Bridget came to pick Greta up hours ago. They were going to stay over at *your* house tonight. They said so." Lainie's heart is pounding. The image of the jock in her mind has changed. Now he's got his hand in Greta's pants. "Are you sure? Maybe you took too many painkillers? Can you check?"

Harper's ability to speak is deteriorating. She's melting on the other end of the line.

"Screw oo. Dey aren't ere, Ainie. Okay? Dare at yer ouse. O ook urself." *Screw you. They aren't here, Lainie. Okay? They're at your house.* That last bit could either be, *Go fuck yourself* or *Go look yourself.* Lainie decides on the latter.

"They're not here, Harper."

Lainie and Peter look at each other. Peter pieces together the scenario from Lainie's end of the conversation. He leans in close to the mouthpiece.

"Harper," he says, overprojecting. "Listen to me: The girls are not here. They're *not*. They said they were staying at your place."

"Dey eyed," Harper says. Then she hangs up.

They lied.

CHAPTER SEVENTY-ONE

The next twenty minutes are a blur of calling the parents of Greta's other friends and classmates, trying to locate Greta. More than a handful have a child who's been caught in the same lie. Phone calls triangulate across the area, bouncing from mansion to mansion. Boozy parents to high ones to righteous ones and indignant ones. They add up to the same sum: Eight teenagers—partiers, jocks, mean girls, all—have woven an elaborate lie. At least complex enough that all their laissez-faire parents, busy with trying not to be parental, have been caught with their proverbial pants down.

Lainie's been taking notes as Peter watches her write through parted fingers that clutch at his face. A name written out, then a line drawn through it if the kid is home. The name circled if they're out, unaccounted for—Greta's is one of them, her name lassoed with pen over and over, the paper close to tearing. The pieces of the puzzle are coming together. Thanks to reliable intel from one mother who seems to give two shits, a clearer picture has formed. Four pairs of teenagers, all saying that they're staying over at one another's houses, but none of them are there. One of the teen's parents are at their house in Palm Beach. . . . *assholes*.

Lainie hangs up the phone and writes the address of the Daehlers' house—the one in Palm Beach—while the other mom calls them in Florida now.

"Dollars to doughnuts they're all at the Daehlers' house," Lainie says.

"The Daehlers'? John Daehler's a prick. If his son is anything like him . . ." Peter says.

"Exactly. And Francine Daehler is an asshole. So you better believe their son, Todd, is a double-recessive prick-asshole," she says.

"Dammit," Peter says.

Lainie works the beads of her bracelet through her fingertips. *Greta Hearts Mom. Greta* Hates *Mom.*

"Do we call the cops? Get them to go over there?" he says.

Lainie shakes her head. She has a different plan. She gathers her bag and car keys. Murphy Brown meows, indignant over her lack of kibble.

"We're driving over there. Now," she says.

"Let me see the address."

Lainie shows him her chicken-scratched note.

"Is that Sycamore?" he says.

Lainie nods and hands him his jacket, puts on her own.

"Do you know the way?" Peter says.

He's always been terrible with directions. She could point him where to go, tell him to walk straight, and he'd still find a way to circle back, demagnetize his internal compass. It's charming.

"I do. Besides, you've had more to drink than me," she says.

"I feel sober as a judge," Peter says.

Lainie opens the front door and they both step out into the cool night air. A triangle of light spills from the house onto the driveway. Peter's and Lainie's shadows follow suit. Murphy Brown bolts out in front of her, into the light.

Next time I'm dreaming . . .

She stops cold on the front landing. "What, Peter? What did you say?" The voice hadn't sounded like Peter, but it certainly wasn't her own.

"What, *what*?" he says behind her. "I didn't say anything. Grab the cat, would you?"

Lainie walks onto the pea gravel and reaches down to pick up Murphy Brown, *Greta Hearts Mom* staring up at her from her wrist. That's a laugh. She carries the chunky cat back and plunks her into the house, closing the door.

Lainie's sure she heard a voice. *Next time I'm dreaming* . . . She casts the thought aside and she and Peter crunch across the driveway to the car. As she reaches to put the key in the lock, her hand opens and the keys fall to the ground. It isn't nerves. She wasn't fumbling. Her hand dropped them, like she meant to do it. Like someone pried her fingers open. She picks them up off the damp stones and, with two hands, puts the key in and opens the car door, unlocking it for both of them.

"Butterfingers," Peter says, and he climbs in the passenger side.

There isn't much to talk about as Lainie and Peter drive the seven miles to the Daehlers' house. The house where eight kids, including their daughter, are partying their asses off.

The road is dark, winding. The sky moonless.

Why couldn't this have been a normal night? How did they get to this place where Greta acts as if she hates them? Where every word out of her mouth is a lie? When Lainie thinks of that little girl on the Mystic boardwalk, holding their hands, eating taffy, unashamed to show affection for them in public, it detonates something inside her. Shards cutting into her soft tissue, making her bleed internally. It feels like it's too late, like the damage is done. Inoperable.

They head into a curve and her bracelet rolls across her skin and then along the steering wheel. Lainie needs to believe that sweet version of Greta is still in there somewhere. Has to be.

"Watch it!" Peter calls out, putting his hand on Lainie's thigh.

She sees the possum in time as she rounds out of the bend and hits the brakes, coming to a stop. The awkward creature's waddled halfway into their lane. It freezes in front of them. Instead of one set of eyes blinking in the beam of the headlights, there are five. No, make it six. It's a mother possum with five babies on her back, riding her like a pachyderm.

Lainie flashes her lights at the possum family.

"C'mon, Mama. Move it along," she says.

The mother possum gathers her strength and carries her load to the other side of the street, descending into a field.

Lainie and Peter give each other a look.

"Irony or metaphor?" Peter says to his wife.

"Both. Definitely both."

They drive on. Their destination is a mile ahead.

The Daehlers' house blazes with life at the end of the quarter-mile-long driveway. It's a monstrosity of columns and chimneys. Four cars are parked out front. One of them Bridget Bower's.

"She's here. Greta's here," Lainie says.

She knew she would be. Part of her hoped this was all a misunderstanding. That Harper was soused and anesthetized to such a degree that she forgot that Bridget and Greta were safely ensconced in Bridget's bedroom, brushing each other's hair and telling ghost stories.

Fat fucking chance.

"Let's get this over with," Peter says.

The trauma isn't hers alone. She can see it in his eyes, hear it in his voice. Greta no longer belongs to them. The hero's cape is off.

Lainie reaches over and takes his hand, squeezes it.

"Whatever happens, we'll be okay. Let's not lose our tempers. Let's get her home and safe and take it from there. Right?"

Peter nods, but it doesn't look like he's buying it. Lainie's not so sure she buys it herself.

They pull up front and the headlights shine into the living room, illuminating a table surrounded by bodies in various states of undress. From her vantage point, Lainie can see Greta. Next to her, Todd Daehler—lacrosse jock, prick-asshole—is kissing her neck.

Her daughter is topless.

CHAPTER SEVENTY-TWO

They don't bother knocking. Lainie and Peter bust in like cops raiding a speakeasy.

Taut bodies scatter. Chairs fall to the floor. Clothes are strewn everywhere, surrounding a table that must have cost a fortune, sticky with spilled cups of beer, divots from quarters doing permanent damage to its lacquered surface.

Strip quarters. Really? The more things change . . .

If this wasn't her daughter they were talking about, if this was someone else's story being told at a drunken dinner party, it'd be hilarious. A laugh riot. It's not someone else, though. It's Greta, Peter and Lainie's only daughter, and she's standing (barely) butt-ass naked except for a black lace thong that Lainie didn't know she owned.

Lainie stares in wonder at how beautiful Greta's become. Even in this absurd, beer-stinking cacophony of teens yelping and scattering and Peter saying angry, Dad-like things that Lainie can't quite make out, Lainie is taken by Greta's physical beauty. The power that's surging through her daughter's seventeen-year-old skin that she has yet to harness. Greta's approaching the peak of her female storm while Lainie's is blowing out to sea. Dissipating.

She envies her.

Crazy but true, part of Lainie wants to sit back and cheer on her wildly disobedient and drunk daughter from the sidelines. She remembers what it felt like, how each move of the body was part of a greater chess match. Was it a wonder that Greta hated them? Or thought she did? They were trying to take it away from her, to control her wattage that could light up a city.

I'd hate me, too.

Mother Lainie kicks in again. Greta's standing, bewildered, eyes spinning with alcohol as her friends dash to other parts of the house. Bridget Bower runs out the front door and into the night. Lainie picks up Greta's clothes and brings them to her.

"Put these on," she says, handing her a bra, jeans, and a T-shirt.

Greta's teenage breasts defy gravity. Lainie can't recall the last time she saw her daughter naked. She watches as Greta fumbles. Drunk as a skunk and unable to figure out which way her bra should go.

"Let me help you," Lainie says. But no sooner does she try to help Greta with her bra straps than her daughter pushes her away.

"You don't . . . tell me . . . what to do." Greta's words are slow, hard to mold in her mouth. She taps her index finger into Lainie's sternum after each word for emphasis.

Lainie thinks of Harper Bower's strangled speech. *Dey eyed.*

Todd Daehler and Peter are in the kitchen, talking. If Todd wasn't naked and holding his hands in front of his junk, it might look like they were having a normal chat. Lainie wonders what Peter's saying to him. Did he threaten to kick him in the balls?

Greta's managed to get herself dressed—Lainie spotting her as she loses her balance with each attempt at putting on a pant leg; Greta swatting her mother's hand away every time. Her T-shirt's on backward. So what? The house is in chaos. It's *Lord of the Flies* and Peter and Lainie are the only grown-ups here. Too bad. Not their problem. Everyone else's parents know the deal. They'll come collect their children if they want to. Lainie and Peter have theirs. That's all that matters.

They flank Greta, Peter taking her left arm, Lainie her right, and drag her drunken sack of a body out the front door and toward their car, jacket draped over her. Greta's feet scrape across the grass. She's all but passed out.

They deposit her in the back seat, Peter holding up his daughter's torso from one side of the car while Lainie fishes around for the seat belt from the other. She secures it in place and Peter props Greta upright, only to have her slump all the way down again, face-first into the leather.

"It's okay, Peter. Forget it. She's strapped in at least. Let her sleep it off."

Peter closes the rear door and sits in the passenger seat up front. Lainie pushes the hair out of Greta's face and is about to get out herself when Greta paws at the bracelet on Lainie's wrist. The one she made when she didn't hate her mother.

Eyes closed, Greta whispers, "Next time I'm dreaming, I will remember I'm dreaming."

CHAPTER SEVENTY-THREE

Lainie's trying to make sense of the words that came out of her drunk daughter's mouth. The same ones that she'd thought she heard as they left the house. Peter didn't hear Greta, or, if he did, it didn't register. There has to be a logical explanation for what's going on. Lainie just can't figure out what it is.

"That was a nightmare," Peter says, as they turn out of the Daehlers' driveway.

Lainie looks into the rearview mirror. Greta is a rag doll, passed out on the back seat.

"Lainie? You okay? You're white as a ghost," he says. "It's like you said before: We'll be all right. Let's get Greta home in one piece and take it from there. Right?"

Lainie nods.

Her eyes are focused on the road in front of them. The truth of the dark exposed for only as long as the beams flash across it, before retreating again. Lainie tries to picture what the scene will look like when they get home, when they carry Greta back inside their house, what they'll say to her, each other. Each time she attempts to imagine it, she can't see beyond this moment, beyond where the light is shining right now. It's as though the future doesn't exist.

"Lainie? Hey, slow it down a bit. The worst is over."

They're coming into a series of sharp curves, flanked by trees that date back to the Revolutionary War. Gnarled oaks and maples, multiarmed monsters caught by the high beams, waiting to pounce.

Next time I'm dreaming, I will remember I'm dreaming.

The voice is clear. It's a woman's. Lainie's certain of it. The words bounce through the interior of the car, ring inside Lainie's head. The world slows around her. Quiets. In her periphery, Peter's fingers grip the seat, his right leg extends forward, depressing a brake pedal that isn't there. Lainie has the sensation she's not alone within her body, that a hidden hand is manipulating her. She looks up to the rearview again. Her breath pulls out of her like a string.

A woman is sitting in the back seat alongside her passed-out daughter.

The woman's there, but she's not there. Her mouth moves in the mirror's reflection, but the words come out in Lainie's head. Over and over: *Next time I'm dreaming, I will remember I'm dreaming.* The woman is familiar in a way Lainie can't process. Her hair is auburn and wavy. Her cheeks sharper, more mature. Creases around the eyes where once it was smooth. Lips ripe for gloss. *No*. No, no, no. This can't be. None of this can.

It's Greta. But it's not Greta.

It *is* Greta. Older, wasting away. Two versions of her daughter in the back seat. Lainie screams without making a sound, shuts her eyes tight. Her manipulated arms try to right the steering wheel. They've overcorrected, and a maple finds its opportunity to lunge at the windshield.

Lainie's forgotten she's driving. Time is elastic. She has all the time in the world and no time at all. The curve is too sharp and the wheels have locked. They're sliding. Careening forward toward the dark, toward the truth that lurks there. Toward a place without a future.

A form materializes from the shadow, unravels like a bolt of black silk next to the passed-out version of Greta. A lever-like arm extends out, reaches toward Lainie. And then . . .

Nothing.

CHAPTER SEVENTY-FOUR

A force lifts Greta's body up from the back seat, sits her upright. Places her like a doll on a shelf.

The scene before her makes no sense. She's in the car with her parents. Not *she*, but *they*. Grown Greta and teen Greta, overlapping. Her mother is driving, her father is in the passenger seat. They're sliding, hurtling toward a tree.

Next time I'm dreaming, I will remember I'm dreaming.

Greta isn't drunk anymore. She's aware, sharp. A voyage. She's on a voyage.

Emerging from the shadow next to her is a being made of soot and black. A long arm unhinges and fingers extend out. They reach for her mother's wrist as the tree closes in on the windshield, its roots writhing and aglow. *The Collector.*

Greta grabs it before it can touch her mother. Her hands sink into a membranous inky mass. Rivulets of blue static swarm across her skin, charge over her head and neck. Her hands move up further, plunging into the torso of the thing, pulling it toward her and away from her mother.

The Collector pushes back against her. The thing isn't solid. It's sticky like a spider's web, and Greta gets caught in it. Blue flashes of lightning cover her as she digs herself deeper and deeper into it. If the thing is in pain, it gives no sign. The Collector's body is malleable, compressible like a cloud of cotton candy. With each grab and twist, Greta's mobility decreases. She's tangled in it. Wrapped in black. Paralyzed.

A human hand tears through the oblivion of darkness. It's a woman's hand, bedecked with rings, azure light shuddering across it. On the thumb, an ornate ring of gold roots and leaves of emerald squirms to life, digs into the hand's flesh. Just as fast, it retreats back into the pitch. But Greta saw it.

Miranda. The Collector *is* Miranda.

The shadow's head leans in close to Greta—any sign of Miranda gone. It's a black mirror. In it, Greta sees her own reflection. The teenage Greta is gone. She's the thirty-seven-year-old woman who walked into the Found Object Society carrying a baggie with her mother's bracelet in it. The one she died wearing. The black of the Collector's head flares, wraps itself around Greta's face like a hood. Greta can't breathe. She's inside a great void of space, filled with stars.

Did I do it? Greta thinks. *Did I stop it?* Then the horrifying truth of it comes to her.

She didn't stop anything. She caused it.

CHAPTER SEVENTY-FIVE

"Greta Davenport. Greta Davenport, can you hear me?"

It's Miranda's voice. She's patting Greta's cheek. She can't feel it. The door to the cabin is open and Big Daniel Craig stands halfway in and halfway out. He's worried. Miranda's calm, beaming, almost backlit. A red light pulses behind the rectangular cabin window. Greta's immobile, far away. Miranda puts two fingers to Greta's neck and leans in, her ear close to Greta's mouth.

She wants to see if I have a pulse, if I'm breathing.

The spirals inside Miranda's ear are a beguiling nautilus of cartilage. What does Miranda smell like? Greta can't remember. All her senses are fading.

"Mr. Somers's light's gone red now, too, Miranda," Big Daniel Craig says.

Mr. Somers. Ezra. Ezz-raaa.

"Good. Go to him," Miranda says. "I've got this one."

"Miss, maybe just this once—"

Miranda cuts him off. "I said go, Daniel."

BDC is gone. Greta's scope of vision narrows.

An impossible thought gasps for air in her fading mind: *The crash was my fault*. Though not in the way she'd thought, not because she'd lied. No, her mother swerved out of control when she saw her adult daughter in the rearview. *Future* Greta.

"It was me," Greta says to Miranda, her voice no more than a whisper. "I made this happen. And you're—"

"I'm putting you out of your misery, remember? You can't exist in both places, Greta. You've made your choice."

Miranda lives inside the eyepiece of a kaleidoscope, images falling like colored pieces of glass: Zephyrine sinks into silt, her blood staining the surrounding water; Lassiter's eyes swell shut as he chokes out the word *Mother*; Colleen jumps to the side as Tyrone falls; Lainie, Lainie Davenport, hurtles toward a tree, Peter next to her, Greta in the back seat.

Words can no longer form in her mouth. Instead, Greta nods in silent agreement to an unfathomable outcome.

Behind Miranda, a shadow forms—rising and enveloping her like a cloak. Miranda's latex-gloved hand removes the beaded bracelet from Greta's open palm and places it in a wooden box.

G-R-E-T-A ♥ M-O-M

CHAPTER SEVENTY-SIX

Greta pulls the tissue out from between her toes. Her toenails are dry—dry enough. Bridget will be here soon. She twists the cap back onto the bottle of Sleepover Squad and puts it down next to the uncorked mascara. She looks in the mirror. This lip gloss is all wrong, too. It's brown. *Gross.* She wipes it off and tosses the used wad next to the other ones. She settles on an opalescent peachy-pink.

The voices of her parents rise up from downstairs.

Her mom laughs and says, "Peter!"

Greta cringes. Everything her parents do and say lately ticks her off. Even a simple laugh that has nothing to do with Greta feels like running into a stop sign. Why is that? Tonight, Bridget's telling her nightmare of a mom that she's staying over at Greta's, and Greta's telling her parents she's staying at Bridget's. Then they and a bunch of friends are going to party at Todd Daehler's, whose parents are in Florida. *Hot* Todd Daehler.

Greta turns on the water and soaps up her hands. Under the flow are two sets of hands—hers and another that looks kind of veiny . . . *old.*

"What the fuck?"

She pulls her hands out and holds them up. One pair. Just one. *Weird.* Murphy Brown stands outside the bathroom waiting for her. She yawns and meows at the same time.

Bridget will be pulling into the driveway any minute, and Greta wants to get out before her mom bitches at her again. It's always something. She grabs her sneakers and heads to the stairs. Murphy Brown follows alongside her, collar bell tinkling. There's another set of feet following in sync with Greta's. Like her hands, the feet look older, too. The toenails are deep purple, almost black. Dizzy, Greta loses her balance. She grabs at the handrail with four hands. *Four.*

Greta's falling, almost floating. Murphy Brown runs ahead of her and turns into the living room, where her parents are hanging out by the fire. Only she can't hear them anymore. They've stopped talking.

Greta catches herself before she reaches the bottom.

There's a knock at the front door. Bridget wouldn't knock; she'd honk. Bridget never comes to the door—like *never*. A dread creeps through her as she slows her motion. The scene around her shifts, morphs. The same colors assuming a new shape. Her body feels . . . different.

Knock-knock.

The front door is gray. It's supposed to be white. Why are her parents being so quiet?

"Mom? Dad? Can you answer the door?" Greta says.

There's no answer. The flicker that should be bouncing off the windows in the living room from the fireplace isn't there.

Knock-knock.

The Davenports' living room is empty. Well, it's sort of their living room, but not. The chimney juts through the middle of it. All the shelves with Mom and Dad's books and knickknacks are gone. It's one giant open room. What's happening? Is she dreaming? Having a nightmare?

There's someone at the door. Greta needs to open it.

She puts her hand on the doorknob and sees her distorted reflection in the brass. It's her, but not her. Like the living room. All her same parts, rearranged. Grown-up.

Heart pounding, Greta opens the door.

A handsome Black man stands there. He's wearing a sports coat and jeans, casually elegant. Todd Daehler's got nothing on him.

Ezra, Greta thinks.

The last thing she remembers is . . . Miranda, the Collector, reaching for her mom's bracelet. The Found Object Society. *Mr. Somers's light's gone red now, too, Miranda.*

"Ezra," she says out loud.

"Greta," he says. He looks happy, vibrant. His cheeks are fuller, shoulders broader.

Beside him, holding his hand, is a young boy. He's a miniature of his father blended with someone else, his eyes more hazel, a softer chin. He's wearing navy pajamas covered in little owls—and a life vest.

"I want you to meet Jake. Jake, this is Greta. My very good friend, Greta."

Jake reaches out to shake Greta's hand. It's warm. Such small fingers.

Behind them, the trompe l'oeil mural of the Brooklyn Bridge rises, blooming with life. Cars vibrating across it rumble in the distance. On the Brooklyn side, Jane's Carousel shines and spins like a distant galaxy. A hand that had held a curtain back in a window recedes, and the curtain closes.

"Jake and I thought you might want to join us at the carousel," Ezra says.

Jake tugs at Greta's sleeve. He hands her a checker piece. "Look what I found. You can have it," he says.

"Thank you, Jake." Greta takes it, puts it in her pocket. She looks up at Ezra. "It worked."

"I guess it did," Ezra says.

Greta looks back. The door to her house has closed. In front of the trio, the passageway under the word ARCADE takes form, depth. Pedestrians walk through it and toward the East River. Greta, Ezra, and Jake follow the flow through to the other side.

Greta's mom catches her teenage daughter at the bottom of the stairs.

"Jesus, Greta. Are you okay? You could've broken your neck."

Her father's standing next to her, holding her from the other side. Greta must've gotten dizzy as she ran down, lost her balance. The headlights from Bridget's car sweep across them through the windows. She honks twice.

"I'm okay, Mom. I just slipped, I guess."

Her mom sighs, lets go of Greta, and both her mom and dad step back. Usually, Greta recoils from any affection from either of her parents. This time, she's sorry they've moved away.

"You're staying at Bridget's house?" her mom says.

Honk-honk.

Greta nods and heads to the door. As she opens it, she feels an object in her jeans pocket. She reaches in, then pulls out a round plastic disc. It's warm to the touch. A checker piece. Something shifts inside her. It's indefinable, but it's as though she's being reconfigured. The same pieces of her, put together in a new way.

Through the windshield, Bridget motions for her to come over and get into the car. Her hand still on the doorknob, Greta steps back.

This version of Greta Davenport waves goodbye to Bridget and shuts the front door.

EPILOGUE

THREE YEARS LATER

She stands outside of Baggensgatan 23 in Stockholm's Gamla Stan neighborhood, pulled here by a power greater than the mysterious invitation that appeared under her hotel door three nights ago. She brushes the snow off her coat.

The past three years have sucked the life from her, turned her world a dull gray. What she experienced in the office (or whatever it was) on Drottninggatan, with the American woman Eileen, had cracked something open inside her. Light had poured in, sensations, smells—color. It isn't simple curiosity that brings her here tonight, nor the transfer of an absurd amount of money into an anonymous bank account, but the need to feel something again, to awaken her mind and body, which have grown numb with regret. Deadened by the guilt of *I should have done more. I could have done more.*

The blue-domed camera above the ancient stone-and-iron entrance clicks her in before she has a chance to say anything. They're expecting her. The hallway is long and dark and at the end of it, a gleaming monster of a vault door shifts and clacks, opening with a gasp of air.

A man of fairy-tale-like proportions stands at the entry and smiles.

"Welcome to the Found Object Society, Miss." His accent is cockney, not Swedish.

She walks into an orgasm of color and musk. The wallpaper

dances with images of humans and creatures copulating, images of violence and death. The handsome giant is speaking to her. Only part of her brain is listening. She hands him her phone, her coat—that much she heard.

"Miranda will be right out, Miss."

She nods and runs her fingers over the wall. The texture is raised, like hives.

"Welcome." A goddess. A Miss Universe. A Miss Goddamned Queen of the Solar System—with her astounding cheekbones, bosom, and near-black hair—stands before her in an electric-blue Victorian-era gown. "Please follow me."

As they walk through a heavy velvet curtain, her eyes adjust and the Jolly Green Giant sends her off, saying, "Enjoy your death, Miss."

Miranda is talking, explaining things. It's important, it must be. Her mind is on overload, and it's all she can do to keep herself upright. She follows the blue and the *shushing* of the silk as the woman's gown brushes across the floor. Stretching before her, no end in sight, are shelves upon shelves, filled with hundreds—thousands—of cubbies of varying size.

She only catches fragments of Miranda's well-rehearsed speech: "The Collection Room . . . the objects that you will choose from for your voyage . . . cataloged by regions and time period."

A tiny bell sounds as one pin light after another pierces the dark, illuminating seven different cubbyholes. In the distance, something clatters as it moves through a pipe, followed by the suck of a pneumatic tube.

"Take your time," Miranda says. "Your first voyage is your most important. It will set the tone for the rest."

The beams of light are identical. One in particular takes hold like a tractor beam. Heart pounding, she stands in front of the cubby and reads the catalog number: *NEUSA21C-51274. Northeast United States of America, early twenty-first century.*

When the card slid under the door of her suite at the Grand Hôtel, it elicited a memory she couldn't put her finger on. Something she hadn't understood until right now: It was the same card Greta had shown her in the kitchen that day three years ago.

Hand shaking, she points to the object in the cubby.

"Is this the object you've selected, Ms. Carr?" Miranda says.

"I think *it* chose me," Lis says.

"That's often the case. You have discerning taste, Lisbeth. One of our specialty Paradox Voyages. An excellent first choice—*very* complicated. You won't be disappointed."

Miranda reaches into the cubby with a pair of golden forceps and places the object inside a wooden box, the interior matching the shape and size of the beaded bracelet, handmade by a child. Handmade by her best friend, Greta Davenport, who vanished three years ago.

Blue static dances across it as Lis reads what the bracelet says:

G-R-E-T-A ♥ M-O-M

AUTHOR NOTE

Though many of the locations I use in the book are real—most notably, 273 Water Street, the Edgewater Beach Hotel in Chicago, the Richard Haas mural in the South Street Seaport, Baggensgatan 23 in Stockholm—I have taken architectural and design liberties with them to better suit the story. The same can be said for the real-life characters of Christopher "Kit Burns" Keyburn and the (true) one and only Greta Garbo. Any errors and omissions are my own.

ACKNOWLEDGMENTS

In late 2019 I started writing my first novel. What I knew about publishing was minimal (save for a yearlong stint as an editorial assistant at Hyperion Books for Children decades earlier). I didn't have an agent, nor did I know any of the authors I swooned over other than reading their books and devouring their acknowledgments at the end when I finished them. Fast forward to now, and I find myself calling many of those authors my good friends and colleagues . . . all as I write my own acknowledgments. To loosely quote a post from the great Marie-Helene Bertino: *There is no such thing as speculative. Look around!*

I wouldn't be here if it weren't for my ferocious genius of an agent, Victoria Marini. Thanks for rejecting me twice and each time asking, *What else have you got?* A totally non-hyperbolic thank-you-times-one-billion to my incredible editor at Hyperion Avenue, Chelsea Cutchens. When we had our first call, I knew you were the one. It was as though you'd been writing *The Found Object Society* alongside with me. You got me, you really did. This book is all the better for your tenacious insight and your willingness to call me out when I'd strayed. To my fantastic publicist and fellow *Anchorman* aficionado, Kathleen Carter, thanks for going on this debut ride with me. WV, always.

If you weren't aware, it takes a massive team of dedicated, overcaffeinated, and caring humans to get a book out into the world. Thanks to these folks at Hyperion Avenue: art director

Amy C. King (a big thank-you for your patience and bringing my vision of the cover to fruition); the copyediting gurus who get that I don't get commas—Meredith Jones, Sylvia Davis, Dan Kaufman, and Rachel Warren; copy chief Guy Cunningham; managing editor Sara Liebling; senior marketing manager Daneen Goodwin and marketing manager Greta Shull; and my publicist at Hyperion Avenue, Daniela Escobar. Deep gratitude to Faceout Studio and Spencer Fuller for the stunning cover design.

Giant hugs to Dawn Ius, my earliest editor and champion when no one else knew my work. She also gets a special shout-out for sending me a picture of the perfume bottle that later became the end of poor Zephyrine. To my workshop mates from the Yale Writers' Workshop and our instructor, Rebecca Schiff, who read the very first words of *The Found Object Society* and encouraged me that I was heading in the right direction, thank you. To Lizzie Carr (also from YWW) for being an early reader and supporter—and also the namesake of Greta's best friend, Lisbeth Carr—keep going, you are a writing talent that will be recognized.

Georgina Cross, Jennifer Fawcett, Vera Kurian, Laura McHugh, Danielle Trussoni, Tessa Wegert, your early friendship, blurbs, and support (from first interviewing agents to my book deal) means the world to me. Each of the following people deserve their own paragraph for their multifaceted support and kindness, but future PDA and cocktails will have to suffice: Jason Allison, Kathleen Barber, Julia Bartz, Allison Buccola, Mindy Carlson, May Cobb, Kellye Garrett, Danielle Girard, Lee Matthew Goldberg, Rich Green, Katy Hays, Jennifer Hillier, Tullan Holmqvist, Angie Kim, Kirby Kim, Jean Kwok, Amy Landecker, Melissa Larsen, Sarah Lawton, Vanessa Lillie, Mark Mann, Jessa Maxwell, Clémence Michallon, Dennis Michel,

Wanda Morris, K. T. Nguyen, Alex Segura, Gretchen Stelter, Sarah Tomlinson, Wendy Walker, Ashley Winstead, and CO in Rhinebeck for the serene writing space. Megan Abbott and Lou Berney: your superhero use of voice is a constant inspiration.

Enormous gratitude and love to Fiona Davis and Greg Wands, Clare Mackintosh, Sheila Crowley, and Molly Waxman.

To all the Bookstagrammers, librarians, indie bookstores, booksellers, and, most of all, readers, thank you. None of us would be here without you.

To my parents, thanks for keeping it weird, and thanks to Dad for taking me to horror movies and graveyards for ice cream when I was far too young. It stuck.

And most of all to Tom, for being right there with me for every Act (and there have been many) since 1997. This version of me, any version of me, loves you.